Jubilee Day

Also by Michael Sky

Thinking Peace

Breathing Lessons

Dancing With the Fire

This is a work of fiction. Names, characters, places, and incidents either are the product of the author's imagination or are used fictitiously. Any resemblance to actual persons, living or dead, events, or locales is entirely coincidental.

Copyright © 2011 by Michael Sky

All rights reserved.

Published in the United States by lulu.com

Library of Congress Cataloging-in-Publication Data

Sky, Michael, 1951-

Jubilee Day: When America Changes Its Mind
About All the Big Things

ISBN: 978-1-257-12442-8

Jubilee Day

When America Changes Its
Mind About All the Big Things

by Michael Sky

Lulu.com

For Lily,
my lucky charm

Day One

Sunday, November 6, 2011

No sane person seeks a world divided between billions of excluded people living in absolute deprivation and a tiny elite guarding their wealth and luxury behind fortress walls. No one rejoices at the prospect of life in a world of collapsing social and ecological systems. Yet we continue to place human civilization and even the survival of our species at risk mainly to allow a million or so people to accumulate money beyond any conceivable need.

—*David C. Korten*

Chapter 1

As she raced her way through the early Sunday morning streets, Dr. Joss Morgan replayed her conversation with Varnum: four prominent Americans had died during the night, all in their sleep, of apparent natural causes. At 8 a.m. Eastern, an email arrived at every major media outlet and dozens of online blogs. The subject line read: "A Message for the Dominators." The content: "Six will die, every day, until you begin to share wealth and power. Jubilee."

"We just got word that Mallard died," said Secretary of Homeland Security Bill Varnum. "In his sleep. Dick Mallard, for Christ's sake. We're assuming there's two other deaths we haven't discovered yet. The nation's on full alert. We're under some kind of attack."

"Who were the others?"

"Chuck Davis. Wallace Griffin. And Howie Croft."

Republican firebrand in the House. The Chief Justice of the Supreme Court. The president's Chief of Staff. And Vice President Richard Mallard, supposed power behind the last president and unofficial leader of the Republican party.

As Varnum put it, his voice quavering, "Bigger than 9/11."

It was some kind of terrorism, but no strapped-on bombs, no exploding airplanes. No civilian casualties. Not your average terrorists.

Joss parked in the underground garage and, ten minutes and several security checkpoints later, she walked into the already churning First Response Team meeting.

FRT was a cross-discipline group of specialists tasked with doing an initial analysis of any Homeland event and making recommendations for future actions. Some members of the group came to every initial meeting; others were only called in when the situation touched on their area of expertise.

As the DHS chief profiler, Joss was always called in, and often remained part of any ongoing investigation.

There were already a dozen participants in the room, all familiar to Joss. She took a seat at the large rectangular table, turned on her government-issued tablet, and connected to the collaborative file for this case. FRT leader Henry Trenton was running the briefing. Trenton was the oldest on the team, and had been in military intelligence since Vietnam. Gray buzz-cut, gray-blue eyes. Trenton was dressed in civvies, but could step into a full dress parade without anyone noticing.

With a quick nod to Joss, he continued: "All four were East Coast: Davis and Croft in DC, Griffin's Virginia, and the vice president, New York. Hard to imagine men of this stature going unnoticed past mid morning, so if there are two more they're probably West Coast. Or some other part of the world."

"I could nominate a certain North Korean dominator," muttered Kenji Nakamura, the go-to guy for all things East Asian. Kenji was second generation Japanese-American, fluent in several languages, including Chinese, Japanese, and Korean.

Trenton asked him, "Did they receive the email?"

"No indications yet. But they'll know soon enough; we've got reports of the email in Japan, China, and South Korea, large numbers. Looks like it started in English and then was translated as it was forwarded."

"Same in Israel, Egypt, Iran, and Iraq," said Neda Soltan, Middle East language and culture expert. Neda was Iranian, and like Kenji and Joss, she was born and raised in America, but was fluent in the language and steeped in the culture of her parents' homeland. There was a running joke that she and Joss were twins since they shared several features: slender bodies and pretty oval faces framed with jet black hair. She was another FRT regular since most events had a Mideast connection. Like everyone else in the room, she was tracking multiple feeds on her Book.

All relevant documents in an investigation went into what was called "the Book." Investigator notes, interviews, tips, whatever—went into the Book. Photos, audio and video files, all recordable by the tablet, copied to the Book. Hot links to dozens of databases, a full range of communication links. While Trenton oversaw the process, he considered the Book to be in charge.

"Unfortunately," said Neda, "some of the translations have, uh, embellished the original message, adding 'Death to Israel' and 'Praise Allah' and such. Which isn't helping. There's already noise out of Israel about retaliatory bombing if a single Israeli dies. Any Mideast victims and things could get ugly in a hurry. We really need to get in front of this. Get people to see that something else is going on here. This isn't the same old holy war crap."

Nodding heads around the room.

"We'll know a lot more tomorrow, assuming they strike again," said Trenton, "For now focus on what we have. Work the bodies and crime scenes. Find some witnesses. What about the email? What's it tell us about the bad guys? Joss?"

Joss came up through the FBI as a profiler and had been recruited to DHS and the FRT by Trenton. "Not a lot to go on but it's colloquial American except maybe for the use of 'the dominators.' More formal than 'the rich,' or 'the elites,' or 'fat cats'—suggests educated. Left leaning. 'Jubilee' could be a signature, but also might be part of their message—it refers to a universal forgiveness of debts. Whatever it means, the message is as much polemic as threat. Think abbreviated unabomber," she said, referring to Ted Kaczynski whose mail bombings had been justified in a 35,000 word manifesto that the *New York Times* and *Washington Post* published.

"Except," she added, "only nineteen words. Also, this isn't a solitary perp. These are highly-organized, multiple killers, not leaving clues. Protected targets. And some sort of weapon we've never seen before."

Trenton turned to forensics lead, Wade Donnehy. "What have we got on cause of death?"

Throughout the meeting, Donnehy had been tracking coroner and forensics reports for the four known deaths. "No signs of violence. No signs of intruders. Estimated time of death for all four is 4 a.m. Eastern. For the three that have progressed to autopsy, they're calling it hemorrhagic stroke, probably due to an aneurysm. A blood vessel in the brain ruptured. Death was sudden, quick, most likely without waking."

Donnehy paused for a breath. The room went quiet as everyone pondered how.

"Primary risk factor for ruptured aneurysm is traumatic injury to the head. After that, the usual lifestyle sins—diabetes, obesity, hypertension, smoking, alcoholism. Too little of the nutrient copper, or too much zinc can contribute. Obviously, none of these apply here.

"Could be an exotic poison. Or some sort of GM nano organism. Something that can be delivered from a distance and timed for effect. Or implanted and then triggered. Whatever it is leaves no traces, at least nothing that has shown up so far in the autopsies and tox scans."

"What about something like sound waves, or radiation, ELFs, something that could be beamed from a distance?" asked Cam Woodstein, the team tech guru. At 28, he was the youngest team member. He was also the most casually dressed—T-shirt and jeans—a source of irritation for Trenton, but one that he overlooked because Cam produced.

Everybody looked to Trenton, who turned to Lieutenant Sam Pollard. Pollard was the only active military man in the group. He had a classified background in Special Forces and black ops and was the team weapons specialist. An expert's expert on explosives. He was in the loop on all Pentagon weapons programs and was knowledgeable about, and often friendly with, arms merchants around the world. Like Trenton, he tolerated the civilian dress and other informalities of the group, but no one called him Sam; he preferred Lieutenant, would answer to Pollard, and he used last names only for everyone in the group, except Trenton, who got "Sir!"

"We've got a big problem," Pollard said, "with any kind of beamed or radiated attack: three of the victims were in bed with partners, all unaffected. Victims were all men, partners all women, so maybe whatever it is can discriminate by gender. But I've never heard of anything like it, not in development, not even on a Pentagon wish list."

"Got a theory?" asked Trenton.

Pollard hesitated, and Joss had a feeling that he wanted to throw something out there, but after a few seconds he answered, "No sir, nothing yet."

Trenton also paused for a long moment.

Lead political analyst Darrell Wells broke the silence, stating flatly, "Whoever did this killed the former vice president of the United States. Out of office for three years but still a major player. As were Davis and Griffin. Vocal, disruptive critics of the president's policy. If it turns out that this is some radical left group there's going to be aggressive blowback from the right."

Wells was a longtime Washington insider, a blue-blood Democrat in thousand-dollar suits and trendy haircuts. Joss had a hard time understanding why he was even in the room. He brought nothing in the way of defending against terrorism or catching bad guys. His job was to assess the political ramifications of any event and to advise the administration on effective responses. Important work, Joss figured, but more appropriate in the White House situation room. The politics of the victims and perpetrators should have nothing to do with gathering evidence and solving crimes.

Feeling piqued, she said, "What about Howie Croft? First he got the president elected, and now he's chief advisor and major fixer. Should make the right real happy that he's dead."

"Absolutely," Wells answered, frowning. "I'm just seconding what Neda said. We need to get on top of this before it spins out of control. And we need to be stressing Howie's death to keep the right at bay."

Classic Wells. Even when he agrees with you it feels sleazy.

"Well, here's something more for them to be pissed about," said Cam, reading from his Book. "Joint Chiefs General Bob Eisley has died in his sleep."

Chapter 2

At just past 2 p.m., Joss pulled up to Chief Justice Griffin's Virginia residence. The house was at the end of a long, gated driveway and the police had held the press and inquisitive neighbors back at the street. There were several official vehicles in the parking area, some with lights flashing. Uniformed police guarded the perimeter of the old Victorian, in anticipation of reporters hopping the fence. Others were systematically combing the grounds in search of evidence.

Trenton wanted her to assess at least one of the crime scenes this afternoon, in advance of a statement from the president scheduled for six. The email had quickly become the most widely-disseminated in the history of the Internet. Everyone online had received at least one copy, and the traditional media had informed everyone else. It was the only topic of conversation on the network and cable news channels, as well as the blogs, Facebook, Twitter, and the rest. Accusations and incriminations, theories and counter-theories, threats and counter-threats. Everyone was angry, many were afraid, and no one had any idea who the enemy was.

FRT had quickly expanded to thirty investigators, with some dispatched to the known crime scenes, while others sifted through internet traffic, NSA communications, various criminal, financial, and travel databases, all in search of—anything. They had two critical missions. First, to give the president something to reassure Americans that progress was being made and that the terrorists would soon be apprehended. Second, they had fourteen hours to stop another six deaths.

Minutes after the confirmation that General Eisley had died at his family home in San Diego, they learned that Senator Bernard Tofer had also died, in his sleep, at his home in Provo. Another icon of the right. Tofer was a darling of the Tea Party and had led the opposition to just about everything the president had tried to do in his three years in office.

Once they had Tofer, "six will die, every day" became a ticking timebomb. That prompted a discussion of preventive measures, which led to nothing but questions. How do you protect the millions of Americans who might be considered 'dominators'? How, for that matter, do you define 'dominator'? Why Howie Croft but not the president himself? And while the president is one person that they would do everything possible to defend, how do you defend against invisible death rays or whatever the hell was at work here?

Lieutenant Pollard had finally closed the conversation, harking back to something Trenton had said: "We need more data. These guys will make mistakes, or leave some pattern of behavior. We'll track them down, but more people are gonna die first."

Wells had lost his cool, almost shouting, "Are you nuts? We need this stopped *now*. The president's polling was hovering below fifty percent before any of this happened. This will kill him."

Mercifully, nobody killed Wells, though some imagined it. The meeting ended with Trenton handing out assignments, including a minor bombshell for Joss. "I'm calling in Alex Mendelsohn to partner with you. Start at Judge Griffin's. Figure out how they're doing this. At least come up with a plausible theory."

"Go get 'em, Scully," said Cam, to a few snickers. Though Joss had only watched *The X Files* once—and found it utterly ridiculous—she'd seen enough to understand the reference. Scully was the rational, skeptical doctor-agent who partnered with Mulder, the conspiracy-believing agent for all things weird, alien, and paranormal. Joss had never met Alex Mendelsohn, but she'd heard of his reputation for out-of-the-box thinking and tactics.

Yet however much Mendelsohn might mirror Mulder, Joss was no Scully. As the child of a Chinese mother and multiracial father, Joss had grown up with a deep appreciation for the mysterious forces driving her and her world. Her best of all memories was sitting cross-legged on her parents' big bed in the mornings while her mother tossed the I Ching to divine the lessons and leanings for the day. Her mother saw messages and portents everywhere—in sudden changes in the weather, in the ringing of a telephone or doorbell, in the flight of birds, in colored circles around the moon. "The outer world," she would say, "is a reflection of your inner world. They are connected, Joss. Understand one and you understand the other."

And so it was that for all her scientific education, Joss was at least comfortable with her mother's world of unseen forces. Didn't quite agree, but neither could she dismiss it. Things were rarely black and white, but rather shaded gray and obscured with fog. Science had its limits and there was more than one path to the mountaintop. Still, she wielded a mean skeptical edge when faced with things overly woo-woo, so maybe she'd be doing some Scully after all.

Actually, her only concern was that Trenton thought she needed help. Though, of course, he was right. She had no idea what was killing these people, but whatever Trenton and Pollard were pondering was something out of the ordinary. So she was looking forward to Mendelsohn's take.

As she approached Griffin's front door, it swung open and out stepped a grim-faced, shaggy-haired FBI-agent. He was already extending his hand. "Doctor Morgan," he said, more statement than question.

"Special Agent Mendelsohn," Joss replied, shaking his hand. "Been here long?"

His weathered face suggested years of experience, but the rest of him felt young. He pondered the question, then smiled and nodded. "Long enough to know that something's happening here and it ain't exactly clear."

She half-sang, "What a field day for the heat." His eyebrows bounced up in surprise. "My parents were hippies. I was raised on sixties music."

Mendelsohn's smile got bigger, briefly, then he turned serious. "If the other five sites are the same as this, and that's the word so far, then I hope you like puzzles." He turned, and led her into the house, still talking.

"Doors were locked, alarm on. Absolutely no sign of physical intrusion. No deliveries or visitors in the past few days. We're still running tests on the air, water, food, but Beth Griffin spends more time in the house than the judge and she's fine. We're also testing the judge's meds. It would be a way to do it, but I'm not optimistic. The coroner says it doesn't look like poisons or toxins, but he'll be doing more tests."

He paused to look around. The interior of the house had been gutted and remodeled, swapping the cramped Victorian style for open and airy Scandinavian, with lots of off-white, and blond wood, and sleek modern furniture. Joss picked up a framed photo showing the judge and his wife and two teenage girls.

"We heard that his wife was in bed with him. What about the kids?"

"Photo's a few years old," he answered. "They're both in college. One at Dartmouth, the other Harvard. They're heading home under protective custody now. Let's go upstairs, check out the scene."

The bedroom continued the Scandinavian design, with a king-sized bed facing large windows opening to the west, an overhead skylight, and scattered track lighting. The bed had been stripped and the room was still cluttered with forensic detritus. They both stopped to stare at the bed, listening for some sort of sign of what had transpired.

Joss's training was in psychological forensics. Her talent was taking in the human elements at crime scenes—signatures, props, method, style—and teasing out a profile of the perp. It was equal parts left-brain analysis and right-brain intuition. She *always* got something.

But today, nothing. Didn't even feel like a crime had happened. As if a phantom had drifted in through an open window, stolen the judge's soul, and drifted out again.

"Now I know why they called in Agent Mulder."

Mendelsohn smiled at that and, shaking his head, he said, "I never heard of *The X-Files* until they started calling me that. Thing is, while there is no actual FBI collection of x-files, we do get weird cases, not often, but they happen. I had some success on one my second year with the Bureau. I've been Mulder ever since. But I spend most of my time working on computer crime."

"So you're on the trail of that Nigerian prince who keeps sending me emails?"

He laughed. "Right, right. He's a slippery fellow. And just one of many using computers to steal money, ideas, identities, stalk kids, hack into databases, disrupt systems—"

"Any computer angles to our puzzle?"

"Well, start with the email. It's not difficult to make email untraceable, but it does require some level of sophistication. Then there's the likely fact that this is an organized group, spread out around the country—they gotta be using the Internet for communications. Also, if they're homing in on their targets, GPS." He turned to Joss, cocking an eyebrow. "Then there's the mystery weapon."

"Homeland's tech guy suggested several forms of beamed-in attacks."

"But how to account for the unaffected bedmate?"

"Exactly."

Mendelsohn was nodding. "Rules out a lot."

Joss stared at the bed. "So, after you eliminate all the improbables, you're left with—?"

If he had a theory, he wasn't telling. "Let's go talk to Mrs. Griffin."

With a final glance back at the empty bed, she followed Mendelsohn down the stairs and into the kitchen. In a small breakfast nook, they found Beth Griffin nursing a cold cup of coffee. Still dressed in her nightgown and robe, she looked frail, tired, and too young to be a Supreme Court Justice's widow.

"Mrs. Griffin," said Mendelsohn, "This is Dr. Joss Morgan, lead investigator for Homeland Security."

She nodded at Joss, who said, "I'm very sorry for your loss. We just need to ask a few questions. If you're feeling up to it."

Though Beth Griffin had not been online all day, or watched television, she'd had several phone calls and knew that her husband had apparently been murdered, along with several others. What had been just one of those sad things that happen—waking with the morning light to realize that you're curled up to an unnaturally cold body—had turned into something much worse.

"He was only fifty-six," she said. "He was going to be the longest-serving Chief Justice in history. There was so much he wanted to do."

Joss and Mendelsohn sat still while she softly cried, then struggled to regain her composure. Finally, she took a deep breath, straightened, squared her shoulders. "We were sleeping. I. . ."

Another round of tears. She shivered and started shaking her head.

Joss didn't think they'd be getting much out of Beth Griffin today, if indeed there was anything to get.

As the crying subsided, she asked, "Did your husband travel away from home in the past few days?"

"No, when the Court's in session he stays home, keeps very regular hours."

"Did you have any unusual visitors recently?"

"No, I already said, no visitors, nothing unusual. We live a very ordinary life."

"Had your husband ever suffered a serious blow to the head, or ever had a concussion?"

"Not that I'm aware of. We met in college. I—he—I suppose he could have been injured before then."

Mendelsohn had mentioned that the judge's medications were being tested, so Joss didn't go there.

"Can you think of anything that was different, or out of place, or in any way unusual as you went to bed last night?"

Joss regretted that her question had ended with "last night." Beth Griffin said nothing for a full minute, her eyes closing and opening. Was she trying to remember her husband's last night? Or to rewrite what happened?

She opened her eyes, looked right at Joss and said, "No, nothing different."

"Did you wake up during the night?"

"No."

Joss sensed that if she pushed for anything more all they would get was tears. She was about to close the interview when Mendelsohn asked, "Do you remember if you dreamed?"

Chapter 3

Source: President's Press Conference

JASON DANIELS, *CNN*: Mr. President, can we assume that this is Islamic terrorism?

PRESIDENT CARVER: At this point, Jason, we're not assuming anything. We don't have all the facts yet, but every investigative agency in America is hard at work. Our nation is under attack. We are on world-wide full alert. I will not let this stand. We will hunt down and capture those responsible and bring them to hard justice. Donna?

DONNA MORGENSTERN, *L.A. TIMES*: Mr. President, in past terrorist attacks, there have been warnings and clues that were missed, dots that weren't connected. Was there any intelligence that this was happening?

PRESIDENT CARVER: Today I've received reports from all relevant organizations and at this point I'd have to say that no one saw this coming. So we've got our work cut out for us. Charles?

CHARLES BACKLY, *WASHINGTON POST*: Mr. President, you said that while the cause of death was cerebral hemorrhage, the method was still unknown. I've spoken with a dozen medical experts and none of them had a viable explanation for how the murders were done. Do investigators have a working theory for means of death?

PRESIDENT CARVER: Charles, I'm a politician, not a CSI specialist. I'm not going to speculate. Let the investigation run it's course. We should have answers soon.

BACKLY: Soon enough to stop more killings?

President Carver: We are doing everything in our power to stop these killings and bring the guilty to justice. My solemn duty is to protect the American people. I will not rest until I know that we are safe from these cowardly killers. Last question—Mark?

Mark Bonner, *NY Times*: Mr. President. Any anxiety about going to sleep tonight?

President Carver: None at all.

Source: The Jim Franke Show

Jim Franke: People, some great Americans were killed last night, murdered while they slept! And what was their only crime? Loving America! And loving it so much that they stood up to our so-called president, and stood up to the liberals and the health-care nannies and the welfare statists, stood up to the regulation fascists, stood up to this whole socialist takeover of our country!

I watched Misleader's press conference and you know what? He didn't look surprised by any of this, did he? Of course he's not worried about getting killed tonight! Of course not! Why should he worry, it's just his enemies, the very men who are trying to stop him that got killed!

Oh sure, he talked about Howie Croft, they're all talking about Howie, saying Howie proves this is a bipartisan anti-American plot. But people, we know better, don't we? What if Howie knew what they were planning and tried to stop it? Right? Are you getting this? What if Howie Croft tried to stop his boss's plans? Huh? What if Howie Croft was one brave American who stood in the way of a terrorist cabal, a so-called president and his fascist friends?!

Sleep well tonight, dear Misleader—your days are numbered. I'm here to tell you, we the people are coming for you. It's past time to cleanse the tree of liberty and it won't be our blood this time, it'll be the blood of tyrants! We're coming for you!

Source: The Daily Liar

I have to say right off that in ten years of writing for this site I have never been so utterly baffled. The only thing we know for sure is that six major players in American politics died last night. Beyond that, what to believe? Do we believe that all these men died of identical cerebral hemorrhages? Do we believe that these medical events were acts of murder, that someone somehow caused blood vessels to burst in the brains of each of these men? Do we believe that six more will die tonight, victims of the same mysterious killers?

I don't know what to believe. Or who. Never been a conspiracy buff but now I'm wondering. The official explanations, such as they are, just aren't credible. It's too big a coincidence to be natural causes and just flat out impossible that it was done by Islamic terrorists or any other group of anti-American nutbags. No, this had to be an inside job with someone very near the top calling the shots.

It always comes down to means, motive, and opportunity. However these men were killed, the murder weapon was something way out of the ordinary, the sort of complex, experimental weaponry that only the government would have. And, government agents would have easy access to the schedules and locations of these powerful men. There's your means and opportunity. As for motive—this will cause the same growth of the security state and consolidation of power within the presidency that we saw after 9/11. Scare the bejeezus out of the American people and they'll surrender all their precious freedoms. Just promise to keep them safe.

A promise that President Carver made no fewer than seven times during his press conference.

Oh, and a bonus for the prez: several of his enemies were taken off the board.

Source: DC•PM

MATTHEW CRISSOM: Don't you think you're being a little hard on the president? I mean, unless you've joined the nutters who think the President of the United States is running a murder racket, what more could he have done today? And what about Howie Croft? His oldest friend and closest confidant. It looked to me like he was genuinely mourning his death. And all the others. I mean—

GEORGE DEEDS: *Cui bono,* Matt, *cui bono*. The chief beneficiaries of these deaths are the president and his party. And it's hard to imagine a crime of this dimension happening without the president's knowledge, however plausibly deniable it might be.

JUDY ROTHBERG: Oh come on, George! Are you serious? The president plotting mass murder?

DEEDS: Someone is plot—

Crissom: Next you'll be accusing him of running drugs and sleeping with interns and ripping off Savings and Loans—oh wait, we've already seen that movie.

JONATHON ROBART: I'm with George. Something smells here, and fish always rot from the head.

ROTHBERG: That's just the stink of your and George's vile accusations.

DEEDS: All I'm saying is—

ROTHBERG: What you're saying is just—

ROBART: Judy, even if he and the Democrats are totally innocent of these killings, they're not leveling with us now. Nobody in the medical or scientific community thinks these guys died the way they're saying. The president lied to us tonight. And in Washington the cover-up is always worse than the crime.

CRISSOM: So there you have it, folks—President Carver turns out to be a stone cold killer. Or the right wing in this country turns out to be bat guano crazy. That's all we have time for on DC•PM. Get a good night's sleep everyone.

Chapter 4

After yesterday's FRT meeting broke up, Henry Trenton spent the rest of the day in consultation with superiors from the State Department and Homeland Security. He was in charge of one of several parallel investigations. Every effort would be made to coordinate information and to avoid stepping on one another's toes, but they wanted everybody on this. Unlimited resources. The first thing he did was boost the number of analysts working the midnight-to-nine shift, so that now, at two in the morning, there was a furious flow of activity at Homeland headquarters. He had people monitoring the Internet, telephone traffic, financial transactions, and all travel sectors. Others were watching real-time satellite reports, with special attention on Washington, New York, Chicago, Dallas, and Los Angeles.

Of course, nobody knew what they were looking for. The hope was that if there were more deaths something would show up for one or more of the monitors. Some little squib of whatsit that they could trace back to whoever. It was a great plan, equal parts futility and frustration. They weren't looking for a needle in a haystack; they were looking for one blade of hay that stood out from all the rest. With thousands of haystacks to sort through.

The thing is, Trenton was baffled. Multiple autopsies by the nation's best had turned up nothing. Ditto crime scene forensics. Assuming the next round of deaths was a repeat of the first, with the same lack of physical evidence, sooner or later they'd be forced to conclude that something non-physical was killing these people. Whatever it was, how could they hit their target but not the person lying right next them? How could they even know where in the house the target was? They were looking for a weapon that could strike with pinpoint precision yet leave no signs of surveillance or targeting or delivery. And could do all of this in six locations, more or less simultaneously.

Which is why he teamed Alex Mendelsohn with Joss Morgan, even though he considered Mendelsohn borderline nuts.

At the FRT meeting, he'd thought that Lt. Pollard was holding something back, so later he asked him straight out, "Just speculating, if you had to guess—what are we dealing with?"

"If I had to guess—some form of psi. ESP. Psychokinesis. A combination of remote viewing and object manipulation. Or maybe post-hypnotic suggestion. One way or another, the enemy is getting into the target's brain. Sir."

Trenton nearly laughed. He'd been expecting some new and off-the-books weapon program, something too secret to raise in the group. But psychokinetics? Mind control? Certainly explains Pollard's reluctance to bring it up. Still, wasn't like they had any better theories.

"Tell me more, Lieutenant."

"Sir, the government's been experimenting with mind control and mind-powered weaponry since the fifties. All highly classified. Playing with LSD and other drugs. Hypnosis. Telekinesis. Influencing at a distance. Story is that nothing ever came of any of it and it all shut down years ago."

"But?"

"In '85 I was sent to an off-base research facility and went through three days of what they called psych testing. They had us trying to see the images on hidden cards, and guessing at numbers, and trying to move ping-pong balls with our minds. Even did some airy-fairy meditations. Seemed like a huge waste of time to me and after three days I was back with my unit, never heard dick about any of it. Told it was classified, but a couple years back I got talking with an Army lifer who went through it, had the same experience. Was like we'd been tested for something and failed."

"So, you're saying that some other guys passed the tests, and went on to become psycho-killers?"

"Sir, I just don't think they'd be pursuing something for forty, fifty years if it wasn't producing results."

Chapter 5

Andrew Matson couldn't sleep. After two hours of restless-everything he stopped trying and sat on the side of the bed, with elbows on knees and face in hands, and listened to Muriel's gentle breathing behind him. He'd grown accustomed to sleepless nights, especially in the four years since the banking crisis got going. It was a perilous time; he was under so much pressure, his role at the Fed, his earlier years at Marsdale Lipman, then the confirmation battle for Secretary, the bailouts, and the stimulus. All while jobs tanked and bankruptcies soared and healthcare imploded. Then the fucking hearings.

At this point, the only non-banker in America who didn't think that Andrew Matson should be drowned in a vat of toxic assets was the president. Pundits left and right made the same accusation: Matson was handpicked by the financial industry to carry its water. The bankers were in fact more than satisfied with his work. A boom industry through four bear-ugly years, they now owned all the important politicians, starting with the president. Despite all that had happened, Matson had the most secure job in the world.

That didn't stop the sleepless nights. Not even Ambien was stopping them lately, just made him groggy all day. He was trying not to take one, especially tonight.

He wondered how many other rich men like himself had been sweating it since the news broke today. How many others figured they qualified as a "dominator?" There's a few million American millionaires, a few hundred billionaires—were they all endangered? At six a day, 2190 a year, odds favored most of the rich surviving. Good odds. Plus they were bound to catch whoever's doing it long before then, worst-case within a month, that's just 180, even better odds. Unless.

Unless you're an especially prominent dominator, one of a small group that's in the public eye, everyone watching what you're doing and digging through your history and looking at your personal finances, you're sitting in meetings and hearings all day defending the system, doing your job, not your fault politicians let things slide so long and so wrong—

The headache just happened. A sharp pain at the back of his skull, it started small and quickly got bigger, harder, louder, pushing his head down, his body collapsing, then a horrible nausea, thinking of Muriel, feeling cold, hot, sweating, *this is how it ends*, he thinks—

He stopped thinking and slipped off the bed, hitting the floor with a loud thump that awakened his wife.

Day Two

Monday, November 7, 2011

One person's savings are lent out to become other peoples' debts. So the "magic of compound interest" to savers means an equal "magic of exploding debt" to somewhere else in the economy. . . . In every known society, the effect has been to concentrate wealth in the hands of people with money.

—*Michael Hudson*

Chapter 6

Joss woke at four-thirty, seconds before the alarm went off. She lay there for another ten minutes, stretching and contemplating her day. Today they find out if the email threats are real. Could already be happening. She slipped out of bed, now wide awake and moving with determination. She'd make Homeland by six.

She and Mendelsohn had called it quits yesterday after finishing at Judge Griffin's. Not much to investigate and even less to learn. "We just need to wait till morning," Mendelsohn had said. "Meanwhile, let's follow one of the first rules of war—sleep when you can. Unless," he'd added, smiling, "you're worried that the Sleepy-Time killer's gonna get you."

That had led to a discussion about the naming of serial killers. Joss thought it important that the name be a good fit and that it come from the killer's method—Jack the Ripper—or signature—The Zodiac Killer. "But who gets naming rights," asked Mendelsohn. "The press? the cops? And how is that decided, and what if no one likes the name they pick?" They agreed it would be best to avoid the whole matter. And besides, these guys had named themselves. Jubilee.

Fresh-brewed coffee was waiting for Joss when she entered the kitchen. She filled a large mug and then fired up her Book. Nothing had made the news feeds yet, but there was a message from Trenton. There were already two probables: Treasury Secretary Matson and Marsdale Lipman CEO, Donald Sachs. Sachs was in New York; Matson was local. His wife called 911 just after four;

the site was secured and waiting for them. Mendelsohn had confirmed that he was en route.

Five minutes later, Joss was speeding through mostly empty streets to Matson's suburban home. Her GPS directed her to a curving, tree-lined street of modestly upscale homes on half-acre lots. She didn't need the address to know the house—it was the one with all the vehicles in front, the flashing lights and crime scene tape, the cluster of suits and uniforms gathered on the sidewalk, sipping from styrofoam cups, waiting. As she stepped out of her car, Mendelsohn emerged from the group with a bright "I'm-a-morning-person" greeting.

Joss and Mendelsohn had wanted to see a fresh crime scene, before it was overrun by an army of responders, which explained the early morning waiters. They told the others they needed fifteen minutes. But as they entered the house Joss was thinking more like five. Already felt like a repeat of yesterday.

The house was an elegant if small two-bedroom. The Matson's had no children. The downstairs consisted of a large living room to the left, dining room on the right, and kitchen to the rear. Though lights were on in every room, there were no signs of invasion or disturbance, nothing askew. Of course, that's what the CSI guys were for, to take a much deeper look for whatever's askew. But Joss's gut was saying nada. In the kitchen she eyed the same brand coffee-maker as hers, with a fresh-brewed pot. She and Mendelsohn shared a brief look of "coffee would be nice" but thought better of it and headed upstairs.

At the top of the stairs they found two open doorways. They stepped into the nearest, and saw, they assumed, Muriel Matson sitting in front of an open laptop, holding a coffee cup and talking on a cell. Yesterday, Beth Griffin had still been in her nightgown and robe; Mrs. Matson was dressed in worn but stylish jeans and a black cashmere sweater, ready for the day. She acknowledged them with a quick nod and continued her conversation.

Entering the bedroom, they found Andrew Matson's pajamaed body crumpled on the floor beside the bed. Looking just as you'd expect for someone who died of a sudden cerebral hemorrhage. Joss made a cursory examination of the body, eyes only, touched nothing, saw nothing. She expected the autopsy would report nothing.

As at yesterday's scene, she was getting zero sense of the perp. No sign of his presence; no trace of his crime. She took a deep breath, letting it out with a forceful sigh.

Mendelsohn was shaking his head. "May as well let the crew get to work. Let's talk to his wife."

Muriel Matson was just finishing her conversation as they entered the combination home office, library, and media den. She directed them to two open chairs, closing the phone, saying, "His parents—John and Marianne are both in their eighties. Andy was—this is so hard for them."

They made introductions. Joss said, "We're very sorry for your loss, Mrs. Matson—"

"Please, call me Muriel."

Mendelsohn said, "Muriel, we're assuming that your husband was murdered, same as the six men yesterday. At this point we don't have a whole lot to go on. We're hoping that as you were present while the crime occurred perhaps you experienced something out of the ordinary. Were you awake at all last night? Have any trouble sleeping?"

As Muriel quietly pondered the question, Joss was struck by her air of serenity, not at all your typical new widow. "No, I rarely have trouble sleeping, and last night was no exception." She paused, again pondering. "However, I did have a dream." Muriel let these last words hang, like a subtle challenge.

She held Joss's gaze for a long moment, then did the same with Mendelsohn, who finally asked, "And you remember the dream?"

"Yes, I remember it perfectly." She paused, eyes closed, then open and looking at them, like she was debating confession. "Are either of you familiar with lucid dreaming?"

Joss nodded as Mendelsohn answered, "Sure, that's when the sleeper becomes aware that she is dreaming."

"That's right. Becomes aware within the dream and, with experience, becomes able to influence events and circumstances in the dream world. Which, according to some, has carryover effect in the real world."

Joss winced slightly at this last bit, just enough to show her doubt. Muriel nodded and said, "If I dream that I painted my house pink, then I don't expect to find my real house painted pink when I wake up. But if I dream that you and I are in some sort of conflict and we work it out in the dream, then it absolutely shows up in our relationship. Absolutely. Crazy as it sounds to say that dreams can affect physical reality, it's equally crazy to say that they don't affect psychological, subjective, interpersonal realities."

"Which can affect the physical," mused Mendelsohn.

Muriel arched an eyebrow and smiled at Mendelsohn. "Andy and I were married twelve years ago. A pair of economics majors, he was rising in the Fed and I was doing taxes for friends and family. For the first few years we were happy and in love. Then we hit a horrible patch. We fought a lot, tried counseling, were heading for divorce.

"I did some therapy, attended a few weekend workshops, scarfed up dozens of self-help books. On the advice of my therapist I started keeping a dream journal and got to the point where I always remembered my dreams. Then I picked up a book on lucid dreaming and was inspired. Took me six months of practice to have my first LD, been a most-every-night thing ever since."

Joss wasn't sure she saw the relevance, but veiled her impatience.

"That was five years ago. I started right in on Andy and me, holding a question about our relationship as I fell asleep and then dealing with whatever came up in the dream. And, long story short, our relationship steadily improved. We just got better. The love was back. Andy was as work-obsessed as ever, but I felt full when he wasn't around and totally appreciative when he was. We were happy."

She picked up her mug for a few sips of coffee. "I never told Andy about any of it, though he knew I was 'into my dreams.' I think he thought it a harmless trifle. But I know that the dreaming saved our marriage. And more. Without it we would have been crushed when the banks blew up. He was being attacked by everybody. But Andy not only came through it, he rose to Secretary. And I was dreaming solutions the whole way." Deep breath and a long, slow exhale. "Though, I must say, I'm not always successful. The magic doesn't always work. Some mornings I wake up stressed and frustrated, means there's more work to do. Or that I just can't help."

Muriel paused again for coffee. "I first encountered this—whatever—four nights ago. I couldn't do anything with it. When I heard the news yesterday I knew it was connected to the dream. And that it was coming for Andy. I debated all day whether I should tell him. We could have slept somewhere else. Or maybe stayed awake all night. But no way to know what would work and Andy would have just thought I was being crazy. Then it was all moot because he didn't get home till past one and was totally exhausted and needing sleep. I kissed him good night—thinking good-bye—and then fell asleep.

"It's a simple dream. Andy and I are in this room and he's sitting behind this desk, but is turned and facing the windows. I'm about where you are, standing, looking at the back of his head. I'm trying to get his attention, trying to say something, but I can't get any words out. Just can't make speaking work. Then, and this is how it goes in the dreaming, I figure it out, I start talking, but now the words are too soft. So I make my voice louder, but now there's this huge noise coming from outside the house. I look to the window and there's a fire raging, outside, as if the outside is on fire and it's spreading to the inside. It's getting hotter, the noise louder. Then I'm facing Andy. He says, 'This is how it ends.' And I wake up. And Andy's gone."

Joss and Mendelsohn sat quietly, giving her time. This was the closest Muriel had been to visible grieving, but still she maintained an air of calm. She's at peace, Joss thought, then asked, "Muriel, in the dream, are you able to discern any human presence?"

"Do I know who the killer is? No, sorry, nothing like that." Another big sigh. "I realize this isn't all that helpful."

"Actually, you've been a lot of help," said Mendelsohn. "You've pointed us in the right direction. And I hope that you'll keep dreaming and let us know what you find."

Another barely perceptible wince of skepticism from Joss. Muriel saw it, smiled, and said, "I know it's hard to believe. That's why I never told Andy, or anyone else, till this morning. I'm not always sure what I believe myself. But this—I just know that Andy was attacked mentally, whether by another dreamer, or ESP, some form of thought control, something that I almost touched in the dreaming.

"The thing is," she continued, "whoever did this made a mistake when they killed Andy."

"Mistake?" asked Joss.

"They're trying to remove the power elites, right? Well, for all of Andy's high profile positions and fancy titles he wasn't making economic policy—he was just implementing decisions others were making. Why not go after his predecessor, John Morton, who had real power? Or Carver's chief economic advisor, Richard Winters, another former Secretary. Or Carver himself. Why kill Andy? Why not his bosses?"

While Mendelsohn replied, Joss opened her Book for an update. Then, interrupting, she said, "We have four more confirmed deaths—John Morton, Richard Winters, Donald Sachs and OmniBank's David Stansbeck."

Muriel Matson gasped when she heard the names of Morton and Winters.

"Well, you got that right," said Mendelsohn. "Keep dreaming. And keep us posted."

Chapter 7

In 1969, as a nineteen-year-old sophomore at Harvard, George Washington Carver stood at a crossroads, one of those you hit in life. He was black—no longer "Negro" but not yet "African-American"—and light-skinned enough that he could pass for white, the result of his mother's Irish genes. It was something that he thought a lot about doing.

His father Robinson, born and raised in Roxbury, had come home from the war in '45, a decorated and much celebrated hero. He'd spent the first couple months recovering from injuries at Dorchester Hospital. There he became the prime concern of nurse Mary Moriarty, of South Boston. Their courtship and eventual marriage was mildly scandalous, the issue mitigated by Robinson's hero status, so long as they settled, and remained, outside of Southie.

While a few of Mary's people—her mother, a brother, and two nieces—maintained the relationship and even came to Roxbury for visits, for the most part she was cut off and did her best over the years to mesh with the local community. It was testimony to her fundamental decency that she largely succeeded. She and Robinson would eventually have six children, four a deep ebony like their father, and two, Wash and his sister Lettie, closer to their mother's alabaster.

Of course, naming him George Washington Carver gave the secret away to anyone who knew African-American history. But he'd been "Wash" since childhood, and never used George. And names are easily changed, if he had wanted to really start anew. None of which would ever have occurred to Wash if his parents were still alive. But his mom went four years ago, followed months later by his father, in a clear case of "can't live without you." So it wasn't like he'd be denying his parents by changing his name, or his father by changing races.

Wash still had five siblings to think about, and lots of relatives. But the sixties had been so tumultuous and he wanted so much to *be* someone, was already thinking about a future in politics. Yet "black in America" meant either that you kept low and out of sight or that, should you try to stand tall and assert your rights, they'd kill you. So he appreciated that strangers and new acquaintances assumed he was white. Made for a less stressful existence and one with more options.

A product of the times, he never questioned the law or custom or whatever it was that made a man black if he had even a single great-grandparent of African ancestry. It was just the way it was and Wash knew that, however much he might pass for white, it would never change the fact that he was black.

He was deep into these big questions when his poli sci professor assigned a long essay on "the single most important change you would institute if you were king or queen of the world." Wash was dating a Japanese-American girl at the time and they had marveled over their mutual absence of racial biases. With the paper deadline looming, he'd had a post-coital epiphany. As king of the world he would decree that for three generations all people would have to marry and procreate outside of their race. Once all the races were thoroughly mixed, a major cause of human conflict would disappear.

It was good that no one had ever dug up that old paper. It would give the Carver's-a-radical camp a pretty horse to flog.

Last year of college, he met Danni, and his race-switching plans were quickly forgotten. She was unambiguously black, and proud of it. They had a torrid romance, two beautiful kids, and an exciting rise in Boston politics that would bring him a few short steps from the White House when Danni took ill. That she was not here with him, that she'd never gotten to be the nation's First Lady, was a deep well of sadness that would never go dry.

So much had changed in the twenty-four hours since Howie and the others died. An hour after the email arrived, President Wash Carver called a meeting of his advisors, selected Cabinet members, the vice-president, several senators, the directors of the CIA and FBI, and three of the Joint Chiefs. After all the reports and updates, the president summed up. "So, we've got some serious bad guys who are most likely not Islamic terrorists and who are killing people with a weapon we've never seen before. They're going after prominent Americans in leadership positions and say they'll be killing more. Six a day. Well, I want every law enforcement agency in America working on this, every one. No lead too small to follow. We're not officially under martial law, but until these guys are caught we need to do whatever it takes. Whatever. I want them stopped and I want it done now."

This was as angry as the president had ever gotten, despite three years of unremitting crises and disappointments. "They've already done major damage to this administration. The right'll be angrier than ever because they just lost five of their own and figure it's somehow my fault. We need to get a new Supreme Court Justice confirmed. And appoint a new Chairman of the Joint Chiefs. And with all this happening, we've lost Howie."

The president stopped, visibly saddened. He and Howie Croft went back to Carver's early days as a community organizer in Boston's south end. First colleagues, then friends, they'd worked and played together for thirty years. Carver gave Howie credit for winning him the presidency. Sought his advice on everything from nuclear arms treaties to planning his daughter's wedding.

The rest of America did not share the president's love for Howie Croft. To the right, he was an attack dog in expensive suits with a penchant for profanity. To the left, he was a triangulating pragmatist with a compass pointing to center-right. He'd viewed politics as blood sport—play aggressively, no rules, to the death. He'd been an imperious chief of staff, fiercely protective of the president, and disdainful of anyone who did not obsequiously curry his favor.

So the president also needed a new chief of staff and was thinking *irreplaceable.*

"Here's the thing," Carver continued. "Whoever's behind this is using violence to try and force political change. That's terrorism. And we do not bargain with terrorists. We cannot give in to their demands. Cannot in any way change our policies. Can not and will not."

"Mr. President," said FBI Director Wilson Russell, a holdover from the previous administration and by far the most conservative person in the room. "We need to be careful that we not approach this like previous acts of terrorism. This is a new scenario, hell, it's a whole new paradigm. First, every person in this room is presumably a potential target and at this point we're not sure how to protect ourselves or anyone else. Second, it seems to me the enemy may favor your policies, given their targets. They're eliminating barriers for you, starting with the chance to remake the Court. Judge Griffin was fifty-five. He had another thirty years. Short-term, once you appoint a liberal, the five-four votes start going your way."

"Wilson," said Carver, "you make it sound like I'm behind this, or that I might be glad it's happening. I don't think we need to give the conspiracy theorists any help—they'll be out in full force soon enough."

"No sir, and not my intention at all. I'm just trying to understand the killers. They're after 'dominators.' But they didn't kill the president. Or the Senate majority leader. They're targeting conservatives. In fact, I'm probably the most endangered person in this room."

"But how do you explain Howie?"

"That's what I'm getting at. First, Howie Croft was, according to your supporters, a strong hand directing you to the right. Second, he was certainly one of the most powerful men in Washington, and a millionaire several times over. And third, his death gives you cover—only the real crazies will think that you engineered the death of a good friend and advisor. This isn't an anti-Republican thing per se, more an anti-rich-and-powerful. Whatever their politics, all six of the dead men were in the financial upper crust. This is good old-fashioned class warfare, only it looks like the poor have got themselves a weapon."

There was an uneasy silence as a room full of millionaires contemplated this last point.

As the meeting was ending, Vice President Ian Riles tried to boost the mood, saying, "You know, we're just assuming there will be more attacks. Couldn't they just be bluffing?"

"To what purpose, Ian?," answered CIA Director Thomas Kanofsky. "People bluff when they don't have a winning hand. Right now, the enemy can strike with impunity. They'll keep killing until we stop them, or we submit to their demands."

By eight the next morning, they had six more deaths: the current and the previous Treasury secretaries; the president's top economic advisor, himself a former Secretary of the Treasury; the CEOs of the nation's two largest banks; and the CEO of the world's biggest oil company. Russell's assertion about class warfare appeared to be right on the money. So to speak.

Chapter 8

Brew Tinsley should be on a roll. Heading into the third hour of the Morning Brew, callers lighting up the board, and the juiciest fucking topic ever. Though Day One of what Brew was calling the War on Achievement had been pretty scattered—the news was breaking while he was on air, for chrissakes—he began Day Two with a half-hour, commercial-free monologue that laid it all out there, made crystal clear what was going down. The people with the power to design the weapon were the people benefitting from its use. None other than the democrats and the magic Negro himself.

Ladies and gentlemen, we're witnessing the first ever political coup led by and for the people already in power. But instead of overthrowing a bunch of worthless government bureaucrats, these cowards are killing off the best and the brightest in America. They're killing the doers and achievers, the very people that make this country great. A conservative chief justice. A conservative five-star general. The most powerful vice president in history. Conservative senators. Conservative CEOs. They even killed Howie Croft because he wasn't liberal enough.

Let that sink in for a second. They killed the president's good buddy because he wasn't liberal enough. Well the one thing that I'll say about Howie Croft is that he knew how to get things done. That was his real crime. Liberals don't like people who get things done. Don't like the people who start and run businesses, don't like the achievers and the doers, don't like the hard-working men and women who make this country go.

So they've declared a War on Achievement and they're killing us off, one by one, they're killing off the movers and shakers, the risk tak-

ers, the entrepreneurs, the so-called fat cats, the wealthy and the powerful and everyone who aspires to wealth and power, everyone who stands in the way of their socialist security state, they won't be happy until we're all dead and out of their way.

First they tried to regulate us out of existence. When that didn't work, they tried taxing us to death. Still couldn't defeat us, so now they've resorted to the most cowardly and vile—most evil of tactics, they're coming into our homes and killing us while we sleep.

It was potent stuff and had lit a fire under the Brewskis. Not that his listeners needed help getting angry, not even for day-to-day liberal shit. But this. John from St. Louis pretty much said it all:

Brew, the liberals have fired the first shots of Civil War II. They started it, just like the Pearl Harbor Japs and 9/11 sand niggers. They went after our leaders, trying to decapitate our movement. We need to stop them yesterday and start getting even. Book says, eye for an eye. It's lock and load time folks, get your weapons ready. For every leader on our side, we kill two of theirs, starting with the Mau Mau—

Though Brew had had to cut the caller off, with a token disavowal of his final words—can't be calling for the President's assassination without getting an unpleasant visit from Homeland Security—he did nothing to blunt the overall tone and message. And each subsequent caller pushed it further.

God bless the Second Amendment, this is exactly the reason the Founders included it. Weren't worried about any outside invaders, their main fear was out-of-control government. . . .

Howie Croft was trying to stop them. I heard that he went to Carver, told him he couldn't support killing Americans, so they killed him first. . . .

Carver's not behind this, Brew, he's not smart enough. It's the people pulling his strings, the liberal puppet-masters, the Kennedys, Streisand, Soros. . . .

In fact, Brew had no idea who the killers were, though Barbra Streisand was a stretch. You could obviously rule out all conservatives, including the more militant Tea Partiers and radical militias. And the word was it wasn't al Qaeda, just didn't come anywhere close to their style or capabilities. Had to be some leftist group and whether the president knew about it or not, they were working on his behalf. Really on behalf of the whole leftist, liberal, socialist cause. Which made them the enemy in a war for America's soul.

About halfway through the second hour, a caller said something about "joining Brew's Army" and how "you got us standing up to these cowards" and "it's time to win the war on liberals." It triggered a scary realization for Brew—he'd been pushing the "war on liberals" for more than twenty years, casting himself as a leader, General Brew, the liberal-slayer. All sorts of acknowledgment and plaudits from conservative politicians attesting to his power and influence. Year after year the most influential in talk radio. As the promos put it, "The most powerful conservative voice in America." Fuck.

Went right to commercials and sat for five minutes in a cold sweat. His vision went blurry, couldn't even read the names of the callers. Felt dizzy. Started thinking, it's already happening, I've been poisoned, or shot with gamma rays, or however the fuck they're doing it. Shit. Just before coming out of the break he managed to regain control. He registered that he was still alive and the sweats were passing. Just stress, he thought, you'll get through this. But he still felt queasy and for the rest of the hour he had trouble staying focused.

Now, settling in for the third hour, Brew couldn't shake the thought that how he felt now was irrelevant since it was still morning. They were killing people in the middle of the night. Wouldn't happen till he was sleeping. The only thing he knew for certain was that he had to be high on the list of likely targets. Fuck me.

Chapter 9

Mendelsohn turned his car over to another agent so he and Joss could travel together. It was nearly eleven on a bright autumn day when they finished at the Matsons. As Joss pulled away from the curb, Mendelsohn said, "We're just wasting time at crime scenes. Nothing inside of nothing wrapped in nothing. Gotta be really frustrating for the forensics folk. But lets keep interviewing family members, especially any bed-mates—though I doubt we'll come up with another witness as good as Muriel Matson."

"So, I take it you believe her account? You believe the lucid dreaming stuff? That she encountered the killer in her dream?"

"What's not to believe, doc? Lucid dreaming clearly happens, and among the various cultures that practice it, it's accepted that the dream world can influence the real world. I thought she explained it pretty well. No one's saying the 'dreaming' or 'dreamtime' affects brick-and-mortar, physical reality. But that's not all there is, is it?" He wasn't really asking. "We also have this subtle, mental, vibrational reality. Where mind-over-matter happens, ESP, telepathy, faith healing. Where lucid dreamers do their thing."

"Uh, faith healing? Have you been talking to my mother?"

Mendelsohn laughed. "So the aging hippie has issues with her daughter, the doctor?"

"More the other way around. She loves that I'm a doctor, couldn't be prouder, even when I switched to psychology."

"Psychology was Plan B?"

"Yes, I started out wanting to be a surgeon but just couldn't deal with the blood. Shifted briefly to pediatrics but couldn't face the reality of dying children. Turned out to be a slow progression from the physical to the mental. But even after I got my degrees it didn't take me long to realize that I didn't really want to deal with the mentally ill either. Then I learned that with a little extra training the feebs could build on my medical background and turn me into a profiler—psychological forensics.

"My mother thinks it's all great. But she simply and politely refuses any Western doctoring, won't take modern meds, doesn't listen to any of my professional advice. She thinks I've adopted a limited worldview. Calls me a scientific materialist. Expects me to grow out of it."

"Well, 'scientific materialist' is kinda harsh. For hard-core materialists, if you can't detect it, if you can't somehow measure it with accepted devices, then it simply doesn't exist. Period. Anyone who suggests otherwise is a know-nothing fool or lying charlatan. You can't even have this sort of conversation about it." He studied her profile as she maneuvered through the heavy traffic. "But you strike me as more 'middle way.' Your mother's world and medical science are both valid."

Joss was uncomfortable with both his scrutiny and the analysis. But really couldn't disagree. She'd been straddling the two worlds for as long as she could remember. Growing up, her mother's doctor was the wise and wizened Mr. Lee, with his acupuncture needles, burning *moxa,* and foul-tasting herbal concoctions that would brew on the stove for hours, stinking up the house. Her Americanizing father went to Western doctors and worried about his cholesterol and took whatever pharmaceuticals they thought he needed. As did, and still do, her two older brothers.

But Joss's health had been her mother's responsibility, so she too was in the care of Mr. Lee. Fortunately, she was a healthy enough kid that appointments were rare. She never really noticed her family's medical split until she was a teenager and started comparing notes with her friends. Seemed like they were all seeing smart young doctors, with their miracle vaccines, brilliant surgical techniques, organ transplants, healing cancer and heart disease and everything else soon enough. And she was seeing an eighty-nine year old coot who spoke broken English and went on barely decipherable expositions about *chi,* the five elements, and the state of something called the "triple-warmer meridian."

None of which was at all relevant to the current crisis. So she nodded agreeably, and said, "We've got an hour till the meeting. You hungry?"

They stopped for sandwiches and coffee and ate in silence until Joss said, "If you're right, if they're somehow dreaming these attacks, I still don't get how they actually cause hemorrhaging. Isn't that a brick-and-mortar, real world effect?"

"Just speculating, okay? We know that dreaming about sex can cause actual arousal to physical climax. Or that just imagining an athletic performance can have many of the physical benefits of actual practice. So they could be causing the victims to have a dream that has the effect of increasing the pressure or heating up blood vessels in the brain." Shaking his head, "Like I said, just speculating."

"Problem is," said Joss, "Andrew Matson was probably awake when it happened, given his position on the floor."

"Of course, you're right, missed that completely!" Mendelsohn stopped to rethink. "Maybe it's the killers who are doing the dreaming, and with way more ability than Muriel. And in their dreams they visit you and—what?"

They rode the rest of the way to Homeland in silence. Joss was thinking about her mother and Mr. Lee, who liked to say that if she wanted to change her body she must first change her *chi.* Whatever the hell that was.

Chapter 10

Some thirty hours into the crisis, the president's command that everybody take part in the investigation was coming together, and without the chaos some had feared. The FBI was coordinating efforts at the state level through their local offices and passing leads and findings to DC. Federal efforts, including the FBI, CIA, NSA, CDC, DoD, and every branch of the military, were all coordinated at Homeland. The usual turf battles had been suspended. Most Americans wanted the killings stopped and were willing to temporarily forego civil liberties, as the country slid into quasi-martial law. The largest manhunt in human history was underway—all databases were open to government scrutiny, including those of banks, doctors, schools, ISPs, major search engines, the military, and the judicial system.

Howard Trenton was still in charge at Homeland Security; they'd dropped the FRT designation and were now simply Homeland. His group had expanded to include representatives from each of the major federal agencies. Every bit of intel, from anywhere in the country would make its way here and into the Book; decisions, alerts, and action plans would emanate outward to reach the whole nation.

Though he had tried for a few hours sleep last night on the office sofa-bed, he'd had to settle for one brief nod-off. There'd been too much to think about and too many questions to ponder, not the least being whether or not he'd survive the night. *How the fuck are they doing it? Can they only get you if you're asleep? What if you're not sleeping at home? With so many "dominators" to choose from, how are they picking their victims?* Trenton had seen a lot of combat, dangerous, scary situations, and had always managed to sleep, but here he was, anxious as a teenage girl over a late period.

He was hardly alone. In a 10 a.m. conference call that included four Secretaries, two five-stars, the directors of the FBI and CIA, and the president, a major concern was how to structure the investigation so that it wouldn't create targets for the enemy. The President had posed a scenario where those in leadership positions were killed and then their replacements were killed until there was nobody willing or able to catch the killers. Carver'd apparently had a sleepless night himself worrying over who to appoint to the suddenly open positions at the Court and Joint Chiefs. And now Secretary Matson and a new Fed chairman. Plus replace Howie Croft, and all without putting new people in the line of fire.

FBI Director Russell pointed out that while the sample size was still small—ten to twelve deaths—the victim profile was clear: wealthy white men in positions of power, center-right politically. And so, he suggested, they should make the public face of the investigation a liberal, minority female of modest means. The president could do the same for any positions that had to be filled quickly; where possible he should just delay until the killers were caught. The trick was to keep the government running without seeming to cave into the killers' demands.

The president expressed relief that his press secretary, Marsha Switt, should be safe; still, in the near term he'd be making most of the public statements about the crisis. Everyone agreed that presidential presence and confident reassurance was critical. Just one day of this had amped the public mood to menacing, fear-driven crazy.

As for the public face of the investigation, Trenton offered that Joss Morgan and Neda Soltan were both highly capable and perfectly matched Director Russell's criteria. It was quickly agreed that, even though this looked like homegrown terrorism, an Asian doctor would work better than anybody of Middle Eastern descent. So Morgan it would be.

Trenton decided to hold the spokesperson announcement until the end of this morning's meeting. When everyone was settled in he offered a perfunctory greeting and then updated what was known. They now had verified six new deaths and he did a quick summary of each, confirming that they matched yesterday's, and that the crime scenes were yielding no information. He noted that seven of the victims were not alone in bed and that at least one, Secretary Matson, was out of bed and possibly awake when he died. FBI was reconstructing the movements of all of the victims for ten days prior to their deaths, looking for any points of intersection. They were also going building-to-building within a one mile radius of every crime scene, inspecting sites and interviewing occupants. And all relevant satellite footage and local security cameras were being scrutinized. So far, nothing to report from any of it. Finally, he pointed out the obvious victim profile—rich, white, conservative male—while thinking to himself that there were only a few potentials in the room, wealth being an eliminating factor for several, including himself. Then he asked Cam Woodstein for an update on the email, the only piece of evidence they had so far.

Cam cleared his throat. The fact that someone so young could be addressing such a sober, seasoned group was testament to the fact that youth ruled the Internet. "They used a single gmail account, doing a mass mailing to a batch of addresses in the media and government. Soon as the first deaths were announced it went viral. They signed up anonymously for the gmail account a year ago from a public computer in Europe. Same thing yesterday—they used a public computer in Portland, Oregon to do the sending. Gotta figure they covered their tracks, but we're checking out the computers, in case they messed up."

Everyone in the room had the same thought: these guys don't mess up.

Trenton then asked Joss for an update on the profile. She was nodding her head as she answered, "It's still hazy, but a picture's forming, based on three factors: the email message, the targets, and the manner of death. We're looking at a small, tightly-organized group. Pacifists, though could be ex-military, with deep convictions coming out of some bad experiences with authority. Highly-educated, upper-middle class. Male and female. Middle-aged and older. Think 'revenge of the nerds, senior edition.'"

Joss stopped for a quick smile. Remembering Mendelsohn's comment about her mother, she thought, so, we're at war against a bunch of aging hippies. And they've got the most massive military machine in history quaking in its imperial boots. It's gotta be driving the tough guys in the room nuts. Wait'll they hear the rest of it.

Joss and Mendelsohn had decided on her to present the Muriel Matson interview. Figured Scully would carry more weight with this group. She continued her report.

"We've interviewed two spouses, Beth Griffin and Muriel Matson, who were in bed with their husbands when they died. Both confirmed that nothing out of the ordinary had occurred in terms of the house, no odd deliveries, no changes in medications or diet, no deviations in their husband's routines. And nothing unusual during the night, at least for Mrs. Griffin.

"But Mrs. Matson has an, um, interesting story to tell." Joss laid it out for them: the process of lucid dreaming, Muriel's years of "dreamtime" experience, the problem solving, the question of real-world influence, then the dream itself and Muriel's conclusion that someone had "mentally" murdered her husband. Joss wasn't sure what she'd expected—laughter, derision, harrumphs and pshaws? In fact, as she spoke the room went still, with everyone on alert. After she finished there was an uneasy silence, as if she'd just proclaimed her faith in the flying spaghetti monster.

Sam Pollard spoke first. "So, you're saying that someone is thinking their way into people's brains and causing blood vessels to explode?" Though Pollard was all tough guy, Joss thought he sounded surprisingly un-skeptical. Like he'd already been heading in this direction. She glanced at Trenton and got the same feeling.

"I'm saying that a sincere, intelligent, and not-at-all-flakey witness thinks that. I'm not sure what I think. If you'd asked me yesterday if Uri Geller could really bend spoons with his mind I'd have told you it was a total crock. This is a thousand times harder to believe. I want to think that we're dealing with an exotic poison, or a GM nanobot, something that could be engineered to go active at a set time, and yet be undetectable. That's way easier for me to believe. But the truth is, everything we've learned so far points to a non-physical weapon, really, six such weapons, that can operate at a distance, that can differentiate between two people lying next to each other in the dark, and then get into the brain and trigger a specific hemorrhage. And leave no trace of how it got into the body, how it caused the death, or where it went after."

She stopped for a sip of water. "Couple all of that with Mrs. Matson's statement and, um, call me a reluctant sorta believer. Or," looking at Pollard, "give me some tangible super-weapon to believe in."

"No such creature," Pollard said, frowning. "We've got various energy beams—sonic, microwave, laser—but nothing that comes even close to this. Likewise, biotech. All sorts of nasty critters being cooked up in government labs, but nothing that fits these specs. Afraid I'm with you doctor, and have been since yesterday. This is some kind of mind control."

A few people were shaking their heads, visibly disturbed. Darrell Wells spoke right up. "Are you people kidding? You expect me to go to the president and tell him, what, that some swami is killing people with his thoughts? Jesus, Morgan, when did Homeland start believing in voodoo? This is nuts! And every second we spend on this crap is time lost finding the actual enemy and his actual fucking weapon."

Trenton held a hand up and slowly looked around the table, taking the pulse. He stopped at CIA liaison Mark Whittle. "CIA's been involved in this kind of stuff for years, hasn't it?"

Whittle had to override his natural impulse for denial. "Yes sir, going back to the sixties. Remote viewing, precog, telekinesis, telepathy. Driven by Cold War fears that the Soviets were way ahead of us in psi warfare. Far as I know it was one empty hole after another and they shut it all down in '95."

"That said," Whittle added, "I'm with the mind control theory, until we get tangible evidence of something else."

"The thing is," said Trenton, looking at Wells, "you're right. Going after a highly advanced but more or less conventional weapon is a whole different investigation than going after a psi weapon. If we choose wrong, we're wasting time while more people die."

Trenton took the temperature of the room again. Now more heads were nodding affirmatively, with only Wells in clear disagreement. Hard to shake a position that included the doctor, the top military man, CIA, FBI, and Trenton himself.

"For now we leave all of the other investigations, including FBI, pursuing the conventional. But we start after the psi. Specifically, we need to know everything the government has ever done in this regard. We need lists of all the subjects involved. We need some expert—someone who was there—in this room. We need to rethink means and opportunity and recalibrate accordingly. Mostly, we need to start asking a whole new set of questions."

Chapter 11

Source: The Progressive Report

SALLY TIGER: Good evening, and thank you for tuning in. Tonight I'll be spending the full hour talking with longtime antiwar activist, Nobel economist, and progressive icon Nathan Kane. Nathan, thanks so much for joining us. This has all been such an extraordinary turn of events. Your initial take on the dominator murders?

NATHAN KANE: Sally, like everyone else, I got the email before the first deaths were reported, before the government had made any connections. Didn't know that anyone had been killed, or how. Frankly, while I was intrigued that someone thought they could force a dominator culture to change, it struck me as quixotic in the extreme and another example of internet flimflam.

TIGER: Then the deaths were reported—

KANE: Right, and when I heard who had died and the way they were killed, I went back to the email and suddenly the message was clear, concise, and like a neutron bomb going off in American society. Eliminating key individuals while leaving everything else untouched. The ultimate military decapitation.

TIGER: Decapitation?

KANE: Remove the leadership and you might not have to fight the war. The U.S. has tried it with a string of foreign leaders going back to Castro. It's never been the most successful tactic. These days they use aerial bombing, which depends on perfect intel, which they never have, which is how we end up destroying family homes and wedding parties when we're aiming for Saddam and bin Laden.

TIGER: Explain what you mean by dominator culture.

KANE: It's all about the distribution of power. Any system or organization—be it family, business, NGO, government—has a choice as to how it makes decisions, sets priorities, establishes rules, settles disputes, allocates resources—how it manages its affairs. Who has the power to do what? How do you resolve conflicts?

You can either share power, with all members cooperating for the common good, or you can have a dominator system, where those who have the greatest capacity for dominating others take control and hold power over everyone else. So it's either "power-with" or "power-over." The primary ways of dominating—of asserting power over others—are through the use of force, the use of wealth, and the use of religion. So, in any dominator culture—and modern America is the most dominant ever—the people in charge, the people making all the decisions and reaping all the benefits, are those who have the greatest capacity for aggressive force, or the most money, or the blessings of the dominant religion. Usually a combination of all three.

TIGER: If America's a dominator culture, then what about democracy? Where does the will of the people as expressed through voting fit in this picture?

KANE: Well, unfortunately, it doesn't. Democracy is a great system for a communal or cooperative culture. It is the essence of "power-with"—everyone has an equal voice. From each and to each accordingly. But in a dominator culture elections get perverted. Candidates don't run on the issues or their skills as legislators. Instead, the one who raises and spends the most money buys the seat. Once in office they spend more time fund-raising than legislating, and most of the fundraising is nothing but legalized bribery. We end up sending rich people to Washington to make decisions and enact laws that increase the wealth and power of themselves and other rich people. It's all farce and a long, sad way from "one person, one vote."

TIGER: So then Nathan, having spent a lifetime struggling against dominator culture, only to see it grow stronger and more entrenched, what are your feelings about these Jubilees? Should we be rooting for these guys?

KANE: Sally, as you know, I served in Vietnam and came away with deep doubts about all wars, even so-called good, necessary wars. I've been a pacifist ever since and cannot and will never condone the use of violence—except in cases of self-defense from clear and present dangers. Which, I'm not sure we have here. Unless, well, I suppose you could make the case that this is an act of self-defense in the American class war.

TIGER: American class war? Are we allowed to say that on the air?

KANE: (Laughing) No, it's not exactly a favored topic, it it? But that doesn't change the fact that America is suffering from a profound class struggle. I'm reminded of something Warren Buffett said when asked whether a new proposal to tax the rich was a form of class warfare. "There's class warfare, all right, but it's my class, the rich class, that's making war, and we're winning." The rich, the overclass, have been winning for a long time, but democracy was always a mitigating factor. Over time, the underclasses got the right to vote and other minor liberations and, theoretically, their voice got louder, more powerful.

In reality, the overclass just increased its grip, especially in the last fifty years. Wealth and power has concentrated in the hands of the top two percent, while the many have gotten relatively poorer.

TIGER: The poor are losing the war.

KANE: Losing badly, and inflicting little damage on the overclass. Until now.

TIGER: So, these killings are a good thing?

KANE: Violence is never a good thing. But if we are indeed in a class war, which, after all, the rich started, then violence is already being inflicted against the poor. Which makes what the Jubilees are doing truly defensive, in which case, I'm glad that somebody is taking on the rich and doing it, so far, without killing civilians or increasing the suffering of the underclass.

TIGER: You're saying the men who were killed were combatants, rather than civilians?

KANE: Sure, all of the men who have died so far played active roles on behalf of the dominators. They all added to the misery of the underclass, even if they had little awareness of doing so. So no, not civilians.

TIGER: And does that make this a just war?

KANE: You know, I hadn't thought of it, but yes, I believe this fits the parameters of Just War Theory. Is the cause of the underclass just? Have they exhausted all other possibilities before resorting to force? Is the inflicted suffering proportional to the suffering they've experienced? Have they used the least force possible? Yes to all, and the only way to say otherwise is to think that the lives of these twelve men are of greater value than the many millions of suffering poor. So yes, we can call this a just war.

Chapter 12

The thing about being president is that not even the current mega-crisis could stop all the other necessary business from happening. Though he'd cancelled a number of appointments, he'd managed a keep-the-oil-running meeting with a Saudi prince, and the signing ceremony for a jobs bill that had been three years in the making. It was a shame to feel so deflated at what should have been a celebration of a major accomplishment for his administration. Plus, in the ensuing photo-op no one was interested in what he had to say about jobs—all the questions were about the Jubilee killings.

What could the president say? They were no closer to identifying much less stopping the terrorists. They were no closer to identifying the means of attack. They assumed six more men would die tomorrow, but hadn't a clue as to how potential victims could protect themselves. And while they had a clear picture of which Americans were most at risk, what could he tell America's rich and powerful? Leave the country? Stop sleeping? Give their fortunes to the poor?

Secretary Varnum had made the point that as panic-stricken as the nation was, very few Americans had anything to fear. This was like a virus that only attacked ultra-blue blood. At six victims a day, it would be sixteen months before they reached the 9/11 body count, and they'd be stopped long before that. There should be a way, Varnum had reasoned, to dial back the fear and panic and put the nation at ease.

The president gave it his best shot, at one point telling the gathered reporters, "Look, we know that the terrorists are threatening only a very small number of the wealthiest Americans, the people they consider 'dominators'. The vast majority of Americans have nothing to fear. As FDR warned years ago, the worst thing we can do is give in to our fears. So I implore everybody, starting with you in media, to take a deep breath, realize that you and your families are safe, and keep this from snowballing into something bigger than it has to be."

It was like he ran it up the flagpole only to watch in horror as the flagpole exploded into a thousand bits of maiming shrapnel. While there were few "dominators" among the White House press corps, they spent their time working for and with such people, and most aspired to the anchor position or best-selling book that would get them into the club. So they were on the side of panic and didn't appreciate Carver's patronizing tone. The Beltway consensus was that he'd showed callous disregard for the present and future victims, that he was not doing enough to catch the terrorists, and that he was secretly pleased with what was happening.

After the press conference, lesson learned, the President issued a memorandum telling everyone in the administration who was not directly involved in the investigation to go home and be with their families. It was no longer a matter of whether one fit the at-risk profile or not; irrational fears could be as crippling as legitimate ones—more so, precisely because they cannot be dealt with rationally. And with all of this unfolding on the Internet—well, how successful would FDR's fireside chats have been at calming the people if they'd been spending sixteen hours a day plugged into the world wide wack?

According to the online chatter, millions of Americans were taking evasive actions, moving into hotels or homes of less prosperous friends and family. Every night flight on every airline was supposedly booked, and private jets were fueled up and ready to go, in the belief that if you were in an airplane between 3 and 6 a.m. Eastern, you'd be unreachable. It was generally agreed that you needed to stay awake all night. There were stories of parties being arranged, private airplanes stocked with coffee and amphetamines that would carry the rich overseas until the danger had passed.

Official reports from FBI and Homeland described a more modest situation. Airline bookings were up, but not outrageously so. Only a small number of the rich and powerful were doing anything more drastic than booking a few nights in a local hotel. Some were just too busy. As one of the president's billionaire advisors put it, "Real dominators don't take vacations." Others flat out refused to let the terrorists dictate their behavior; those powerful enough to be on the hit list, were not about to be pushed around.

Whether people considered themselves at risk or not, everyone was tuned in. This was a 24/7 reality show—the only topic of conversation at lunch counters, office water coolers, dinner tables, and every form of media, old and new. Major newspaper editorials, TV pundits, and radio talkers, were all echoing the government's position, presenting it as an act of terrorism with tragic losses. In such outlets, there was little discussion of the email's message, nor speculation about the nature of the perpetrators. This was war, they were the enemy, and all that mattered was hunting them down. In the absence of any new developments to report, they went to spin-brushed profiles of the heroic dead.

But on the Internet, a thousand blooming Facebook pages and blogs were in support if not outright celebration of the killers. The math was simple: when the writer or speaker was a millionaire or better, they were screaming bloody murder; for most everyone else, the Jubilees had become populist heroes of the highest order. Petitions of support were circulating via email, and musical paeans to the terrorists were flooding YouTube. One site, thank-you-thank-you-thank-you.us, had collected celebratory photos sent in from all over the world, thousands in its first twenty-four hours online. Most outrageous of all were the online gambling sites, offering odds on the next to die, with increasing winnings for each one you got right.

During lunch, Carver turned on the TV and watched Nathan Kane couch the whole thing as a case of "just war," not quite saying that Howie and the others were combatants in the war against the poor, so they had it coming. And really, how could the left—and, to be honest, Carver and his administration—not be high-fiving the deaths of Mallard, Griffin, Senator Tofer, General Eisley, and Chuck Davis? They'd gained more with their deaths than they could have hoped for in several election cycles. And six more to go, every day.

The reaction on the right had been slower to take shape. With the exception of Matson and Howie (and the bankers, who everyone hated), the victims were all conservative rock stars, so there'd been an initial burst of grab-your-guns rage. As Stewart Conlin, crown prince of the neocons proclaimed, red-faced and terror-voiced, "They're killing America's best and rightest!" With the second day's deaths, the nature of the beast had come into stark focus. The terrorists could strike anybody, anywhere. Didn't matter how strong and tough you were, or how many guns you owned, or how many bodyguards you had, or how much you spent on the latest security system, you were vulnerable. Helpless. Many endangered conservatives—Republican politicians, military hawks, billionaire bankers and CEOs—retreated into please-don't-notice-me silence.

Less upscale conservatives, who mostly understood that they were not threatened, had a more complicated reaction. Because a few liberals had been included in the murders, some were pointing out that America's real fault line ran more top to bottom than left-right. Four years into the worst economy since the thirtie's, most people understood that they were barely scraping by on the bottom while the rich—liberals and conservatives—partied up top.

Still, the largest and loudest voices on the right were making the case that Carver was at least complicit in the murders, if not the actual killer. Which made for a simple storyline, quick to propagate—the liberal President is killing off conservative heroes. So while a small percentage of the right's not-so-prosperous base wa[illegible]ng the eat-the-rich, populous fever, the majority, and e[illegible] the movement's upper echelons, were uneasily alig[illegible] the government and mainstream media, at least on the key points: this is a terrorist attack; good Americans are dying; we must do everything we can to stop the killers and bring them to justice; and, we must absolutely resist in any way yielding to their demands. And, oh, by the way: the president is a mass murderer.

The religious right—what Carver secretly called the "not so religious and rarely right"—was emphatic in its anti-terrorist response. The Bible was clear in its condemnation of murder, at least when it's your own getting killed. Plus, so many religious groups these days were run by millionaire evangelists preaching a testosterone-laced mix of prosperity thinking and male domination. Though no religious leaders had been killed as yet, most were smart enough to recognize themselves as fat targets. Some were fighting back, with sermons denouncing the evil witches who were stealing souls in the dark of night. Others were sneaking away on urgent sabbaticals.

The rest of America was either secretly or overtly on the side of the Jubilees. For what were the deaths, in their sleep, of a dozen privileged men compared to the hardships that the average American suffered every day during these hard times? Some who had been out of work for years now; millions living and dying without health insurance while overfed legislators took years to craft inadequate legislation; families that had lost their homes to foreclosure and their dignity to bankruptcy; the utter disappearance of small-scale farms; millions of veterans, home from failed wars, facing a shameful lack of physical and mental health services—really, for most Americans, not to mention the rest of the world, the Jubilees were dealing hard truth and long overdue justice to a pack of pampered fools.

They eagerly awaited the morning news.

Chapter 13

As Jim Franke pulled into the parking lot of the Vermont Crest Motor Inn, he was still debating whether to keep right on to Canada. He wanted to be far away from his Manhattan condo, but close enough to get back for tomorrow's show. Getting completely out of the country would add another hour to the trip. Plus, he'd have to show his passport and bang, the government would nail him.

Franke had no doubt whatsoever that Carver and the liberals were behind this. Who else but the United States government could pull off such a crime? Who could have developed such sophisticated weapons? Who could manage nationwide surveillance of multiple citizens without being noticed by the government? And who's benefiting from the deaths of America's leading conservatives? America's leading liberals, of course. What could be more obvious?

Franke had hammered away at these points in today's show. *Just because you're paranoid doesn't mean the government isn't out to get you, hmmm? Because Uncle Jim is here to tell you, this government is out to get you, and me, and all of us who believe in Life, in Liberty, in the American Way. The people who make this country what it is, the greatest country on earth. The people who stand in the way of the liberals and their dream of a One World, anti-capitalist, pro-abortion, socialized everything, nanny state. Carver's Killers are coming for us all, the capitalists, the entrepreneurs, the small businessman and the homeschooling mom and the born-again Christian, they're coming for you, they're gonna stop you in your sleep if we don't stop them first!*

Of course, Franke knew that few of his listeners were at risk, while he may as well have a neon target painted on his back. He debated just offing himself, leaving a long note excoriating Carter and rallying the troops. His selfless martyrdom could spark the Second American Revolution. He'd be quoted hundreds of years later, like Nathan Hale. *I only regret that my show didn't have a longer run.* But no, that'd be surrendering to Carver, letting him win without a fight, and Jim Franke was not a quitter.

But sometimes you retreat, to better fight another day. Which is why Franke bolted from the studio at the end of the show, talked to nobody, told no one where he was going, got out of the city fast and all the way to Vermont without using toll passes or credit cards. He checked into the motel with a fake ID and wearing shades, paid cash, and went right to his room with a bag of groceries he'd picked up along the way. He had his laptop but had left his cells behind. He was ninety-nine percent sure that they had no way of tracking him.

Unless. Halfway to Vermont he'd started thinking about bio-chips, like the tracking devices that they put in pets, even in children. What if they'd gotten a chip into him somehow? Like when he had his appendix out last year. That was his only hospitalization in the last twenty years and he was pretty sure the chip technology wasn't on line before then. Had to be the appendix. Or the dentist. He'd had several fillings and a couple crowns in that time also. But the dentist could only put a chip in your teeth and Franke was pretty sure these chips were at the base of the skull. He was out cold for the appendix, had to be then.

Sure, people laughed, joked about tinfoil hats and all, but think about it—what other explanation is there for the murders? Phantoms? Voodoo? Mind vampires? Or, a cutting-edge nanochip, sitting right next to the vessel that brings blood to the brain, timed to explode or triggered by remote control, and bang, you're dead in your sleep without a trace of evidence.

Notice how none of the government experts had even suggested it? All the proof Franke needed. He was kicking himself now for not going straight to a doctor, somebody who could remove the chip. Of course, they probably put the chips in all the doctors first. And, oh shit, what if the chips had GPS, like pet chips? What if they knew exactly where he was? Or, fuck, if it was on a timer it didn't have to track you, didn't matter where you were, when the timer hit zero, bang, so did you. Fuck!

His hand went to the back of his neck, probing, searching with his fingers for anything that felt foreign. He considered going to a hospital, but he'd have to identify himself. Plus, most ER docs are liberals, that'd be playing right into Carver's hands. He was remembering an episode of *24* when Jack cut a chip out of his body with a knife, but if he didn't know where the damn thing was. He shivered at the thought. Plus, no knife.

After a while, his mind went blank. Couldn't think about it anymore. There were no good options. He turned on Fox, but they were rerunning his morning show, so he booted up his laptop and went online. Ten minutes of surfing turned up nothing but the same speculations that started the day. So there'd been no news, no arrests, no end to the killings. He closed his laptop, stretched out on the bed, and stared empty-headed into space until falling asleep for the final time.

Day Three

Tuesday, November 8, 2011

If we help the poor we undermine their initiative, we are told. We presume that poverty spurs enterprise. If we reduce the income of the rich we also undermine initiative we are also told. But here we presume that being poorer does not foster greater resourcefulness.

This unusual way of thinking has led us to be one of the most miserly countries when it comes to helping the needy while being one of the most generous when it comes to elevating those with more than enough. The result is concentrations of wealth of biblical proportions.

—*David Morris*

Chapter 14

In lieu of other witnesses like Muriel Matson, Joss and Mendelsohn were interviewing those who led psi experiments for the military or CIA during the sixties and seventies. It was long enough ago that anyone involved was at least in their fifties, and those who'd been in charge even older. Thus, it was a short list of names. First was Dr. Joseph Wiggenstern. "This guy's eighty-three," said Mendelsohn. "We better talk to him while we have the chance." The doctor lived in the northwest and wasn't up to flying to DC and they didn't have time to go to him and back, so they set up a video call for 9 a.m. his time.

They met in the vid room five minutes ahead of the call. While Mendelsohn went over the doctor's profile, Joss checked her Book for updates. Today's target was apparently the news media, because the four confirmed deaths included two Fox news hosts, venerable Times pundit Lester Gross, and Mr. Talk Radio himself, Brew Tinsley, the "Senator from WGOP."

"Still missing two," she announced, "but how about Tinsley?"

He frowned, looking almost dismayed, and it occurred to her that he'd seemed a tad off all morning.

"Don't tell me, you're a big fan."

His head was bobbing, halfway between nodding yes and shaking no. "Well, definitely a long-time listener, anytime I'm in the car between eight and eleven. In fact, almost turned it on yesterday when we were coming back from Matson. Too bad, would have been nice to hear the last Morning Brew. I'll have to get the podcast."

Joss was now staring at him like he had confessed to serial pedophilia. He caught the look and smiled. "Found him totally offensive. Hated his politics. Was never a 'Brewski' and never listened anytime except in the car. But my dad listened religiously, and he got me started, and it became a way to connect with him. They even sounded alike, so I could close my eyes and imagine my old man speaking." He paused, smiled, and continued, "He died three years ago, but I could always get him back by listening to Brew."

Well shit, that got her teary-eyed.

"Brew Tinsley, Lester Gross, Hal Dempsy, and Oliver Bagwell," she said, moving on. "Major conservative voices with significant audiences. All four had been fighting back hard the past two days. Bagwell did his show in his old Marine uniform, declaring open season on liberals, voicing one outrageous speculation after another. Gross's column in yesterday's Post was part tirade, part taunt, and had the title, 'Bring It On'. Dempsy's shows were unhinged rants accusing Carver of everything from overdue parking tickets to genocide. *Most* conservative leaders are playing it safe and quiet, hoping to slip under the Jubilee radar. These four were the most vocal and now, easy-peasy, they're dead. Talk about sending a message. Fox just became more interesting to watch."

"Shut him up but good," Mendelsohn muttered. "I wonder what the 'Brewskis' will do without him and Dempsy and Bagwell to listen to?"

Joss wanted to say "Who cares?" but instead asked, "What do we have on this doctor?"

"Joseph Wiggenstern is eighty-three years old and was the staff psychiatrist for a series of psych experiments the Army ran, starting in '61. He was with the project until '69, when he retired from the Army. Spent twenty years in private practice, mostly out patient care for the Seattle VA. It's unclear when the Army's experiments were halted."

They made the call and the doctor came up on their large screen: lanky but unstooped, with a mop of white hair and alert blue eyes. He was sitting in what appeared to be a library, the background lined with floor-to-ceiling bookshelves.

"I'm glad we could do this," said Wiggenstern, after introductions. "I don't travel so well anymore."

"Not at all, Doctor," said Mendelsohn, "Thank you for making time for us."

"At my age, time stops being an issue. So! You have quite a mystery on your hands. How can an old man help?"

"As I mentioned on the phone," began Joss, "one avenue that we are exploring, with some reluctance, is that the killers are using non-physical means, some form of mind control, psychokinesis, ESP, or something we've never even heard of. But somehow using their minds."

The doctor was nodding vigorously. "So you wanted to talk to someone who was part of the government's long-ago mind-control experiments? Maybe I'd know the killer? Might even be the killer?" His eyes were actually twinkling.

Mendelsohn answered, "More like we're hoping for a clear picture of just what went on and where it may have led. And, yes, if there were any individuals who stood out as especially adept at whatever it was you were doing."

Wiggenstern took his time framing an answer. "My father came home from fighting the Nazis physically whole but emotionally ruined. Classic PTSD, only then they called it shellshock, if they talked about it at all. Mostly, he just suffered in silence. I always figured he felt ashamed. I was sixteen when he came home, old enough to know he was damaged by the war and I wanted to help. I majored in psychology when I got to UW and after graduation I enlisted in the Army so that I could study firsthand the effects of war on our soldiers.

"Unfortunately, I was fifteen years ahead of the curve. The military was still ignoring the problem. The push to acknowledge what they first called post-Vietnam syndrome didn't come till the seventies. So instead of healing minds I was put to work looking for ways to make more effective warriors."

Wiggenstern paused for a sip of water, then continued, "Nonetheless, the project started off with some promise because the first thing they had me studying was LSD. A new pharmaceutical with extraordinary properties, some were saying, perceptual breakthroughs, instant enlightenment. Later I'd learn that the CIA had already been experimenting with it for several years and we were one of several projects the government was running.

"As a doctor, my prime interest was in the drug's healing potential. I felt then, and never stopped believing, that properly administered, it could help my father and others like him. But . . . that wasn't the mission. The Army was looking for a weapon. Or an interrogation tool. But LSD is just too unpredictable, and if what you want to do is hurt or kill the enemy there are far better ways."

"How many subjects did you have?"

"As many as eight, never fewer than three. Twenty-seven altogether during the time we spent on LSD. All army enlistees who volunteered for the study. Every session was followed up with a combination of psychological testing and counseling.

"As I understand it now, the CIA spent twenty, thirty years on interrogation, with all sorts of quasi-ethical and flat-out evil experiments, only to conclude what any hippie could have told them after a single trip—LSD rather undermines one's grasp of hard facts. Plays games with your memory. Any testimony you give while under the effects is pure fantasy. And coercing or, God forbid, torturing a person on LSD just pushes them further into incoherence."

Again Wiggenstern paused, and this time he looked down and slowly shook his head.

"How long did the study last?" asked Mendelsohn.

"Three years," said the doctor, "then the Tim Leary scandal broke at Harvard and the Army pulled the plug. It was very frustrating. We'd proven that it couldn't be used as a weapon, civilians like Leary were pointing to possible benefits, and I thought, here we go at last, we're discovering its therapeutic effects. Instead, LSD became taboo and we were assigned to precognition, telepathy, and telekinesis. And with the same agenda—are these mental abilities real and, if so, how can they help us win the Cold War? It was such a waste of time. At this point, soldiers were starting to come home with PTSD, made a thousand times worse because of the antiwar environment they were returning to. It was on my mind all the time. I debated leaving the army, going counter-culture, and becoming an underground LSD doc. Instead, I spent my days testing soldiers' psi abilities—guess what number I'm thinking of, predict which card will turn up next, travel out-of-body to a specified location and tell me what you see. Utter nonsense."

"So," said Mendelsohn, "you're a skeptic?"

"Well actually, no, I am a confirmed-by-experience believer. Telepathy, precog, out-of-body travel—I've seen convincing evidence of all of it. What was nonsense was the whole military-industrial approach we were taking.

"Look, if you'll grant an old professor a brief lecture: everyone agrees that love is a genuine force in people's lives. It's a real, verifiable phenomenon, a vital part of the human experience for thousands of years. A central element in human culture, yes? But what do we know scientifically about love? Two people fall in love, the oldest story in the world, a universal experience. But has science ever explained how and why people fall in love? Why, out of so many choices, this person? And why some stay in love forever while others fall apart?

"Now, many of us, by a certain age, have satisfying answers to all of those questions, born from personal experience. But that's subjective, it won't work for everybody else, may not even work for us all the time. Science can't help us with love, can't nail it down or map it out. But that doesn't make it unreal or unimportant. Quite the contrary."

Though Joss was getting antsy, Mendelsohn was locked in. There was *something* about the doctor. . . .

"The thing about love," Wiggenstern continued, "and this holds true for psi and ESP and LSD-induced experiences, is that they all derive from the human interior and so are shot full of thought and emotion. Good luck quantifying either. They're more art than science, and very soft science, at that. So we can't approach them with hard science protocols, nor should we expect to find predictability or certainty. Think back to your own experience of falling in love: if, at the moment it was happening, you and your lover-to-be were transported to a laboratory and hooked up to various monitors, then told, 'OK, continue,' while a team of scientists looked on, taking notes, well, you see the problem. Yes? That is more or less what we were doing, first with LSD and then with psi. Like going to the zoo to study wild animals."

"So, if the protocols were all wrong," said Mendelsohn, "how did the studies convince you that psi was real?"

"Yes, well, a lot of it came from personal experience, after my army years." He looked at Joss, smiled, and winked. "I've been married for sixty-one years, and like a lot of longtime couples, Eva and I have had many experiences of telepathy, still have them. Far too many to write it all off as coincidence, or to say that we're reasonably anticipating each others thoughts. When it happens, you know it. Same as when you think of calling an old friend moments before the phone rings, them calling you. It's clear to me that such experiences are proof of telepathy, but hard science rejects it all. Says, 'Come into the lab and replicate.' Yes? But of course, we can't. We're not sure why it happens and have no control over how or when. Certainly can't weaponize it. None of which means it isn't real. Or shouldn't be paid attention to when it occurs."

"Dr. Wiggenstern," Joss asked, "in the work you did for the army, did any of the men stand out as especially adept or show any extraordinary or even above-average abilities?"

"No, not at all. We were playing parlor games. Though I saw what I considered evidence of psi, it was pitifully soft. Whoever is doing this—and I gather that you think there is more than one perpetrator?—they can replicate the practice at will and have full control over who, how, and when. Nothing soft about it. If there'd been even a whiff of these abilities back then I'm sure the government would have secured it for its own purposes."

Which, of course, was the favored theory among cranks, conspiracy nuts, and the Republican Party. Which was not where Mendelsohn and Joss were wanting to go. They thanked the doctor for his time, he apologized for wasting theirs, and they ended the call, no closer to finding the bad guys.

After switching off, Joseph Wiggenstern heated some soup and bread, and sat before the TV tracking the latest on the story while he ate. Leo had sent out the new email, causing a whole new burst of frenzy. He wanted to call Eva, but rules are rules. After eating, he bundled up for a brisk walk in the chilly autumn air. Straight out the back door and onto North Beach, then a fifty yard walk to the rocks, and slowly back again.

He and Eva had lived on the island for thirty years, though he'd kept his Seattle apartment for a good chunk of the time, working four days a week at the VA, then back early Friday for three days in paradise. Ironically, it was because of those hated separations that they discovered the dream.

When he got back to the house, he turned and faced the water again and closed his eyes, and breathed in deeply the ocean air. As he'd been doing intermittently the past three days, he looked inside for change, guilt, damage. The inevitable karma.

If it was there he couldn't see it.

Back inside, he made tea, then sat at the computer and went online. The new email had already spread to every inbox in America and was the topic of chatter everywhere. He visited several sites, some news, some psych-related zines and blogs, the same sites he visited everyday. Then he logged onto the super-secure website Brett had put together for this time, for what Leo called 'the shift.' There were posts from Tom, Mia, and Eva, all doing well as Day Three unfolded. He posted his own item, relating his interview with the Homeland investigators. Logged out, moved on to several more sites, just idle surfing, then turned off the computer and stretched out on the sofa for a nap.

Chapter 15

At noon Eastern, another batch email went out to the same list of media and web addresses. Like the first, it was from a closed gmail account which would prove impossible to trace, even with Google's full cooperation. As with the first one, the subject was, "A Message for the Dominators." Should anyone doubt the email was from the actual killers, the message read:

Jim Franke and Thomas Harrow died far from home.

The gap between rich and poor is unsustainable.
It undermines society in myriad ways.
If we are to survive, we must reduce the gap,
must live in fair, equitable and just cultures.
For the common good.
Jubilee

It took less than an hour for the new message to spread to every computer, TV, and radio in America. Franke's death was immediately confirmed; the clerk at the Vermont motel where he spent the night had recognized him during check-in. Media mogul Thomas Harrow was harder to track down. He had flown out of New York the night before on his private jet, bound for France. He arrived at 7 a.m. local time, went straight to his Paris condo and laid down, as was his custom, for a one hour power-nap to sleep off the trip. His personal assistant realized he was dead a few hours later and first called Harrow's lawyer, who delayed announcing the death for business reasons, but disclosed it when contacted by the police.

Two points were clear. Only the killers could have known about Franke and Harrow before the email went out. And they knew that both men were "far from home" but got to them anyway. Investigators soon established that Franke and Harrow died at the same time as the others, despite being in hiding and as far away as Paris. Which strengthened the case that the Jubilees were using some sort of voodoo, witchcraft, demon-thought-control, which was ratchcting the fear up several notches.

After reading the email, the president immediately convened a meeting. This latest batch of deaths was especially disturbing to him. Five of these men had been publicly berating him, calling him names, accusing him of the most awful acts, doing everything in their power to derail his administration, while the sixth, Thomas Harrow, had been signing their paychecks and urging them on. The president had wished all of these men ill, had, in his heart of hearts, grown to despise them. He was not at all sorry these six were dead—a new and unpleasant feeling for him.

Most of his advisors were at the table, while a few would be joining via video links. Several aides were seated along one wall. The president asked Henry Trenton to summarize what they knew and didn't know so far.

"We now have eighteen deaths, identical in every way. Time of death is 4 a.m. Eastern, give or take ten minutes, including Harrow. Seven were alone, eleven were sleeping with their wives, and six had children sleeping in other rooms in the house. One had a pair of relatives in the guest room. Except for two of the wives who reported vivid and, they think, meaningful dreams, everybody slept through the night, with nothing out of the ordinary to report."

"At least none of them died cheating on their wives," muttered CIA Director Kanofsky. Nobody laughed.

"Crime scenes have yielded nothing, and after the Franke and Harrow killings, we'll be putting less effort into the scenes.

We already knew that the killers weren't entering the homes; now we know that they are not outside the homes, nearby, and aiming some sort of weapon at the targets. Nor are they surveilling sites," Trenton concluded.

"Well then," asked the president, "how are they doing it?"

"Sir, there are two theories at this point. We think it entirely possible with current technology to engineer a nanobot, inserted at the base of the skull, which, at a programmed time, would explode or heat up, sufficient to cause an aneurysm. This might satisfy the lack of evidence and, as I said, is considered feasible."

"But how do you get it inserted?" asked Carver.

"Without the person knowing," added FBI Director Wilson Russell.

With Howie gone, the president's closest advisor was Zia Carillo, his National Security Advisor. Like Howie, she went back to Carver's Boston days. She tended to save her input for private time with her old friend, but today was different. She said, "Some crazy on the radio today was saying that the government put something in the flu shots this year, infecting everybody with a bio-weapon that could be turned on when they, that would be we, wanted to get rid of someone. But that puts you back at turning it on for one person, but not the person lying next to him. Or turning it on for Harrow, halfway round the world."

"Right," said Trenton. "They'd have to insert it in advance, since access to VIPs would get harder once the killings started. For some of these men, I don't see it ever happening without their knowledge."

Trenton nodded to Russell and said, "Wilson's people are doing deep backgrounds on all of them, looking for common points of intersection. It'd be nice if they were all former military, or saw the same doctor, or ate the same breakfast cereal." He was shaking his head. "We're having no such luck finding links, and six more dead tomorrow makes it that much more difficult. It's a feasible theory, but with major problems."

As everyone sat with Trenton's conclusions, the president scanned the group, looking for someone who was itching to say something, some epiphanic insight that would explain it all with a huge "aha!" Instead, he saw—nothing but frustration on the faces of some very smart people.

He nodded to Trenton. "The second theory?"

"Mr. President, when we eliminate all possible physical explanations what we're left with is a non-physical method of attack. Something that we can't see or hear or measure with the standard tools."

The president lifted his hand. "Excuse me, Howard, but it sounds like you're trying hard not to say that they're killing people with their minds."

Trenton grimaced. "Yes sir, something like that. But, I have to say, we may as well claim they've employed a team of ghost assassins. Or invisible ETs. If we have no idea how they're doing it, then we have no idea how to stop them. It means admitting that any one of us could keel over dead right now. Because someone somewhere thought it."

Kanofsky broke in. "We don't need to know how they're doing it, we just need to find the bastards and shut 'em down. If their minds are lethal weapons then we pump 'em full of drugs. Give 'em lobotomies. Disarmed, crisis over."

As the person in the room most likely to keel over dead, the CIA director's impatience was understandable. The president gave him a sympathetic nod, then turned back to Trenton. "So what are we doing to find them?"

"As you may know, the government has been involved in a number of psychic studies, going back more than fifty years. Military, CIA, some academic. We started looking in that direction right away, and have pulled together a comprehensive list of all such studies and participants. We're looking for any studies that stand out, or any subjects who showed the sort of ability that we're dealing with here—influence at a distance, telekinesis, astral projection. We obviously need access to everything," glancing in Kanofsky's direction, "no matter how deeply classified.

We're assuming that abilities such as this don't just appear one day, that there'd have to be some history of development."

The president looked to Kanofsky and then General McAdams, Chairman of the Joint Chiefs. "Gentlemen, let's be sure that everything in any way pertinent to this investigation is made available to Howard's team."

McAdams answered with a clear "Yes, sir," while Kanofsky simply nodded.

The president held his gaze for a long moment, then said, "OK, what else? What about the note?"

FBI was doing its own profiling, so Russell took over. "The second note confirms Henry's observations and adds a lot to the profile we've been building. This is not a bunch of young, angry hotheads. Or sociopaths. Nowhere close to the usual terrorist profile. There's more than one, but not a large group, we're thinking less than twenty. Probably male and female. They're older, say middle-aged and up. American citizens, white, well-educated and well-off. Leaning hard to the left, anti-capitalist, anti-corporate. Passionate about their cause though not out of personal grievance. They're willing to kill non-combatants to force political change, though they may view the victims as combatants in a class war. They're convinced their cause is just."

"Is this religious?" asked Carillo. "Isn't Jubilee a Christian thing?"

"Well, yes, that word has raised some questions. Is it intended as a command or a signature or both? As a command, it has roots in both Judaism and Christianity. While the details differ, the main thrust is the same—Jubilee is a time of—I guess you could say religiously-enforced power-sharing. A time to forgive all debts, to give slaves their freedom, and to release all indebted prisoners. The rich were to return land and property to its original owners. Could include God's forgiveness of sins, like a universal pardon. There have been numerous 'Jubilee Years' throughout history, the most recent being 2000, when there was a big push to forgive poorer nations of their debts. Not much came of it, but we should definitely be looking at advocates of debt relief."

"So," asked the president, "by calling themselves 'Jubilee' they're telling us this is what they want?"

"Yes sir," said Wilson. "People on the left and the right have been clamoring for something like this since the early days of the financial crisis, basically a citizen's bailout to match the ones that, they say, Wall Street got. Instead, they got foreclosures, bankruptcies, unemployment, lost pensions. They're still hurting, still in debt, angrier than ever at how well things have gone for people at the top. Damn, I think we'll see a lot of people lining up behind a call for a Jubilee. Which, to answer your question, Zia, makes me think this is not coming from any one religion, but it is following a religious impulse that goes back a long way."

Yesterday, the president lost both his Treasury Secretary and his chief economic advisor. He asked William Atkison, who'd served in the treasury under Reagan, to sit in. Atkison had spent much of the past three years criticizing the administration's approach to the financial crisis, and become an unlikely spokesman for the populist cause. The president looked to him now. "William, how would it work? I mean, is a national forgiveness of debts even possible? I just want to get clear on what they're asking. What would it look like?"

Before Atkison could say a word, Kanofsky nearly jumped out of his seat. "Mr. President, we can not give in to these bastards. We should not even be thinking about it. No negotiations, no accommodations, nothing. You cannot let a small band of psycho terrorists dictate major policy changes. Besides, what have they done? They've killed eighteen people. They've declared war on us, they've fired the first shots, and we're taking casualties. But we cannot be talking surrender."

Carver welcomed dissent in policy discussions and now was no exception. As he was framing a reply, the usually taciturn General McAdams spoke up. "Director Kanofsky, though I would never advocate for surrender or appeasement, I don't think you're appreciating the implications of what these people are doing. This is pure political decapitation—take out the leaders and win the war. Same as we tried at the start of the Iraq War, only they're hitting their targets. Instead of struggling through a bunch of pawns, taking casualties the whole time, you go right for the king, mate, and game over. Good strategy, and, compared to our efforts, these guys are grand masters."

Kanofsky started to answer, but the general held up his hand and continued talking. "Point is, these eighteen deaths have already impacted America more than the 3,000 on 9/11. They didn't just remove men from key positions and silence strong voices of opposition. They've sent a clear message to anybody who would take their places—change the policies or suffer the consequences. If the president replaced Judge Griffin with another conservative I have no doubt that the replacement would be the next to go."

"So we just don't make any appointments or any large policy decisions until after they're caught," said Kanofsky. "And likely targets keep their mouths shut." He smiled, and added, "And maybe I take my own advice."

"If I were them," said the general, "I'd punish inaction. First, I'd go for the most visible, most vocal, most meaningful targets. As they've done. Then any replacements who try to sustain their predecessors' policies. A few rounds of that and you've ended vocal opposition. Then you go after those who just aren't following their commands. At some point, and I would think soon, if there's no serious movement toward their demands, they'll start killing liberals too." He paused, looked at Kanofsky, and continued, "And I don't think we'll be catching them anytime soon. They're obviously smart, a small, tight-knit group that's been planning this for a long time. Disciplined. These guys are playing a game for which we have no defenses."

"They'll make a mistake. Criminals always do."

"Underestimating this enemy would be the worst mistake we've ever made."

Chapter 16

Ryan Weathers always wanted to be the president of a bank. His father worked his entire life for Capital Bank in the small town of Collswood, New Jersey. They'd lived just three blocks from the bank and Ryan's earliest memories were of his father, dressed in suit, tie, and hat, briefcase in hand, kissing his mother good-bye, and then out the front door to walk to work. Some days he'd walk with his father to the bank and then sit beside the huge roll-top desk, watching him talk on the phone and dictate to his secretary, until his mother came with doughnuts and coffee, and cocoa for Ryan. Sometimes his father took him into the vault—still, cold, quiet and overflowing with goodies. When Ryan was seventeen, his father made vice president of the bank and started driving the three blocks in his new Cadillac. A few years more, he was president. He ran the bank another twenty years until his retirement at sixty-four, a wealthy and supremely satisfied man.

It was all Ryan ever wanted. So he went to Harvard and graduated cum laude with his MBA. Then right into a position at Bank of Boston, and into what he was now beginning to look upon, nostalgically, as his golden years. He and Carolyn, young, hot, in love. The Back Bay apartment, and every morning he'd kiss her good-bye and walk through the Public Gardens to the bank, where he spent his days doing pretty much what his father did, only with better tools and for much better money. It was the early nineties, the boom was on, and it was their story to write, happy endings as certain as the year-end bonuses.

Carolyn got pregnant. Not exactly planned, but great news nonetheless. Only problem was the apartment—already tight, no room for a baby, and besides, it was time for them to own. They started searching, looked at in-town condos, suburban homes, but nothing felt right. Ryan kept saying that he could live anywhere, but Carolyn thought she would know it when she saw it, like there was only one house in the whole world for them and she had to find it.

Then came the Marsdale Lipman offer. One of the nation's top investment banks wanted Ryan to come to work in their Mergers and Acquisitions division. The offer came with a sweet deal on a three-bedroom Manhattan condo. With Carolyn's parents in Brooklyn and Ryan's in Jersey, the chance to be closer to all with a baby on the way was the sign Carolyn had been waiting for. This was their new home.

Fifteen years later, the move was a mixed bag for Ryan. Personally, he could not have been happier. Joe was fifteen, Cari twelve—two great kids, smart, funny, and full of life. Carolyn thrived in the city, loved being a mom, and negotiated a long list of daily to-dos with efficient grace. While Ryan worked fifty- and sixty-hour weeks, his time with his family always rejuvenated him. It helped that the long hours brought in enough money to answer the material wants, including the larger condo, the shore house, the private schools, and the latest fashions.

Professionally, he'd had a rougher time, though no one but Carolyn was aware of it. At Bank of Boston, he'd spent his days doing things for people—listening to their stories, vetting their proposals, arranging loans, working out qualifying details, coming up with second and third ideas when the first fell through. At the end of the day, he could point to a young family moving into their first home, or a new café on Newbury St., or a future college education "in the bank." He could look at it all and say, "I did that." Often, the young wife or the café owner would send a thank-you note, proving that he did indeed do something that mattered.

He'd only been at Marsdale Lipman a few weeks when he realized that many of his co-workers spent their days selling securities that were devoid of any tangible value and didn't follow any of the rules of good banking. It was speculation, pure and simple. Casino banking. Account managers acted like Vegas gamblers, only better dressed and with an arrogance that comes from always winning. Ryan was more than disappointed, he worried he'd get entangled in the shady ethics and possible crimes. But he kept these thoughts to himself at work. He reasoned that the security speculation was just one piece of Marsdale Lipman. While his work in M&A had its own ethical gray areas, at least it was real, and entirely legal.

The one thing he never really considered was quitting. As somebody—Sinclair Lewis? Upton Sinclair?—once said, "It's hard to get a man to understand something, when his livelihood depends on him not understanding it." He and Carolyn were financially wed to the firm, at least until the kids were grown and on their own. So Ryan overlooked, ignored, denied, rationalized, excused. Whatever it took to keep plugging away. Over time, the casino bankers became the firm's superstars, as they innovated ever more exotic instruments for taking the gamble out of speculation.

When they started securitizing subprime mortgages, Ryan could no longer keep quiet. He knew the mortgage business. There are rules that should never be broken. Such as keeping the cost of housing near thirty percent of monthly income. Or the simple fact that housing prices could not keep rising forever. The vast majority of these subprimes were heading to default, the housing bubble was bound to burst, and all the derivatives that the firm was peddling were essentially worthless. Ryan became convinced that the US was heading for financial armageddon, with catastrophic effects worldwide.

In '05, he managed his first private meeting with CEO Donald Sachs. He calmly made the case against subprimes, and recommended that the firm get completely out of the business and discreetly move to unburden some of their biggest clients. Sachs gave the impression that he was listening; in reality, Ryan may as well have shown up in a long robe, holding a sign proclaiming "The End is Near, Repent!"

"Well," said Sachs, after Ryan finished talking, "you make some interesting points, but really, you should stick to your strengths because I'm afraid you don't understand investment banking. We're not making loans to naive, young married couples. We're dealing with large institutions and sophisticated investors. Everything we sell is government regulated and top rated. Frankly, nobody agrees with you, not me, not the overseers, and especially not our customers. They very much want what we're selling."

"They may want it, but they have no idea what it is. Derivatives, I mean, if the underlying loans are crap then so is anything derived from them."

"Mr. Weathers, I don't appreciate your tone. And, again, you're simply wrong. Some loans will default, that's always the case, but that's why we bundle them, to balance the bad paper with good. Now, I shouldn't have to tell you that doomsaying is bad for business. You're doing excellent work in M&A, for which you're being well compensated. I suggest that you focus on your work and leave the investment bankers to theirs."

Ryan did as he was told. He became the M&A go-to guy. He enjoyed ever-increasing salary and bonuses. He tuned out the crazy stuff. It was none of his business.

Two years later, it was everybody's business. The subprimes hit the fan and nearly took down Western civilization. Though nobody said, "You told us so," Ryan's standing in the firm shot up. First, because everyone knew he got it right, and second, because unbeknownst to Ryan they did in fact take his advice, sort of—after his meeting with Sachs they started short-selling the very products that they were pushing on their customers. So the firm made money selling the damn things, then made more money when the damn things defaulted. As the crisis unfolded, Ryan hated being a banker, hated everything about it, could barely face Carolyn and the kids. He expected that all the banks, starting with Marsdale Lipman, would be broken up, with bankers being frog-marched off to jail.

To his surprise, the firm took a lead position in resolving the crisis. Actually, was given the lead position, first by Bragg and then by Carver, thanks to the Marsdale Lipman alumni in key government positions and all the millions spent lobbying. It was an astonishing turn of events. For all the populist anger at the banks, for all the political yammering about tighter regulations, and for all the financial suffering of the nation as it struggled through four years of the Great Recession, the firm grew more powerful than ever, nobody lost their jobs (much less went to jail), and the rich were, no surprise, getting richer. It was a grotesque amorality play; the bankers were paid outrageous sums to not really clean up their own mess and there was nothing the American people could do but whine about it.

Until Day Two of the Jubilee murders. The first day was a Sunday, and the killings had all been political, so everyone showed up for work Monday morning talking about it, but not feeling at all threatened. But then as the news hit—Sachs, Matson, Morton and Winters—the firm went certifiably batshit crazy. Their stock tanked, all deals-in-progress halted, and the phones rang incessantly with customers wanting out. The firm was not only missing its CEO, it had lost the three men, all Marsdale Lipman alumni—who were steering the government through post-crash waters. It was impossible not to think that the firm was under direct attack, that everybody working there was in the cross-hairs. Even the secretaries felt it. Though the email had said "six a day," if they could kill six, why not more? They obviously had a hard-on for Marsdale Lipman; they could wipe out the entire firm tomorrow. Everyone who had sick days left early.

Day Three, and though no more bankers were killed, the financials were all heading in the wrong direction, fast. The Executive Committee held an emergency meeting, a group of twenty, which included Ryan. Senior vice president J.T. Clayes, now acting CEO, led off the meeting with another shocker. After paying somber respect to Sachs and the others, he said, "As for going forward, I am sorry to say that I am resigning from Marsdale Lipman, effective immediately." He waited thirty seconds for the room to quiet. "For nearly forty years this firm has been my life, my true family. And it's no secret that I've been working toward being CEO. But not this way, not under these circumstances. If I were in charge, I would do everything to continue, to emulate the exceptional work that Don did. I wouldn't change a thing. But of course, that's the problem, isn't it? These killers are apparently from the blame-the-bankers camp, and they seem to have particular animus toward us. And they're saying, change your policies or die. Well, I refuse to change but don't want to die. Much as I love my work, and this firm, it's not something worth dying for. Not like this."

"But John," said Harold Leonard, who, Ryan was pretty sure, was next in line for CEO, "why not just stall for a bit, doing nothing provocative, until they catch these assholes?"

"Sure, we can. Sounds like a reasonable plan. But how do we know if they're on board with it? Maybe tonight they take me, you, and the next four in line. Till they get somebody who will do whatever they want. Whatever the fuck that is. Are you willing to make the gamble? I'm not. I've got all the money I need and grandchildren to play with."

CFO Jay Little spoke up. "Stalling is not an option, anyway. Investors are bailing on us already, and it's picking up steam. The numbers are just sick. Any more bad news and we've had it. Really, we can be gone like that," he said, snapping his fingers. "We sure as hell can't count on the government to come to our rescue, can we? We've lost Andy, lost Richard, John—there's nobody left over there. People, we are screwed if we don't do something, today, something strong, affirmative."

Clayes was nodding, but in agreement with the futility of their situation. He had lost the will to fight, no question, as had, Ryan thought, just about everyone around the table. Finally, Leonard said, "Well, fuck if I'm standing by while a bunch of ghosts steal everything I've busted ass for. I nominate myself as CEO. I propose that I call an emergency meeting of the Board and major investors, press included, later this afternoon. I'll talk about the tragedy of Don's death, murdered in his sleep for the crime of running the most successful bank in the world, and make it clear that we're the victims here, that the American people are the victims, and these ghost fucks are everybody's enemy. And that Marsdale Lipman has no intention whatsoever of giving into threats, and turning into some communist institution. We can't let this happen. I won't."

It was a rousing enough speech to get a few heads nodding affirmatively. Everyone else looked like they just wanted to get out of the room and far away from Marsdale Lipman, as quickly as possible.

Chapter 17

For all his preaching about heaven and hell, "America's Pastor" spent little time contemplating his own death. Paul Sheppard considered himself a righteous if flawed man, like the apostle for whom he was named. He never doubted that a lifetime of good works would outweigh his minor transgressions on Judgment Day. Sheppard was strong and fit at seventy-five, no reason he couldn't live to a hundred, like an Old Testament prophet.

He just had to pass this test. Dear Lord, what a test. These ghost killers, these voodoo witches, stealing souls in the dark of night, come to test America, like Jesus in the desert. Tempting America to surrender, to give up power. To renounce the Lord for some secular tyranny.

But didn't the Bible say that men should command their wives and children, that preachers should command their flocks, didn't God say right in Genesis that man was given "dominion over the fish of the sea, and over the fowl of the air, and over every living thing that moves upon the earth?" Didn't God say, "Subdue the earth?" Subdue! Command! Dominate! The Bible is one long story of men wielding absolute power over others, because God commands it.

Paul sat before the microphone in the BFC studio, feeling the Holy Spirit flowing through him, speaking through him. In the years since he founded Broadcasting For Christ, he'd done thousands of radio and television shows. For the really important messages, radio was better. Nothing but the Word, plain and simple.

Do we discount the Bible over an anonymous email? Do we abandon our faith over the threats of godless criminals? Do we deny our Lord because we're afraid? Is that who we are, helpless children, quivering in fear, pleading for our lives, trembling before heathens and devil worshippers? The Lord is my shepherd. I shall not want. Though I walk through the valley of death, I fear no evil! My brothers and sisters, we are in that valley now, death surrounds us, a smothering cloak woven by the devil's own hand. But we fear no evil! Death comes to steal away the Holy Spirit, to steal away the light. But we fear no evil! We fear not!

People were saying, on the Internet, the cable shows, even some whispering at BFC, that he was on the list, doomed. Ultra-conservative, mega-rich, Christian dominionist. Currently, number four at six-a-day.com. It was like he was standing in the colosseum, surrounded by the howling Romans, calling for his death, turning thumbs down. But it just pumped him up, got him going. He couldn't keep quiet, couldn't tone it down, could not. Paul had seen right off that this was a test—not just testing him, the man; this was a challenge to God Himself. These ghost killers had some sort of power, no question. So they needed to be shown the power of Jesus. Rub their noses in it. It was time, time for the world to bear witness. Time for God to defeat evil, in clear sight, in the world of men.

His followers, bless them, had risen to the challenge. Someone on the Internet proposed coming together in one great prayer circle, praying through the night, surrounding Pastor Paul with love and light and protection. The idea had gone viral and now millions, many millions of believers from all sects and denominations were adding their prayers, creating a holy shield around Paul Sheppard. He was humbled almost beyond words.

Tonight, my friends, the forever war between good and evil reaches its climax. Tonight, the forces of good will pray the mightiest of all prayers. We will demonstrate, now and forever, that there is but one God in this world and He rules! But one God, and He commands. One God, and He overcomes all evil! Let the word go out, to all who can hear, let the message spread to all nations, join us in this battle, join us in this prayer, join us in your thoughts and dreams, join us! When the sun comes up tomorrow, we will all be there, together, alive with the Holy Spirit, victorious, and the world will know the awesome power of our God!

As he pushed away from the microphone, he was shaking, quaking with the spirit, quickened with the power of a million blessings. He'd never felt so alive, so vital. He would do more than just survive the night, he would wake up in the morning ten years younger, healed by the combined power of human prayer and God's love. It would be a modern miracle—undeniable evidence of the one true God and the only true religion.

Paul was ready. Ready for sleep, ready to meet these demons, to face them and defeat them. *I will fear no evil.*

Chapter 18

The two men in the *DC•PM* green room were sitting as far apart as the room would allow, each wondering how they got roped into an appearance with the other. George Deeds, of course, was a regular on this and many other news and opinion shows, as well as a longtime columnist for the *Post*. But Nathan Kane, though a Nobel economist, prolific writer, and staple in college curricula for some forty years, rarely appeared on prime time TV, not even PBS. People assumed it was because he was too far left for the average viewer, but Nathan knew otherwise. He just didn't fit the format. For these shows you needed to talk fast and loud and in short, easily-digested sentences. And you had to adhere to the accepted narrative, what he once called "the manufactured middle."

But extraordinary times, he supposed, called for frumpy old college professors. The Jubilee killings had set into motion an unprecedented political realignment in America. The corporatist right was experiencing an acute power vacuum as nobody stepped forward to replace the recent departed. Today they lost their most prominent media voices and, again, it seemed unlikely anyone would be taking their places soon. On the left, quite the opposite; power sharing, debt forgiveness, demilitarization, redistribution of wealth—a batch of old lefty daydreams—were now on the ascendant, finding a place in the national conversation. And people wanted to hear what Nathan Kane thought about it all.

A young woman stepped into the room, said "five minutes," and stepped back out. Nathan and Deeds made eye contact and held it long enough that Deeds began nodding his head. "USC, 1986. We were on a panel discussion about Reagan and the contras. I was defending the great man and you were arguing treason and proposing war crime trials." He smiled.

Nathan returned the smile. "You, the three other speakers, and the moderator, as I recall, all defended Iran/Contra. Making me the Reagan-hating radical."

Deeds just nodded. Hard to tell if he was agreeing that Nathan had been treated unfairly or that he was indeed a hate-filled radical. The moment was broken as they were called to the set. After introductions and a smatter of small talk, Matthew Crissom cut to the chase.

"George, as you know, we had trouble getting anyone to come onto the show. I mean, just to come and talk! The president's put a temporary ban on administration appearances, presumably so no one says anything that might get them killed. And conservatives, after Tinsley and Franke, I mean, that was only this morning and we've already had a wave of cancellations. So, I appreciate your coming and have to ask, are you worried about what you say? Does it feel like maybe you're on trial here?"

"Well, I just don't think you can hide, not with a public record like mine. And if I start talking like a liberal it'll just feel phony and they could kill me anyway. But I do sense an ethical streak in these killers, these Jubilees. It seems to me they are not targeting conservative ideology so much as—well, I'm not sure what you call it, I'll leave that to Nathan, but—the greedy bankers, the corporate fat cats, the military-industrial complex. Seems they're going after the men who actually run the country, or, someone like Brew Tinsley, who has a huge following, Jim Franke, also a huge following, who saw themselves as generals, directing their armies of listeners and viewers and such. I certainly don't have millions of readers hanging on my every word, ready to storm the White House when I say go."

"Have you checked out your position on six-a-day?"

"I consider that and all the other sites glorifying these terrorists to be public obscenities. So, no, I have no idea if I'm a good bet to die tonight, or not," Deeds replied.

Crissom turned to Nathan. "You've spent a lifetime advocating for the sort of change, the social justice that the Jubilee killers are trying to force. What do you think about what they're doing? And what about the public reaction, the websites and Facebook groups and now a rally in DC in support of them?"

Nathan paused for a breath and could feel Crissom's instant impatience. No on-air dead time. Speak up! "Well, there're several questions there, Matt. They are, as you say, trying to force a change, and the irony, or really the conundrum, is that they are trying to force America to stop governing by force. The men who died all had great power—a combination of money and access to or control of state-sanctioned violence—and they used their power to force decisions and policies that often went against the democratic choices of the American people. This is what the Jubilees mean by "the dominators"—people, mostly men, who can force others to submit to their will."

"I'm sorry, Nathan," said Deeds, "but 'state-sanctioned violence'?"

"Well, we call it the rule of law, but it's basically a protection system for the rich and powerful. The only thing that's keeping out-of-work, foreclosed, and bankrupted Americans from storming the estates of the bankers who made millions while committing financial murder are legal enforcement agencies—police, FBI, the National Guard, private security firms, all ready to use maximum force. That's state-sanctioned violence, and it's no different than sending the Marines into third-world countries to protect corporate interests, otherwise known as local resources. We can fancy it up with hallowed documents and parliamentary procedures but anytime the powerful are seriously threatened, they bring out the guns."

Nathan took a quick sip of water. "But when those same bankers decide to foreclose on some poor schlep who's underwater and out of work, they flat-out invade his home and throw him and his stuff on the street and send the sheriff to make sure he goes, and if he's foolish enough to fight, they arrest him. Or worse. The threat of violence underlies all dominator systems, whether we're talking about a country, an organization, a business, a family."

Crissom cut in. "I'm not saying that I agree with your analysis, but how does this tie into the Jubilee murders?"

"Well, it's really an ancient dilemma: if I am living in an unjust situation, under the violent domination of others, and I resort to violence to overcome my oppressors, then I become that which I was fighting against. Now I'm the dominator using violence to control others. It's why so many revolutions end poorly, however righteous their origins. Why it's so hard to break the cycle of violence once it gets going. So, the Jubilees are up against this problem: how to violently eliminate what they perceive as the bad guys without taking their place and starting a new cycle. I'm not sure it can be done, though they've come up with an extraordinary approach."

"Sounds like you approve of what they're doing," said Deeds. "Do you condone these murders?"

Nathan suddenly understood why he'd been invited on the show. Crissom pressed the point. "Before you answer, Nathan, this is from a conversation you had with Sally Tiger yesterday."

They ran a clip of him, sitting across the table from Sally, making the case for class warfare: *If we are indeed in a class war, which, after all, the rich started, then violence is already being inflicted against the poor. Which makes what the Jubilees are doing truly defensive, in which case, I'm glad that somebody is taking on the rich and doing it, so far, without killing civilians or increasing the suffering of the underclass.* Then: *I believe this fits the parameters of Just War Theory . . . the only way to say otherwise is to think that the lives of twelve wealthy men are of greater value than the many millions of suffering poor. So yes, we can call this a just war.*

Then Crissom, with gotcha glee, said, "Not quite breaking out the pom-poms, Nathan, but it sounds to me like you're taking sides. Do you condone these killings?"

Nathan didn't squirm or get defensive or complain about being quoted out of context. He did take his time framing a reply, which had been incubating since his conversation with Sally. "I'm a pacifist. I could personally never do what they're doing, or order others to do it, or provide material support of any kind for their actions. That said, I view what's happening as potentially positive. For the very reasons I gave on the clips you just showed. America is being torn to pieces by class warfare, and the poor and middle-class are suffering enormously. The Jubilees are fighting back, effectively, and within the bounds of Just War Theory."

"Oh come on, Nathan." Deeds had lost the having-a-friendly-chat smile. "These men are being murdered for the crime of success, of making and investing money and, in the process, creating jobs for the very people you say they're at war against. They never intentionally targeted another person, never wielded a weapon, rarely even thought about the so-called underclass, much less wage war against them. You certainly can't hold them responsible for the failures of the poor. Just absurd."

"The Jubilees apparently disagree, George," remarked Nathan.

"Look," said Deeds, "America clearly has it's failings, and the rich have huge advantages over the poor, whose suffering is lamentable. But you're justifying—you just called cold-blooded murder 'potentially positive'."

"Which Americans do every day we're at war, don't we? When we hear that one of our drones has accidentally obliterated an Afghani wedding party, do we rise up and demand an immediate end to the war? Do we worry over how we can condone such killings? That kind of atrocity happens on a regular basis in Afghanistan, in Iraq, in all wars, but it never ends the carnage, doesn't even slow it down. We might not call it cold-blooded killing, but I assure you the survivors do. Instead we say, it's collateral damage, all wars kill innocents, it's just the way it is. Bottom line, big picture—we see it as potentially positive. We hope in the long run it furthers our objectives."

"But Nathan," said Deeds, "those are real wars, necessary wars, and yes, all wars kill indiscriminately. This class warfare you're talking about—it's pseudo war, a liberal fantasy, undeclared, undefined, the so-called combatants don't even know they're fighting or that their neighbors are really the enemy. Sounds like you want America to have a second Civil War."

"Well, no. It's more that I agree with Warren Buffett, who said the war's already on and the rich are winning. Casualties are strewn across the American landscape. It's estimated that forty thousand Americans died in the past year due to inadequate access to health care. While that's better than the fifty-five thousand who were dying before the reforms, it's still a lot of collateral damage. Add in several million foreclosures, twenty percent real unemployment. All casualties of something, whether or not you call it war. And what can these beleaguered people do? Our vaunted democracy has devolved into oligarchy—everyone in and out of government knows that corporate money is running the show—so what recourse is left when voting is rendered meaningless?"

Deeds was shaking his head in vigorous disagreement. Nathan continued, "These years since the financial meltdown we've seen a building populist rage, but it's been blind rage, inchoate and not entirely rational, with the underclass fighting among themselves. Now they have a champion. If you ask me, the biggest surprise of the past three days is that the militant right, with all their weapons and hatred of Carver and threats of secession, has been so quiet. After the initial, knee-jerk accusations that it was all Carver's doing, it now looks like they're standing down and waiting to see how it all unfolds. They might not entirely like the Jubilees' agenda, but I think they appreciate their methods. If the Jubilees can unite the left and right factions of the American underclass, while simultaneously weakening the overclass, we might avoid a second Civil War for something better—the second American Revolution."

Chapter 19

It'd been a busy day for Joss and Mendelsohn. Interviews all morning, a working lunch at Homeland, up to Manhattan to see Olivia Harrow, then the late afternoon press conference, and flying back to Reagan National. Now they were having a late dinner in an airport restaurant, chosen not for its food, but for the airport ambience that allowed them to peck away on their Books while eating. It didn't take either of them long to catch up—Day Three had seen no breakthroughs, no hot leads.

Joss snuck a look at Mendelsohn, chewing his food while thumbing a text message on his phone. This was the third meal they'd had together now, kinda like a couple. While they'd been professional in their interactions, Joss had to admit that she was enjoying her time with this interesting, funny, and not unattractive man. She'd been single for more than a year, ever since showing Corey the door. Much as she liked being on her own, it was a work-obsessed existence that at times left her feeling unfinished. Like she had a vague but persistent itch that she couldn't reach without help.

She and Mendelsohn of course, mostly talked about the case when together, but there'd been a few stretches of personal revelations, enough that she could piece together some of Mendelsohn's story. Three years older than she, he'd graduated with a law degree from Michigan State and applied immediately to the FBI, his lifelong dream. Fell in love with a schoolteacher, got married, divorced a year later. All work and no play, just like Corey and herself. No kids. Second year, he was a junior analyst working the tip hotline. He'd taken a call from a psychic who claimed she'd "seen" a little girl who'd just been kidnapped in the night from her Atlanta home. The family was following the kidnapper demands—no cops, no FBI—so the Bureau didn't know it had happened. Mendelsohn encouraged the woman, listened, and asked questions. She responded with such detail—street names, an auto body shop sign, three men, a white guy with thinning, dirty-blond hair pulled back in a ponytail—that the Atlanta office thought it worth a look. The surveillance team saw a skinny meth-head with a scraggly ponytail enter a building with a bag of groceries. An hour later, the Hostage Rescue Team had an unharmed ten-year-old in hand. No casualties, just two dead perps; ponytail would live to go on trial. Mendelsohn was an overnight sensation. The *X-Files* hero.

"The thing is," he said, "they praised me for my instincts, but dismissed the psychic as a fraud. Said she must have known somehow, had some connection with the kidnappers, which they failed to unearth after a lot of looking. Threatened to prosecute her for aiding and abetting. I mean, shit, she'd never been out of Ohio." Shaking his head. "Made me damn curious, if not an outright believer. The Bureau's official position was 'try not to think about it.'"

Joss had listened sympathetically and without comment. She felt herself naturally inclined toward the Bureau's position, but after the past two days—well, at least she *was* trying to think about it. Just didn't know what to think.

They'd been sent to interview Olivia Harrow, widow of billionaire media giant Thomas Harrow, because she'd mentioned having a "weird dream" to investigators. If they were hoping for a repeat of Muriel Matson, however, it was not to be. For starters, she wasn't even with her husband, who was several thousand miles east in Paris. Nor was she an experienced dreamer.

"I never remember my dreams," she declared, speaking directly to Joss. "But I'll never forget this one. Thomas was in a round room, with windows all around. He's by himself, but it was like I was there. Then there was an orange glow in the windows, in all of them, and it grew brighter and brighter, and then got really hot. And then it just bursts into flame. And I woke up. I looked at the clock and it was 4:05. Thomas died a little after 10 a.m., they said, in Paris. It was the same moment. I dreamed it."

They took her through it three times, but they weren't going to get any more. Up since four and traumatized by her husband's death, Olivia Harrow was starting to crash and interrogation wasn't helping. Joss gave her a card with the perfunctory, "If you remember anything else, please give me a call," and she and Mendelsohn were on their way.

Once they were settled in the cab, Mendelsohn mused, "Trapped inside a small room while a fire rages outside, then fire inside the room, extreme heat—and then he dies. Same dream as Muriel Matson's."

Joss was not totally buying 'death by dream,' so she squinted skeptically at Mendelsohn and said, "Quite a coincidence, huh?"

Mendelsohn just smiled. At least he didn't laugh at her.

They rode in silence for a stretch, then Mendelsohn asked, "Ready for your moment on the big stage?"

She'd hardly had time to think about it since Trenton informed her yesterday that she'd been chosen as the public face of the investigation. She'd been fine with it, "as long as it doesn't stop me from actually investigating."

Trenton assured her that all it required was, at most, a daily press conference. Maybe some interviews. He would feed her whatever they had, and whatever they did or did not want said, and she would update the American people. "With any luck it'll be a short gig," he'd added. When Joss asked if she was chosen as a minority female, he answered, "Actually, minority female of modest means."

In other words, she ain't dominating nobody, so let the lady speak. She figured that if she hadn't already been killed for trying to solve the case, then they probably wouldn't kill her for telling everyone how lost the investigation was.

The room was packed. As Joss approached the podium she felt a wave of anxiety. No matter what she said, she was bound to disappoint them. She started with a blunt recitation of what little they knew—who died, where they were, time of death, and a medical description of the cause of death.

"We still do not know how they were killed. The scenes are all clean, with absolutely no forensic evidence. So we can say for sure they're not coming into the homes. We're searching for a weapon that can alter brain chemistry from afar. Or a poison or nano-weapon that could be administered in advance. We're exploring all possibilities. Whatever it is, it is something new, something we've never seen before."

Trenton had told her to avoid the whole mind control angle if possible, so she stopped there and opened the floor to questions. Which got frustrating, for everyone, in a hurry. The first several questions were all variations of who's doing this and how are they doing it? How many ways can you say, "We have no leads?" Finally, a voice from the back of the room shouted out, "It's been three days and every law enforcement agency in the country is working on this. Are you saying that no progress has been made?"

"No, not exactly. But mostly we've been eliminating possibilities. As I said, we now know a number of things that they're not doing, so we're not wasting time and energy on non-starters."

"Dr. Morgan, isn't it true that the government maintains a number of top-secret weapon projects? Has done so for decades? And what do you say to those who are claiming that only the government could create such an advanced weapon?"

"Yes, well, there's no question that the U.S. defense establishment is always working on new weapons systems, some quite exotic. I assure you that this was among the very first possibilities we looked at. And eliminated. The U.S. government has never developed a weapon like this. Which is not to say that there haven't been theoretical discussions of such capabilities, but when you separate the science from the science fiction, there's really nothing there, going back more than fifty years."

"Are you suggesting this is foreign?"

"No, in fact we're confident that it's not." As she spoke, she realized she'd just opened a door into the profile, which Trenton and company had hoped to avoid, though he'd said it was probably inevitable.

Sure enough—"Are you saying there's a profile of the killers?"

"Yes . . . of course, there's always a profile, though it's still developing. We are confident that this is home grown, that the Jubilees are Americans, that they are college-educated, that they are well-off, if not wealthy, and that they are motivated by a sense of social justice, as opposed to, say, vengeance, or ethnic or religious hatred, or a lust for power." This was the problem with discussing the profile—it was hard not to sound sympathetic. A fury of voices and raised hands confirmed her worries. She called on a red-faced jaw-grinder in the first row. Bull by the horns.

"Are you suggesting that these eighteen murders are just?"

"Not at all. I was describing their profile. *They* think they're furthering the cause of social justice. *We* think they're killers who must be stopped."

The questions went on for another ten minutes, but nothing new was asked or answered. She promised another press conference "tomorrow, when we will surely have more to talk about." She and Mendelsohn had a plane to catch, so they bolted from the room as quickly as possible without seeming to run away.

Two hours later, they were finishing a late dinner in an airport restaurant, and catching up on a day's worth of messages. She ran through phone, email, and Facebook. She was just about to close her Book when she heard the blip of a Skype text.

Somebody named Jubilee wanted to connect. Probably a crank, but easy enough to delete them, so she okayed the contact. There were five messages waiting.

jubilee: Andrew Matson is the only one who died awake and out of bed.

jubilee: The second email was served from a computer at Good Vibrations, a Portland internet cafe.

jubilee: If you try to trace this message, we will know, and we will sever our connection with you.

jubilee: We need your help.

jubilee: Please, hear us out.

Joss glanced at Mendelsohn, who was absorbed by something on his Book. What to do? The first two lines established their bona fides—only a few investigators and the killers knew about Matson and the email source. She wasn't a techic but the third line sounded feasible. And the last two, well, they got her attention. She was intrigued. She made a quick decision: nothing to be gained, at this point, in reporting the contact. It would be untraceable, they would learn nothing, and they'd be no closer to stopping the killings. On the other hand, communication is always a good thing.

She typed, **I'm listening**.

Chapter 20

Harold Leonard didn't think of himself as courageous. He'd never served in the military, fired a gun, or been in a fist fight, not even as a kid. Didn't climb mountains or go on wilderness treks or any such macho adventures. Though his work at Marsdale Lipman involved a lot of high-stakes risk management, the risks were mainly to the clients and investors; he earned his money whether the deals panned out or not. Like everyone else in the industry, he flattered himself that he worked hard for a living, but except for the long hours, there was nothing hard about it.

So how to explain what the secretaries were calling "Leonard's Last Stand?" He certainly didn't see it coming, but when that prick Clayes just up and quit—I've got my money and I'm outta here—something snapped. Next thing he knew he was the CEO of the largest bank in America and he had hours, not days, to halt the market slide, reassure the shareholders, and stabilize the customer base. And do it all without getting zapped by these Jubilee freaks.

He'd called Ginny right after the meeting with the news, thinking she'd be thrilled with the major bump in money and status.

"You did what? Are you serious, Harold? Why don't you just paint a bulls-eye on your forehead?!"

"Gin, we can't just run and hide, and if we don't act, and act fast, the firm is history. And I'm in for a major fall—everything I've worked for. A whole lot of money—just—disappears. Gin. Our money. The kids' future. I mean, Christ, three days ago Marsdale Lipman was the center of the universe. Sachs was a fucking god. And Clayes just quit, the pussy. I was the only one to stand up, the only one who fucking gave a shit."

"Right. The only one. Think, Harold."

Then she started crying. In between sobs: They're going to kill you. I'm too young to be a widow. What about Jason and Brooke? Brooke, pregnant, your first grandchild. Tears and more tears.

He couldn't placate her, or continue listening. She was not helping. Besides, he had to get crosstown for the emergency shareholders' meeting.

Leonard hadn't known what to expect for a meeting called with just three hours notice, but they packed the Four Seasons' largest conference hall. Proof that Marsdale Lipman was still alive. Scanning the room as everyone got seated, he noted that a serious chunk of their stock was present, as well as several major clients and a gaggle of cameras.

He introduced himself and quickly explained how he came to be CEO, while managing a few not-so-subtle digs at Clayes and the other quitters. Then he spent a few minutes eulogizing Morton, Winter, and Sachs—the firms last three CEOs, as well Andy Matson, another alumnus. He lamented the terrible losses to the firm and acknowledged that the damage now extended beyond the four deaths. The firm itself, its stock, its brand, its reputation, were all suffering.

"Some are saying it's fatal, they say the killers mean to destroy our firm, and that we don't have a chance, period. The market, of course, has been reflecting those fears. And, as I said, at this morning's board meeting several trustees gave into the fear and quit. I imagine some of you are feeling the same, thinking you and your money will be safer if you get as far from Marsdale Lipman as possible. But before you make any decision, please hear me out."

Leonard was as curious as everyone else to know what was coming next. Those who had voiced the most public opposition to the terrorists all died this morning. The day before that, the nation's top bankers. So how to take charge and provide leadership without getting killed? And how to set clear goals for the firm going forward without contradicting the Jubilees' socialist pap?

As he spoke, he felt a warmth welling in his chest, the first inkling, in his entire life, of genuine courage.

"Let's be clear about what's been happening to our country these past three days. Because this is bigger than Marsdale Lipman. This is about how we, a free and democratic nation, run our affairs. From colonial times to the present day, free-market capitalism has been the life blood of America. It is the essence of the liberty that we value so highly and the envy of the free world. Free enterprise, America's blessing and gift, makes this the greatest country on earth.

"Like any system made up of people, capitalism has its shortcomings. There's always room for improvement. From time to time, it fails, sometimes spectacularly, as it did in '08. But it always recovers, and comes back stronger, lessons learned, and there's no better example than this firm. Marsdale Lipman has delivered increasing profits every quarter since the crash."

Trouble. A statement like that would ordinarily trigger a fist-bumping ovation, but today, only a smattering of tentative applause. More troubling, it was starting to piss him off. Ungrateful fucking cowards. He pressed on.

"The Jubilees,"—he'd decided against calling them terrorists—"want to tear it all down. They view capitalism as a criminal enterprise and have taken to executing its most prominent practitioners. Their goal is something more radical than socialism. When they call for the 'dominators',"—he flashed finger quotes—"to share power, they're talking about a massive redistribution of wealth. When they call themselves 'Jubilee',"—more finger quotes—"they're telling us how to do it. Comes from the Bible, and it means the forgiveness of all debts. They want us to forgive everyone's debts. Just think about that. If they mean zeroing out credit card balances, mortgages, personal loans, corporate financing, just like that, all debts are forgiven—well, for Marsdale Lipman and I dare say for many of you, it would be instant bankruptcy. Same for the other banks. America would really crash, worse than three years ago, worse than the Great Depression."

He paused to scan the room, gauging the mood. Still timid and unsure. Skittish, like they might bolt from the room at any moment. He was playing their tune but they'd forgotten the words.

"Maybe the moneylenders don't belong in church, but they are essential on Main Street and Wall Street. Without the ability to borrow money, you'd have a hard time running a lemonade stand, much less a modern corporation. Hell, without the ability to take on debt, the government would cease to function. We're all debtors at different points in our lives. Carrying debt responsibly and paying it back on time, honoring your commitments and contracts—it's not just good economics, it's good morality and ethics, the fundamentals of a good life.

"Now I want to speak directly to the people behind these attacks. I appeal to you: let's focus on where we agree. The country is still suffering from a crash that was in part caused by imperfections in the financial services sector. The FSA corrected many of the problems, and Congress added legislation in the past eighteen months that's taken it even further. So the bad times are behind us, unemployment is back below fifteen percent, foreclosures and bankruptcies are tapering off, inflation is stable, and the market has gained back nearly everything lost in '08. Is there more work to do? Yes, of course, it's still a big undertaking, but think of how much more we could accomplish as partners, rather than adversaries.

"As CEO of Marsdale Lipman, this is my plea, and my pledge: let's work together on this. If you will stop the violence and make clear your vision for America, I promise to meet you more than halfway and to do everything in my power to make it happen. I'm giving you my word and offering my hand."

Now he saw many heads nodding yes, more than a few smiles, and when somebody started clapping, the whole room joined in. Marsdale Lipman would survive at least another day.

Would he?

Chapter 21

Leo sighed. It was, as Dorothea said, just something they had to do. She'd been adamant, though for his lovely wife that was like saying "she breathed." If she'd had her way they would have acted during Clinton's first term, right after Gingrich and gang took over Congress and the scandalmongers were going full force. She'd been throwing-things mad for weeks on end, she wanted so badly to just shut them all up, dead and done. Her anger, of course, was one good reason they couldn't act. Cooler heads prevailed then, and now Dorothea was the first to admit how wrong she'd been. Truth is, this wasn't a task for youthful passion, Bret, Mia, and Ali aside. Nor was it for the sick and dying, which is why, in the end, Dorothea had driven them to act.

A few years back, Leo had come to accept that they would never unleash their terrible weapon. For if ever there was a right time for it, it had to be the Bragg years, starting with the election. They'd all wanted to act, but the anger problem had metastasized throughout the group. It was so hard not to hate Bragg, Mallard, the whole lot of them. Seemed like everything that happened—9/11, Iraq, Guantanamo, the financial meltdown—was furthering the ruination of a great country. Desperate times. But they could never get clear enough of the hate and anger to pull the trigger on their desperate measure. What awful years! After Bragg's reelection, Leo and Dorothea seriously discussed just leaving the country, moving to Vancouver, Europe, anywhere to get away. But they stuck it out, and the country not only survived, it replaced the pitiful Bragg with the promising Carver.

They'd all gathered on the island after the election and it was like a life sentence had been lifted. Carver, the breakthrough president, signaled a profound shift in power dynamics that would utterly transform American culture. They'd felt relieved of their dark charge. There would be no need to resort to mass murder.

But by the end of his first year in office, Carver had overseen a massive transfer of wealth to the very crooks and liars who caused the crash; escalated the war in Afghanistan; strengthened the security state; forced the entire country to become customers of the blood-sucking insurance industry; pushed for nuclear energy, "clean coal" and more offshore drilling. A likable guy and great speechifier, but he was just another politician doing what the big money demanded. After Leo and the others got over their initial disappointment, they realized that they were needed more than ever and, the key point, that they were no longer angry. They didn't hate Carver, didn't hate the government, didn't even hate the bankers. Everyone was just playing out their parts in a system that corrupted everyone. So they started thinking "maybe." Then Dorothea got cancer and they started thinking "now."

Leo stared at Joss Morgan's reply, his fingers poised. Another big sigh and he started typing.

jubilee: I can imagine you feel conflicted about this, talking with the terrorist.

joss: My feelings are irrelevant. I'm only talking to you to see if I can convince you to stop the killing.

jubilee: Which is more or less why we need your help. Not so much to stop the killing, but to limit it.

joss: ??

jubilee: We have a weapon which—sorry for the cliché—must never fall into the wrong hands. If you succeed in catching us, it will, inevitably. Once it's out there, others

will learn to use it, may even improve on it. Imagine a world, doctor, in which there's a wide-spread ability to kill one's enemies or competitors without risk and without leaving evidence.

joss: You should have thought of that before you started.

jubilee: We did, I assure you. We thought about it long and hard, twenty years. We thought there was a fail-safe. But that was in the abstract. Now that it's real, we're not so sure.

joss: Sounds like you want this lethal power all for yourselves. You're crazy if you think I'm going to help. You need to be stopped.

jubilee: We will stop on our own, at sixty deaths. That's our limit. We need your help to keep it. If we finish without getting caught, we and our doomsday weapon vanish, never to be heard from again. We will acquire no financial gains, no position or power for ourselves, no recognition, no special status, nothing. But America will be a better place, more equitable, healthier all around.

joss: You think you can fix the country in ten days?

jubilee: Yes, I do. We've been planning this for a long time. So far it's unfolding pretty much as expected.

joss: Except for the fail-safe problem.

Leo didn't answer.

joss: Why should I believe you?

jubilee: You built the profile. You know us. We're not evil. We're not sociopaths. This isn't about revenge or hatred or amassing fortunes. We're ordinary people who have spent our whole lives on the losing side in the permanent class war that defines America. We've marched, protested, sat-in, written letters to legislators, signed petitions, contributed

to candidates, worked on campaigns, supported initiatives, joined unions, started co-ops, run for office, and voted. And year after year, nothing but increasing casualties on our side. America has just about lost its soul. No one should want that to happen. We can't allow it to happen. Finally, we have a means of fighting back that can make a difference. How could we not use it?

For the first time since they started, there was a long pause in the back-and-forth. Though he was confident that Joss Morgan was their best option, you never really know somebody till they're called. Problem was, if they were wrong about her that would be it for this approach. They would not be trying this with anybody else. He'd already revealed too much.

The decision to reach out to the investigation had only been made last night. It took the first two days for them to comprehend what they had wrought and then to start fretting over how badly things could go wrong if they were caught. Eva was the first to ask, "What if we're wrong? What if it's easily learned?" and the anxiety just grew from there. They didn't want to quit too soon, but they absolutely could not be captured and interrogated. So they would reach out to somebody in the investigation. After talking with Morgan and her partner this morning, Joe had pronounced her a good prospect, and Leo'd had to concur after watching her in the press conference.

He heard the blip of a new message.

joss: OK, I need to sleep on this. How exactly am I supposed to help you? You realize I'm just one of thousands of investigators looking for you?

jubilee: Yes, though you're being modest. We wouldn't ask you to stop doing your work, or to sabotage the work of others. All we want is a heads-up if you're getting close.

joss: Why sixty? Why not more? Or less? Why not stop now?

jubilee: If we stop now, the system will take it's losses and rebound. Nothing will change. Things might even get worse, could be a wave of reactionary oppression. Beyond sixty, we run out of ammunition. But sixty should be enough. We see several tipping points colliding in the next few days. Enough to shake things to the core. Breakdown into breakthrough. Can't make things any worse, but could make them better.

joss: OK, gotta go. What happens next?

jubilee: You continue to vigorously pursue us. I'll check in once a day. If the investigation starts to zero in on specific individuals, let me know.

Leo pushed away from the computer, stood up, and did a quick series of stretches. Then he sat down again, went to the website and posted a report on his interaction with Morgan. He read through four other new posts. He closed the computer, went upstairs, and ran water for a bath. It was just after ten. Harold Leonard had three more hours to live.

Chapter 22

Source: The Daily Liar

Wow. Day Three of the Jubilee phenomenon, and what can we say? These guys aren't effing around. And they're cutting like a scalpel at the cancerous rot that's afflicting America.

I spent a few minutes searching back through ten years of daily posts—3774 and counting—and guess which liars have shown up a lot in these pages: Dick Mallard, Howie Croft, Senator Turncoat Tofer, the Marsdale Lipman wrecking crew of Morton, Winters, Matson and Sachs, Dennis "Gulf Spill" Hastings, neo-con media czar Thomas Harrow, and wingnut loudmouths Brew, Franke, and Gross. Even Bagwell and Dempsey have had several mentions. It's a bullshitters gallery lacking only W. G. Bragg to be complete—not that I'm calling for the ex-prez's assassination. Much.

I'm not saying the Jubilees are reading this blog but—we're certainly drinking from the same coffee pot. As today's message makes clear.

When I haven't been railing against the nation's high-level liars, I've been railing for economic justice, fairness, equity. Closing the effing gap between the filthy rich and the rest of us. Cutting down the obscene and utterly ridiculous salaries and bonuses that we allow rich assholes to walk away with while regular folk suffer. Instead of bailing them out, treating them like the losers they really are: let their failed schemes sink their companies and then send them to jail for fraud and theft.

Just one more thing—Mr. Jubilee, are you listening?—start taxing the fuckers. Eighty, ninety percent, like the good old days when the American economy still worked. Before the anti-government, anti-regulation greed-heads started buying our congressmen and senators. And presidents.

Source: The Sarah Meadow Show

SARAH MEADOW: Ladies and gentlemen, we have a very brave guest tonight. Harold Leonard, a senior executive at Marsdale Lipman on Monday, took over today as CEO for Donald Sachs, who was jubileed on Tuesday. And he did so, I have to say, with a speech that seemed a bit defiant, given what we've learned about the Jubilees and their not-at-all empty threats. I should also make clear that Harold Leonard asked to come on this show. Though I seem to share much of their politics, the last thing I want is to in any way lend support or encouragement to what the Jubilees are doing.

Harold Leonard, thank you for coming on the show. I've read the transcript of the speech you gave at your firm's big meeting today and, as I said, it sounded somewhat defiant, given the circumstances. Was that your intention?

HAROLD LEONARD: No, Sarah, not at all. And I appreciate your giving me the opportunity to clarify what I said. The Jubilees may not have access to the full feed from the Marsdale Lipman meeting today, so this seemed a good way communicate directly with them.

MEADOW: Then, if we assume they're listening: after today's new message, it seems like what they'd most want to know is how you—Marsdale Lipman—intend to share wealth and power so that the gap between rich and poor is reduced and we move toward a more fair, equitable and just society.

LEONARD: Well, the key word there is "fair," and I'd add two other important words: efficient and effective. We can agree with their goal of reducing the gap between rich and poor, while questioning whether raising taxes on the rich is fair—since the wealthy already pay the lion's share of federal taxes, while the poor pay none at all. It's also been proven that raising taxes on the rich is neither efficient nor effective; the best way to increase the wealth of the poor is to leave the wealthy free to make decisions and investments that start new businesses, add jobs, and improve everyone's economy.

MEADOW: Sorry, but isn't that exactly what the previous three CEOs of Marsdale Lipman were saying before the Jubilees came along?

LEONARD: Yes and no, Sarah. It's true that allowing businesses and hard-working Americans to keep more of their earnings so they can participate fully and freely in economic activity is a basic tenet of free-market capitalism. But it's also true that the system isn't perfect, as demonstrated by the problems of the poor and, uh, by, um, periodic crashes, such as we recently experienced.

What I'm proposing, and I'm speaking to the Jubilees when I say this, is that we work out a solution that uses the talents and wisdom of the wealthy, rather than punishing them with death and increasing taxation. That we incentivize rich people to help the poor, rather than force them. Otherwise, we could end up with a society where no one is willing to work the long, hard hours of founding a new business, or inventing a new product, or discovering the next miracle medicine.

MEADOW: But again, I'm not sure I'm hearing how this is different than the status quo of the past several decades.

LEONARD: The difference is that, it is unfortunately true that people like me have tended to ignore the problems of the poor in the past. We just left it to the government to fix—

MEADOW: While claiming that the government couldn't actually fix anything.

LEONARD: Well, yes, again, we didn't always make good decisions. What I'm calling for now is a partnership between all stakeholders: the rich and poor, the government, and the Jubilees. I'm confident that our problems are not insurmountable and that, if we work together, we can create an America that works for everyone—fairly, equitably, and justly.

MEADOW: Sounds good to me, here's hoping it sounds good to them.

Day Four

Wednesday, November 9, 2011

All accumulation, therefore, of personal property, beyond what a man's own hands produce, is derived to him by living in society; and he owes on every principle of justice, of gratitude, and of civilization, a part of that accumulation back again to society from whence the whole came.

—*Thomas Paine*

Chapter 23

Muriel lay half awake, her heart racing, the sheets damp with perspiration. The dream again.

She's in her office, Andy is looking out the window, seated, his back to her, and the fire is outside, coming closer, light pouring through the window, and she's trying to say something, to warn him, but she can't talk, or, she's talking but not making sound, and then the fire's in the room, with a deafening roar.

Three nights ago, that's when she woke up to find Andy fallen to the floor, dead. The past two nights she'd sensed somebody standing behind her, over her right shoulder, but she couldn't turn to look. Tonight, she sensed him again—it was a man—and then she sensed another presence, a woman, also behind her, more to the left. But she couldn't move her head, couldn't turn in either direction. Then she woke up.

She slowed her breathing. Let her body sink into the bed. Felt for the dream thread, taking her back into it.

She's there for a beat and then the room changes and she's standing on her lawn, in daylight, and there's a crowd of reporters and photographers at the street. A woman emerges, walking toward her. She's Asian, smiling, offering a handshake. It's Joss Morgan, the detective. She says the name "Malcolm Carney."

Malcolm Carney. Muriel awoke, turned, and reached for her journal and light-pen. She jotted down the name and a few other details, clicked off the pen, and lay back again. For well over an hour she lingered in a twilight state, part dream, part meditation, part reflection. She roused a little past six, did thirty minutes of yoga, showered, dressed, made tea, and sat down at the computer with her first mug of the day.

She googled Malcolm Carney, thinking that this could be her husband's killer. The first several pages listed were all for a retired Army general, Malcolm T. Carney, and the top links went to a speech he gave yesterday. It was quite a tirade, blaming the Jubilee murders on Muslims, though later in the speech he used the term "Arabs." His main thrust was that Carver was in cahoots with the Muslim-Arabs, using them to weaken American resistance to a Muslim-Arab-socialist takeover of the country. He called for a "red state secession," for the impeachment of Carver, and for nuking most of the Middle East, starting with Iran.

Safe to say, not Mr. Jubilee. But a good candidate for Jubilee martyrdom. There was nothing on the news sites yet, but it wouldn't be long. If Malcolm T. Carney is one of the dead, then, Muriel thought, I may have been present when he died. Maybe he was the man behind her in the room, who she couldn't quite see. Does that mean the woman was the killer? Or was Joss Morgan the woman?

Or was this a vivid but ordinary dream that had no meaning beyond her interior world—the dream Morgan, nothing more than a representation of some part of Muriel, or some piece of the puzzle she was working on. It was hard to tell. It sure felt like she was dreaming with somebody, whether Morgan or the killer or even General Carney. But that was the thing with dreams. When you start wondering which dream was more real than the other—she let out a loud sigh.

Though, if Carney turns up dead—that's pretty damn real. She opened the desk drawer and took out the detective's card. If Carney turned up dead, she'd be calling Joss Morgan.

Chapter 24

Day Four of the Jubilee murders was just underway—half past seven and they had three confirmed deaths—and Henry Trenton was in a cab racing to a meeting with the president. Any other case he would have just told the man, "Sorry, sir, I've got work to do." Three new deaths to investigate, three others pending, all added to eighteen open cases, with six more a day for however long. Any other time and he'd be full throttle with all the work: crime scene reports to pore over, autopsies, lab tests coming in, questioning witnesses, debriefing investigators, integrating all this data coming from hundreds of different sources, looking for the common threads, the patterns, the clues. "Sorry, Mr. President, no time for talk, we're hot on their trail."

Not this time. Seventy-two hours since it started and he was chasing ghosts. Phantom perps with invisible weapons. Death by mental. No leads, no clues. What was he supposed to tell the president? Truth was, if the Jubilees wanted the president dead, he'd be dead now and there was nothing anyone could do to stop it.

Army two-star Malcolm Carney was awake when he died at 4:05, on base, in a private barracks protected by electronic jamming devices, and in the company of two aides, also awake, all three cranking on a combination of coffee, whiskey, and cigarettes. The early statement from the aides was that they were well aware of the time as it approached four. They were engaged in typical gallows chatter, and the general was in mid-sentence, laughing as he talked, then stopped, hand to the back of his head, in obvious pain, and keeled over. He was dead in under a minute.

Grateful as Trenton was for the eye-witness report, it scared the shit out of him.

So maybe it was just as well that he was out of headquarters for a bit. He needed to bring back some kind of good news. Or at least get the panic out of his eyes before he faced his team again.

He'd been expecting another meeting like yesterday's, so he was surprised when they led him to a smallish room a few doors down from the Oval Office. He was doubly surprised when the president entered and sat down for a talk, just the two of them.

"You drink coffee, Henry?"

"Mr. President, that'd be just fine."

Carver nodded to a young woman hovering in the shadows. When she left for the coffee, Carver said, "So, Harold Leonard takes over at Marsdale Lipman and dies the next morning. Apparently, they didn't favor his speech. And General Carney, I assume you've heard?" Trenton nodded. "Awake. With witnesses. I'm afraid this is your option number two, Henry, some sort of psychic attack. Mind control." The president slowly shook his head. They sat in a silence for a few moments. Trenton was about to speak when the coffee arrived. He waited till it was served and they were alone again.

"Mr. President, I wish I had something, anything encouraging to report to you. Yesterday I was worried about how vulnerable we are. Today, after Carney's experience, well, we're beyond worried. They can kill with impunity, anyone they want, anywhere in the world. I'm told the general underwent a series of tests the past two days. MRI, X-rays, blood tests, urine analysis, a head-to-toe, inside-out physical exam, looking for anything planted, inserted, swallowed, injected. Anything that didn't belong. They found nothing. So I'd say yes, we're looking at some sort of psi attack. For which we have no defense, nor means of identifying the attackers. We're hoping to find someone else with similar abilities, but since we don't know how or what they're doing—"

The president didn't look surprised or alarmed by any of Trenton's words. He'd apparently thought it through himself, reaching the same conclusions.

Carver nodded a few times and said, "That's partly why I wanted to meet with you this morning. I'm not sure everyone on our side is fully committed to tracking these killers if it turns out their psychic abilities were actually developed by us. CIA, NSA, every branch of the military, they all have histories of black ops and top-secret projects, typically hidden from Congress and the president. So that we have plausible deniability at times like this. But if the Jubilees began in some government project, then we need to know. It may be our only chance of catching them."

"Sir, I believe you're right and we're looking hard at all such projects. I assure you, every branch of government has been fully cooperating. We've generated a database of nearly two thousand names who participated in some sort of psi or mind control experiments, going back sixty years. Yesterday we conducted a dozen interviews, including a couple of project leaders. We're conducting dozens more today, paring the list down, removing the deceased and the too old or infirm, checking names against the profile, looking for links between individuals. Certainly helps to have the largest investigative team ever assembled."

"Any promising leads?"

"No sir, nothing yet. But it's still early."

"It may still be early for the investigation, but for what they've unleashed . . . it could already be too late. They've got nearly sixty percent approval ratings, can you believe it? And they go higher after each new batch of victims. Never thought I'd live to see the day. My party's totally on board—too bad about Howie, of course, but all in a good cause. Independents are breaking fifty-fifty, but trending Jubilee. Once the Republican middle class figures out this works for them too, then it's all over. Government by assassination.

"I'm damned no matter what I do. With the exception of Howie, Matson, Morton, and Winters, they're removing men who stood in the way or actively worked against my agenda. Puts me in an impossible position. If I try to stop them, then I don't wake up one morning, and the country gets the sort of musical-chairs leadership that Marsdale Lipman is going through. Just keep killing the boss till they get a boss who goes along. Which, the vice president has informed me, he will do if I won't."

The president paused to let that sink in. "He said that, as regrettable as the killings were, and as troubling as it is to give into blackmail—power sharing and debt relief was just what the country needed, what the world needed and, his words, "if you can't beat 'em, join 'em." Not exactly the oath of office. So do I have my vice president charged for treason? Or do I go with the part of me that's starting to think he's right? And if I do that, how will this not look like it was my plan all along?"

Trenton wasn't sure why the president wanted to talk to him. He didn't need a special meeting to get the nothing-update. And Trenton could have reassured him about interagency cooperation in a simple phone call. It seemed like Carver just needed to air his thoughts and had chosen him to listen. Guess it used to be Howie Croft's job.

The president must have read his mind. "You're wondering what you're doing here, right? The thing is, since talking to Vice President Riles, I think I really get what they're doing with this military decapitation. It's always been a good idea—knock off the king and you don't have to fight all the battles. But it's rarely worked, for two reasons. First, the king has the best protection, so you have to battle through all the pawns just to get to him. And even if you can surgically take out the king—say you get a spy in the kitchen to poison his food—what if his successor is more of the same, or he's even worse, especially since his king was just assassinated? Good strategy in the abstract but fails in reality."

Trenton usually had no time for military talk from civilians—calling someone Commander in Chief doesn't make them military—but Carver was a special case. He majored in history at Harvard and before going on to Law School he wrote a slim, but well-received volume on Just War Theory and the legal evolution of warfare. Though he ran and got elected on a peace platform, he'd governed as a true friend of the military and got equally high marks from the stateside brass and the boots on the ground.

"That's right. There's no way to protect the king. Which also solves the second problem because there's no way to protect his successor either. So they just keep killing the Leonards until they get a Riles. Soon enough, they have Jubilee sympathizers running the government and major corporations, they've eliminated dissenting voices in the media, and neutralized the military. Even the religious right will be on their team."

The president signaled to his aide for more coffee. They again sat in silence until it was served.

"When this got started," said Carver, "like a lot of people, I thought, How bad can six deaths a day be? It would take a year and a half to reach 9/11 numbers and we'd catch them long before then. Well, aside from the fact that I'm not nearly as optimistic about catching them, I don't see them doing this for long. A month, maybe less. 'Cause that's all it will take. I mean, they've already shaken the country to the foundations. And it's changing us, already. Remains to be seen whether its good change or not. Ten years ago and it would have been different, but now, with the Internet, it's all happening so fast. Yesterday, I still thought we had time, that I could put off replacing Judge Griffin and just stall on their demands. I actually thought I had some control over the situation. Now it's clear that the only control I have is in the decisions that I make. And if I don't act soon, the Jubilees will move on to President Riles.

"Which is why I wanted to see you so early in the morning." Carver paused for a thought-collecting sip of coffee. "You've already answered this, but I need to ask again. How long will it take to catch these guys?"

"Honestly, sir, I'm not sure we ever will. As long as they're active and killing people, then we can hope that they'll make a mistake, leave some trace, something useful. Or maybe one of them can't handle the guilt, or a wife or neighbor catches on and turns them in. But if you're right and they stop it cold in a few weeks, and they don't break discipline, they just fade away—then we never find them.

"But even if we did, unless they confess," Trenton continued, "if this is pure psi, no weapons or tools outside of their minds, then even if we do identify them, we'll have a hell of a time proving anything. So if we catch one, or even a few, what do we do? Put them on trial and convict without evidence? Or just pump them up with drugs and stick them in a dungeon? What's to keep the ones you haven't caught from eliminating police, prosecutors and judges until we release their friends? I don't think we want to fight an all-out war against these people. Frankly, I'm not sure we want to catch them. And I can't believe I just said that."

"I can," said the president, "because I've been thinking along the same lines."

"Mr. President, if you're asking me to fake or scuttle the investigation—"

"No, not at all. Whatever the dynamics, the fact remains this is murder, terrorism, actually, and they need to be stopped. So, I want you to do your job and everything in your power to catch these—criminals. But I sensed in you an ability, rare, I have to say, in law enforcement and military circles, to see beyond the black and white, the good versus evil. To appreciate the murky grayness of the situation. And to deliver an accurate assessment, including any doubts or misgivings, without the can-do bravado—which is exactly what you just gave me."

Trenton was afraid to say anything more. It bothered him that there might now be a recording of him and the president talking about appeasing the Jubilees. Though, in fact, Carver never said as much, and Trenton wasn't sure what path the president would be taking.

"So, Henry, conundrums and contradictions duly noted, it's time to get to work. We need to catch at least one Jubilee who we can interrogate and/or negotiate with. Even better would be to find a non-Jubilee who knows what they're doing and how they're doing it. We should also be looking for some sort of leverage, something, such as close family members, that we can use to stop the killers once they're identified. You worry about getting that done. ASAP."

Trenton was about to stand when the president added, "You know, it's already been a rough three years: global depression, three wars, congressional gridlock, the oil shortage. The spill, the hurricanes. Hundred-year storms followed by thousand-year storms. Now this."

They say the presidency ages a man so fast you can watch as his hair turns gray and stress lines cross his face. Trenton believed it. He wanted to say something, perhaps lay a reassuring hand on the president's shoulder. But all he could manage was a quick nod and a half-empty promise to stop the killings soon.

Chapter 25

The Jubilee killings first stunned, then engulfed, then utterly remade mass media. It wasn't just that other stories were shoved aside. Producers were replacing their regular programming with Jubilee coverage and racing to put together breathy specials complete with custom graphics and theme music. *Jubilee vs America. The Jubilee Destruction, Day Four. Jubilee Today.* This was especially true of the morning shows—networks, cable, and radio. People no longer cared to start their days with celebrity breakups, congressional peccadillos, or the latest fad diet. By 8 a.m., all anyone wanted to know was, "Who got jubileed?"

The promise of six dead VIPs every day proved a compelling narrative, with infinite possibilities. Part crime drama, part game show, with A-list celebrities getting bumped off in mysterious fashion by ghost villains, apparently in the name of global celebration. The Internet gambling sites had been the first to react, taking bets on who would die next. Though TV and radio couldn't offer actual gambling, they unabashedly exploited the game, with pundit panels running down lists of likely victims and then giving odds on their demise. *Chris, I'm putting the general at three-to-one, but I think the senator lives to see another day.* There were segments devoted to hypothesizing Jubilee strategy, explainer segments on the meanings of "dominator," "power sharing," and "jubilee," and updater segments on the progress, or lack thereof, of the investigations. There were expert guests to discuss the political ramifications to Carver, or the reactions of the Christian Right, or the way it was affecting grade-schoolers, or the stock market, or the military, or our allies abroad. Plus high-end, multimedia eulogizing of the new victims, with special guests to provide insight into their lives and meaning for their deaths.

And that was just the traditional media. The Internet had hung out a sign, *All Jubilee All the Time.* Thousands of websites sprang into being, each offering their own take on the Jubilee phenomenon, while millions of established sites turned full attention to it. People blogged, texted, tweeted, chatted, commented, emailed, skyped, and facebooked, thumbs and fingers clacking away, furiously adding their two megabits to the collective conversation. Others composed paeans to the Jubilees and posted them to YouTube, where several went viral. The Jubilee wiki page was the most active in Wikipedia's history, as hundreds of contributors created a thoroughly sourced and cross-linked history of the events and the individuals involved.

After Joss named herself and Mendelsohn as lead investigators during yesterday's press conference, they shot to the top of media booking lists. Trenton decided that, for the short term at least, managing the public response was as important as catching the Jubilees. "If a major panic gets going," he'd said, "we could have armed uprisings in the streets and full-blown martial law or God knows what else and working the case will be moot." So he assigned them to make the rounds on the morning shows, appearing separately, to get the greatest spread. Solo appearances only—no panel arguments, no screaming sound bites. They were made available for the second half of every hour, and spent the time in between getting caught up on relevant facts or breaking news while in transit to their next appearance. From noon on they would return to the investigation, with a possible late-afternoon presser by Joss.

For her part, Joss was glad to be on her own for the morning as it was giving her time to ponder what to do about her secret contact with Jubilee. She had decided to tell Mendelsohn, because it would undermine their partnership to withhold such a development, and she really valued his take on things. She figured he was rogue enough to keep quiet about it. She also wanted to include Trenton, and perhaps even the president, but was less certain how they'd react. Which was all the more reason to bring Mendelsohn on board. They'd be meeting back at Homeland after this last interview and would talk then.

She'd done three appearances so far today and they'd all gone well enough. One producer-assistant told her she was "a natural, with major telegenic presence." Seemed like a good thing to have and she had to admit she was enjoying herself. Maybe when this was over she'd leave Homeland and take a run at Hollywood. She could already hear her mother.

Sally Tiger had temporarily changed the name of her long-running cable news show to *Jubilee Nation*. An unapologetic and street-seasoned liberal activist, she had a history of tangling with authorities of all sizes and stripes and tended to view government officials as adversaries until proven otherwise. Mendelsohn had been assigned to the Tiger interview but had begged off, "not because I'm afraid to talk to her but . . . um . . . I think she's really hot." It was one of those men-are-from-Mars moments that left Joss pondering a life of abstinence. Maybe skip Hollywood for a nunnery.

"Dr. Morgan, thank you for coming on the show. I'm sure this is a hectic time for you." Joss smiled, nodding. "Could I ask you to begin with a recap of this morning's events?"

"Sure, Sally. Unlike the previous days, we identified all six of the victims before eight a.m. I suppose everyone is so tuned into what's happening now that potential victims all have family and friends watching out for them. Which makes it unlikely that anyone's death would go undetected for very long. Unfortunately, preliminary crime scene and autopsy reports are more of the same—no discernible trace of attackers, weapons, poison, nano-technology—nothing.

"The victims today were two-star Army General Malcolm Carney; Harold Leonard, who just took over as CEO for Marsdale Lipman yesterday—"

"Making it the last four CEOs from Marsdale Lipman."

"Actually, four of the last five; Clayes resigned and lived to tell the tale. So far. Then there were three military VIPs: Cyrus Bird, CEO of Kontrain, the nation's largest private security firm; Lance Withers, CEO of Taylor Dann, the second-largest private security firm; and Douglas McDonnell, CEO of Altamen, the nation's largest defense contractor. And then lastly, the Reverend Paul Sheppard, founder of Broadcasting For Christ, known to many as America's Pastor."

"Who apparently had millions of followers praying through the night for him."

Though the reverend's challenge—the power of Jesus versus the power of the Jubilees—had been widely reported last night, Joss was under orders to avoid all religious discussions. As Alex had said, "If this thing goes religious we're really doomed."

"Yes, I heard that also. A brave man, he stood up to the Jubilees. But you know, the really interesting case last night was General Carney's. We know that he died at exactly 4:05 because there were two witnesses. The general has had a history of making inflammatory statements, long before Jubilee ever got started, but in the past two days he'd been stepping it up, blaming the murders on President Carver, and on Iran, and calling for armed resistance against the Jubilees. He clearly understood the risks because he took steps to defend himself, including a full physical checkup and a range of tests to rule out any injected substances or implanted chips. He stayed awake all night, on a well-defended Army base, in the presence of two of his aides, and separate audio and video recording devices. A detective's best case scenario, you'd think, but not a trace of evidence. Though it does confirm our working hypothesis."

"Which is that this is some sort of psychic attack?"

"That's right, Sally, though I must stress it's still hypothetical. But what happened in the general's quarters is just hard to explain any other way. When you rule out every conceivable physical explanation, what you're left with is the non-physical."

"So, we're talking about mind control? Witchcraft? Voodoo?"

Though the investigation had been tipping in this direction from day one, they'd avoided addressing it head-on with the public because it put them in a weak and ignorant position. It's hard to project confidence and earn the public trust when you have no idea what's happening or how to stop it. They also worried that a psychic weapon would tend to panic people more than even the most lethal physical weapon. Mendelsohn had gone on a bit about how much he enjoyed thrillers, even when they had scary, end-of-the-world premises. "But horror movies, with invisible forces attacking in unpreventable ways—they work on primal fears and scare the beejeezus out of people, even when they know it's just a movie."

Joss didn't want to get into witches and voodoo. She shrugged, with a look of *"who knows?"*

Tiger answered back with a look that said, *"We need more than that."*

Joss said, "As a doctor and scientist, I'm still struggling with the whole concept. Right now we're looking hard for evidence, outside of these killings, of such human abilities. Of course, we're aware that human literature is replete with stories and claims of extraordinary human abilities, arising from all cultures. The more religious a people, the more they tend to believe in such things, but we see it even in modern, scientific cultures. Until now, I would have agreed with those who say there's little proof in support of such abilities, that it's all superstition and old wives' tales. Now I'm thinking those old wives knew a thing or two. But the bottom line remains—however they're doing it, they're not leaving any evidence. Any theories we have at this point are inferred from that lack of evidence—"

"Which basically means you don't know jack."

Joss laughed. "Sure, you could say that." Joss had fielded similar comments in the earlier interviews, so she knew to just acquiesce. No point defending your ignorance or arguing with the facts. *We don't know jack.* All the more reason to talk about something other than psychic powers and ghost killers.

Tiger must have agreed, because she asked, "What do you make of 'Jubilee?' Is it a signature? A command? Or both? And if it's a command, what would they have Carver, or any of these wealthy CEOs, do? What do they want? How does one jubilee?"

"Sally, we are treating it as a command, along with 'sharing wealth and power.' Your question—'what do they want?'—is an even more pressing question than 'how are they doing it?' Because they are killing, first, those who they perceived, before this all got started, as particularly egregious dominators. And secondly, those who, since the first email, have failed to respond to their demands. Take Marsdale Lipman. First, they killed Richard Winters, Douglas Morton, and Donald Sachs, all gone without warning, apparently for past sins. And now Harold Leonard, who just took over yesterday with a somewhat conciliatory speech, though, evidently, not what the Jubilees wanted to hear. Meanwhile, J.T. Clayes, who was next in line before Leonard but chose to walk away, is alive, even though he spent years accumulating wealth as what the Jubilees would call a financial dominator."

Tiger leaned in closer. "So they're trying to change the actions of our leaders by killing those who are least likely to change? They kill Howie Croft, trying to influence the president, but they don't kill Carver, at least not yet, because they think he's reachable."

"Yes, well put. I suspect some were scheduled to die from the outset, men like Croft, Wallace Griffin, Vice President Mallard, General Eisley, Thomas Harrow—all died on the first or second day and nothing they could do to prevent it. They were object lessons for everyone else. But since then, my guess is that the Jubilees are watching the rich and powerful, and that whether one dies or not depends on how he responds to their demands. Those who fight back, like Brew Tinsley or General Carney, are eliminated—more lessons for the rest of us. Those who surrender their power, if not their wealth, like Clayes, are spared. And those who, like the president, neither fight back nor surrender—well, we just don't know how long they'll allow that before—"

As she was speaking, Joss became aware of a wave of movement in the studio audience. A rustle of whispering. Heads looking down, apparently at phones and tablets. She noticed that Tiger was reading the teleprompter, which had been blank throughout the interview. Reports of another mass email.

"Dr. Morgan, ladies and gentlemen," said Tiger, "a new communication, ostensibly from the Jubilees, has just been released. It's authenticity has yet to be confirmed by the government, but here's what it says: . . . ."

Chapter 26

Halfway back to Homeland, Joss got a call from Trenton redirecting her to the White House for a meeting with the president. Trenton had had a meeting with Carver this morning and gave her a quick rundown on what to expect. His take was that the president knew he had to act soon—on the Jubilee demands, as well as appointing replacements for Judge Griffin and Secretary Matson—but was struggling to get beyond the usual Beltway thinking. Which is why Carver was taking meetings with non-politicos like him and Joss. He added that (and here Trenton may have been projecting) while the president was not about to overtly join with the Jubilees, it felt like he was tilting toward their demands.

Joss was aware of the polling that showed sixty to seventy percent of Americans favoring the Jubilees. More to the point, she'd felt herself drifting in that direction, and could sense the same in Trenton and Mendelsohn. The president too? The whole line of thinking made her uncomfortable. Add in last night's still-secret communication and she was starting to feel like anything but an objective servant of the law.

A White House aide had seated her in a spacious room that seemed familiar to her—or maybe she was remembering scenes from *The West Wing*. As she waited for the president, she sipped her coffee and opened the latest from Jubilee on her Book. This time they'd used Facebook for message dissemination. Started with a few thousand friends and it just went from there. They

may be older, as the profile suggests, but they definitely have a geek on the team.

Like the last mass email, and her private chat, today's began with identification: ***David Stansbeck died in a locked bank vault.*** Stansbeck, the CEO of OmniBank, was a Day Two victim. He did indeed set up a cot inside his bank's vault and lock himself in for the night. It was one of the details Trenton kept out of reports and discussions. Outside of a few people at the bank and a few more at Homeland, nobody but Jubilee knew about it. It wasn't quite as convincing as naming Franke and Harrow before they were discovered, but it was authentic enough for her.

Establishing authenticity was critical because in the past twenty-four hours a number of emails started making the rounds, all signed "Jubilee." Homeland was discrediting them as quickly as they popped up, easy to do since none came with insider information, nor were any proving difficult to trace back to their origins. Probably why the Jubilees switched from email to Facebook. Joss had no doubt they'd covered their trail there just as well. More evidence of their tech-smarts.

The Jubilee Manifesto

1. Progressive federal income tax, starting at $500,000 annual income

2. Progressive value-added taxes for the states

3. Cap executive compensation at no more than 100 times the minimum wage

4. Cap interest on all borrowing at no more than 10%

5. Take half of all current military spending and redirect it to positive, productive social spending

6. End the wars, wind down the empire, and refocus the military strictly on rational defense of the American homeland

7. Public financing of elections with tight limits on corporate "speech"

8. A one-time forgiveness of all debt

Well, they weren't asking for much, w
ed her of some of the wish lists that made the
Carver was elected. Dismissed as nothing more
sive fantasies, they'd come with stern warnings aga
incrementalism. Of course, Carver was never the p
champion they'd hoped for, was in fact a master of incr
thinking. He could be frustratingly centrist and seemed far committed to reaching out to Republicans—most of whom despised Carver—while paying little attention to the progressives who, he knew, had no other options. As Nathan Kane had put it, borrowing from Churchill, "Carver is the worst possible leader for these times, except for all the others." Disgruntled progressives had swallowed their frustration and come to feel grateful for his most mincing half-steps. Scraps from the table while Wall Street feasted, but hey, after eight years of Bragg, it was something.

The president entered the room, thanked her for coming, and apologized for making her wait. This was her first time meeting Carver and it was just as others had reported—however you felt about his politics, it was hard not to instantly like the man. If she was a "major telegenic presence," what did that make Carver? You needed a word that was a thousand times better than "major."

After a quick round of pleasantries, he nodded at her Book. "The manifesto?"

"Yes sir. I was just noticing how much it resembled the progressive agenda in '08. Weren't all of these items advanced in one form or another just after your election?"

"Well, I don't believe anyone talked about forgiving all debt, but the rest of it, yes, I noticed that too. So, does that mean we should be looking at my supporters? At Democrats, at liberals? We certainly can't turn anyone who's ever advanced one or more of these ideas into suspects, can we?"

"No, sir, not at all. We are casting a wide net for previous usage, in speeches or writings, of any of these terms, though I doubt that they'd make such a mistake. But we're thinking this group goes back long before you came on the scene. They may have been in favor of your candidacy and election, but most like-

out an overt show of support. They've been flying below radar for a long time. I think they gave you a few years to see if you could engineer this revolution they deem necessary. When it didn't happen, they acted."

Joss was aware that she was speaking less from the profile now, and more from what she'd gleaned after last night's chat with Jubilee. The writer had made a point of how long they'd worked the political process, and how little they'd achieved. She placed them in the countercultural upheavals of the sixties. Hopefully, in visible leadership positions that left a mark. She'd shared as much with Trenton and he was directing the searchers to look hard at that time period.

The president nodded and said, "I spent three years figuring out how things work around here, meeting with the opposition, making compromises, working with House and Senate processes, dealing with the press, the military, all the interest groups, and all with an eye to achieving what the American people sent me here to do. Despite the hard times, so much of it inherited, I thought we were doing pretty well, and getting better as we went along. Then this comes along and I'm supposed to just drop what I was doing and join up with a bunch of assassins."

Now he was shaking his head. Trenton had mentioned just this sort of moment in his earlier conversation. It felt kinda like he needed a sounding board, maybe because Howie is gone, or maybe he's just being careful not to expose any of his top advisors to Jubilee scrutiny. She decided to just listen, unless Carver asked for a response.

"The thing is," he said, still shaking his head, "I'm not sure I could do what they ask even if I wanted to. An American president cannot take orders from anonymous terrorists, just can't. Wrong in a dozen ways and bound to be illegal, in someone's eyes. We'd spend the next six months in impeachment hearings."

He smiled, and fixed his penetrating eyes on hers.

"Like your boss, you're wondering what you're doing here."

"Mr. President, I am honored, and thrilled, to be here. But

yes, I do feel a bit out of my element. I'm really not very political." She quickly added, "Though I do vote!"

He was still smiling. "I understand. You're not the first scientist to notice that political reality often contradicts, denies, even attacks the scientific worldview. If the government was run according to scientific principles, rather than politics, global warming would never have gotten started, we'd have cured cancer years ago, and automobiles would be running on sunlight. We wouldn't be wasting our time legislating against gays or women's bodies or whatever else gets some group of fundamentalist crazies in a tizzy. If scientists ran the government, the environment would be pristine. Energy would be free. Corporations would not be able to get away with externalizing all their costs into future disasters. They most certainly would not be considered 'persons.' We'd choose leaders based on their knowledge and vision and proven abilities, rather than their capacity for kissing babies, mouthing soundbites, and collecting bribes."

Now it was Joss's turn to smile. She was tempted to say, Mr. President, this is why I voted for you; you were going to usher in a whole new world. What happened? As a doctor, she had to ask. "A cure for cancer?"

"Well, first of all, if we were a 'scientocracy' it wouldn't have taken us fifty years to wind down smoking. The science on tobacco's been clear since the sixties, when I was lighting up my first Marlboros. But big tobacco's been a major lobbying force all these years—you'd think the legislators taking their money would have trouble sleeping over the millions of lung cancer victims or turning children into addicts. But that's our system. Politicians say yes to whoever pays their bills. The case against tobacco eventually got so strong that we were able to enact meaningful legislation and get smoking rates to decline. But no such progress with the tens of thousands of potentially toxic chemicals we pump into the environment. Now, I'm not a doctor or a scientist, but it has always seemed obvious to me that the rise of cancer paralleled the rise of industrial chemical pollution. When you have DDT and other toxins showing up in breast milk—well, like

I said, seems obvious to me. But the big chemical companies use the same playbook as big tobacco—purchase the right politicians and you don't have to worry about scientific evidence. Hell, you can stop science from even looking in the right direction."

Wow. It was a side of Carver the world had never seen. She was getting her first inkling of why he wanted to talk to her.

"Here's the thing, doctor. Most politicians don't start running for office so they can become paid toadies for corporations. We start with good enough intentions—public service, helping our constituents, making America a better place. But our system, hell, once you get elected it just takes over. Every politician eventually makes the same devil's bargain—if you want to get re-elected or move on to higher office, here's the money you'll need and this is what we want you to do. Or not do. It's a crazy way to run a country, foolish in the extreme. But railing against it is wasted breath. Just look at healthcare—in the end, every item in that bill had corporate approval before it ever reached the floor for a vote. I mean, in America, big money has totally co-opted the democratic process. And anything that doesn't kill it only makes it stronger. So you end up with someone like me—and it would surprise you how many politicians would be comfortable with this conversation—but for all our power, we stand by helplessly watching things fall to pieces. Someone like Teddy Kennedy, who worked for single-payer healthcare all his life only to be posthumously credited for ushering in a bill that drove a spike through the heart of single-payer once and for all."

He paused for a sip of coffee.

Joss said, "So, if change from within the system is impossible, the big changes can only happen due to external forces? Major pressure from outside the system, like wars or eco-disasters? Economic collapses?"

"That's right. During the Bragg years, someone called it 'the shock doctrine.' When society suffers a great enough breakdown, it's ripe for deep, structural change. It's really about shattering the status quo, something that can't be intentionally done *as* the status quo. Takes an outside force."

"Like Jubilee."

"Like Jubilee. They're killing the men who most embody the status quo. Take Dennis Hastings—that damned oil well has cost Petroleron some $100 billion and counting, not to mention damage to their brand and a permanent mark as the company that poisoned the Gulf of Mexico. But not only did he survive, his personal wealth unaffected, Petroleron came through it with only a few cosmetic changes and still making money. The status quo prevailed and stronger for it. At least until Jubilee. Now Hastings is gone, Petroleron is teetering on the brink, and the Petroleron board knows it can't replace Hastings with more of the same. Or they'll get the Marsdale Lipman treatment. The status quo will not prevail this time because Jubilee will just kill it."

"So, Mr. President, it almost sounds as if—" She couldn't say it.

"It's not that I approve of what they're doing, any more than I would approve of a catastrophic hurricane or earthquake. But it's happening, no one can stop it, and . . . at the very least it's created an opening for the total system-wide change that the country, that the world really needs. Frankly, whatever reservations I have about Jubilee's methods and ultimate goals—even if they go on to kill a few hundred rich men, hell, even if they decide to kill me—it's worth it if it works. If it initiates positive change. Because, without such change, there will be thousands, millions of unnecessary deaths. Environmental collapse. Global economic depression. Resource wars over oil, water, food. Planetary chaos. Billions will die. And our world, right now, is *that* close. If killing a few hundred men will stop that, even give us an outside chance of stopping it . . . I'm thinking it's worth it."

All the better, then, if they only kill sixty. She had to tell him.

"Doctor Morgan,"—his best smile—"Joss. This is a once--in-forever opportunity to remake the world. I'm convinced, it's the right thing to do, but I need some help, beyond what the Jubilees are doing. I need people who can help me think through the implications—with a hard eye toward unintended consequences.

Then work out the details of implementation. I really don't need Beltway wisdom or realpolitik. Howie, for instance, would have been all wrong for this, which was probably why they eliminated him right off."

"That and the fact that it gave you cover."

"That's right, that too. Which is why I can't use anyone too wealthy or too entrenched in the power hierarchy. I need some smart, talented people, but no millionaires, no political royalty, no celebrities. People willing to stick their necks out. FDR had his kitchen cabinet. I need a Jubilee cabinet—unofficial, unseen, and unacknowledged. To guide America through these terrible times to something—better. Something, I have to believe, much better."

He paused to let it all sink in. "What do you say, Joss? Will you join me in this?"

She answered without hesitation, "Yes, sir, of course," wondering, Did the President of the United States just ask me to join him in an act of treason? She took a slow, deep breath, exhaled, and said, "And I have something pretty amazing that I've been itching to tell you. Last night I had a most interesting communication. . ."

Chapter 27

Carolyn Weathers drove in silence to the Marsdale Lipman stakeholders meeting, the second in two days. She worried that it was already too late for the firm and that she and Ryan should cut their losses and move on. Literally move on, since it would mean downsizing their daily affairs, starting with the Manhattan condo. But Ryan, staring silently out the passenger window, harbored no such thoughts. He was laser-focused on what he'd called "the transformation of American finance." She could not be prouder of him, of both of them.

They'd been up at dawn and learned of Harold Leonard's death soon after. Ryan was not surprised. Though he hadn't known when it would happen, he knew Leonard was doomed the moment he seized control of the firm. New CEO, same as the last. When Ryan had told Carolyn about yesterday's meeting and Leonard's defiant speech, she'd agreed. There's a fine line between bravery and foolhardiness and Leonard had crossed it several times.

So she and Ryan had sat at the breakfast table, unable to eat but guzzling coffee. They had the sort of big-issue conversation that took her back to junior year, Sunday mornings on the quad. Twenty years as wife and mother had crowded out such things, not that she'd ever complained, but she knew she'd been living in a well-appointed box. Until this morning, when she and Ryan blew it to pieces. Now she was tingling with anticipation, feeling rejuvenated, like she'd just been to a brain spa. Ryan was proclaiming nothing less than an all-out, top-down revolution.

"It's our karma, Carolyn. We were part of the problem, made money during the meltdown, got fat while the rest of the country starved. This is our chance to make amends. Help make things right again. Maybe."

"Big maybe," she'd said, feeling less skeptical than it sounded. Which was saying something because Ryan had always been the romantic, starry-eyed fool, while she'd been the practical one, given to bouts of gnawing doubt. So when Ryan would say they were soul mates, fated to fall in love, Carolyn would answer that love's nothing to fall into, like some lucky break, and no such thing as soul mates. "Real love is intentional," she'd say, "something you have to work at, something two people make out of nothing. We *make* love."

"Some of us find love," he'd say, turning on the look, "just happen upon it, an unexpected blessing."

"The problem is," she'd say, "people who just happen into love can as easily happen out of it. They wake up one day and kiss honey and the kids good-bye because 'it's just not happening anymore.' Well, to hell with that. If the love is fading then it's time to work harder."

It was their favorite argument. Ryan could never quite let go of believing in soul mates, though he'd come to appreciate that love is work and well worth doing. Carolyn didn't believe in soul mates, but she did believe in him. And never more than this morning.

They'd managed to get Joe and Cari out of bed, through breakfast, and off to school without having to explain why dad, usually gone by seven, was still around. The kids of course knew about Jubilee and the problems at Marsdale Lipman, and must have at least pondered their father's future. But at twelve and fifteen they had their own problems to deal with, far more serious than the havoc Jubilee was causing. She envied their naiveté, if not the adolescent angst.

Once the kids were out the door, Ryan started making calls and sending emails. The news of Leonard's death would result in a major sell-off of Marsdale Lipman stock when the markets opened. But the firm had considerable cash reserves—nearly three hundred billion—enough, Ryan hoped, to facilitate the firm's reorganization into something that would meet Jubilee terms. "Sharing wealth and power" seemed clear enough: an end to the megabuck salaries and bonuses, reducing or eliminating fees, reducing the rates on loans, in general paying bankers and account managers a lot less than they'd grown accustomed to. It meant an end to all of the shady and unethical practices, the high-stakes speculation, the exotic derivatives that nobody understood, shit like selling short on customers. Time to return to real work, producing real products, generating real wealth.

And the signature, "Jubilee," was all about the forgiveness of debts. So maybe they'd cut loose all the toxic assets and under-performing debt, just tear it up, get it off their books. Felt good just thinking it.

The meeting was set for 10 a.m. Same as yesterday—remaining board members, large stakeholders, and the press. Though the markets had already opened, the news of the meeting should at least slow the sell-off and give them a chance.

Or not. Carolyn had gently offered that they just shut things down, using the cash reserves to facilitate a soft landing and then giving whatever's left over to charity or the government. Ryan could go back to Bank of Boston or take off in a new direction. Write a book about it all. It's not like he was ever that attached to Marsdale Lipman. The money was great, but his whole time there had been a struggle. "Ninety percent of what we do is gambling, not banking," he'd told her early on. Years later he modified it some—"There's no gambling at Marsdale Lipman, any more than the house gambles in Vegas. It's fraud and theft, plain and simple."

She was ashamed now to admit that whenever he talked like that she'd try to smooth it over. "It couldn't be as bad as you say and besides, you aren't doing the bad stuff." "The only way to change things is to hang in, keep working, and eventually have enough power to make a difference." Then, the clincher—"Right now we really can't afford your idealism, Ryan. Maybe when the kids are grown."

They were stopped at a light just a few blocks from The Four Seasons. Carolyn reached over and gave his hand a squeeze. Ryan squeezed back and smiled. Starry-eyed, but no fool.

They strode into the large, chandeliered room a few minutes before the ten o'clock starting time. The crowd was about the same size as yesterday, though with fewer stakeholders and more press. The mood was funereal. If corporations were people, then what could be sadder than the impending death of a 112-year-old icon? Ryan headed straight for the podium. The fact that nobody questioned his authority to call and take charge of the meeting showed just how completely things had unravelled. In just three days.

He quickly introduced himself, thanked everyone for coming, and expressed his sorrow over the recent deaths, including this morning's. "Yet, if I could borrow and bend a line from Shakespeare, 'We've come to bury Harold Leonard, but not so much to praise him.'" It struck a discordant note that sent an unsettling jolt through the crowd. "Because," Ryan continued, "what Harold promised when he stood before you yesterday was a return, with only minor concessions, to the status quo. Marsdale Lipman, the other banks, our whole financial system, going back to business as usual. Though he made a show of wanting to accommodate the Jubilees, in truth his tone was mocking and his intentions clear. The lowest point in his speech, to my ears, was when he boasted about the fantastic profits we've been raking in the past four years." Another discordant note and even Carolyn got fidgety. Fantastic profits are bad? In this group? She imagined sitting in church on Easter morning while the minister proclaimed his conversion to atheism.

Ryan plowed on. "I'm sorry, but such thinking epitomizes the mess we're in, acting as if the ever-increasing wealth of a small group of Americans is in no way connected to the ever-increasing suffering of the rest of the nation. Acting as if the financial gap between the upper and lower classes—yes, I know we hate that word 'class,' but that's the reality, two distinct classes—we're acting as if the stratification of American society into such financially disparate groups doesn't matter. Doesn't have any negative consequences and it shouldn't concern us that Main Street is underwater as long as Wall Street is flying. But the reality, painfully clear since the crash, is that it hurts in countless ways and, bottom-line, it is unsustainable. We cannot go on this way. The Jubilees have forced the issue but let's be clear—America was in dire straits before they came along."

Ryan paused for a few breaths, listening for the next words. The room was anxiously subdued, as if waiting for biopsy results.

"I realize what I'm saying is, uh, hard for some of you to hear. Goes against the free-market principles we've spent our lives celebrating. But Harold's death makes clear that we don't really have a choice here—or, we do, but not the options we'd like. Marsdale Lipman will either reinvent itself, more or less in alignment with Jubilee demands, or it will cease to exist. Maybe it'll be nationalized and reborn as Carver Marsdale Lipman." Finally, some laughter. "Or broken into pieces, scooped up by our competitors at fire-sale prices. Unless Jubilee destroys them also. We can try turning back the clocks, we can try stalling—but down that road the firm's finished. Employees out of work and shareholders out of luck. No, there's really only one choice before us, the Jubilee way, and really, let's face it . . . even if there were a viable alternative, if it means bucking the Jubilees, who's going to stand up and lead the way?"

Carolyn and Ryan had talked about getting to this moment and the importance of making it very clear that there was no overt opposition. So he waited for a full minute, letting who's going to stand up hang in the air. No one so much as blinked. Whatever they might be thinking, they weren't stepping into Harold Leonard's unfortunate shoes. Still, silencing opposition was not the same as winning it over. As Carolyn had said, "Motivation by fear can only get you so far. You need to get them buying into the new deal."

Ryan waited, waited, until the media folk started whispering among themselves, then said, "So. Let's talk about the Jubilee alternative."

Chapter 28

Dorothea stood before the bathroom mirror, brokenhearted at the rapid decline. A lifetime of beholding her mirror-self flashed past, like a movie montage. As a child, "dress up" had been her favorite game and standing before the mirror and preening, the best part. At thirteen, the full-length mirror on her bedroom door was her first stop every morning and last before bed; she'd worry over each pimple, however tiny, while marveling over the ever-so-gradual appearance of breasts and hips. Then the thousands of hours before a thousand different mirrors applying make-up. And, best memory of all, standing sideways to the mirror when pregnant with Mia, thrilled by the curves.

A good, strong, beautiful body. Sixty-nine years of grace and pleasure and now this. Cancer taints everything, inside and out, and there was nothing she could do about it. The doctors said it had spread everywhere and was beyond treating. Her fault, they hinted, for spurning their services all these years, never getting her early-warning tests. But she was secretly glad to be too far gone for the five-hundred dollar pills, the medicine that makes your hair fall out, the hospital heroics, and insurance company hassles, the whole fight, fight, fight. Better to make peace with what is than go to war against it. The truth was, her see-no-doctors approach had worked damn well for a long time. No regrets here.

But poor Leo. For anyone else, other than Mia, he'd be right there, defending her desire to go gently into night. Hell, this was his philosophy as much as hers, and he had a few more years of no-doc living in the bank, as well as the most keep-your-frikkin-hands-off-me living will ever written. No one could rant on the medical profession like Leo. More than anything, she hated what her cancer was doing to him, hated to see him tied up in contradictory thoughts, actually pondering chemo and other horrors. Well, it would all be over soon enough.

The upside to her illness was that it had pushed circle into action. They had hung on the verge for nearly twenty years, knowing what they were capable of and believing it necessary, their cross to bear, their duty, for the benefit of all humankind. But it just never happened in the nineties, never found the right moment. The problem was, they still believed in democracy back then. And, truth be told, abstract theorizing was all well and good but none of them really wanted to start killing people.

Then came the odious Bragg and his wrecking crew of an administration. She'd gone eight years, wanting to kill that man every day of it. Got very close to "fuck it, I'm doing it" a few times. But hate is just like cancer, it eats away at you, destroying from within, and they'd had to accept that they couldn't move against anyone who inspired such antipathy. It wouldn't work and could do serious damage to the dreamer. Which was the only reason Warren G. Bragg was still breathing.

Carver was such a huge relief after Bragg that, while they didn't quite recover full faith in the system, it made sense to practice a little patience and give things a chance to play out. So they'd bided their time, waiting and watching, hoping for the best, but were not all that surprised when Carver failed to transform the nation. One by one they all gave up on him—not blaming Carver so much as the staying power of the status quo—until only Mia and Brett were still holding out. Younger by decades than the rest of them, they'd only been part of circle since '06. They hadn't experienced the years of futility that leads one to hard choices and desperate measures. There ensued several anxious months with a series of awkward meetings while the old farts tried to persuade the kids to stop acting like a pair of cautious old farts.

They would not be moved. Leo had started to worry that they would never change their minds, that they'd turned against the project and might not even be trusted with the secret. Dorothea started feeling threatened, by Mia, of all people. Took her back to when Mia was in middle school getting indoctrinated in drug-war nonsense and Dorothea worried she'd turn her mother in for smoking pot.

Leo and Brett had some heated discussions, to no avail. Dorothea and Mia had several equally fruitless talks. Though none of the others said as much, they were becoming impatient. She feared circle might split into squabbling factions, which really would have been the end of it.

Did the stress from this period make her sick? They say that not all stress is bad for you, but that what hurts most are the stressors you can't do anything about. The worst case scenario is major-league stress combined with utter helplessness: pretty much describes her world during the months her cancer got going. She of course never verbalized this to anyone, not even Leo, and if she were at all religious she'd be praying hard that Mia never make the connection. Because yes, she knew her cancer was triggered by the intense external pressures of the time—shit everyone was dealing with—made worse by her conflict with Mia.

Or, silver-lining time, her body had taken charge and done the one thing that would get everyone committed. When she sat down with Mia to explain what the doctors had found and what they were predicting, the clouds that had darkened their relationship instantly lifted. Mia argued with the facts ("Since when do you care what doctors say?"), bargained ("Have you gotten second opinions? Have you checked out any alternatives?"), then wept for a stretch, wrapped in Dorothea's embrace, until they were sobbing, then breathing, as one.

Eventually, a calm and serious Mia said, "Dee, this means we have to act. Soon, real soon. We can't do it without you," pausing for a few brief tears, "and you may not . . . there's no way to know . . . we just have to . . . right?"

Dorothea felt all the tension of the past year drain out of her. Screw the cancer—in that moment, staring into her daughter's beautiful eyes, the two of them subsumed by love, she'd never felt so good, so whole.

"That's right, honey, it's now or never."

"So be it. And don't worry about Brett; he'll do the right thing."

Chapter 29

Talk about your perfect timing. One hour before the start of the show, Jubilee sent out their latest message—an eight-point manifesto with specific instructions for remaking the financial system. And who did Sally Tiger have scheduled for *Jubilee Nation*? The Nobel economist, old friend Nathan Kane, and libertarian icon, Win Deggars. They'd been invited to come on for what she'd thought would be an abstract discussion of the concept of "jubilee." Thanks to all the specifics in the new message, their conversation was entirely relevant and, for economics, rather lively.

She found it interesting that Jubilee had turned Nathan into a media star. Despite a Nobel Prize, dozens of books, and universal recognition of his intellect, he'd been a rare guest on any television or radio shows other than her own. She figured he was just too counter to the conventional wisdom that drove American media. Even after the economic meltdown totally validated his unconventional wisdom. But now, since Jubilee, he'd been on with Crissom once and was scheduled for an appearance on the Meadow show later today.

Win Deggars was similarly contrarian, though from the opposite direction. He'd been another strong voice in the pre-crash period, warning against the policies and practices that would eventually cause the economy to implode. But in his telling the problems were mostly with the government and not the financial community. He'd opposed the bailouts as unwarranted government interference and advocated letting unhealthy companies and people fail. In the post-crash period, the conventional wisdom had gravitated toward him, blaming everything on the government, while opposing tighter regulations on and criminal investigations of the financial community.

Sally held a printout of the Jubilee message. "Nathan, just two days and eighteen bodies ago you were on the show talking about dominator culture and class warfare. At that point, we didn't know what they meant by 'sharing wealth and power,' but here come the details. Starts with a call for progressive taxation. Federal income tax, starting at $500,000 annual income, and value-added taxes for the states. Your comments?"

"Sally, I would include the third item—the cap on executive compensation, tied to the minimum wage—they're clearly targeting the unequal distribution of wealth in this country."

"Income distribution—isn't that what you won the Nobel for?"

"Yes, that's right. My work was in the eighties, when the gap between rich and poor in America was expanding rapidly. In a cross-cultural study of First World countries and US states, I showed that for eleven social indicators, such as physical and mental health, homicide and suicide rates, teen pregnancies, incarceration rates, use of the death penalty, drug abuse—that each of these social issues correlated negatively with disparity in levels of wealth."

"Meaning?"

"Meaning, the larger the gap between rich and poor, the unhealthier, unhappier, less stable, and more violent a society becomes."

"Seems like one of those times the Nobel committee was sending America a message," Tiger said.

"May have been, but as with all such messages coming from the European social democracies, America wasn't listening. Anyway, the first step is a return to the kind of progressive taxation we had until JFK began dismantling it. Taxing the rich is the fairest and simplest solution to our financial problems. It's fair because—*they can afford it*. Even after they send billions to the IRS they'll still have enough left over to live the very good life. You have to understand, ninety-nine percent of Americans fall below the $500,000 per year mark. This only affects one percent of the population. If, at the same time, we tie executive compensation to the minimum wage, then the net effect is that the gap between overclass and underclass shrinks dramatically."

"We just have to eat the rich."

"No, more like soak the rich. Get some real trickle-down happening. But remember—they can afford it. If you make a billion dollars and have to pay ninety percent in taxes, you still have one hundred million dollars. Woe is you, right? So, our options: we can solve our problems, *maybe*, by belt-tightening and budget-cutting that seriously impacts seventy, eighty, ninety percent of the population. Or we can persuade one percent of the population to be satisfied living with mere millions."

"Persuade?"

"Better to persuade than force, which never works anyway. The rich have to see that this works in their favor. They have less money but they live in a better world."

"How can you call what Jubilee is doing anything but force?" asked Deggars.

"I hear you, Win. I grant that they're walking a very thin line. I liken what they're doing to a demolitions expert who can bring down a tall building with a few small but well-placed charges. What they've done so far, with a few well-placed victims, is breaking up the prevailing power structure. The key going forward is, 'can they persuade us to adopt the changes in their manifesto'?"

"What about the second point," asked Tiger, "consumption taxes for the states?"

"Shows a libertarian streak, I think, though Win might disagree. The federal government has no business in most of what happens at the state level so federal taxes should not be going there. Instead, each state needs it's own dedicated revenue system and, rather than taxing income twice, they should go with consumption and value-added taxes."

Tiger nodded to Deggars and said, "Win? Your take on the first three points?"

"Well, Nathan's right, I'm amenable to the solution for the states—taxing consumption is the best way to raise revenues because it gets the incentives right. Those who work hard and live frugally are rewarded, whereas spendthrifts and wasters are taxed. Makes the most sense, so why not for the federal government also? Instead, they're proposing that we intensify the practice of punishing the most productive members of society. Which is crazy. Taking money out of the pockets of the wealthy just means shrinking investment in the businesses that make America go. Means fewer entrepreneurs, fewer venture capitalists, fewer startups. Less jobs. Shrinking production and declining GNP."

"But don't we have all of those problems now?" asked Tiger, "At the culmination of years of reduced taxation?"

"Sorry, but you can't pin the bad economy on our most successful and productive citizens. Federal income is only half of the equation. Spending is the other half and we're in the mess we're in because of several decades of runaway spending. It's the entitlement system in this country that needs regulation and reform, not the markets. They need less regulation, so that the incentives make sense and freedom can work its magic."

"So, you'd advocate cuts in Medicare, Social Security, food stamps, unemployment benefits?" asked Tiger.

"Yes. Along with—and here I agree with the Jubilee message—deep cuts in military spending. As they say, shut down all of our foreign bases and bring the troops home. From everywhere. Close down the empire and no longer engage in offensive wars of choice. Self-defense only."

He paused for a round of applause from Tiger's peacenik audience. "But if I could go back to the whole 'soak the rich' bit. We simply cannot countenance the government seizure of an individual's hard-earned wealth. Or capping anyone's compensation. It's just wrong. It's never worked, anywhere it's been tried. Punish your hardest working citizens and what you end up with is a mediocre and underproductive populace. It's a recipe for massive failure and goes completely against our founding principles."

Now the audience responded with scattered boos. Nathan jumped in. "Win, I'm not sure what I find more disagreeable—the implication that average Americans don't work hard and deserve to have what little benefits they now receive cut back and taken away—or, the notion that billionaires work hard for all their money. When in fact they don't work at all for most of it, don't perspire—no calloused hands, no aching muscles. They don't have to be smart or right. Hell, even when they're total screw-ups, they still get get rich. Their money does all the heavy lifting and earning for them. The so-called magic of compound interest is the only thing laboring here, and it's a labor of lust and greed that increases individual wealth without producing anything real."

"That's just not fair, Nathan," said Deggars. "This is what class warfare gets us—demonization of the people who do the not-at-all-easy and absolutely essential work of running the largest and most complex economy in history. If you want to see the total collapse, not just of our system, but of the whole global economy, go ahead and put it in the hands of the so-called 'common man.' I put my faith in the men and women who guided us through the meltdown. They're the real heroes and deserve every penny we pay them."

"More like every penny they extort," said Kane.

"Nathan, we get it," said Deggars. "You don't like rich people."

Nathan laughed. "Actually, I'm a happy member of the top five percent. And some of my best friends are—"

"Rich people," said Deggars, smiling. "So, how do you deal with all the filthy lucre?"

"Voluntary taxation—we give everything we don't need to charity."

"But there you go, don't you see? It's voluntary. That's the essence of libertarianism—free people making smart choices. Income and estate taxes generate the opposite—coerced people with limited and generally stupid choices. Faceless bureaucrats deciding how to spend your money, invariably pissing it away on foreign entanglements and social boondoggles. Then turning to their most productive citizens and saying 'give us more.'"

Tiger spoke up. "If we could go back to the list . . . I want to make sure we discuss the final two items before we run out of time. Sounds like we're in agreement on the fourth and fifth points, regarding the military and winding down the empire. The sixth point—public financing of elections and limitations on corporate speech—is huge, but let's save that for another show.

"The question of the hour is how do we deal with debt? Jubilee's calling for a ten percent limit on interest rates and, their words, a one-time forgiveness of debt. Win?"

"Ha," shaking his head. "Good luck persuading creditors to forgive their debtors. Just try running this nation, running a business, managing an economy without debt. It's absurd, like banning oxygen. And reveals an anarchist streak, hiding inside all the socialism. If they really cared about creating a fair and just society they wouldn't be advocating the mass repudiation of personal responsibility. And the cap on interest rates? Just means that there will be no more credit for your underclass, Nathan. Any lender that extends low interest loans to high-risk borrowers is doomed to fail. Business 101.

"Also," Deggars continued, "we need to remember that 'jubilee' is a biblical term referring to the periodic forgiveness of debts. Used to be called for every fifty years. And that Christianity, Judaism and Islam all condemn usury, which can mean either excessively high interest rates, or the whole practice of charging interest. Hence Jesus chasing the money-lenders from the temple. So it seems these Jubilees have a strong religious streak to go with the anarchism."

"Too much religious influence for you, Win?" asked Tiger.

"Well, I'm a practicing Catholic, so I believe that religion has its place—just not in the statehouse, nor on Wall Street. And I'd think it would worry those of you on the secular left that the country's on the verge of being run by what appears to be a christo-anarchist assassination cult."

Everyone held their breath for a moment, half-expecting Deggars to keel over with a brain aneurysm. Tiger turned to Kane and said, "How about it, Nathan? Win's right about the historic antecedents. In fact, they've got us all using a term, jubilee, that originates in the Torah. Does it worry you that we're being pulled into some really old-time religion?"

"No, not at all. They're not telling us what to do with our money, that we should give it all to the church or tithe regularly or not spend it on this or that sinful behavior. They've sent us three messages and I really don't detect a trace of religion in any of them, aside from their use of 'Jubilee'. And while the forgiveness of debts and proscriptions against usury both go back to biblical times, in the here and now they go to the core of modern culture, secular and religious.

"Because, as Win points out, just about everything and everybody runs on debt—it's as ubiquitous and essential to life as oxygen. The problem is—and here's where we part ways, Win—without sensible, enforceable regulations, it turns from life-giver to life-destroyer. We needed a clean air act to keep oxygen working for us, now we need a clean debt act to get money working for us. Without it, the gap between rich and poor keeps expanding and America keeps declining."

"Speaking as an economist, Nathan, can what they're calling for even work?" asked Tiger. "And, if so, how would it work?"

"Well, there's two parts, each necessary to the other. The first, the ten percent limit on interest rates, fixes the practice of moneylending so that borrowing and debt work better going forward. You know, they're not saying that businesses, governments and individuals can't borrow anymore. They're saying that the practice must be better regulated. Otherwise, wealthy lenders invariably get richer, at the expense of borrowers. You simply cannot allow the rich to set the terms or write the rules because they will always pursue greater profits for themselves. It's human nature and corporate law, so no blame attached, but a culture of unregulated financial transactions favors the wealthy, as a matter of course. Frankly, I see ten percent as a cap, but would prefer rates at half that."

"Nathan, nobody's forcing people to borrow, high or low. It's their choice. And lenders likewise should get to choose whatever rate the market will bear," said Deggars.

"Spoken like someone who's always had choices. Most people don't, Win, not always. At some point, when they go to college, or when they get really sick, or they lose their job, or the car breaks down, they have to borrow, at whatever rate they can get. As you just pointed out, it will be a high rate precisely because they are in such bad shape. Borrowing at a high rate redistributes money upward, by definition and design. This is why, historically, Judaism, Christianity, and Islam all banned usury at one time or another—it concentrates wealth and rewards greed. In modern terms, it creates *trickle-up* economies. And really, no one's saying that lenders can't lend out for more than their costs. But one to three percent over costs would be fair, and manageable. That's a far, far cry from our current situation.

"So, we establish sensible regulations for all future lending. Then, we reboot the economy with a one-time top-to-bottom debt amnesty. Most debts are forgiven. Consumer credit, car loans, mortgages, the whole panoply of financial products. The national debt."

"That's just crazy, Nathan," Deggars nearly shouted. "The global economy would grind to a halt. We'd go into a depression that might last decades. I mean . . . you can't be serious. Plus, you're talking about seizing trillions in assets from people who did nothing wrong but invest their money."

"No, this wouldn't affect savings, nor investment in tangible goods and services. It would devalue prices, but that would be across the board, so goods and services would retain their relative value. You might even be able to separate out and retain some debts; for instance, housing prices could be tied to the real-world assessed values, and mortgaged at three to five percent. But unreal goods and services, financial and real estate bubbles, all of that would disappear.

"Look, it goes back to interest rates and usury. The fair amount of interest to charge on any loan is that which covers the lender's costs—the cost of the money to them, plus their operating expenses—plus, and this is key, a decent wage to the lender. But when lenders are free to set their rates as high as the market will bear, it's usury, and the end result is that they're making thousands of dollars an hour as glorified clerks. Multi-million-dollar bonuses to coked-up gamblers who produce nothing of tangible value. Since having so much money increases their power in society, the longer it goes on, the worseit gets. Until, in our current situation, it can no longer be dealt with in half steps or simple measures."

"Time to reboot," said Tiger.

"That's right, nothing to lose but our debts," Nathan concluded.

Deggars was shaking his head, but looking less emphatic about it. "You're asking one group to—I don't know, it just seems unfair. You're breaking promises, rescinding contracts, making one group suffer for everyone else. It's like reverse discrimination or something."

"I hear you, Win. Still, anyone who's had so much money and opportunity but hasn't taken steps so they can come through this in good shape—well, if somebody has to lose, why not them?"

Chapter 30

"When the call comes," his father always said, "there's them that stand up and there's them that run. Which you gonna be, Boyd?"

He'd snap to attention, salute, and answer, "Stand up, sir!"

Then his father would say, "When the Jews and niggers try to take over this country, there'll be them that appease and them that fight. Which you gonna be, Boyd?"

"Fight sir!"

And, "When the gov'ment tries to shut you up and take your money and come after your guns, whatcha gonna do, Boyd?"

"Fight harder, sir!"

Then, when Boyd was little, his father would smile and reach out and mess his hair, say "That's right, boy," maybe pat him on the back. When Boyd got older, the old man, Jake, would smile, then shoot a hard jab to his shoulder, leave a bruise.

Though Jake Hardin had preached respect for the military, he had issues with it too, going back to the '60s when they wouldn't take him because he was twenty pounds overweight. The Army wouldn't take Boyd neither, same reason. Kinda bullshit that lost a war to a bunch of skinny gooks in pajamas and was losing one again to sand niggers and towelheads. Pissed Boyd the fuck off.

Jake died three days before Carver's election. He'd been sick for a long time, laid up, got real skinny, taking oxy for the pain, so he was kinda crazy high, raging on like some old Bible prophet. If he'd had the strength he'd-a walked to Washington, rifle in hand and shot the motherfucker dead. Loved his country that much. Good thing he wasn't around the past three years of mud people rule.

Stand up, fight, fight harder.

Hadn't been any fighting yet, but they were ready, been ready two years. Militias in 42 states, arsenals filled, training out in the open, and nothing Carver or the feds could do about it. Too busy trying to prove he ain't some Communist, running hard from the Tea Party crowd, making like he's a gun lover in support of "well-regulated militias." More like he's scared shitless and doesn't have a choice. What's he gonna do, call in the military? Most of them voted against him, can't stand the fuck, hate that he ran against the wars, hate that he let fags serve with their dicks out, hate his kissing up to Arabs and Jews, running round the world apologizing for his country. Every branch is filled with militia men, training hard, getting ready for the call.

And the private contractors? Kontrain? Taylor Dann? Shit, they *really* hate him. No sir, Big Nigger, when the call comes you and yours is going back into chains. If we don't just wipe you out, good and done.

Since the Republicans took back the House, and with Carver's approval ratings in the shitter, the plan'd been to just wait it out till the election, throw him out of the White House and maybe spare the country an all-out civil war. Boyd and some of the others weren't so sure—Republicans could be just as lame-ass as Democrats—but if they could get the right man at the top, it'd be a better solution. Spare a lot of homeland destruction and save their bullets for all the foreigners who need killing. Had to go along anyway, since the strategy was coming from big-shit military brass.

Like soldiers throughout history, they'd been waiting for the call. Keeping their weapons clean, stocking up, training hard, getting ready.

Then these Jubilee fucks came along.

Started out a mixed bag—good riddance to Carver's Jew advisor, and both the dead senators were Republicans-in-name-only—but the Griffin court had been damn good, specially on guns, and Dick Mallard was a genuine hero, best politician since Reagan. The shocker was General Eisley, five-star Army chief of staff, on record for supporting the militias and off-record their top dog. Boyd wanted to start the shooting then and there. But at that point they were calling it a terrorist attack on *America,* making the enemy whoever was doing the killing, not Carver and his crew. Day Two just added to the uncertainty—bunch of ass-wipe banksters, all Jews or Jew lovers, the very fucks who engineered the so-called collapse to enrich themselves. Boyd wasn't the only one who said "amen" when he read that list. The online conversation started showing some support for the killers. You had to like their style, and maybe Carver'd be next.

Day Three put an end to that. Fucking disaster. They lost five public voices, men who provided daily inspiration and aided in spreading critical intel. And Thomas Harrow was more than just the owner and producer of right-wing media—he'd been channeling buckets of money into the movement. Clearly, *we* were under attack, not America, and the thinking was that Carver had sacrificed a few of his own to sow confusion. No one ever said he wasn't smart, the fuck.

So they'd called for this meeting, a hundred and fifty movement leaders gathering on the grounds of the Sons of Liberty, in Lebanon, Kansas, chosen because it was the geographical center of America. Meeting start was one in the afternoon.

Boyd had left Texas late last night and drove straight through, only stopping for coffee and gas, turning into the Sons' driveway at twenty o' one. Went through one identity check at the top of the drive, then a half-mile through wooded grounds came out to a large old barn with an adjacent field full of cars. Another ID check—more informal now because these guys knew him—and he entered the barn. The men were milling about, coffee cups or beers in hand. A lot of private conversations going on and everybody was talking loud and looking pissed.

Boyd knew why. He'd had the radio on and around eight they started reporting the latest Jubilee killings. First was General Carney, the man who took over when Eisley went down, the man who should've been stepping up to the mic right about now. Then Bird and Withers, heads of Kontrain and Taylor Dann, either them or their people woulda been here too. Fuck. And Paul Sheppard—Boyd didn't give a shit about religion but a lot of the men here did and for them Sheppard was a big deal. And then another Jew bankster, okay, better off dead, 'cept for the message it sent. Like Carney, he'd been next in a leadership line, so the meaning was clear—whoever takes over for Carney, Bird or Withers better change the game or they're dead.

Jesus fuck!

As the men started taking their seats, Boyd made three observations. First, there was less than a hundred men present, closer to eighty, half of what was expected. Second, it was just militia, no military, no private security. Looked like no one would be standing up to take Carney's place. Third, this didn't feel nothin' like an army gearing up for battle.

Sons leader Wendell Fretskin walked up to the mike and gave it a few taps. Whip-thin, head-shaved and camo-clad, Fretskin was nominal leader of the militias, if only because they were meeting on his land. When the barn quieted down, he started talking, slow and deliberate.

"I just got off the horn with Major David Booth. Some of you know him— General Carney's top aide. Booth was with the General when he died." As Fretskin gave his report, the room got whisper still. "The General was thoroughly checked for microchips, poisons, anything inserted or swallowed that could be a danger, nano-bots, GM viruses, all that bullshit. He was clean. Which convinced him that it was some kind of energy weapon, laser technology or sound weapon or something, and they thought they had protection, or at least detectors, in place. Well, Booth says, made no difference. He and another aide were right there, wide awake, watched the general just seize up and die. No sign of anything. Says it's gotta be psychic, mind murder, but who the fuck knows."

He paused to let it all sink in.

Someone shouted out, "Lock, load, and fire. That'll stop them!"

Nobody bothered pointing out the obvious.

Fretskin continued, "Major Booth says we need to just wait this out. That we stick with the pre-Jubilee plan and make sure we win next year's election, at all levels, from Carver down to school boards and dogcatchers."

That pissed everybody off—them that wanted to avenge the murders of Carney and Eisley and the others, them that wanted to take down the Carver administration, and them that just wanted to break things and kill people.

Fretskin held up both hands and waited, stern-faced, until he got their attention again. "Listen up. One, you can't wage a war without clear leadership and we ain't gonna have clear leadership until Jubilee is stopped. Truth is, I feel like some sniper's sighting in on me just standing here. Two, can't stop them if we can't find them, and good luck finding them when the feds have picked over twenty-four crime scenes and twenty-four autopsies and don't have shit. Three, they've been content so far killing six a day, but who's to say they can't do six hundred? Who's to say they don't wipe out the entire movement tonight? Point is, we don't know. Fighting from a place of ignorance just makes you more ignorant. Then it makes you dead. Four, Paul Sheppard had several million Christians praying for him last night. Took the Jubilees head on. Didn't work any better than General Carney's plan. So now some're saying that 'Jubilee' is from the Bible, that it's a Christian thing, so they're going over to the Jubilees. Explains a lot of the empty chairs in this room right now."

Boyd couldn't stay quiet. "Sounds like you're saying we should all just climb on the Jubilee train," he said, almost shouting. "Pray they don't kill us. Pretend we're okay with their share-the-wealth agenda, just ignore the fact that we'd be sharing with mud people. Fuck that."

Boyd heard a few "amens" and saw more than a few nodding heads.

Fretskin held up his hands again and waited for quiet. "I'm with you, brother, all the way. This ain't surrender, it's tactical retreat. Orders coming from up the chain. We're just letting things play out until we have better intel so we make better decisions.

"One last point. You all saw the latest message—well, there's some things to hate about it, but there's also some to like, 'specially the whole Jubilee part. I'm guessing a lot of us wouldn't mind having our debts just wiped out," he said, with a snap of the fingers. "And borrowing in the future at ten percent or less. And cutting billionaires down to size. All I'm saying's, these guys are doing a lot of our work for us. So we wait 'em out, till they get caught or go away or come over to our side. We keep in shape and stay ready. Our time's coming."

Even more amens to that, so Boyd let it be. There's a time for fighting. And there's a time to go shopping.

Chapter 31

It took a few hours for the new message to sink in, but by late afternoon businesses were reporting phenomenal sales, across the board. All on credit. Of course, after four years of high unemployment and stagflation, a lot of people no longer had credit of any sort and those that did had reduced limits. But any who could still borrow were taking all they could get. Everybody had the same rationale—everyone's doing it.

Mendelsohn called it semi-legitimate looting—crazed people leaving stores with their arms full of goodies, but technically legal. Joss feared the nation was heading for the sort of breakdown that results in more traditional looters, and worse. What happens when the credit runs out or the banks pull the plug? What happens if the downtrodden and spit-upon take Jubilee's message and methods to heart and, pitchforks in hand, go after the rich and powerful? What happens if Carver refuses to do what they want, so they kill him next? That's all it would take right now; a presidential assassination and the country would implode.

Carver was the key—Joss figured they left him alive in hopes he was the right man for the moment. But how much time did he have? When it was only a matter of appointing new people to replace those who had died, no one could blame him for moving slow, for such things always take time. But now, this manifesto. He had to at least address it, tell the country where he stood and what steps he would soon be taking, for or against.

When she had told the president about her private communication with Jubilee, he said, "That settles it. There's no way theyd let me stall much longer. For that matter, this whole thing is on the verge of turning into a runaway train. It's time for a sober talk with the American people. Time to make some decisions." Though he didn't tell her *what* he'd decided, he promised that at a prime time press conference he'd be taking control of the train.

And that was before Max-Out-Your-Credit day got rolling.

After her meeting with Carver, Joss returned to Homeland. She had a quick update with Trenton, who was on his way back to the White House. He listened to Joss's report, including her exchange with Jubilee, and the president's reactions to that and the new message, and said, "Haven't left him much of a choice, have they? What he's going to do?"

Joss shrugged. "I think he's ready to do what they want. But he's looking for reassurances. Mainly, will it actually work? He's had people gaming the Jubilee scenario and so far the results are ambiguous. If he's convinced it'll push the country into civil breakdown, then my guess is he continues stalling, even though it puts him personally at risk. If, on the other hand, he decides to go ahead with Jubilee, then he needs to know that the killings and the messages and the policy demands will stop."

"If he goes forward with their agenda," said Trenton, "there will be serious opposition. Wall Street, the Pentagon—I can't see either giving up without a fight. So the Jubilee killings won't be stopping right away."

"As long as it's clear that Carver, along with everyone else, has been compelled to act. If it starts to look like Jubilee's working on Carver's behalf, killing off opposition to his agenda, then—" She shook her head.

"For that matter," asked Trenton, "what about us? We're supposed to be trying to catch these jokers and more and more I'm feeling like a goddamn co-conspirator."

The conversation ended with both affirming that they were indeed still trying to end the killings and see that some version of justice prevailed. Then Trenton returned to the White House—this time for an all-advisors' planning session with Carver—and Joss finally had a sit-down with Mendelsohn.

He'd spent the morning interviewing three new widows and learning zip. Joss found him less upbeat than usual, borderline morose. But he cheered up when she started talking about last night's exchange with Jubilee.

"Wow. Who else knows?" asked Mendelsohn.

"You, me, Trenton, and Carver."

He slowly shook his head. "You're telling me Henry Trenton's going along with—what do we call it—presidential sanction? Mafioso management?"

Joss nodded. She was a long way from clear about her own position, but she tried to explain. "I think that if we had any leads whatsoever, and were reasonably certain that we could stop the killings, or at least protect the president, Trenton would still be in hot pursuit of bad guys. But let's face it, Alex, we've got nothing. Trenton thinks Carver has to act soon or he's next to go. I'm inclined to agree. He has to do what they want or they kill him."

"Still. Capitulation to terrorists? I mean, for years we've said that you can't even negotiate with them, now POTUS is following their orders, in full public view? How can this possibly end well for Carver?"

"Don't underestimate the man's political skills. I think he'll try to get out in front of it, make the case for most of the manifesto and try to bargain a few items down, as a show of strength. If Jubilee's as smart as we think they are, they'll let him have a minor victory or two. Then . . . we see what happens. If it pulls the country out of the hole it's in, ends the recession and the Jubilees fade away—which is clearly their intent—then Carver can come out of this a hero."

Mendelsohn looked unconvinced. "So what exactly are you and Trenton and I supposed to be doing now? Law enforcement or politicking?"

"We're still law enforcement. If we can figure out who they are and how they're doing it, then it would strengthen the president's hand. But, everybody has to remember, things were falling apart before Jubilee came along. If they were to disappear today, there's a good chance the country just continues to decline and drags much of the world down with it. And Jubilee—well, maybe there are laws higher than American jurisprudence."

"Don't go all Jesus on me." Mendelsohn rolled his eyes.

"No, I don't mean religion, more like economic laws—like when the gap between rich and poor is too great, society suffers. Or a law against usury. Or a law limiting military budgets. Or limiting corporate power. Jubilee's saying, we've been breaking those laws for generations now, and look where it's gotten us. Rich got richer, poor got the shaft, and laws got written to keep it that way. Until Jubilee, there was nothing anyone could do about it. People with extreme wealth and power are immune to ordinary justice. How many bankers went to jail after the crash, despite countless examples of fraud and outright theft? Instead, they all got huge raises. I'm just saying, exceptional times call for exceptional laws."

"Joss, I'm an FBI agent, as were you. We're sworn to uphold existing law. We don't get to pick and choose, or decide that these twenty-four murders were in fact justifiable executions because the rich bastards were breaking some higher laws. I mean, 'higher' according to who? Murder is murder. Do we just condone it? Say 'this time it's cool' and proceed to build our wonderful new world, just don't mind all the angry ghosts?"

Joss had no answer, at least nothing she could put into words. She didn't think she or Trenton or the president were condoning murder per se. Nor the Jubilees, for that matter. This only worked if you accepted that America had long been riven by an undeclared and unacknowledged class war that causes countless casualties every day, all from the middle and lower classes. From there, the Jubilee killings are an unfortunate but necessary evil, like nuking Hiroshima and Nagasaki to end World War II. And really, the deaths of sixty or so rich men do not come remotely close in comparison. Maybe she *was* condoning murder.

They agreed to keep doing their duty, working the case and trying to stop the killings. At the same time, Mendelsohn granted that they ultimately worked for the president and "if he ordered them to line up with Jubilee, then line up they would. Like Nixon said, 'When the president does it, it's legal.'"

"And that worked out so well for him," said Joss. Mendelsohn laughed.

They had to move on anyway, as Muriel Matson was arriving with, she said, new information that Joss especially needed to hear. They met in a small interrogation room. As on the day her husband died, Muriel looked strong and composed, not exactly happy, but at peace with what was happening. Serene. Joss found herself thinking, again, that she really needed to know this lady's secret.

"Thanks for making this time," said Muriel. "I know you must be very busy, so I'll come right to the point—I've had more dreams. Actually, the same dream, but more detailed."

Two days ago, Joss had been pretty skeptical that there was anything of value in Muriel's dreaming. A whole lot had changed since then, including Olivia Harrow having the same dream. Now she nodded, as did Mendelsohn, who said, "Tell us more."

Muriel took them through it, same as the original dream in which her husband died, only now she senses two other people in the room, a man and a woman. But before she can turn to see who they are, the dream shifts, she's outside on her lawn and Joss walks up to her and says the name 'Malcolm Carney'.

"I woke up thinking he was the killer. But after I googled him he sounded more like a potential victim. When this morning's names hit the news, there he was. I called for this appointment right away.

"You have to understand, when someone appears in a lucid dream like that, like you did," she said, looking at Joss, "it can mean that you're dreaming also, that we're sharing a dream—lucid dreaming at the same real time and in the same dreamspace. I think I'm dreaming with the Jubilees also, the man and woman that I couldn't quite see. I think it's the people who killed Andy and then Carney. Which is how you could know about Carney before, or more like *as*, it was happening."

"Whoa," said Joss. "I can't remember the last time I remembered a dream. Never happens, and for sure I've never had a lucid dream."

"But you have several dreams a night, even if you don't remember them. Everybody does. It just takes practice to remember them, and more focused practice to start lucid dreaming. And you don't have to remember or be lucid to share a dream; it's enough that one of the dreamers is lucid and that there's a strong link between the dreamers. I connected with the Jubilees when they came for Andy, and we've shared the same dream every night since. Then you and I made our own connection and that pulled you into it."

Joss was wrestling with her old friend, the healthy skeptic. She tried to keep her expression neutral. "So, how did dream-me know that Malcolm Carney was next to die?"

Mendelsohn had been nodding through Muriel's explanation. "Before you answer that, Muriel, just to be clear: you're saying that the Jubilees are dreaming people to death?"

"No, not exactly. I mean, yes, it's clearly non-physical, and at the very least it's leaking into my dreamspace. But I can't explain it. And you know, I could be all wrong and these are just . . . dreams. Even the Malcolm Carney part—could be I read about him or saw him on the news."

"But that's not what you really think," said Mendelsohn.

"No, what I really think is that they're dreaming their way into people's brains and triggering aneurysms. They just happened to go after the husband of a lucid dreamer. I'll bet they were really surprised to see me there. But it gave me an opening into the murder dream." She turned to Joss. "I'm not sure how you got there."

Joss was shaking her head. "I'm not sure either, but last night, I think maybe they invited me in."

Chapter 32

At four p.m. Eastern on Day Four of the Jubilee murders, the president convened an ad hoc "Jubilee cabinet" of five men and two women. In selecting people he'd had two criteria: first, they had to have displayed some degree of sympathy or agreement with the Jubilees, in their actions or comments over the past few days; second, they had to bring to the table some experience for dealing with specific items in the Jubilee manifesto.

Howard Trenton was his first pick. He'd considered Joss Morgan, but decided it best to keep their communications—and Morgan's with Jubilee—private for now. He chose Bonnie Smithson, the four-term independent senator from Oregon, perennial winner of Most Progressive in the Senate. And Charlie Wick, the Florida representative who, pre-Jubilee, had sponsored legislation to cut military spending in half. Carver skipped active military and chose instead retired General Matthew Gross, long derided as General Peacenik, but an original thinker and the author of several excellent books on the history of war. From his staff, he picked Zia Carillo, his most iffy choice; she'd earned a reputation for being tough and hawkish—perfect for National Security Advisor, but perhaps too law-and-order for what was coming. Still, they'd been friends a long time and he knew she was an Eleanor Roosevelt liberal at heart. From the financial world, he called in Ryan Weathers, the newly seated CEO of Marsdale Lipman, who took control of the company just this morning with a promise to rebuild it on Jubilee terms. And lastly, in what would have been the most inconceivable development pre-Jubilee, he'd asked Nathan Kane not only to join this meeting, but to become the new Secretary of the Treasury.

The "Cabinet members" were all seated at a large round table talking quietly when the president entered the room and gestured for everyone to remain seated. He sat, poured himself a glass of water, then slowly scanned the circle, from Zia on his right to Howard on his left. He took a deep breath, let out a long, slow exhale, and began talking.

"There's an old saying that 'freedom is the absence of choice' which strikes me as apt for this moment. The Jubilees have left me, us, this nation, faced with but one non-negotiable choice—change or die. I've done everything in my suddenly meager power to avoid having to make that choice, to keep our options open. But all our efforts these past four days have been to no avail. It keeps coming back to change or die, and suicide by Jubilee, I'm sorry, is just not an option. Not for me, shouldn't be for anybody. Ergo, we're left with change, we've run out of choices, we're free. Something that doesn't happen a whole lot for presidents.

"For all the talk of being the most powerful office in the world, the presidency comes with a thousand strings and preconditions. Constituents who can't be disappointed. Established protocols that are beyond question. Special interests and K Street and perpetual fundraising. The immovable force of the status quo. All of it determining what you can and can't do. You want to normalize relations with Cuba? Makes sense for a dozen good reasons, but sorry, no. End the war on drugs? Single-payer healthcare? Create a fair and reasonable tax system? End Bragg's idiot wars? All good ideas, sorry, no."

He paused for a sip of water and thought that this was the most at ease he'd felt during his entire presidency.

"Now, it's not what some have speculated. There's not a secret cabal of gray men who sit each new president down and tell him how it works, what he can do and what's off limits. Nor are there veiled threats that you'll get the JFK treatment if you step out of line. It's more banal than that; just follow the money.

The big money. Most of it I'd figured out before the election—which I'd never have won without the help of the aforementioned constituencies and special interests and all their cash. When you start, you tell yourself there's no quid pro quo. Then you're here for a bit and try to make something really important happen, but you can't even get it on the table for serious discussion."

The whole time he was speaking he was slowly sweeping around the table, doing what he does best—gauging the response of his listeners. So far so good.

"Take the wars. I ran as a peace candidate. I have been committed to peace my whole life. I came in here wanting to pull out of Iraq and Afghanistan. Shrink the empire. Rethink the whole global war on terror. But Ike was right when he warned against the power of entrenched special interests, and that was fifty years ago. What he called the military-industrial-complex has since grown monumentally bigger, into a global mega-monster, a blood-sucking, money-gorging leviathan. Call it The Beast. It's hard to do anything in Washington that does not affect The Beast and harder still to do anything that would actually diminish it. I take it as a huge victory that we cancelled one weapons program. One. I'm less proud that we've set timetables for withdrawal from the wars because, frankly, I know it's bullshit. The Beast has no intention of leaving the Middle East, not as long as *our* oil is under *their* soil. Look, Bragg built an embassy in Iraq the size of Vatican City. We're not leaving. Nor are we ending war any time soon. The Beast feeds on war. Especially open-ended wars like the Cold War and the War on Terror."

He paused for a breath.

"I'm not offering excuses. Those who are disappointed in me have every right to be. Maybe I could have fought harder, tamed The Beast. Pushed for single-payer. Made Wall Street pay for their crimes and screw-ups. Frankly, better men than I have tried and done no better. We've all learned to settle for passable half-measures and artful compromises. Just the way it had to be—until now. Until Jubilee.

"So. We have the most incredible opportunity. Nothing less than remaking the world. But it is, as the kids say, some scary shit. If we resist Jubilee then they keep on killing people at the top, could be me next, and then whoever takes my place until we stop resisting. If that happens and we go leaderless for too long, then America fragments into chaos and The Beast takes over in the greatest of all military coups. Once they're in control they'll take the fight right to the Jubilees with martial law, mass arrests, torture, and executions, using protect-you-from-terror to rid the country of everyone they don't like. They can easily neutralize Jubilee's threat—if Jubilee kills six the Beast kills six thousand. Or sixty thousand, there's really no limit to what they'll do once it's war. And they'd only have to do it once to stop Jubilee."

He paused for breath again, giving the horrible vision a few moments to sink in. "Or. We stop seeing Jubilee as an adversary. We stop feeling like we're being forced to adopt their agenda. We make it our own. I mean, there's really no other option. Not if we want America to survive as a free and democratic nation. Not if we want to keep The Beast from taking over."

The president talked for a full half hour, without notes, half campaign speech and half inspirational sermon. Much of it would make it into his primetime address, though none of the Beast stuff. He finished upbeat—"I hope you will join me in feeling grateful to be alive, in this time and place, present at the creation, and given the chance to usher in a fresh start for this nation and the world"—and then smiled and spread his hands outward, palms open, inviting the others to comment and discuss.

"Mr. President," said General Gross, "I share your worries but little of your optimism. Even if we go forward with this manifesto, I fear that we still risk a military coup. If we institute this debt relief and the other changes and it doesn't work, or just not fast enough, or if it gets too crazy for too long, our financial system crumbles, markets are crippled, resource wars flare up all over, and we're back into leaderless chaos and military coups. As for winding down the empire: if you bring the troops home into that kind of economic discord—well, add a million stressed out military families to a populace that's armed to the teeth and psyched for the rapture—you're talking Germany in the thirties, on steroids."

The president simply nodded in agreement. It was his point exactly. There was no way to finesse this, nor negotiate, legislate, or compromise it. Every option led to the same horrible end. Which left them free to go for the gold. The equitably shared gold, of course. He turned to Nathan Kane.

"So, Nathan, can the economic items in the manifesto work? Especially, jubilee?"

"Absolutely. I'm embarrassed to admit that in a lifetime of economic thought I never even pondered it. But if offers an elegant solution to the problem that's most concerned me—the always-widening gap between rich and poor. Jubilee reduces that in an instant because it, the wealth gap, is what the poor owe to the rich. In America, the bottom 90% of households owe nearly 100% of all personal debt. And the top 10% hold nearly all of it. A one-time jubilee fixes that, like rebooting the economy, top to bottom."

While no one was vigorously shaking their head in disagreement, Nathan noted troubled looks around the circle. "I know that's hard to accept, sounds unfair and unworkable over the long term. But here's the thing—it's not meant as a longterm policy, not at all. This is a one time course correction, a round of chemotherapy for the body economic. It's not meant to be fair, nor to be a model for the economy going forward. It's meant to address serious imbalances that have proven unresolvable by other means. After the correction, we return to our free market system, more or less, with a new regulatory regime to keep things from going bad again. In particular, the limit on interest rates, since unfair rates—usury—is what feeds the gap, essentially transferring wealth from bottom to top. When the wealthy are able to set the terms for lending, they inevitably increase wealth, at the expense of the not-so-wealthy borrowers."

"I'm sorry," said Zia, "but how does this not totally crash the economy? Didn't we just do a trillion dollar bailout to the banks to avoid this kind of breakdown?"

"With all due respect," said Nathan, with a nod to the president, "that was a good example of what I'm saying. The bankers used their power to set the terms of the bailout, which resulted in a massive transfer of wealth from Main Street to Wall Street. That's the current system—sure as gravity, the wealthy always win, no matter how unfair it is to the rest of society. As for crashing the economy, real wealth is unaffected by this. Savings and investments in real economic activity are untouched. All of the resources that we were using before the jubilee are still available after. Crops keep growing. Teachers teach, doctors heal. Workers are still able to work, thinkers to think, manufacturers to manufacture, service providers to go on providing valued services. Everybody is able to carry on with business as usual, only now they're not shouldering huge loads of debt. The economy not only doesn't crash, it hums along healthier than ever."

Carver observed that the others were not so much resisting Nathan's explanation, as trying to get their minds around it, which the president himself was still struggling with. He noticed however that Ryan Weathers, the new Marsdale Lipman CEO, was smiling. He shot the banker a quizzical look.

"Mr. President, three days ago I thought Nathan Kane was a smart but dangerous leftist. However, for some time now, years really, I've been thinking along the same lines about what was going wrong in banking and financial services. I protested the rise of casino banking at Marsdale Lipman several years ago. Tried to keep us out of the subprime market and predicted much of the crash, though no one would listen to me. So I was primed, so to speak, for Jubilee's message. I've been running the numbers for several scenarios. And what I'm thinking of as the 'full jubilee' works fine for Marsdale Lipman. Frankly, it'll be a relief to dump the whole lot of dubious paper—loans that were never getting repaid. Everybody's better off just forgiving and forgetting such debts. We've got substantial real assets and talented employees, though they'll have to get used to earning considerably less—"

"While still making very good money," said Nathan.

"Absolutely," said Ryan. "I get it. And my guess is most everyone else will get it too, once it's the law of the land."

"What happens to investors?" asked Senator Smithson. "And what about small companies or pension funds that had everything in securitized mortgages or similar packages? Don't they just get wiped out?"

Nathan answered, "Yes, they do. Wherever the 'asset' is somebody else's unsecured debt rather than something real, it disappears. Of course, a lot of that is happening already, without Jubilee—basically the problem with all bubble economies. You get a bubble when prices are inflated by speculative fever rather than the value of actual things. When the bubble pops, all of the fever-driven 'value' disappears and people go from wealthy to poor overnight. This is truly the mother of all bubbles so there will be losers. But far, far fewer than are losing in the current system which makes it easier, I would think, to provide remedies."

"You know, speaking of remedies," said congressman Wick, "I think their manifesto is missing a few key points. Or maybe it's coming in future messages. Because what we really need now is a European-style safety net—though I suppose we should stay away from the word 'socialism'—"

"First time it's been spoken in the White House since FDR," said Carver, laughing.

The congressman flashed a quick smile then turned serious again. "If we had universal healthcare, free higher education, and generous, long-term unemployment benefits, all to go along with Social Security, then people wouldn't have so far to fall and would bounce back faster. We just need an actual safety net. And the thing is, with the fixes to the tax system, and savings from the military budget, we can afford it now. Easily."

"I'm not sure about easy," said the president, "but just the fact that we're having this conversation—you're right, Charlie, now's the time for long overdue changes. And, with the Jubilee factor, you think we can get things passed, even in the current House?"

"If not now, when?" answered the congressman.

Senator Smithson added, "Good thing they included campaign finance reform. If we can put all this to a vote that isn't dictated by lobbyists and campaign contributions, then yes, we should be able to get it passed."

The president turned to Trenton. "Howard? Am I right in guessing that we're swinging a bit left for you?"

Trenton smiled, slowly nodding his head. "Mr. President, if I'd heard this conversation three days ago I might have called for your impeachment. Sir. But as others have pointed out, the world's changing. More than anything, I'm a pragmatist. I've always been a pro-military, economic conservative because that's the world we lived in. But this is new terrain and, practically speaking, the Jubilee agenda makes sense to me. I don't really follow the politics, but if you think this can happen, that the American people will go along with it and benefit from it and," nodding to the senator and congressman, "if you all think you can manage the legislation, then call me 'Captain Lefty', reporting for duty.

"That said, what worries me most is The Beast. I think you're right—Jubilee could be stopped by holding the American people hostage. Folks would turn against Jubilee fast if they were seen as the reason for mass arrests and executions. So, I think we need to deal with that. Right away."

"Sounds like you have a suggestion?" Carver prompted.

"Yes sir, though I'm not sure you want to hear it."

"Shoot, Henry."

"Sir, I think you should initiate contact with Jubilee. Secretly. Affirm your support and make this a partnership. Impress on them the urgent need to stop any palace coups in progress. And, since we're gonna have the best intel on who's taking charge in the military and militias, we start telling them who has to die next."

"Jesus, Henry. You want me directing the assassination of prominent American citizens?"

"Mr. President, I don't think you have a choice."

Chapter 33

As the president finished talking, Dorothea was squeezing Leo's hand so tightly he thought his heart might break. Carver had just announced to the nation that, in effect, Jubilee had won. Master politician that he is, he managed to make it sound like a combination of his good ideas, the people's aspirations, and America's manifest destiny. At one point he said, "We did not ask for or even imagine Jubilee's actions. We do not in any way condone or forgive the deaths of twenty-four good Americans. I intend to use the full power of my office to determine who is behind the killings and bring them to justice. However, it cannot be denied and should not be ignored that their actions have altered the political landscape in this nation at a time when, frankly, it really needed altering."

Some nifty speechifying.

It's an old question, and one that Leo and the others had discussed often: Does history create great men or do great men make history. "History creates" means that it didn't matter who was in charge when circle acted; events would push and prod until just the right man or woman ascended to leadership and did what had to be done. "Great men make" says if they acted when the wrong person was in charge their efforts were doomed. Leo had always leaned toward the side of history, but now he was glad he lost the argument. Bragg could never have made the leap or given that speech. They would have had to kill him and half his administration and just hope the right leaders emerged.

Difficult as it was to do nothing those eight terrible years, it was clearly the right call.

They sat and watched a panel of commentators dissecting the speech. "I get the feeling they're not quite saying what's really on their minds," said Dorothea. "Afraid of getting jubileed."

"Dear Lord, tell me you haven't heard that usage," said Leo.

He played it for a laugh, but Dorothea wasn't smiling. So he cursed the cancer for taking her sense of humor, but she wasn't buying that either. "It's not the illness, Leo, it's the dreams. It's murdering four men and sitting here with the big-hearted pacifist I've loved for fifty years and knowing we'll murder the fifth in a few hours. I tell myself it's war, that they're all wealthy men who thrived on the suffering of others. It makes sense, in my head, a few sacrificed for the good of millions. Makes sense, it really does, but . . . I feel a darkness in my body, Leo, blacker even than the cancer, eating away. I'm sorry. It's still murder."

That had always been the worry: could they participate in violence without being consumed by it? Long before they developed the dream and started hatching their grand plan, Leo had written an entire book concluding, no, any attempt to answer violence with violence, however justified, changes you for the worse. Because violence is viral; it spreads among all it touches like an emotional plague, making everyone's world more ugly and brutal.

He'd ended that book with more questions than answers. Somehow, the peacekeepers of the world had to neutralize the warmongers and haters, but without warring or hating. Find a way to break the cycle of violence without engaging in it.

He felt certain they had indeed found the way. Except for Dorothea, and maybe Brett, they all seemed to be managing without ill effects. And Dorothea, well, she could dismiss the cancer but Leo didn't. She'd been in pain and growing weaker for a full month before they started. If she hadn't gotten sick. . . .

He tuned back into the television. PBS had switched away from the pundits to reporters covering public reaction to the speech. A string of ordinary people on the street—in Boston, New York, DC, Miami, New Orleans, Houston, Chicago, St.Paul, Seattle, and San Diego—all smiled for the cameras, raised hands in peace signs and solidarity fists, and talked excitedly about Carver, Jubilee, and, as one man put it, "America's rebirth." Several prefaced their comments with, "I didn't vote for the man, but—" and went on to sing Carver's praises. A professed evangelical declared that "the rapture had arrived" and others made religious references to Jubilee. Some talked about joining the newly-forming Jubilee party, and everyone raved about the coming changes—freedom from debts, ending the wars, and Carver's additions to the manifesto: universal healthcare and education and a green revolution, starting with "solar panels on every rooftop."

Then they brought on a pollster who, with the caveat that these were instant numbers, declared public approval for Carver and the jubilees running at ninety-four percent. That got a big smile from Dorothea, so big and beaming that, for a moment, he saw her hale and healthy again. The take-no-guff, kick-in-the-butt, make-it-happen woman who had stormed the ramparts with him more than once. He looped his arm around her so-frail shoulders and hugged her tighter to him, fighting back tears. She always knew when he was getting weepy, and loved to needle him about it. Now she just leaned deeper into him and let the tears flow.

They turned off the TV and sat on the couch quietly breathing it in until it was time for circle. Or, what passed for circle during the shift. They'd long understood and accepted that couples had to sleep separately and at a distance for the dreaming to work, which was why Leo had maintained his own little cabin, just for sleeping, the past fifteen years. For security's sake, they'd decided to also stay apart daytimes for the duration, limiting communications to Skype and cyber-circle. Leo managed to endure three days, but his time with Dorothea was such a precious commodity, he couldn't miss any more. Would not. In the morning circle he'd made the case that, with Joss Morgan agreeing to warn them if they investigation got close, they could ease up on the security concerns. They'd quickly reached a new consensus—families were free to spend their days together, but still no group meetings except online.

At a few minutes before eight, Dorothea went and turned on her office computer. Leo remained on the couch with his laptop. Cyber-circle was about to begin.

Joe had introduced them to circle in '68 and they'd been meeting monthly, more or less, ever since. It began with just the six of them, grew to as many as eighteen in the '80s, and eventually settled at the current twelve, with three replacements along the way. Borrowing from Native American traditions, they would sit on the floor and pass a "talking stick" around the circle, each person talking in turn when they held the stick. Joe called it a practice of true democracy; all points on the circle are equal and everyone has an equal voice. They used it in the beginning, and still do, as a form of individual and group therapy. Over the years, it also became their tool for reaching consensus decisions on everything from when-to-meet-next to the development of the dream, the timing of the shift, and picking those they called sacrifices, or, sacs. The magic of the stick was that, if you had the time and patience to let it keep going round the circle, a best-for-all, consensus decision emerged. Joe felt so strongly that the US Supreme Court should use the process that he'd argued for adding it to the manifesto.

Cyber-circle worked pretty much the same. They log into cyber-circle.us, a password-protected and encrypted site that Brett set up. A little app lists their twelve screen names in random order for the day. The person at the top of the list posts first and then each person follows in turn. If you have nothing to say you just type "pass." When everyone's passing, the circle's complete. During the shift, they were trying to meet twice a day—mornings, to review the previous night's dreams and address any problems or concerns, and evenings, to assign sacs and work through issues. Brett was first today and his post arrived a minute past eight.

Brett: Was that the most amazing thing you ever heard? In four days we've totally turned the world around. And got

the president on our side and actually adding to the manifesto. Full power of the bully pulpit, on our side. Go Jubilee! And the best news—we can stop the dreams. We've won. No one else has to die.

SUSAN: I share your excitement, Brett, we all do. But it doesn't feel like it's over yet. We're just hearing from the people who agree with us. Those who don't are keeping quiet. And somewhere meeting quietly and planning a response.

EVA: Reluctantly, I'm with Susan. There's a backlash coming. No way does old Mr. Overclass just cede power and money. And no doubt they'll figure a way to get the red-state racists and gun lovers and Bible-bangers back in their camp, complaining about socialism and the Black House and big government yadda yadda.

ALI: pass

Leo paused for a moment to ponder Ali's pass. She was the last to join the circle, taking Don's place three years ago after his heart gave out. It was just the eleven of them for nearly a year, the whole project in limbo while they waited for Jane to either withdraw or find a new partner. The initial joy when she announced that she was in love gave way to niggling concerns that Ali was a woman—since the dreaming partners had always been male and female. Their concerns disappeared quickly as they got to know Ali. Strong dreamer, meshed well with Jane, and right there on the need for the shift. But after Brett and Dorothea, she seemed least comfortable with joining the ranks of serial killers. Leo would have liked to hear what she was thinking now.

LEO: I agree with much of your optimism Brett and am already thinking we might not need to do sixty. But we do need to stay focused for a few more days, another round or two of pruning (yes, I know I swore off gardening metaphors). Here's why: we're dealing with a three-headed military these days—the US armed forces, the militia movement, and the private

security firms. While their ranks are filled with underclass schleps, the guys at the top are rich and they're not giving up, not without a fight. And even the poor schleps, much as they might be attracted to our economic message, they're not all thrilled with ending war and winding down the empire. That's how they make their livings, and how some of them get their kicks. So, there's still some leaders and leaders-to-be who we'll need to sac. At best, we get some Jubilee-friendly leaders in place. Shy of that, we keep them too disorganized to mount a counter-attack.

JANE: i agree. and i don't think ali and i should be doing reverend michaelson tonight. we're really not getting any push-back from the religious crowd. nor the banksters. and how cool is it that kane is running treasury? and marsdale lipman is suddenly the good guys? and they're saying chun for the supreme court.

JOE: First, I want to go back and really appreciate what Brett said. Listening to Carver's speech is now one of the high points of my eighty-three years, right up there with wooing Eva and catching Jillie when she was born. For those of us who were there at the beginning, well, we don't have transcripts from those early circles, but Carver tonight? He was literally the vision come true. Only better. Still, Leo's right (he said, for the 10,000th time). The last refuge of power is physical force; I have no doubt that planning for a military takeover is underway. We need to get those leaders. Tonight if we can.

ROB: I agree. We need to carry this through to completion. And Susan and I also need a new target, I think. I heard a bit from Senator Prescott after the speech, and he might just be talking scared, but he was more or less acquiescing. How about two each from the military, the militias, and the private contractors?

DOROTHEA: I had the same take on Prescott, as well as many of the pundits and commentators. That they were just talking scared, afraid of being "jubileed," a term that Leo found hilarious. I think there's some of that in all of them, even folks like Carver and Kane still seem uneasy and are choosing their words carefully. Like they're not sure about us. Or they're not sure how the shift will shake out for them—will they lose all their money, will they retain any power or standing? For Leo's schleps, this is easier because they have nowhere to go but up. But some people are clearly about to lose a lot. I have to agree—they will fight back. Though I so wish it were over, we're not done yet. Personal note: I'm feeling a tad better today. Being with Leo for the afternoon was just what the witch doctor ordered.

MIA: I'll be over in the morning, Dee. Stay strong, everybody.

TOM: The only thing that bothered me in the speech was the lack of a timeline for the jubilee. The whole country went spree-shopping today, all on credit. Merchants are worried they'll never be compensated, and for good reason. We can't stay in this "Jubilee's coming" phase for too long without irrational behavior spinning out of control, on multiple fronts and with serious consequences. For this to work, Carver's got to deliver stability, stat. I would have liked to hear a date or some actual details of a plan.

JESSIE: All the more reason for us to maintain our role. Because, except maybe for Nathan Kane, no one in the government has any idea how to do this. But we do—sort of—because we've been thinking it through for so long. So we need to be telling them—in public messages and our communications with Morgan—how and when it's going down. While also nipping any resistance in the bud.

It took just one more time around the circle to reach consensus on staying the course—Brett conceding that "the gray heads know best"—and three more rounds to settle on tomorrow's sacs.

Dorothea rejoined Leo on the couch and they sat in silence until it was time for him to go. "See you in the dream, sweetie," he whispered, while they hugged good-bye.

"See you in the dream," she whispered back.

Chapter 34

"Not gonna happen," Ted Tiller muttered to himself as Big Nigger finished his speech. Dumb mutt thinks he can turn America into some kind of commie paradise, stealing from the rich to give to the lame and the lazy and the coloreds and the freaks. Wants to dismantle the greatest empire in human history because some assholes killed a few men. America, surrendering after a four day skirmish with twenty-four casualties. Fucking unreal.

An extremely wealthy man, Tiller was not some pompous ass squandering daddy's fortune, nor a prissy blue-blood, afraid of breaking things. He grew up on tough Brooklyn streets, left home at fifteen, barely literate, and without a dollar to his name. Enlisted in the Army at eighteen and did two tours in Vietnam, in country, hard time the whole way. Killing gooks, watching buddies die, doing whatever it took to stay sane. Came out of it with his own form of PTSD—he called it "post traumatic smack down"—best way to deal with trauma is to make sure you're inflicting more than you're getting.

Near the end of his second tour he fell in with a gun-running racket. A couple of procurement sergeants were redirecting a tiny stream out of the rivers of weapons that were flowing through southeast Asia. Tiller's job was to make contact with the buyers and handle the transfers. Dangerous work, but turned out he had a knack for it. After discharge, he ended up staying in Nam through the fall of Saigon. Eventually landed back in the city, thirty-three years old, working on his second million, an established name in the world of international arms dealing. For the next thirty years he plied his trade—much of it legal—piling millions into billions as the number one supplier to the world's varied wars, large and small. Mr. War, Killer Tiller, Tiller the Hun—he'd been called lots of names and they all pointed to one in-your-face fact: he was the strongest, the smartest, and the richest.

From time to time he'd hook up with a woman who'd get to know him well enough to question how he felt about "enabling so much grief and sorrow in the world." Did it bother him that he was "fueling the slaughter of innocents and the pillage of nations?" as one stupid twat put it. Not that he gave a shit, but blaming him for war was like blaming an umbrella salesman for rain. There'd always be someone getting rich on war and it may as well be him. These days he limited himself to bimbo fucks and dumped them the moment they showed signs of independent thinking. Which meant that he mostly lived alone, free of the distractions of nattering females and needy children. Christ, just the thought of children was enough to make him puke.

He had to admit this Jubilee shit had him scared. Mallard and Eisley were both friends, to the extent that Tiller had any. More important, they were close allies in the business of war. Since Carver's election, the three of them were key figures in a small but capable group of wealthy patriots dedicated to taking the country back. Yes, an actual right-wing fucking conspiracy. Called themselves the Freedom Brigade. Plan A was to stifle Carver's agenda, throw continuous dirt at him and vulnerable members of his administration, and poison public opinion so that he and his party would lose big in the mid-terms—mission accomplished—and then be destroyed in 2012. But they'd also mapped out a military response, led by the militias with covert support from the private security firms. General Eisley was critical to that because he'd have to keep the Army and Guard from interfering until the moment was ripe to sweep in and save the day, with new leadership installed. Still, much as they'd all profit from a shooting revolution, the political path was the surest and they were well on their way to success before the Jubilees showed up.

That first morning, after reading the goddamn message and knowing who they had killed, Tiller felt like some satellite sniper was floating overhead, waiting for him to fall asleep. He was sure he'd be next. Went right on counter-attack, starting with intel. But his contacts within the investigation all confirmed they had nothing but six clean crime scenes, no clues, no evidence, no fucking idea who was doing it or how. Except some were already thinking it must be some kind of mind control.

Tiller had spent forty years around bullets and bombs and men who could kill you in two seconds with their bare hands. He'd survived so long and so well that he'd come to fear nothing. But this—what? Mind murder? Invisible assassins seeping through cracks in the wall to kill you while you sleep? He swore he could feel them sighting on him. Fucking ghost snipers.

He did manage to sleep some that first night and the second day's dead list was not so threatening. Bunch of bankers—Tiller had nothing but contempt for the lot of them—and the very wealthy Dennis Hastings, universally despised since the Gulf spill. If this was just about taking down the rich, Tiller still had cause to worry, being a conservative billionaire. But less so since he wasn't associated with any particular corporations and had zero public profile. He'd never been interviewed, had no wiki pages telling all about him, nor a media trail of opinions and utterances and YouTube moments. Even took steps to make sure he didn't show up in Google.

The second night he slept better, but woke to a more worrisome casualty list. Tinsley, Franke, Bagwell, Dempsey, Gross—they'd been the public voice of the anti-Carver movement and they'd been instrumental in whipping up the base and spreading intel. All big losses, but even bigger was the man they worked for. Thomas Harrow was principal funder and controller of the right-wing media machine. With the five of them gone, the Brigade's media presence and communication abilities were severely degraded. Call it a minor massacre, followed by a day of futile investigations and another night of restless sleep.

Then came this morning's news. It was like waking up to incoming mortar fire. Malcolm Carney, Cyrus Bird, Lance Withers, and Douglas McDonnell, along with Harrow and Eisley, were the top tier of the Brigade. Carney was Eisley's replacement, the highest ranking member of the group, tasked with managing US forces if this became a shooting war. He'd intentionally drawn Jubilee fire with his "fuck Jubilee" speech, he'd been so sure they couldn't touch him; his death made it clear how defenseless they really were.

McDonnell ran Altamen, the largest weapons manufacturer on the planet, everything from .22 ammunition to stealth bombers. Most of his work was already done—there were weapons caches strategically placed around the country, disguised as Altamen inventory. He and Tiller had been silent partners and quasi-friends since the early '70s; it pissed him off that Doug was gone, but his business was tight enough that it ought to keep going with whoever takes his place.

The loss of Cyrus and Lance hurt the most. Kontrain and Taylor Dann were the largest and most influential private security firms in America, so big that they had more of their men in Iraq and Afghanistan than American servicemen. Damn good business too, since private contractors were getting many times the pay grade of uniformed grunts, without official oversight, and all on the government checkbook. Tiller had provided startup capital for both companies and remained a major investor. It was a perfect setup—Cyrus and Lance both had lived large, enjoyed the spotlight, and liked owning the best and the latest, all shit Tiller couldn't be bothered with. They even got a kick out of rare appearances before congressional committees. Neither minded that their silent partner was actually calling the shots; they were a team, they had the same goals, and all were more than satisfied with their roles and duties. They were good men who would be missed.

But Tiller was still alive. Which could only mean that the Jubilees don't know about him, which means—the first real clue—it's not the government. Because the world's largest arms provider had done mega-tons of business with the world's largest arms dealer. Tiller was well known in the halls of the Pentagon, the corridors of Congress, and at the CIA, FBI, and the rest. If the Jubilees were at all connected, they would have nailed him on the first day. So that was something.

And it fit the profile from Homeland. They're saying it's a small group, fringe dwellers, off grid, disconnected from the mainstream and been out there for a long time. Probably male and female. Older, at least fifty but as old as seventy-five. Tiller couldn't help but notice that he fit the profile pretty well, except for the participation of women. That got him thinking more about why they'd missed him—had to be his lack of public profile—which meant, he figured, they must be selecting targets and gathering intel straight from the media. Everyone they'd done so far was easily discovered and researched—photos, videos, speeches all a few keystrokes away. As he assembled a new team he'd have to pick men who were harder to stalk.

He'd spent the morning trying to establish new contacts at Kontrain, Taylor Dann, and Altamen, but it was too soon at all three. In each case, the legal number two was stalling—basically in hiding—unwilling to become the new target, much less affirm the policies that got the last guy killed. One thing in their favor was that, unlike the banks, the security industry was in no immediate danger of crashing—one of the benefits of dealing in real goods and services rather than the bubble wealth and derivative crap of the financial so-called industry. Also helped that they were privately held companies with unlimited cash, and didn't have to worry about skittish investors pulling out.

Still, having all the time in the world wouldn't matter if he got snuffed tonight. Tiller needed to figure it out and stop these killings. But even though the Jubilees didn't know who he was, they'd done a good job of isolating him, removing all of his top tier. In retrospect, he should have prepared for something like this. As it was, he had a serious leadership crisis at a mission critical time. The question now was, should he work on pulling a new leadership group together? Or just start getting it done? He was mulling his options when the Jubilees' latest message arrived. Then a few hours later, Big Nigger's speech.

The news folk were devoting all their attention to the end of debt and the new tax structure, neither of which mattered that much to Tiller. But cutting the Pentagon budget in half and redirecting it to the welfare state? Ending the wars and dismantling the empire? Putting Tiller the arms dealer out to pasture? Or into some war crimes prison?

Not gonna happen.

Chapter 35

What a day. Joss spent the morning doing a series of TV interviews. At noon, the jubilees released their manifesto and the nation went on a berserker buying binge (and Joss without a spare moment to shop). Then she had a private meeting with the president, followed by more meetings with Mendelsohn and Muriel Matson. Late afternoon, she did a second press conference so frustratingly futile—no clues, no suspects, no nothing—the joke in the press pool was that for future pressers they should just run repeats of the first.

It all left her feeling tired and deflated, wanting to go home and get fetal under the covers. But Mendelsohn insisted that they go someplace for a quiet dinner "to do some serious unwinding." She was surprised at how tantalizing it sounded and that she felt the warm tingle. They went to Portobello's, a tiny ristorante with red-and-white checkered tablecloths, wine-bottle candleholders, and Italian-accented waiters. It was their third dinner in three days and a big step up in ambiance—was this a date? Hard not to feel a little awkward, so Joss was relieved when Mendelsohn did not hold the door for her. To the contrary, after they were seated and settled in, he opened his menu without so much as a glance in her direction, oblivious to the moment. Which reminded Joss that it was just this morning he was mooning over Sally Tiger.

She resolved to stick to business.

They only had an hour for dinner anyway. Carver had called for a meeting with Joss, Mendelsohn, and Trenton to discuss the secret communications with Jubilee. Earlier today, when she told him about the contact, the president's mood had visibly lifted, especially at the news that—worse case—this would all be over in another five or six days, with no more than sixty deaths. But he also expressed fear at the thought of these communications becoming public knowledge.

"If it ever gets out," he said, "it won't matter how it unfolded or what was said or how well things turned out, assuming they even do. It won't take Oliver Stone to make it look like I was a part of Jubilee from the beginning, like it was all my idea, picking off my political enemies. And that'll do more than just make my life miserable, it would jeopardize whatever positives might come out of all this. So. No one else can ever know, and I'd like the four of us to meet ASAP, tonight if possible. In fact, let's meet a little before the time they connected last night; I'd love to say hello."

So that was the plan, 8:30 at the White House to have a clandestine chat with Jubilee.

After the waiter filled their water glasses and took their orders, Mendelsohn held up his water glass for a toast. "To a grand old empire in its waning days."

They clinked glasses, then Joss added, "Let it be a peaceful transition," to which Mendelsohn nodded affirmatively.

Then he asked, "So what's your take on Muriel and her dreams, now that you're showing up in a leading role?"

"Well, I'm sure it's no surprise that I've been skeptical from the start; it's pretty much my default position in life. At USC I was trained to treat dreams as secondary phenomena, something the mind emitted that, with analysis, could inform you about the mind in question. But that's all they did. They weren't supposed to affect the dreamer's body, much less the external world and other people. As someone put it, or maybe I dreamed it, 'what happens in the mind, stays in the mind.' But now, after what we've seen, I'm thinking more like that army shrink from Day Two, Wiggenstern, the LSD guy—I just can't ignore the evidence. Or in our case, the lack thereof. Given Muriel's experiences, death by dreaming is the most reasonable explanation we have."

She paused and then they were looking into each other's eyes, several seconds past polite. She found it simultaneously calming and exciting. "I haven't forgotten that you were thinking dreams from the beginning, when you asked Beth Griffin if she remembered hers."

"That's true," he said, "I did, but it was just an impulse question. I mean, I'm not a lucid dreamer and never in my life imagined dream killers. But I guess my default position is more an open curiosity. That's what it was with the psychic hotline lady; I didn't necessarily believe her story, but she piqued my curiosity, got me thinking, and before I knew it I was looking at proof that telepathy, or distance viewing, or whatever-the-hell is possible."

"As long as you don't start believing too easily."

"No, not to worry, still have the skeptical edge. But I don't let it limit my vision. You know, I've always thought children had it right—believe in and be curious about absolutely everything and then test, test, test. So you don't close any possibilities out."

"Trust, but verify."

He smiled and said, "Even Ronnie got it right sometimes."

That led to a discussion about the current president and how much he was getting right, or not. They both gave Carver high marks for his handling of the crisis, though Mendelsohn still worried over what looked like a clear decision to join the Jubilees. He agreed that it would ruin Carver's presidency if it ever got out. He thought it would also put an end to his and Joss's and Trenton's careers in law enforcement.

"They always say the cover-up's worse than the crime. Transparency in government really matters. If what we're doing must be kept secret then, frankly, there must be something wrong with it."

On that unsettling note, it was time to pay the check and get going.

Half an hour later they were seated around a low circular table, Joss with Mendelsohn to her right, Trenton to her left and the president facing her across the table. It had been a long day for everyone so Carver got right to it.

"I've already shared this with Joss, but it bears repeating: I am counting on the three of you to keep this secret forever. Even if we project a year or two in the future, say the jubilee is a success, the gap between rich and poor has been reduced, America's back to work, the wars are over and peace reigns, even then, if it were to become known that we were in communication with Jubilee while the killings were happening, I believe it could ruin everything, not just for me or you but for the whole country. However, should circumstances warrant it, then I promise I will make it all public. It could very well turn out that in Jubilee Nation politics will cease to be blood sport and people will be able to listen to and accept our actions, might even celebrate us. But we're not there yet and may never be, so I need vows of silence from each of you." Then he waited until Trenton said, "You have it, Mr. President" and Joss said, "Yes sir." Mendelsohn was nodding yes but then said, "Does the White House now automatically tape all your conversations?"

The president smiled. "No, I can turn it off when I want to and this room is always off so I don't have to think about it. There will be no tapes or notes from any conversations I have on this subject."

"Seems prudent, Mr. President . . . and, uh, I'm with you, though, and maybe this makes your point, I still have reservations about going down this path. It just seems we're partnering with killers and implementing their agenda under threat of death. We're not just negotiating with terrorists, we're doing their bidding. Fetter's cartoon today has you as an Aztec priest sacrificing Howie Croft on the altar of income redistribution, ripping out his heart to appease the Jubilees—"

"Yes, I saw that, just one in a long line of such ugly cartoons, going back way before Jubilee. At least he didn't put the bone through my nose in this one. But if you're warning me that things are going to get rough, my friend, that's how it's been from the day I was nominated. Hell, that's how it's been my whole life. There's about twenty percent of this country that hates me because of my father's skin and there's nothing anyone can do about that. Though, I have to say, we've even got some of them on our side right now—the polls are running at above ninety percent approval for me and Jubilee. Now that kind of approval can be fleeting, I know. Bush was also in the nineties after the Gulf War and managed to lose reelection. Things can turn in a hurry, especially if we make a serious misstep. So that's why we're having this meeting. Right now, the American public, the whole world, wants Jubilee to happen, wants to end the wars. It's a hell of an opportunity and it's up to me not to fumble it."

"Which means not muddying the waters with revelations about these contacts with Jubilee," said Mendelsohn.

"Exactly. It will be hard enough getting this done even with the high approval."

"Mr. President," said Trenton, "as far as the communications go—if they contact Joss tonight, what do you need to happen?"

"Good question, Henry, one I've been thinking about since you brought it up this morning." He looked to Mendelsohn, then Joss. "High approval numbers aside, the ten percent who don't approve are not only extremely rich, they control a large segment of the US military, the militia movement, and the private security firms. We're proposing changes that will cost these men billions. Hundreds of billions and unbridled power, all seriously diminished if Jubilee goes forward. Now, they've been waging a no-holds-barred campaign against me from the day I announced my candidacy and its just gotten more sophisticated and better financed as my presidency has progressed. They bankrolled the Tea Party in the beginning and they've been major funders of every one of these Tea Party candidates that have come out of nowhere to win seats. But they've also gone way beyond politics.

"We've been aware for sometime of a coordinated movement involving uniformed officers in each of the armed forces and CEOs of large defense and private security firms. They've been pumping money into the militias and stockpiling weapons around the country. Our analysts say they're preparing for a coup, an actual military coup, like some banana republic, if I manage to win next year. Well, Jubilee must be onto them also, because they killed several of the leaders today."

This surprised Trenton. "Sir, you're saying General Carney was plotting a coup? And Lance Withers? Cyrus Bird?"

"And General Eisley," said Carver.

"Damn," said Trenton, "I knew he was a hawk—" but that's as far as he got when Joss held up a finger. Jubilee calling.

Joss shared her screen with the others—they'd brought a Book for the president—so they could read along and even add messages, though they'd decided to keep the inputs to Joss and perhaps Carver.

JUBILEE: Hello, Dr. Morgan.

JOSS: Good evening. You should know that also present are President Carver, Henry Trenton, head of the Homeland Security investigation, and Alex Mendelsohn, my partner these past few days.

JUBILEE: I'm glad you're not carrying this alone. And that President Carver is with you. Mr. President, your speech tonight was extraordinary, truly inspirational. Had my wife and me in tears.

JOSS: Now that we know you're a married man, how about a first name?

JUBILEE: Let's stick with Jubilee.

JOSS: Sure no problem.

"Joss," said the president, "why don't I take over?"

"Good idea."

PC: Joss tells me you're worried about being caught because this weapon of yours is too dangerous for the world to find out about. I know this was asked and answered but—how could you take such a risk?

JUBILEE: Mr. President, I could ask the same question: you're taking huge, nation-sized risks now. Why? Because you had no other options, no good choices. And I don't just mean the conundrum that we saddled you with—jubilee or die—I'm talking about the state of the world. Global warming. Peak oil. War without end. Economies collapsing from debt. The planet is seriously ill, crashing on multiple fronts, and no one knows better than you the paucity of viable solutions. Five days ago you were out of options and, frankly, helpless—the political dynamics in this country being such that intelligent debate is impossible, likewise attempts to alter the status quo or redistribute power and wealth. Mr. President, we pondered what to do for a long time and arrived at the same conclusion—the risk of letting the world fall to pieces was worse than the risk of using our weapon.

PC: How did you know I would go along?

JUBILEE: We didn't. But we were fairly certain Vice-President Riles would.

Ouch. Just when Joss was starting to like Mr. Jubilee. She glanced at Carver, who was nodding his head slowly, both eyebrows raised, almost smiling.

PC: Why is Bragg still alive?

JUBILEE: This is not about punishment, retribution, or hate for us. Since leaving office, Bragg has returned to being a pampered prince of no consequence. We pledged from the beginning to do this with as few deaths as possible and to only sacrifice those who would further what we think of as 'the shift.' Instead of collateral damage, think collateral advantage—we are targeting the men whose deaths will produce the greatest good.

PC: And you feel comfortable making those decisions?

JUBILEE: No, not at all comfortable. More like burdened. I suspect you know the feeling.

The president sighed and closed his eyes for several moments.

PC: Inheriting Bragg's wars has been the worst part of this job, worse even than inheriting his economy. Making decisions that you know will result in lost lives. . . .

JUBILEE: And yet you escalated Afghanistan.

PC: Once the war machine gets going there's no stopping it. The only peace it allows is killing a little slower, maybe spending a little less. I call it "the beast." And I admit it's been controlling my actions since I got here. It's controlled every president since Eisenhower, who understood the threat and tried to warn us. But you've changed the dynamic. Still not sure about jubilee, but I see a real possibility of ending our military empire, of taming the beast. You know, I wrote about decapitation as a military tactic. Concluded that it belongs to an earlier time, when the world and its governing systems were smaller, less complex. But you've certainly made it work.

JUBILEE: In a dominator system, the governing logic is perpetuation of the status quo. The overclass use their power to keep themselves in power. The rich use their money to make even more. The strong get stronger by eating the weak. Nothing ever changes because you can't expect those in power to enact laws or create policies that would diminish their power or wealth. In fact, they do the opposite, so power and wealth is always concentrating. The out-of-power typically try to tear down the system, thinking to replace it with something better. Most of the time they just fail. But even when they've overthrown the government and jailed or killed the leaders—

decapitation—the system simply reconstitutes and the rebels become the new dominators. The new wealthy rule the poor, the new strong the weak, and nothing ever changes. If all we were doing was decapitating leaders, we'd be doomed to repeating that scenario. But we're doing more, namely, we're changing the thinking of the overclass. In the end, things can only change if they—you, Mr. President—are heart and soul committed to it. The rich and powerful must willingly make the decisions and initiate the policies that reduce their power and wealth.

PC: How can you say you're not using force? I've certainly felt coerced. And the release of your manifesto, do this or die, undercuts the notion that I'm 'willingly' making decisions and policies.

JUBILEE: Yes but, and correct me if I'm wrong, most of what we're demanding feels right to you. Maybe some of it you dreamed about when you were younger. Or hoped to implement when you took office. That's certainly what we heard in your speech, that you were making the manifesto your own.

PC: All true, but it was still forced. Do this or die. And twenty-four victims to make it clear.

JUBILEE: Such was our concession to reality—some sacrifices were necessary. However, we diverge from the usual scenario in two important ways. First, however forced you may have felt, it was more of a nudge, a firm push in new directions. Once you started shifting, we stopped pushing. Look at what happened at Marsdale Lipman today. That speech Ryan Weathers gave, his whole decision to step forward after the deaths of his predecessors—there was nothing coerced about him, not today. He needed a strong nudge and an altered environment, but everything he said was totally his own.

PC: You said there were two ways.

JUBILEE: The other is that we, the ones doing the killing, are not taking over or making any gains from this. We're not after personal fame, power, or wealth. A week or so from now we're finished, never to be heard from again. So the mantle of leadership will pass to those who did not kill or destroy or crush their enemies to get it.

PC: OK. I understand. But we may have a problem keeping me uninvolved in your actions. Are you aware of the plot to overthrow the government via military coup?

JUBILEE: We suspected as much, but have no knowledge of it.

PC: It's been gestating since the election, reaching into some very high places. Your suspicions were on the mark 'cause you managed to kill eight of the top leaders. That's the good news. Bad news is that we fear you've spurred them to act. You've done major damage and are closing their window of opportunity, giving them no option—other than changing their thinking—than to act quickly. They're not changing their thinking. We believe an attempted coup is imminent.

There was a long pause, nearly a minute, before Jubilee responded.

JUBILEE: And you want to select the next sacrifices?

PC: Just one. The leader of the coup, a billionaire named Ted Tiller.

Day Five

Thursday, November 10, 2011

Four hundred obscenely rich people, most of whom benefited in some way from the multi-trillion dollar taxpayer "bailout" of 2008, now have more loot, stock and property than the assets of 155 million Americans combined. If you can't bring yourself to call that a financial coup d'état, then you are simply not being honest about what you know in your heart to be true.

And I can see why. For us to admit that we have let a small group of men abscond with and hoard the bulk of the wealth that runs our economy, would mean that we'd have to accept the humiliating acknowledgment that we have indeed surrendered our precious Democracy to the moneyed elite.

—Michael Moore

Chapter 36

Muriel awoke with a jolt. She was damp with sweat and shivering, her heart racing. She turned to look at the time—a few minutes past four. She reached for her notebook and penlight and started writing.

Same dream, same room, man in chair facing window, I'm behind, woman on my left, man on my right, light outside window, getting hotter in room, fire outside coming closer, then the man turns, looks right at me, older gray hair, angry vicious teeth bared, bright red eyes, then he looks left at woman and he screams, ROARS, like wild animal beast, and the woman. . . .

What?

Muriel put her pen and notebook aside and tried to get back into the dream. She managed to calm her breathing and slow her heartbeat, but with her nightgown clinging with cold sweat, she couldn't get comfortable. Moreover, she realized, she was terrified. Of whatever he did to the woman, of what he might have done to her.

She got out of bed and took the longest hot shower of her life.

Chapter 37

Leo was awake and in the car speeding home to Dorothea within minutes of the Tiller disaster. He was nearly blind with grief, barely conscious of his driving, lucky that the streets were empty at the early hour and it was an oft-travelled route. When Tiller faced them, when he *attacked* her, she simply dropped out of the dream. He'd reached for her, searched the dreamtime, but she was gone.

He should never have agreed to Carver's request. Should have waited one more night for Tiller, followed the protocols. *Bad move, Leo, stupid old fool.*

Not that he'd decided alone. They'd circled last night after his conversation with Carver and it only took one round to reach consensus. No passes, no stand asides. Dorothea had clearly had reservations but . . . it was hard to know what was the cancer talking and what was her. In the end, she'd said yes.

But they'd only had three hours to get to know Tiller and all they were able to come up with was a half dozen photos and three press clippings that contained nothing helpful. No audio, no video, no publications, no interviews, no biography, no magazine puff pieces about the reclusive billionaire, filled with the little personal tidbits that were needed to run the dream. Didn't have a family. Military in the sixties, Vietnam, and apparently came out of it an arms dealer. Went on to make billions, but without ever creating a public persona.

Without a full feel for the man, he and Dorothea had struggled to bring him into the dream. Should have just stopped, gathered more info, come back the next night. Now—he wouldn't let himself think it.

He pulled into their driveway, came to a skidding stop, and ran into the house. She was still in bed, breathing, but unconscious. He gently tried to rouse her, to no avail. Her skin was cold and clammy. He straightened her body, put a pillow beneath her knees, then filled a basin with warm water and gave her a sponge bath. The whole time he talked to her as if she was present, nice and normal, just Dorothea and Leo having a chat. He tried to keep his voice confident, his attitude optimistic, but he couldn't control his thoughts. *Forty-three years since they'd met, so much life together, and then it just ends? No final words, no good-bye hugs?* All he wanted was for her eyes to open, to see her, to be seen by her, *one more time, please.*

After the bath, he crawled into bed and curled up to her. For a long time he just breathed with her, inhaling her essence, exhaling his love, like a shroud protecting, enveloping her body. *Please.*

Around eight he got out of bed and went to the computer. It was too soon to notify the others—they'd all been needing to sleep past nine after the dream. But he sent Mia an email telling her and Brett to come as soon as they could. And he skyped Joss Morgan, letting her know they had failed to stop Tiller and would need better intel if they were to try again.

Big if. Tiller had decapitated *them*. Now it was Jubilee that might not be able to go forward.

The online news was all about the five new sacs, with much speculation about the missing sixth. Everyone was calling it Billionaires Day. The biggest buzz, as Leo'd expected, was about the Lutz brothers. A recent Times Online piece painted the Texas oilmen as the money behind some of the worst rightwing excesses of the past twenty years. Most of the dirt thrown at Clinton, Gore, Kerry, and Carver originated in Lutz publications. As well as corporate greenwashing. Global warming skepticism. The Defense of Marriage Act. The Tea Party. Conservative campaigns against Muslims, immigrants, the estate tax. You name it and Rufus and Dirk Lutz were in the shadows writing checks.

The other three—Donald Best, John Botman, and Charles Critlin—were equally rich and similarly involved in using their vast wealth to get even richer, with no regard for the health of social, economic, or ecological systems. No one, not even Fox News (still reeling from the death of Thomas Harrow), was mourning these men. For all their billions, for all their businesses, big and small, it was hard to point to anything of real social value—anything that made a positive difference in the lives of ordinary folk—that any of these men had produced. They were parasites of the worst kind, sucking the commonwealth into their personal coffers.

Leo wondered how Richard Brooks was feeling this morning. The decision to go after Tiller had given him a reprieve. Maybe he'll have a come-to-Jubilee moment, give away billions, start a Billionaires for All movement.

Or maybe we've been mortally wounded and all of this is coming to naught.

He received a reply from Morgan and was about to answer when he heard the downstairs door open. He rose to greet Mia, racing up the stairs. As they hugged, Leo nodded to Brett, who had the watery eyes of heavy grief.

"Neither of us could sleep," said Mia, unsurprisingly clear-eyed. She preferred to grieve in private and at a distance. "How is she? What happened?"

Leo explained as best he could, then they stepped quietly into the bedroom. Dorothea looked paler, less . . . there.

Mia kneeled at the bedside, took her mother's hand and pressed it to her forehead. Leo and Brett stood at the foot of the bed, each in their own way willing a miracle. Which, after a few minutes, they received: Dorothea's eyes fluttered open. She slowly looked from Mia, to Leo, then Brett, and back to Leo.

Then she closed her eyes and spoke. "I'm sorry, Leo. I just wasn't strong enough, wasn't clear enough. When he came at me,

I felt so angry, and then so hateful, hateful; I hated him, Leo. And then, I don't know, my body couldn't do it, it just couldn't."

Leo moved to the other side of the bed, sat beside her, held her hand, leaned forward to kiss her forehead. Her eyes opened again and they shared a look that went on and on.

Chapter 38

Joss hardly slept. She was vexed by a cluster of endlessly repeating questions and scenarios that wouldn't let go. The two times she managed to briefly drift off, she awoke with a start, trembling, as from a terrible dream. The second time happened a little past four. Which got her thinking about Muriel Matson and that maybe she'd been in her dream again, maybe been "present" for a murder. After a while, she gave up trying to sleep, got out of bed, and did her morning routine.

So she was already at her computer when Muriel emailed her with details of her latest dream. After making clear that dream interpretation is inexact, Muriel wrote: **I think whoever they tried to kill tonight fought back. I think he survived and maybe even injured the woman. It was for me the most frightening dream I've ever had, including Andy's death.** Joss sighed. Though she couldn't remember her dream, reading Muriel's description felt right. Joss somehow had been there for some part of it, enough that, like Muriel, she'd been frightened by what she witnessed.

Finally, she had to agree: it is possible to dream your way into another's head and trigger an aneurysm. Jubilee was right. This must never become common knowledge.

Joss got to Homeland a little past seven and was at her desk, running through updates to the Book from the many lines of investigation. It was short work. Forensics on yesterday's deaths turned up the same lack of evidence as all the others. Likewise, attempts to find or even imagine a physical weapon was going nowhere. FBI was shifting its focus—all of their investigators were now tasked to finding Jubilee, not through crime-scene forensics but by identifying individuals who might have the capacity for lethal mind control. Which worried Joss. As long as Homeland was the only one looking in that direction, she'd know if Jubilee was in danger of being caught. At the very least, if FBI were to interview Muriel, the idea of "death by dreaming" would attract much wider attention.

Joss was also facing a professional conflict. She'd found several strong tells in Jubilee's text messages. Besides the fact that he gave away that he was a married man, Joss felt confident that he was a writer, or had been once, and that he'd have a paper trail, back in the sixties or seventies. If she ran searches on a few key terms—jubilee, dominator, overclass, underclass, collateral advantage—she thought she'd come up with a short list of possibles.

But not only would she not be entering any of these findings into the Book, or informing the fibbies, she wasn't sure if she should even proceed. Do we want to know who they are? How does that help? Wouldn't it just increase the likelihood of their secret getting out? She decided to wait and talk it through with Alex.

Alex arrived past eight, late for him, but indicative, she thought, of how little there was for them to do. The usual avenues of investigation were all dead ends and they weren't able to pursue the few leads they had. Good thing that Trenton was part of their know-nothing conspiracy. And that nobody else was doing any better.

He walked in, handed her a double shot, skim latte, said good morning, and asked, "Whadda we know?" But before she could answer her computer beeped—the arrival of a Skype message. From Jubilee. She read it aloud.

"Joss, I do not have time to talk now but you need to know: we failed with T. And sustained a serious casualty. Can't say for sure what we're doing next but if we go after T again, we need to know him better. Video's best, or audio. Handwriting samples. Artwork or music or anything he's personally created. Anything you can dig up. I'll reconnect early evening. Jubilee"

"Damn," said Alex, after a long silence, "the one thing we hadn't figured on was them failing. Somebody out dream-zapping them."

Joss just nodded. She brought up Muriel's message, read it to Alex, and said, "I think I was there again, or at least observing. I woke up just after four and though I couldn't remember it, I'd definitely had a very bad dream. And Muriel's description confirmed it—some part of me was there."

"Ghost witness. Let's put together a ghost lineup and see if you recognize the perp."

She smiled. They sat quietly, sipping their coffees, pondering next steps. Then they went and brought Trenton up to speed.

"It fuckin' figures," he said. "Tiller is one tough customer. We were onto him in Nam, part of an illegal arms trade, but never lined up the evidence. He thrived over there, war and post-war. Survivor. Cutthroat. Smart. He was the wrong man to go after half-cocked. We have to hope Jubilee will keep going, though perhaps reduced to five a night." He paused for a few moments. "You know, if you accept Mrs. Matson as an actual witness—I'm thinking Jubilee is twelve people, six teams of two, man and woman, maybe husband and wife." He looked at Joss, then Mendelsohn, and raised questioning eyebrows.

"Works for me," said Alex.

Joss nodded yes, and added, "Mr. Jubilee mentioned he was married. Could be his wife who was hurt."

"So, they need our help more than ever. Alex, go to work on Tiller. Get whatever there is on the man. Find something they can use. The feds have been watching him, might have surveillance recordings. And Joss, I want you to go visit with Matson. Don't have her come here anymore and no reports of this visit. Sooner or later we'll all be on the receiving end of investigations—Muriel Matson was a bereaved widow who said she had a bad dream the night her husband died. Period.

"And Joss, the president wants you at the White House, 2 p.m., for a 'Jubilee cabinet' meeting."

Chapter 39

In the aftermath of General Carney's death, the word was that the killers had to be using some sort of mind control. Major David Booth had been right there, witnessed the whole thing, and Ted Tiller knew the major, now his second-in-command, to be a no-nonsense straight-shooter all the way. Though he'd listened to and more or less accepted the major's account, truth was Tiller had thought it was all bullshit. These Jubilee assholes were clever, but they weren't ghosts. Or psychic demons or witches or whatever the fuck. No, sure as shit they had a weapon, a most amazing fucking weapon, and Tiller'd figured he had to track them down and get his hands on the weapon before they turned it on him.

All that was before last night. Tiller never remembered his dreams—more female bullshit—but Christ, he remembered this one. They'd come at him while he was sleeping. He wasn't sure how many, couldn't actually see them, just knew they were there. Wherever "there" was. And they were doing it, trying to kill him, when he turned on them. Counter-attacked. And then he woke up.

Still, he was prepared to write it all off as a bad dream brought on by the stress of the past five days. Even after he noted the time, just after four, which had been established as the killing hour. He got out of bed, did a two-hour workout, showered, had breakfast, and then went online to see who had died.

By eight they had the five men who, along with Tiller and Harrow, had collectively financed the conservative movement for the past thirty years. Everything from gun rights to tax policy to the modern militias and the Tea Party. Good men, every one, and the fucking sheeple were celebrating it, calling it Billionaire's Day, like they were living in Russia or Cuba for chrissake.

But they only had five, which nailed it for Tiller: he was supposed to be number six. Moreover, the enemy had indeed gotten into his mind. Invisible ninjas. Not bullshit after all, and Tiller knew he better neutralize them before tonight or they'd be back again, wiser for their failure and gunning for him.

He ruled out trying to find them. Not enough time and the feds with all their resources were clueless, literally.

No, they needed to be stopped. Time to counter-attack.

Chapter 40

Sometimes life turns on a dime, don't it. Twenty-four hours ago, Boyd Hardin was fired up and ready for action, but down came the word: at ease and stow your gear. If you got any credit, go out and spend it. Which he did, eventually, but he'd spent all yesterday driving back to Texas, so it was slim pickin's today. The mall was fucking insane, most everything already carted away. Shit, just getting there and back he passed two gas stations that were closed, drained empty by Mastercard and Visa, and the rest all had long lines. Same everywhere he looked—stores were either closed up or mobbed. And this wasn't the richest county in East Texas. If you could believe the TV, the big cities were a lot crazier. He ended up maxing out his cards online. Way things were going it'd be a miracle if any of the shit ever showed up.

But the Jubilee fucks musta hit a nerve with these dead billionaires, musta pissed off some rich fucker with a lotta pull. And just like that Boyd was swinging into action.

The plan was simple. Kill a bunch of innocent people, more than Jubilee has killed so far. Then send out a text, multiple channels—Message to the Jubilees—include proof that we're behind the attack and then make clear that for every man Jubilee kills in the future, we kill dozens, even hundreds, of civilians. See how they do with that much blood on their hands. And how long the public keeps thinking of them as heros.

Boyd had his orders. Steal a car. Fill it with C4, nails, ball bearings. Wire it for remote detonation. Drop it on a busy Dallas street corner, get a safe distance away, and pull the trigger.

See, right there's something great about America. None of that suicide shit, blowing y'self up with the bomb. What's the point of that anyway? Got the guts to do the deed but can't live with it afterward? War ain't for pussies. You ain't OK with killing people, don't put on the uniform.

Killing civilians? Women and children? Din't bother Boyd nohow. Well, maybe a touch. But he'd suck it up and carry out the mission, what soldiers do. This was Jubilee's fault anyway. They started the killing and so fucking smart this was the only way to get at 'em, the fucks.

Five minutes after the explosion, Boyd had been picked up by Bobby and they were cruising, speed limit in a legal vehicle, back to Shiloh. Along the way, he texted the details—the make of the bomb-car and name on the registration. Someone on the other end would handle sending the message to the American people. For now, he was done, ordered to lay low. Six other soldiers would handle tomorrow's bombings.

Chapter 41

Joss had decided that to really keep her times with Muriel looking unofficial, they should stay away from the Matson house also. So they met at a Starbucks, found a reasonably private table, and sipped a latte and a chai while discussing the dream. If the investigations that Trenton feared ever zeroed in on this meeting, they were just two women who struck up a friendship when they first met, getting together to chat on Joss's lunch break.

But there was no time for chatting. The moment they were seated Joss started talking. "Muriel, it still amazes me to say this, but your dream was perfectly accurate. The man they were trying to kill not only survived, he hurt one of them in the process. Just as you said."

Muriel nodded. "Yesterday you hinted that Jubilee had talked to you, I think you said they 'invited you into the dream?' Is that how you know what happened? You're in communication with them?"

Joss had already decided to stretch her tell-nobody promise to the president—they needed Muriel's "inside" knowledge.

"Yes. The first time was two nights ago. They contacted me because of my role in the investigation. They fear, I think for good reason, that if they are ever caught, what they're doing could become common knowledge. People who can kill with impunity, without risk, no way to prove it even if you know they're responsible. They asked for my help. To warn them if we were closing in."

"And you said yes?"

Joss was admitting to aiding and abetting Andrew Matson's killers.

"Yes. As did Agent Mendelsohn. And my boss, Henry Trenton. And President Carver."

If she was wrong about Muriel, she was making a huge mistake.

"We all agreed because we share their fears. This method of theirs cannot get out. There can never be testimony or trials or any degree of public reckoning for what they've done. Right now, you might be the only person in the world with some idea of how they do it. We need to keep it that way."

Joss got up for another round of caffeine, leaving Muriel a few quiet minutes to mull it over. When she returned and handed Muriel the chai, she said, "I thought you were a coffee person. I noticed a pot that first morning at the house."

A sad smile. "No, that was Andy's, on automatic, waiting for him every morning at six. I poured a cup that morning without thinking. I've retired the poor machine." She sighed, and said, "Well, with the most mixed feelings . . . I understand and accept your . . . partnership with Jubilee. No one must ever know. But still, they have to stop. Or be stopped. They can't keep killing people."

Joss nodded. "That was the other thing, in our first communication—they said they'd stop at sixty, or sooner. Something about running out of ammunition. I get the sense that dream murder isn't easy, that it's taxing on them somehow, depleting physical or mental resources."

"Sure," said Muriel. "I get that. It's hard for me just passively witnessing. And what they're doing—intentionally invading others' dreams and causing a precise physical response—that's so much more than the intentional actions I manage in my most successful dreams. I think these people have been practicing for a long time."

"Me too."

"Another burden they're dealing with is karma. Killing another person has to carry consequences for the individual. My sense of them, from the dream, is that they're basically decent people. They'd know they were paying a price for what they're doing."

"You know," said Joss, "when I asked why they did this when they were so afraid of the secret getting out, they said they'd always thought there was a fail-safe, something that would keep it from becoming a common skill. Maybe it's this difficulty factor. As long as it took them and as hard as it's been, they thought no one could ever duplicate their efforts—"

"But then, they had such success, seemed kinda easy after all, they start freaking out."

"Right. They must be really freaking out now that they've had a failure. On the one hand, they've reaffirmed how difficult it is to do, but on the other, there's somebody else, a bad guy, who's onto it, actually out-dreamed them and may be putting together his own dream weapon."

"They told you what happened; did they say 'why' or 'how'?"

"Pretty much. It started with last night's communication. The president was asking the questions and doing the typing. He explained to them that, despite reservations about their method, he thought their agenda was just what the country needs, as he'd made clear in his speech."

"Best political speech I've ever heard," said Muriel. "Things I never thought I'd hear an American president saying."

"I agree, as did Jubilee. And ninety-five percent of the public! But then Carver revealed that the five percent who didn't agree were threatening a military coup, and had the wealth and power to make it happen. Apparently one's been in the works since he was elected. So he wanted Jubilee to eliminate the coup leader, a very rich arms dealer named Ted Tiller. They reluctantly said yes, reluctance which turned out to be justified. What they said this morning was they just didn't have enough knowledge of the man. They need photos, video, speeches, etcetera to make it work."

Muriel nodded vigorously. "Makes sense. I see that. Like they went into foreign terrain without a map."

"Pretty much what they said."

"But, I think, something else too: I think the woman was already weak. She felt vulnerable. Strong enough as long as everything went right, but this time, inadequate preparation and a tougher-than-most target—he went right at her."

Joss said nothing. She felt an unexpected pang of loss.

"And here's another thing. I've been thinking about how they know where people are, even if they take off without telling anyone, like Franke, and Thomas Harrow flying to France. It proves we're dealing with dream time and space, which differs from real time and space. Jubilee goes to sleep, same time and place every night, and it doesn't matter where their prey is or in what time zone, because they're connecting in the dream. Doesn't matter where the physical body is, they're tracking down the dream self. It's a whole different geography with its own set of rules."

Joss was starting to get it. "So, the pre-dream data, the bio, photos, video, they need that to stalk the dream self?"

"It makes sense. They probably stalk their victims in advance; in fact, I'm sure they do because I started having the dream three nights before Andy died. So they establish their dream connection and on the final night it doesn't matter what real-world precautions the victim takes."

"And when they didn't do any of that for Tiller, they paid the price. I'm surprised they agreed, knowing how it works and the risk they were taking."

They sat quietly for a couple minutes, finishing their drinks, Joss wishing they'd just waited a day to go after Tiller.

"One more thing," Muriel added, "now that I think about it, they're not invading people's dreams. Not at all. It's more the other way around. They're pulling people into *their* dream."

Chapter 42

While President Carver worried over a looming coup, the American people, Congress, and media were all fixated on the economy. If emotions drive markets, then the American economy was being steered by a schizophrenic, bipolar, paranoid captain afflicted with panic attacks. The stock market was a runaway roller coaster, slow rises followed by fast falls, down 3600 points in the past three days. International markets were only a tad more stable. Nobody had a handle on what was happening or what was coming next. You could throw away all your charts and statistics, your rules of thumb, your definitions—traditional measures were obsolete. The nation could be heading for hyper-inflation or a dismal deflation, unemployment going further up or finally moving down. The spending spree had certainly been fun and exciting, inventories were down, factory orders would presumably jump, all good signs. But if the banks and credit card companies don't release funds to the merchants then how would the factories get paid and how would their suppliers get paid and so on? And that was just one of many reasons to worry.

Start with an economy so sick that it loses trillions in personal wealth in a year. Then add a so-called solution that legislates a $5 trillion redistribution of wealth to the top two percent. Let it stew for two years of twenty percent real unemployment, four million home foreclosures, two million personal bankruptcies, tight credit, rising energy costs, rising healthcare costs, several environmental mega-catastrophes, and two revenue-sucking wars. Then, unleash Jubilee, the forgiveness of debt meme, and national Max-Out-Your-Credit Day. Followed by Billionaires Day. What you're left with is an economy that no one can begin to understand, much less fix.

The one thing most everyone did agree on was that the Jubilee genie was out of the bottle and there was no getting it back in. Things were too far gone. The only way forward, and the only hope for a healthy, functioning economy, was to more or less implement the Jubilee manifesto. And do it fast.

All of which prompted President Carver to submit Nathan Kane's nomination for instant confirmation. He explained to congressional leaders that the secretary needed to start work immediately. He pointed to the markets, to the polls, to the post-spree facts on the ground, and asserted that they had twenty-four hours to present a plan to the people and the Congress and pass the enabling legislation. Congressional leaders from both parties complied and by noon Nathan was the new treasury secretary.

The president told Nathan he had one job: figure out the mechanics of a national Jubilee. He wasn't to worry about the other items in the manifesto—the limits on interest rates, the new tax laws, campaign finance reform. Carver already had legislators taking the lead on each of them and Nathan should assume their legal enactment in his calculations. He should also assume that they'd be moving quickly on a number of steps to strengthen the social safety net.

But first Carver wanted him to sell it to the people.

"It may seem like we're putting the cart before the horse," the president had said, "but if you can get the public solidly behind this, it will make everything else we're doing much easier. We know they like the concept. You just need to close the deal."

So it was that the leftist economist and national scold found himself sinking back into the leather seats of a presidential stretch limo, sipping a sparkling water. Seated next to him was Ryan Weathers, his temporary consultant. Nathan asked Ryan to join him in part because of Ryan's credibility with the bankers and financiers, never big fans of Nathan Kane. He also was thinking

Ryan would make a great treasury secretary when Nathan's time as a member of the establishment, which figured to be short, was over. That is, if Ryan could be coaxed out of Marsdale Lipman. Seated across from them was Ginny Parks, Nathan's personal assistant for the past ten years. Ginny was an edgy progressive who never in a million years expected to be working in the White House. A Harlem girl, joining the Carver administration at such an historic time—well, she was lit up like a Fourth of July sparkler.

They were en route to Georgetown University to lead a nationally-televised, modified town hall meeting on the coming Jubilee. Modified, because the participants would be carefully screened to only allow those expressing support for Carver and the Jubilee. They wanted real people asking good questions and expressing their concerns about moving forward. What they didn't want was a bunch of angry old white people screaming about taking their country back.

"So," said Ginny, "how exactly do you present the plan and talk through the issues and concerns when you haven't had time to work out the details?"

It was a good question. But it wasn't true that he hadn't had time—he'd been researching and thinking about the practicalities of a national Jubilee since the Day One message and signature. Historically, there was little to go on. Though there were several instances going back to biblical times and up into the fourth century AD, finance was just too different then to draw any lessons for the present day. There had been several attempts to make one happen in modern times, but the focus had always been on forgiving the international debts of poorer nations. Most recently, such an attempt was made in 2000, with disappointing results.

The closest parallel for today's America would be the pre-2004 bankruptcy laws, which made it possible for people to walk away from many of their debts without penalty, assuming a lack of attachable assets. The skewing of those laws in favor of the banks and credit card companies was one of reasons the crash of '08 did such serious damage to the middle class. Nathan had done a quick study of the old law, marking the pluses and minuses.

He'd also found a handful of online sites and writers advocating for a jubilee. It was enough of a community to have many long discussions debating the details of this approach versus that. Nathan had found it stimulating and helpful, so much so that, in fact, a plan was coming together. He was ready to start telling the people.

He smiled and answered Ginny's question with one of his own. "What's the best way to learn something?"

Ginny smiled back. "Teach it."

Nathan turned to Ryan. "Sorry, inside office joke." He continued, "You know, I read your speech and thought you made an impressive case for Jubilee, especially given your audience. It got me wondering: what's your biggest worry about going forward with this?"

Ryan's eyebrows shot up at the unexpected question. After thinking for a few moments, he answered, "My wife was talking this morning about 'viral anarchism'—what if people everywhere, all worried about money, already angry about how much they've lost the past several years, now convinced they're going to lose more—what if some out of control protests get going and it just spreads."

"The powder keg scenario," said Ginny.

"With a few endangered billionaires eager to light the fuse," said Nathan.

Ryan nodded. "All too possible and very scary. But then we decided that Jubilee was just the opposite, a positive virus, already spreading far and wide, affecting everybody, and, if we're lucky, counteracting the bad stuff."

Nathan was about to say they'd be needing to make their own luck—this was not a time to be counting on prayer or fate—when they pulled up to the university auditorium.

Fifteen minutes later, Nathan stood before a packed hall making introductions. The audience was young, diverse, and friendly. Scattered through the group were older faces, most of them professors from Georgetown and other area schools. They'd also invited a number of non-university, non-government locals. After Nathan introduced himself, Ryan, and Ginny, and went over the format—a short lecture with questions from the floor after—he started talking.

"As somebody who's been studying economics and finance his whole life, now tasked with bringing a national Jubilee Day to America, let me say right off that it's been a real challenge. There is so much about 'forgiving all debts' that flies in the face of all we've ever known or believed to be true. It's easy to be swayed by the voices warning that this will destroy the banks and eliminate credit and lead to angry mobs enraged at losing money owed them. Voices that warn of grave moral hazards. Voices that say that Jubilee would reward scofflaws, slackers, cheaters, and losers, but punish the productive, the successful, and those who have played by the rules and managed debt responsibly.

"I can only say this: Jubilee is a one-time corrective for our badly damaged and too-far-gone-to-fix financial system. Jubilee is not a substitute for our current system, nor a model for future systems. It's not the right way to run an economy. It's not fair, it doesn't even try to be. It would be better never to reach the point that a Jubilee is called for. But, of course, we reached that point some time ago. The American economy is like a cancer patient facing a slow, painful death that might be spared by a round of aggressive chemotherapy. Despite the fact that chemo brings its own miseries, it's the only hope of getting better. But, once it's worked, you're done with it. This Jubilee will be chemotherapy for our economy—not entirely pleasant to go through, but our best chance of getting better and once we've done it, it's over."

Nathan scanned the audience and liked what he was seeing: nodding heads and friendly faces. It made him eager to get to the Q&A, but he had another point to make first.

"Now, after the Jubilee is when we do have to make serious changes to the way we manage our personal and collective finances. The manifesto has given us the broad strokes: make state and federal taxes more progressive, tie executive compensation to the minimum wage, pass real campaign finance reform, cut military spending in half, and tightly regulate interest rates on all types of debt. The president and Congress are hard at work on each of these. At the same time, they're strengthening aspects of our social safety net, all of it so that, post-Jubilee, we will be able to sustain positive growth without repeating past mistakes. Moreover, these changes are essential to helping many Americans get through what could be tough times. If you don't have to worry about healthcare, retirement, unemployment benefits, or that your house will be foreclosed on, then any economic dislocation you're going through is much easier to deal with."

Nathan went on in that vein for a bit more, then started taking questions. Though, at Nathan's insistence, they hadn't screened the questions, the first was just what he wanted. An earnest young man asking for details.

"The manifesto says 'forgive all debts.' Does that include the federal debt? And how about mortgages? Much as I'd like mine to go away, the material and labor costs that went into building the house—it has to be paid for somehow, doesn't it?"

"Great questions," said Nathan. "Two things. First, the manifesto gave us the broad strokes, but it's up to us to work out the details. And we don't see all debts being forgiven. Second, the manifesto does not proclaim debt as intrinsically evil or say that it should be abolished. It's just opposed to usury, a term that encompasses a range of unfair and unregulated lending practices.

"So, we are looking at and will deal with each form of debt, each lending practice or instrument, separately. Some debts will simply be written off. Others will be written down—principals will be adjusted to compensate for past unfairness and interest rates will be lowered; the individual will go forward with more manageable debt. Then there are some debts that may be written off, but with the government providing compensation to the lender. Finally, those debts that were not in any way usurious or unethical may continue per contract."

A thousand hands shot up. All wanting to ask the same questions: what about credit cards? what about home mortgages? what about my debt?

Nathan continued. "I know you want more specifics, but I don't have them yet." After yesterday, he didn't want to tell them that credit cards were already on the "simply written off" list. "We're still working on it, but I promise that all will be revealed in a day or so."

He called on an unsmiling older woman. "What do you mean by 'unfair' rates? And how do you decide what's fair and what's not?"

"Sure, let me answer the second question first. We start by looking at the lender's income and asking, 'What's fair compensation for the work involved and the service provided?' Now, this is a question that gets asked all the time about other professions. We wonder how it is that rock stars and actors and professional athletes make millions while teachers and nurses barely scrape by. Though it seems unfair, upon reflection we find that these millionaire stars typically work very hard at mastering their skills and then provide goods and services that huge numbers of people value—we pay for the CDs and the movie tickets and the cable service and all the products that attach to the stars through advertising and endorsements. So, you can trace clear line between their production of tangible goods and services and their compensation.

"When we look at these high-rolling financiers, hedge fund operators, currency speculators, mortgage bundlers, the whole panoply of exotic investment products, it is much harder to see the productive work, or tangible goods and services, and certainly nothing that merits tens of millions in compensation. Not even remotely close. These men are being paid ten thousand dollars an hour for fifteen-dollar-an-hour paper-shuffling. They say, "We're taking big risks!" but they're typically risking other people's money and, as we've seen, they get their fat bonuses even when the risks don't pan out.

"And that's what's unfair. Their earnings are divorced from the free-market principles they claim to champion. It is the ancient problem of usury and moneylenders: they are being paid not for an honest day's work, real labor, the production of something of value. Rather, they are exploiting their access to and control of money. Their money is working for them, making them wealthier with no human effort involved. To the extent that society allows this to happen without regulation, the rich get obscenely richer and the gap between the rich and everyone else ever widens.

"So, a fair interest rate on a bank loan or credit card purchase is that which covers the cost of the money—the amount the lender is being charged by the feds or the amount that it is paying in interest to savers or dividends to investors—plus the overhead costs of running the bank, plus a decent wage for the banker. It's a formula that would keep credit cards below ten percent, and home mortgages around five or six.

"That's where we're going. And the only way to get there is through government oversight and regulation. You cannot allow the people who benefit from financial dealing to set the terms. They will always act to maximize personal profits, to the detriment of society. We cannot let that keep happening. Banking, moneylending, is an honorable profession, essential to the functioning of a modern economy. It must be intelligently regulated."

The next question came from another student. She directed it to Ryan, and asked, "You're now the CEO of America's largest bank. Does it worry you that our new treasury secretary sounds a lot like Karl Marx?" Is was a good-natured jibe and got a big laugh from the crowd, Ryan and Nathan included.

"Actually," said Ryan, "we were singing union songs the whole ride over here, in perfect harmony, all about working in a socialist paradise." More laughter. "I will say this about our new secretary—"

At some point during the laughter, Nathan noticed heads turning down to focus on laptops and handhelds, then people talking quietly, with the urgent vibe of an emerging event. Before he could respond, Ginny appeared from off-stage, apologized to the audience for interrupting and announced "a five minute break while we all digest this news."

She turned off their mikes, then said, "About an hour ago a car bomb exploded in Dallas. Thirty dead and counting, lots of wounded. Soon after that an email went out. She read from her tablet: 'A Message to Jubilee. The car was a red Mazda registered to Stanley Smathers. Stolen from the Kwikmart on Brady and Tenth, in Austin.'" Ginny looked up. "Just like the Jubilees, providing ID, then the message: 'For every man that Jubilee murders, another bomb will go off. The blood of innocents is on Jubilee's hands.'"

Chapter 43

Leo had begun to accept that Dorothea was dying. Though she'd rallied some, managing to get out of bed, she was so fragile that every slow, shuffling step she took looked dangerous, like her bones might just crack and crumble. He was afraid to even think about the pain she must be feeling. She couldn't eat, could only take tiny sips of water. Wouldn't even consider swallowing pills. They'd stockpiled some morphine for the end stage and though she was saying no to it now, he knew it wouldn't be long.

Mia and Brett were still at the house and planned to stay right up to bedtime—if they even went home to dream tonight. If not, they'd be sitting vigil until she passed. Mia was with her every moment, while Brett was communicating with the others. Everybody wanted to come to the house. To hell with security, to hell with the whole thing, was the prevailing thought. Joe and Eva would indeed be coming by with food around dinnertime, but Brett told the others to wait. By the time they all drove up from Seattle and ferried over—well, even if they made it in time for Dorothea, with everyone on island there could be no dream. They really needed to circle to make such a major decision. They set a time for three.

Which got Leo thinking, *Dorothea's last circle*. A lifetime of sitting with the most precious friends a person could ask for, listening. Speaking your truth and being heard. Loving and being loved. What more is there? *It's a good life, sweetie; we've been so lucky.*

He was on the sofa with Dorothea and Mia, the two of them talking softly. He couldn't quite make out the words but was enjoying the cadence of their voices and basking in the mother-daughter glow. He got to thinking about their wedding day and how that morning, Joe had taken him aside and said, "Pay attention, catch each moment, then you'll have it always." It was 1969, an outdoors ceremony, and the bride wore paisley. Joe became a ten-dollar "Universal Light Church" minister to perform the service. Jane, with the long red hair down to her butt, played the guitar and sang a soft acoustic version of "Gimme Shelter" that had folks laughing and crying. By the time the after-party was winding down, even the most conservative family members, even Dorothea's father, were calling it a great day and beautiful wedding.

Leo remembered every moment. He would have it always.

At two, Dorothea liked to listen to an NPR talk show, so Mia turned the radio on, low volume. As Leo listened, he thought it might be good medicine because the conversation was all about the positive moves that Carver was making and how optimistic everyone was about the coming Jubilee. But then the host announced breaking news. *A car bomb in Dallas, dozens dead. Followed by an email that—the only part he heard was the final words—the blood is on Jubilee's hands.*

Before he or Mia said a word, Dorothea moaned, a sound of terrible anguish. She turned to Leo and said, "back . . . head . . . pain." And she died.

There was no need to check for a pulse. He could feel it, inside, the world had changed. Mia moved off the sofa and knelt before Dorothea and Leo and lay across their laps. Leo was still gripping Dorothea's hand. He slipped his other hand through Mia's hair. Brett came into the room, took it all in, then sat behind Mia, leaning into her, crying softly.

They stayed like that until Brett said, with a deep sigh, "It's time for circle, Leo, Mia. We need to let them know. And we have some hard decisions to make." He and Mia retrieved their laptops and came back to the living room, remaining close to Dorothea. Leo went to the upstairs office to use her iMac.

At a few minutes before three, Leo posted.

Leo: Sorry to jump the line and sorry that there is no better or easier way to do this. Dorothea passed an hour ago. She was badly hurt by last night's dream, it seemed the cancer just exploded. We managed to get her out of bed around noon, but she wasn't eating. She was in a lot of pain, but not complaining. Talking only in whispers. But Mia and Brett came by and we were having a sweet time. I think we all knew she was nearing the end, she clearly knew, but she was so looking forward to this circle. I know she wanted to be with all of you again, even if just online. Truth is, she didn't have the energy for much more.

We were listening to the radio, just playing in the background, when the news about Dallas hit. They read the email and when they got to the part about blood on Jubilee's hands, she groaned, looked at me, said "back, head, pain" and died.

Anyone else would assume that Dorothea had been describing the physical sensations proceeding her death and to an extent that was true. But to circle, 'back-head-pain' was both the name and the mechanism of their weapon. It was what they invoked in the dream to cause the aneurysms. Part incantation, part mantra, part computer code. Brett called it a "dream app."

Leo: So, the news from Dallas triggered the karmic blowback she'd been so worried about. She kept saying that the dream was killing her. I kept not quite believing it. I rationalized that the cancer got going months before we started. She'd answer back that the cancer was caused by the long-term stress of contemplating serial murder. Now I know she was right, at least for her. Before we even think of going forward, each of us needs to take a hard look at how we're doing, how we're being affected. I ask that anybody who feels at all at risk for what happened to Dorothea, please let's talk about it.

Last thing I need to say now is how much Dorothea loved all of you. We had a few end-of-life discussions these past weeks and in every one she affirmed how satisfied she was with her life, how full it had been, how very grand, and how she owed all of it to you, her beloved circle.

Eva: I'm so sorry Leo, but so glad that you and Mia and Brett were there. Glad that it was sweet. Glad that we all had last weekend. I'm leaking all over my keyboard, pass for now.

Brett: pass

Ali: Echoing Eva. I remember the first time I came to the house, Jane's too young new friend, the tattooed lesbian, come to take Don's place in the circle. I was so scared walking up the steps, and the door opened and Dee was there, and not all smiling arms open, but a little squinty-eyed, looking me over, and just when I was about to turn tail and run, then the big smile. She took my hands in hers, I remember how very warm they were, and she said, "Welcome Ali, welcome aboard." I'm just so glad that I got to know her. Though it was only a few years, I'm a better person for having her as a friend and mentor. And now the world is a poorer place.

They continued in this way for three full rounds, eulogizing Dorothea, expressing their own sorrows, telling Dee stories, passing when they were too choked-up to type, or when, at last, they'd said it all.

Leo: Thank you all, for loving her so. I feel it to my core. I also know that, if she was speaking now, she'd be saying that we have some pressing business to take care of and time to get to it. The biggest question is, do we continue? Do we take the personal risks of saccing any more people? And do we take the now greater risk of causing more bombings? And, if yes to those, what do we do about Ted Tiller? And what about me?

EVA: We continue. We have to. If we stop now the reactionaries take over and all that we've accomplished is making things much worse. I remind everyone that when Dee was first diagnosed, even though she was already seeing the risks in the dream, she said it made the need to act more urgent. She understood, I think, that as much as we've altered the circumstances of war, we're still perpetrating violence, and there would be casualties.

BRETT: This will be a surprise: we continue. When it was threatening her life, I wanted it to stop. But now, I think Dee knew all along that she was herself a sacrifice. I think she took it on so the rest of us could go forward and finish. My only worry now is that I am definitely hating Tiller and the people behind Dallas. So I need to do some serious shadow work. As for you Leo, there's obviously no time to find a new partner. So, unless one of us decides to drop out, perhaps you join a couple to create a really strong threesome, strong enough to sac Tiller.

ALI: Well said, Brett. We continue. How about if Leo joins with Joe and Eva—the three strongest dreamers to take on Tiller and whoever else emerges as top dog. I wish I felt as good about continuing in the face of more bombings. But the truth is, these people are mass murdering everyday, all over the world, whether with bombs or environmental destruction or poverty. We have the power to stop them. We continue.

TOM: We continue. And we tighten our partnership with Carver. They need to stop the bombings. And they need to ferret out the sacs and get us the data so there's no more Tillers.

JANE: we continue. we don't go after anybody without a sufficient profile. we get help from Carver. now what do we do with you, Leo? Ali, it's a nice idea having Joe and Leo and Eva become a threesome, if a tad scandalous. but they've never done it, we've all been dreaming in pairs for thirty years, all that time with one partner, except for me, of course. if they had time to practice, then maybe, but there would surely be kinks to work out. we can't be practicing these next few days, we need our best. I think we're strongest if Leo sits it out and we reduce to five a day.

SUSAN: We continue. Yes to everything Jane said.

MIA: We continue. And Leo, I've been contemplating having you join me and Brett. But, you lost Dee today and you were there last night and it seems like a good idea for you to take a break from the dream. Take time to mourn and heal.

ROB: We continue. Yes to the rest.

JESSIE: We continue.

JOE: Well, we have clear consensus on continuing. No one has expressed any individual mal-effects, which is certainly good news. And we will make sure that we do not go after anyone without the full dope. For that matter, we won't even know who we're going after until we've connected with Morgan and Carver—which means we should be connecting with them earlier in the day, right after this circle's over.

But I need to buck the tide on the Leo question until we hear from him. I suspect my old friend is not happy with the thought of sitting out right now. And, he and I have had a number of conversations over the years about the 'power of two' in the dreaming compared to the lone dreamer. We've both felt for some time that several of us were capable of going solo. But there was no need to go that way—except during the interval between Don and Ari, when we almost brought it up—and besides, we just preferred the harmony of six equal pairs.

Whatever you're thinking Leo, I know you'll be doing what's best for circle and for the country.

Leo: Thanks Joe, and thanks everyone for looking out for me. But Joe's right. I've been thinking about and doing tiny tests with solo dreaming for quite a while. Dorothea was also. The problems last night were the lack of info and her weakened state. Assuming better data from Carver, I want to go back and finish Tiller. I hear you Brett, about hating Tiller, and we're all going to need to stay on top of our emotions now, if there are more bombings. I assure you I've been doing the work, I feel clear, and I am ready.

Not everyone was immediately sold, but with Joe and Leo in agreement, it was as good as decided. Still, it took two more times around the circle to reach near consensus. In the end, Mia "stood aside," meaning that she disagreed with the decision—she just lost her mother and was terrified of losing Leo—but would not stand in the way, and would support it energetically.

One final decision was quickly made: the mainlanders would all come over on the early ferry tomorrow, to recharge with an island afternoon together, saying farewell to Dorothea.

After Leo and Brett had carefully laid Dorothea's body on her bed, and Mia had found Dee's favorite shawl to cover her, Joe and Eva came over, bringing dinner. Although they had all sat around this table together hundreds of times before, since Brett joined with Mia it had been either four or six of them. Five felt wrong, awkward, flat, and they broke up early, each to absorb their huge loss, and the Dallas catastrophe, in their own way.

Chapter 44

President Wash Carver had a theory about elections. The candidates' positions on the issues were of little importance. What mattered to the voters was which candidate was the most comfortable in his skin. Applied to presidential candidates, it meant that your positions and policy statements were consistent with your personal philosophy and that all this came across in your public presentation. Nixon was famously done in by the televised debate in which his sweaty demeanor screamed uncomfortable in his skin. Eight years later, he'd grown more relaxed with the process, while Humphrey was desperately trying to pull together segments of the Democratic party that he vehemently disagreed with. Came across as uncomfortably conflicted. Reagan was the ultimate in blissful self-assurance and blew away first Carter, then Mondale, despite glaring problems with his positions. Likewise Clinton—nothing shook the feeling that, no matter what his failings and weaknesses, he knew who he was and what he was about. Then the utterly unqualified Bragg, who nonetheless was utterly sure of himself. The voters went for it, choosing the man "they'd most like to have a beer with."

Carver was clear that that's what got him elected. Not the beer, but his unshakable self-confidence. He'd been comfortable in his own skin, literally and figuratively, since his sophmore year race epiphany. During the campaign he never lost his cool, displayed no fatal hypocrisies, was never caught weaseling away from his own deep convictions for political expediency. Despite the unending shit-storm of his first three years as president, none of that had changed. Nor was it changing now, in his response to Jubilee. Though it would be characterized as capitulation by some, there was nothing in the manifesto that really went against his own thinking, after a couple of days pondering it. Which is why yesterday's big speech went over so well: he'd been perfectly comfortable in his skin while delivering it.

He'd be damned if this bombing, and any others to follow, would change that. He had set the country on a new course and it was full steam ahead. No backsliding, no equivocation, no second thoughts, no doubts, not a one. And that's what he needed to communicate loud and clear to the somber-faced group of advisors before him.

"Henry," he started, nodding to Trenton, "what do we know about Dallas?"

"Mr. President, we have thirty-seven dead, with six in critical condition. Another twenty-two injuries. It was C4 explosives, with six-inch nails and ball bearings added to increase the carnage, detonated remotely. We've confirmed the car and registration from the email and that it was reported stolen by the owner yesterday. We have an excellent shot at the bomber: the dirtbag didn't check for security cams. We have him parking the car, we know which direction he walked off in, and there are further cams along the way that should give us more. We've got people all over this, new info coming in by the minute. We're going to catch this guy. Today."

"Good work, Henry," said the president.

"Circumstances aside," said CIA Director Kanofsky, "after five days of chasing ghosts, it's good to be chasing dumb-ass criminals again."

Carver noted a few reluctant nods around the table. It was hard to feel too good with thirty-seven dead.

While Homeland was pursuing the Dallas bomber, FBI was in charge of catching the next wave before they struck. The president turned to FBI Director Russell and raised his eyebrows.

"Have to say, Tom's got a point," said Russell. "The past few days my people have been sitting around twiddling their thumbs. We've gotten nowhere on the Jubilees. But this? I've never seen the Bureau more fired up, sir. Effective within thirty minutes of Dallas, we've beefed up surveillance on every radical right-wing group: the militias, anti-abortionists, white supremacists, Christian dominionists, gun nuts, anyone who's even mildly threatened the president or any other government official. Because the whole law enforcement community was already mobilized for the Jubilee hunt, we've got no shortage of eyes and ears out there, some close to these groups. We have people in the groups. We have several wiretaps going and satellite surveillance on known leaders.

"Also, one thing Henry didn't mention is that the C4 was stolen from an Army depot. Every branch of the military," Russell gave a quick nod to the Joint Chiefs chairman, General McAdams, "is now conducting a fast but thorough inventory of weapons and explosives."

McAdams added, "We're also sending a clear message down through the ranks: anyone involved in these bombings or plots to take over the government—or remaining silent about the involvement of others—will be caught and is in for a world of hurt."

As bleak as Carver felt when the Dallas news first hit, the change-the-world optimism that Jubilee had sparked was coming back. If they could stop these guys. He turned to Kanofsky. "I have to admit I've had my eye off the international ball for a couple days, Tom. How's this playing with friends and foes?"

The CIA director was tempted to say that he too had been distracted, had barely slept since Day One, so certain he was that Jubilee had him on their list. A Republican holdover from the last administration, his many disagreements with Carver were one of the Beltway's worst-kept secrets. But living through five days of internal turmoil while the country spun through such monumental change had worked some sort of magic on him. He found himself beginning to like Carver and warming to the Jubilee agenda. Even the demilitarization. Even Nathan Kane. Of course, he was still an old spook, so he kept this all to himself.

"So far, Mr. President, it's been an almost universal non-response. First, because of the timing. If this had happened pre-crash, then we'd have seen markets tumbling everywhere and a slew of desperate and unhappy reactions. But post-crash, when America sneezes, the rest of the world does *not* catch cold. Though, if we declare that we're repudiating our foreign debt, that could change in a hurry.

"Second point is the talk of a military wind-down. While most of our allies' leadership may approve of American military bases on their soil, few of their citizens want us there. Nor, of course, do our enemies. I suspect the whole world is busy making plans, getting ready for us to pack up and go.

"Last point is same as we're seeing domestically: everyone knows that Jubilee can strike anywhere. There's simply no percentage in saying anything that might put you or your country on Jubilee's hit list. Better just to stay quiet and enjoy the show as America finally gets its comeuppance."

The president slowly nodded his head, agreeing with Kanofsky's analysis, if not the tone.

"Let's see if we can disappoint them some," he said. "We're going to show the world that—post-Jubilee—our best days are ahead of us. We're at the end of the old America, but just getting started on the new. And we're not the only ones who need to make this shift; we're just the first to go and, as such, we'll still be leading the world. The problems with usury and debt especially—they affect everybody, so it might be the Jubilee needs to be universal. Nathan, what are your thoughts? And what's your sense of the timing at this point?"

Nathan had been sitting there, listening to the others but barely hearing. He was going through some personal shock and awe at the turn of events that had seated him at the table with the president and his chief advisors. A new America, indeed.

"Mr. President. As you know, we're taking each form of debt separately and asking one question: were the interest rate and terms of contract fair? Where the answer's a clear yes, we sustain it. Where it's a clear no, we repudiate. And for those in the ambiguous middle, we do some combination of repudiation, restructuring, and government pay-down. In terms of foreign debt, I'm recommending that we forgive without qualifications all third-world debts and encourage the rest of the world to follow suit. As for our foreign debt, much of it is fair, and has done more good than harm; it's generally a plus to have other nations invested in us. But that which isn't, we repudiate. Same for the federal deficit; we repudiate the unfair debt, but sustain the good—treasury bonds and such."

Nathan paused for a breath, and to let the others comment or object or call him a dirty commie or throw him out of the room. But everyone, including the directors of the CIA and FBI, the chair of the Joint Chiefs, the Senate majority leader, and the president himself all sat in silence, pondering his words. No one looked happy, but they all seemed clear that this was the path they were taking. He kept talking.

"Domestically—well, here's the deal with credit cards. There is just so much in the industry that violates fairness, not to mention basic human decency. Such a litany of shady ethics and outright fraud that there's no point wasting time and money sorting through it to separate out the good from the bad. High rates, dishonest contracts, fraudulent fees . . . all rife throughout the industry, all the instruments of a massive, massive transfer of wealth upward. That needs to be stopped and the whole industry shut down and reset. Period. A total Jubilee. All credit card accounts go to zero and are closed. Credit card companies are required to settle their merchant accounts in full. Everybody cuts their cards in half and learns to live with debit cards until a reconfigured industry starts offering new cards at fair rates—"

"Hard as I try to accept this," said National Security Advisor Zia Carillo, "it feels as unfair as what you're trying to fix."

"Well, it *is* unfair," answered Nathan. "Which is why it's important to keep stressing that this is a one-time corrective, not the economy of the future. In order to correct huge, long-term, destructive imbalances, we're taking steps that will hit some folks hard. But the numbers of 'unfairly treated' will be far less in the corrective than in the current system. And because we're pumping money and resources into the safety net, no one has to take too bad a beating. But you raise a good point, and it's worth exploring just who the losers are when we erase all credit card debt.

"There are four groups to look at," Nathan continued. First, are the merchants who do not get reimbursed for recent sales. We'll command the credit card companies to pay, but some will inevitably not have the reserves. I'm proposing that the government pay those off—think of it as stimulus money going directly into businesses. Then, there are the people who don't use credit cards; they've missed out on a lot of free gifts. There's nothing we can do for them except point to the improvements in their world. Likewise, the people who used cards, always paid their bills on time and kept their balances at zero. As you said, Zia, it feels unfair, it is unfair, but it's in a good cause. And, really, neither of those groups are actually injured by what we're doing. We're not bankrupting them, or repossessing their property, or breaking their kneecaps or anything.

"The group that is injured is the industry executives, the men and women who have been raking in millions. The folks who loved it when Ronald Reagan said 'Life is unfair.' Well, it's finally caught up to them. And frankly, most of them will come through this still wealthy, just not as obscenely so. For society, a very small price to pay, inconveniencing a tiny elite, forcing them to get by on less, to the benefit of everyone else."

Nathan ran through a few more credit sectors. Car loans would be sustained with some restructuring. Student loans would all be forgiven, with some government pay-down. Going forward, Nathan proposed the establishment of free higher education at public colleges. Private schools could continue offering their unique or superior experience for whatever the market would bear. The goal would be to stop sending new graduates into the world saddled with debt.

"The way it works now," said Nathan, "we are graduating debtors into the world. That's why there're more plastic surgeons than GPs. Why so many MBAs go for financial services. Doesn't matter how well-intended and altruistic you start out, if you're twenty-five years old and two hundred thousand dollars in debt you need to think about making money, in a hurry. Bad for the individual, bad for society."

Zia spoke again. "Well that one makes tons of sense to me, based on personal experience. And I'm starting to get how all of this goes together, that it can only work if we do it all at once."

"And what about the formula for home mortgages?" asked the president.

"Yes, well, the speculators and bundlers have made a major mess there," said Nathan. "You really can't have a German pension fund holding the paper on a bungalow in Florida, but that's what we've got now: loans that have been repackaged and resold and spun through several accounts until nobody is responsible or accountable for them. Which is nuts. Home mortgages are too important and run for too long. They require an easily contacted, if not local, interested and invested lending partner. Someone who can carefully and effectively vet the application before the loan and then help folks through any rough spots over the long term. Someone approved by and subject to federal regulators. These subprime mortgages, all the people underwater, the ones facing foreclosure—most had no such lender to begin with and it's difficult now to even know who owns the house if they default.

"So, we'll need an agency, something like the Resolution Trust, that will over the next year restructure the nation's mortgages. For some eighty to ninety percent, we just lower their rates to six percent or less, then calculate the amount they overpaid during the course of the loan and subtract it from their principal. The banks get squeezed a bit and consumers have more in their pockets.

"For all of the failing loans, I propose that the government take them over. Determine a real price for the house, take into account what they've paid, and set their principal accordingly, at the new rates. The government gets a nice revenue stream to help with the transition and people stay in their now-affordable homes. When they sell, the new buyers have to work with a bank. So, eventually, we're out of the housing biz. Who's hurt? Whoever got stuck with the paper last. Fair or not, the best thing for society now is to move on. Basically, we just throw the whole mess in the incinerator."

"Nathan," said Kanofsky, "I must say I'm impressed with the plan." He smiled. "And no, I'm not just saying that to curry favor with Mr. Jubilee. Like Zia, I'm getting how it all fits together. But, this is like planning for war, and what we know there is that plans go out the window once the shooting starts. I still have trouble seeing anything but total chaos when we announce this."

"I share your concerns, Tom, and wish I could offer assurances, but we really are casting off into unknown realms. Sometimes you just have to leap."

"Leap when?" asked Carver.

"Assuming we've stopped these bombers—how does tomorrow sound?"

Chapter 45

Alex Mendelsohn was on his way to the White House for a late-afternoon meeting with Carver, Joss, and Trenton and, it was hoped, a contact with Jubilee. The Dallas bombing had taken the already chaotic situation that Jubilee created and thrown it into an industrial blender with several volatile new ingredients. Made for a huge fucking mess. One silver lining was that the nation's entire law enforcement industry, thousands of agencies and tens of thousands of investigators, were already hard at work on Jubilee. Fifteen minutes after the bombing, the whole lot was redirected to catching the bomber and stopping any others in their tracks. After five days of chasing phantoms who never left clues, it was a relief to everyone to be working forensics again and pursuing bad guys who were most likely already known to those monitoring the militia and white supremacist movements.

This meant that, Mendelsohn figured, till the bombers were caught, nobody would be looking for Jubilee, which was another silver lining, because he was pretty sure he'd found them. Took one Joss insight, a few hours on the computer, and a lucky break.

He started with her suspicion that the Jubilee of their secret communications was a writer and that he was politically active going back to the sixties. She'd suggested a search for several key terms—dominator, overclass, underclass, income gap, and jubilee—in Nexus, Authors in Print, and Google Books, with a range from 1960 to 1980. After a dozen searches and some data manipulation, he had forty-one names. Because of the time frame, they were all seventy and older, and he was able to eliminate twelve who were dead or seriously infirm. Then he began to put together in-depth bios of the remaining twenty-nine.

He started working the names in random order and fifth on the list was Leo Sharpski. And that's when they got lucky. There was nothing that leaped out in Sharpski's author bio, except for a single line at the very end: "Leo lives with his wife on a small green island in the Pacific Northwest." A tiny bell dinged as he read the words—they'd interviewed another old-timer who lived on a little island off the coast of Washington. Doctor Joseph Wiggenstern, head of Army psi studies in the sixties, the man they interviewed on day two, who joked about being a suspect. Ha, ha. A little more digging confirmed that Sharpski had been in the Army from '60 to '65, stationed at Fort Lewis, same time as Wiggenstern, and that they were both thirty-year residents of the same little island.

It was a little past two when he knew he had them, but before he could pursue it further, his Book beeped with the news about Dallas, followed by orders to get to the White House for a four o'clock meeting.

Chapter 46

Source: The Sarah Meadow Show

SARAH MEADOW: Ladies and gentlemen, welcome back from the break, and if you're just tuning in, we have a special one-hour, news-maker interview with Ryan Weathers, who yesterday became the new CEO of Marsdale Lipman. I should say again that yes, it was just two days ago that we had Harold Leonard on the show—who was the new CEO of Marsdale Lipman for about twelve hours before he was jubileed.

Ryan, you were just starting to talk about the Jubilee Manifesto and what it all means to a company like Marsdale Lipman and, bigger picture, for the nation's economy.

RYAN WEATHERS: Well, of course, there are so many unknowns here. We're looking at a total overhaul of our economy and the way we do business, taxation, spending less on the military, strengthening and expanding social services. That's a lot to consider even before you throw in the Jubilee.

Here's how I laid it out for our current board and investors. We're closing down all of the financial services that weren't actually serving anybody except ourselves. It had come to represent an embarrassingly large portion of the firm. They've been shown the door, along with all their so-called products, derivatives, credit-default swaps, all the stuff that existed just to make us money.

Our sole work now, our sole reason for existing, is to support the American business community. We'll do that the old-fashioned way—by channeling investors' money into what we consider to be viable businesses. Helping businesses with financial reorganizations, capital expansions, mergers and acquisitions. Helping investors by putting their money into safe, solid portfolios, with modest returns.

Modest is the word of the day. All employee salaries, from CEO to janitorial, will be in line with the Jubilee formula—I will make no more than one hundred times the lowest-paid in the firm, who will make more than the minimum wage. No more year-end bonuses, no more gambling incentives, no more rewards divorced from one's actual work.

SARAH: My word—and, uh, how is everyone taking this?

RYAN: Well, we had to let a lot of folks go, because we just don't have work for them now. Some may return as we get back on solid ground; others may be better off just going to Vegas since that's where their true talents lie.

Source: The Daily Liar

What is it about the fucking rich in this country? It's so important that they hold onto all their goddamn money that they're willing to destroy everything else? Willing to blow up a crowded city street, kill innocents, kill women and children, kill anybody who gets in the way of their insatiable appetites for more, more, more? Doesn't matter that 96% of the country is ready for Jubilee and welcomes the changes? Doesn't matter that the rest of us badly need these changes—to hell with all of us because a few rich assholes think they need to get richer still?

And don't tell me we started it by killing a few of them. America's class war has been on for generations with nothing but millions of middle and lower class casualties. A few dead rich men and they start screaming about fairness. News flash: this is as fair as it's ever been in America.

Frankly, this is the first big test of Carver's New America. If we go hard after all of the men responsible for today's bombing—from the low-level creeps who carried it out to the high-level fat cats who ordered it done—if we go after all of them hard and throw all of them jail, then we'll know things are really changing.

Source: DC•PM

George Deeds: No, I'm not saying that the bombing was justified. Please don't put words in my mouth. I'm merely pointing out its inevitability. From the moment America's Commander in Chief made clear that he was siding with the terrorists there was bound to be a backlash. The president's actions have left the nation vulnerable to what happened in Dallas, and much worse.

Judy Rothberg: I see, George. A small number of angry white men don't approve of the way things are going, so they slaughter a bunch of women and children, and it's the president's fault?

Deeds: His choices led directly to today's bombing. Yes.

Rothberg: Have you been paying attention at all? Really, what choice did he have?

Deeds: He could have—should have stood up to the Jubilees. Like a real Commander in Chief, like the most powerful man in the world. It would have inspired the rest of this once-brave nation to pull together and put an end to Jubilee once and for all. Instead, we got Neville Chamberlain all over again, surrender and appeasement, pretending the Jubilees are our friends.

Matthew Crissom: Except for one small problem, George. He'd be dead now, another ill-advised resister, like Harold Leonard and General Carney and Paul Sheppard. The only thing he'd be inspiring is full compliance with Jubilee.

Deeds: Better a dead martyr than a living traitor.

Rothberg: George, I think you need to listen to Carver's speech again. He's not appeasing, he's leading. He took the Manifesto and added to it, and he's talking about the Jubilee almost like it was his idea all along.

Jonathon Robart: "Almost like?" More like "always was." This is what George and I have been saying from the start, that this has Carver's fingerprints all over it. He pretended to be upset by Howie's death, pretended to go after the Jubilees, but days later, the best law enforcement agencies in the world have nothing and the president has turned Jubilee.

Crissom: So, then, you're with George? Dallas is a justifiable response to the president's supposed treason? More bombings to come, and you're rooting for them? Whatever it takes to stop America from becoming fairer, more equitable, more peaceful?

Chapter 47

Eva hadn't hurt this bad since they lost Jillie. They say there's nothing worse than losing a child, and you'd get no argument from Eva; she'd been carrying that heartache since a drunk driver killed her only child two days short of sweet sixteen. Eva had fallen into a terrible despair, a dark, crushing cloud that obscured everything—Joe, her work at UW, her own health, the future. She'd had to quit teaching and for months barely left the apartment. Joe still went off to the base each morning and did his Army thing, then came home for a dreary dinner. They barely talked. He'd had a vasectomy after Jillie was born, a practical and noble decision, at the time, that Eva became obsessed with. Her child had been torn away from her and there was no getting her back. No getting her motherhood back. She'd started taking pills and thinking about suicide.

Then Dee came into her life.

In 1966, Dee fell in love with Leo, who, along with Don, had been participants in Joe's first LSD experiments. They'd both enlisted in the Army in '60 and were barracks-mates at Ft. Lewis when Joe's study was announced. Leo and Don were the first two volunteers and stayed with the program through LSD and into psi, until their discharges in '65. By that point, the two of them and Joe had discovered co-dreaming. They continued as friends, getting together on a regular basis to work on the dreaming and experiment with LSD, MDA, peyote and other psychoactives.

Joe was fifteen years older than Leo and Don, and had gotten to know them both in a professional shrink-patient relationship, which remained the case even as their friendships developed. But when Jillie died, the roles flipped. Their meetings became Joe's therapy, the two younger men, his guides. Between their good counsel and the dreaming, Joe slowly returned to life. Along the way, the trio became master dreamers and developed the rudiments of what would eventually become "the dream."

Though Eva had continued sinking deeper into depression, even as Joe healed, she did not begrudge him his good fortune. Nor did she feel left out or abandoned. At that point, she was ceaselessly blaming herself for Jillie's death. There was no sense to it, but she couldn't stop thinking: *bad mother, bad mother, bad mother*. She deserved her suffering. So she wrapped herself in it, a thick cloak of self-loathing and recrimination. A woman like her should not hope for healing or happiness or friends. It hardly mattered anyway, she was not long for this world.

Joe, of course, had never abandoned her. As he once put it, "I was following the airline stewardess rule: First place the oxygen mask on yourself, then on your dependent." He'd had to save himself before he could help her. When he was ready, he took a four-week leave from the Army to devote himself full-time to Eva. First thing he did was persuade her to try LSD.

Eva hadn't paid much attention to Joe's work with the drug. She'd never been a drinker or smoker and, until the accident, had no use for pills of any sort. But she knew that he'd been looking for a way to heal the wounded psyches of combat veterans and, he said, LSD had shown great promise. She knew that in the past six months he'd been doing it himself with his friends, and it had clearly helped him. So she said yes, if only because it might dull the pain.

Their apartment was too noisy for the experience—Joe could go on for hours about the importance of "set and setting" when you do acid. They used Leo and Don's, a quiet, Seattle double-decker, set back from the road and surrounded by trees. The plan was for Leo and Don to be the guides while Joe, being too close to "the subject," would passively observe. What Joe didn't know was that Leo's girlfriend, Dorothea, had recently moved in with him and that Leo and Don were thinking it would be better for Eva if she wasn't tripping alone. Joe trusted their judgment, so he went along. Eva didn't much care; Dorothea seemed sweet, if effusive with the never-burned innocence of the young.

Twelve hours later, she and Dee—in one hilarious interlude Eva had been unable to pronounce "Dorothea"—had become long-lost friends, sisters, and forever soul mates. Eva fully recovered her motherhood by surrendering to Dee's mothering. Though they never got sexual, their intimacy was so potent that the men fled downstairs to Don's. The women stayed up all night, had the most profound conversations, epiphanies galore. They cuddled, while playing the same albums over and over. Laid side by side with eyes closed for what seemed like hours, but might have been seconds, and went on hallucinatory journeys that at some point merged, both of them in the same vision. When the sun came up, they wandered out into the dewy Seattle streets in search of coffee and got giddy watching the straights all rushing to their cubicles, the suit-and-tie lemmings, people with no idea, who couldn't see the real world, the light, the indwelling enchantment.

Talk about your magic potion. Eva was to-her-core healed in a single day. She and Dee gave unforgettable birth to a love that would last forty-five years. Cherry on top, that was the night Eva learned to dream.

Chapter 48

At five o'clock on Day Five, President Carver went before the American people for his second major speech in two days. They'd debated sending Joss—might have been fun now that she had something to report—but Carver felt that people needed more than an update on the case, they needed to know what was happening to their country, where things were going, and what he was doing to make sure it all worked out. And they needed to hear it from him.

So Joss was at the White house, but watching the speech on TV with the rest of America. She was seated in the same room they'd met in yesterday. At some point, Mendelsohn and Trenton would show up, then the president, and then they'd touch base with Jubilee.

Carver started by addressing the Dallas bombing and expressing his sorrow for the loss of so many innocent lives. He was building into a righteous, this-will-not-stand, presidential anger when Joss received a text.

It was from Alex: ***b there in a bit. btw, i know 2 of the Js. u know 1. c u.***

What a tease! And damn his timing. She wanted very much to listen to Carver but . . . Alex was saying she already knew one of the Jubilees? Someone from pre-Jubilee life? Somebody everyone knows? Or someone from the investigation? She decided to let her subconscious work on the puzzle and turned her attention back to Carver.

"—caught, tried and spend the rest of their miserable lives rotting in prison. Now, I want to speak directly to those who may be planning more attacks against this country. Whatever revolutionary glory you might have imagined for such actions is utter bunk. It is neither courageous nor patriotic and it is most definitely not what the American people want. You are on the wrong side of history—"

Joseph Wiggenstern. Had to be. The Army shrink who led the psi experiments, a second-day interview. Right age and fit the profile like a glove. Actually joked about being a suspect. She smiled, despite herself. She remembered him as likable if a bit frisky for his age.

She tuned back into Carver who, having addressed the threat of anti-Jubilee counterattacks, was now talking about the changes coming to America. She wouldn't have thought it possible to match yesterday's speech, but—wow. His words, inspired as they were, almost didn't matter—the man was on fire, positively aglow.

"—rarely get the opportunity that's before us now. This is more than a second chance. We've been called to totally remake America and the choices we make today will resound for generations to come. It behooves us to dream big and choose wisely.

"Do we want an America without poverty? An America without hardworking people financially ruined by hospital bills? An America without homeowners facing foreclosure due to bankers' incompetence and greed? An America without the gross and unhealthy disparities between the very rich and everyone else? We can have that. We can have all of it. We can make it all happen *now*.

"Do we want a peaceful America, one that prepares intelligently for its defense, but ceases the empire-building, the foreign invasions and resource wars, all of the international entanglements that our founders so wisely warned against? Do we want an America that channels its productive work into creating rather than destroying, that builds schools and highways and hospitals instead of arsenals, an America that invents life-enhancing technologies rather than better ways to kill? We can do that. We can do that *now*.

"Do we want an America that finally and resolutely sloughs off its racial and ethnic and religious conflicts, steps clear of the old hatreds, free of the foolish—"

The door opened and in walked Alex, followed by Trenton. They both were looking almost upbeat, like they'd had their best day since Jubilee got started. Joss figured that identifying two Jubilees would account for Alex's good mood; for Trenton, it must mean they've made real progress not just on Dallas, but on the threatened reprisals.

She muted the sound, but was keeping one eye on Carver, who continued to beam we-can-do-it-all.

"Did you figure it out?" asked Alex.

"Dr. 'how-can-old-man-help' Wiggenstern?"

"The very one," he said, grinning, then to Trenton, "Eighty-three, but a real live one. Pretty much laughed in our faces. But more or less told the whole truth and nothing but, as far as he went."

"So how did he slip up?" asked Trenton.

"Nothing directly. I followed a couple of our profiler's tips," with a nod to Joss, "which led me to a writer named Leo Sharpski. I noticed that he lived on an island off Washington State. Which I remembered from Wiggenstern. Turned out Sharpski was part of Wiggenstern's psi studies back in the sixties.

"Of course, that's all circumstantial. We still have nothing tying them to the crimes and likely never will, unless we bring them in for some 'enhanced' interrogation. But if the situation were to unravel and we needed to stop them, at least now we know where to apply the pressure."

"Great job, Alex," said Joss. "What's really good is that you found them with leads that only we had—through our interview with Wiggenstern and then the clues that Jubilee left in our private communications. So, as far as their being discovered by others and their secret getting out, we should be okay."

"So Henry, what's the deal with Dallas?" asked Alex.

"We've identified the bomber and are taking him down right about now. Dirtbag named Hardin. Known member of the Sovereign Texas Militia. We've got him at a big anti-gov meeting in Kansas yesterday, then in Austin late this morning. Asshole uses plastic for everything. I guess they didn't cover that in toy soldier school. We have him halfway from Austin to Dallas around one local time, then a positive ID off a surveillance cam getting out of the car in Dallas, two minutes before it blows. His next charge is in Big Sandy, twenty miles from his home. An assault team is on site and has confirmed he's there." Trenton looked at his watch. "He's either dead or in custody by now."

It was too soon for hallelujahs, but they were all breathing easier. "So, now we just have to stop his friends," said Joss.

"FBI's all over that. They're tracking everyone who was at that meeting yesterday, and anyone else on their radical-right watch list. Gonna be nearly a hundred predawn raids; they're sweeping up the whole movement, gonna keep them locked up till after the Jubilee. S'what we should've done after Oklahoma City, just shut the militias down. Would've if not for Waco and Ruby Ridge. You just can't let a bunch of angry assholes parade around with loaded weapons spouting anti-government BS. If you ask me, not that anyone has."

Trenton continued to surprise Joss. It's like Jubilee had awakened his inner liberal. She liked the idea of military types with progressive values.

"Meanwhile," Trenton continued, "I've had our team working on the Jubilee hit list. We've got a strong dossier on Tiller now—going all the way back to his childhood, kinda shit the Jubilees love, apparently—and we've prepared similar files for our own Most Unwanted list. So they can pick the ones that work best for them and not have any more Tillers, we hope."

Joss nodded, then raised a finger, and unmuted the TV. Carver was finishing up.

"—will stand with me, shoulder to shoulder and heart to heart, we will not just dream a better world, we will make it so. We can do it. We will do it. Because, my friends, we *must* do it.

"God bless you all and God bless these—more than ever—*United* States of America."

Chapter 49

Five hours into life as a widower, Leo realized he'd already done his grieving. Unlike with Don's heart attack—one moment here and then gone—they'd had time to get ready for Dorothea's passing. The moment she decided to forego medical treatments, the clock had started ticking. He'd been quietly grieving ever since, doing the inside work. First, the obligatory bargaining—had he really argued that she try chemo?—then he got angry, raging at a God he never believed in. Finally, for several days he just focused on her, how she was feeling and what she wanted. Took him to acceptance, then resolution, the final stage of healthy grief.

So he wasn't hurting. He wasn't even missing her, not like you'd think. How could he ever miss her? She was present in every nook and corner of the house, her singular vibe, reverberating, glowing. He was surrounded by artwork, knickknacks, and memorabilia, each one with its own Dorothea story and when he listened he could hear her telling the stories, her voice, her laughter, sounds that had filled his days.

Leo had been a cabbie and aspiring writer when they met. He'd had one or more projects going ever since, all of it nonfiction, and she'd always been his audience—the reader he was writing for and making his case to. Instead of talking to himself or an abstract audience, he had his inner Dorothea. When he was working something through, the process was an internal dialogue between the two of them, going back and forth, debating the fine points, sometimes arguing passionately. *Leo, are you sure you want to say this?* Or, *Great first para, Leo.* So she'd been living in his head, chatting away, for a long time. The conversation hadn't stopped when she passed and no reason that it ever should.

Then there was the dreaming. Back when Jillie died, Eva and Joe had been plagued with recurring nightmares. So the six of them had committed to co-dreaming every night to re-envision her story. They dreamed her high school graduation. Then graduation from UW. They dreamed her wedding. Dreamed her children, Eva and Joe's grandchildren. Dreamed her a mature, wise woman, sitting across the circle, holding the stick, sharing her life. All these years later, Leo still had Jillie dreams. He always awoke from such dreams feeling happy, fulfilled, the dream events affecting him as deeply as if they had really happened. Which, of course, they had. For there was no death in the dreaming. He'd be reunited with Dorothea—strong and beautiful—every night until his own passing. Who knows what happens then?

Still, he wasn't sure he wanted to see her in tonight's dream. At least not until Tiller was done. Truth was, even with the package Carver's people had put together, going after Tiller alone was a huge risk and he'd be lying if he didn't admit to some anxiety, especially after what happened last night. But talking with Carver had made it clear that stopping Tiller was essential and that it really needed to happen tonight.

When it was time to connect, he just hadn't had the energy for typing, so he clicked on the audio button instead. They accepted the call and a woman's voice said, "This is Joss Morgan, with the President, Henry Trenton, and Alex Mendelsohn. Good idea switching to voice."

"Yes, well, it's been a hard day," said Leo, "for all of us, I suspect, and this is just easier. Also, a better experience of communication, at least for this old-timer. Too much of the person is lost in email and texting."

"This is President Carver speaking and I couldn't agree more. I've been wanting to ask all day . . . I understand that one of your . . . friends may have been injured last night, in this business with Tiller?"

"Yes, it's true. She was already very sick." Leo's voice thickened as he was hit with an unexpected wave of sorrow. "Given our lack of preparation, it just proved too much for her. She passed this afternoon."

"I am very sorry for your loss," said Carver. "When the full history of this time is written, which eventually will happen, she'll be praised for her courage and heroism. In fact," he added, "I would award her a medal myself, if I knew her name."

Leo smiled. He appreciated the president's gesture, as well as his gentle attempt to lighten the moment. Though he was tempted to just go ahead and introduce himself, that was a decision for circle to make.

"Let's leave that for your investigators to discover. If they haven't already. But I will drop another clue and tell you that she was my wife of forty-two years. She died for something she believed in with every fiber of her being. Her death just makes it more vital that we succeed."

Nobody spoke for a long moment.

"Sir, this is Henry Trenton speaking. I just sent you a compressed file that contains video, photos, audio and an extensive bio on Ted Tiller, plus similar packages for ten others who we've determined to be the top threats. It should be more than what you asked for, but I trust that if it's not, you'll let us know. Especially, that you won't go after Tiller unless you're sure."

Leo clicked on the icon to start the download.

"Yes, well, you're right, of course, and I appreciate your concern. From what you've said it should be more than ample."

"Still Trenton speaking: We also want you to know where things stand with today's bombing and the threat of future retaliations for your actions."

"Which," said the president, "I imagine must have been very troubling for you and your friends, the 'blood on your hands' part."

"Well, it was, though it only strengthened our resolve. Truth is, we expected much worse. And we had no way of knowing how you would react. But we saw the possibility that we could end up being the most hated people in America, the nominal cause for a second American civil war."

Leo paused to collect his thoughts. It was important to him that they understand this.

"But. We were convinced, are still convinced, that that's right where the country was heading anyway if we didn't intervene. We really felt we had no choice but to act, worst-case scenarios be damned."

"From where I sit," said Carver, "you were right."

"From where I sit," answered Leo, "you and the people you've pulled together made it work. Medals for everyone!"

It sounded to Leo like all four of them laughed.

Trenton then went over the state of the coup and counter-coup. Today's bomber had been apprehended and, while he wasn't cooperating, he'd been so sloppy in his villainy that they were working a slew of leads back to his masters. Early tomorrow morning, same time as the sacs, the FBI was coming down hard on the whole radical-right movement, locking up the militiamen and gun nuts, the anti-governmenters and religious loonies, shutting them all down until the Jubilee was well underway, the troops were coming home, and the new economy was humming along.

"The troops are coming home?" asked Leo. "War Incorporated is going along without a fight?"

"More than I'd ever have expected," said Carver. "Seems the more authoritarian and hierarchical an organization, the more effective decapitation as a strategy. When you knocked out the main command—the generals, the arms dealers, the propagandizers, the most hawkish legislators—the whole military climate in this country started shifting. Then came the bombing. To whatever extent there were coup sympathizers within the ranks, most did an abrupt about-face after Dallas. Fact is, most of the people in the military are good people doing what has always been necessary work. Why wouldn't they want the America we're describing? Plus, pocketbook issues trump everything; there are few millionaires in the armed services, even fewer stockbrokers and hedge fund managers. But there are hundreds of thousands of working-class families who are dealing with debt and inadequate healthcare and trying to raise children in a positive environment."

"So, the pawns are on board. What about the kings? The empire builders?"

"Again," said Carver, "it starts with your efforts, removing the top dogs and getting into the heads of the next in line. Put a real damper on any resistance, but even more, it's changing their thinking. Just look at what happened at Marsdale Lipman. The rest is up to us—making the case that we can retool the arms industry and keep everybody employed, including returning soldiers, doing the constructive work that America really needs. Frankly, as the picture clarifies, as people get what it means to have everyone home, doing good work, well, it's an easy sell for all but a handful of rich men, and they just don't have the power they used to have. Once they get that they are able to retain much of their lavish lifestyles, it makes more sense to join us than fight us."

"Just like you drew it up, right?" said Mendelsohn, speaking for the first time.

"More or less," answered Leo. "Of course, the big unknown was always the president. Or, during the Bragg years, how many players we'd have to remove until we got the right person in charge. We weren't even sure it was possible for an American president to come over to our position, to accept and work on behalf of the manifesto. It was the biggest risk in all of this."

"So why did you finally decide to act?" asked Joss. "Why now?"

"Yes, well, why now?" Leo had to pause again for another small wave of sadness. "Like a lot of progressives, when President Carver took over we were filled with optimism. Ridiculously so, when we stopped to think about it, but you gotta believe. Two years into it we could see that, with all due respect, Mr. President, the system wouldn't allow substantial change. Then the midterms made it that much more hopeless. You were spinning your wheels and, in some ways, actually hurting progressive causes. Made it clear to us that all of the unhealthy indicators in American culture would just keep getting worse, that the country was sliding inexorably into some very bad times.

"So, we started planning. Then my wife got sick, and—" Leo couldn't finish the thought.

After another long stretch of silence, Joss said, "Though I never knew her, what makes me really sad now is that she missed Jubilee by just one day."

Though he shouldn't have been surprised—it was, after all, the end-point of all their dreaming—it still came as a jolt. *Jubilee in one day*. Imagine that.

We did it, Leo, we really did it.

You did it, sweetie, you really did.

Chapter 50

If there was one thing that Ted Tiller should have learned on his way to amassing $470 billion in assets it's that you get what you pay for. The best things in life cost the most and only losers and fools think otherwise. Skimp on the cash and what you get is second class, Tiller always said. So when you're hiring someone to engage in criminal behavior, if you want the job to succeed—which includes not getting caught—then expect to pay a lot. If you're not paying a lot, then don't be surprised when the idiot gomer screws the pooch and points law enforcement in your direction. The stupid fuck.

The first reports had been perfect. The look on Matthew Crissom's face, trying for just the right gravitas on the tube as he broke the huge story, was priceless. Couldn't keep the terror out of his eyes. Shock and awe, asshole. When the email went out, "the blood is on Jubilee's hands," Tiller knew he had the country by the balls. Total domination. Enemy on the run. Americans would abandon the Jubilees in droves, looking to the strong to keep them safe. Enter Tiller and company to the rescue. First, they'd stop Jubilee and then go after Carver. He could fucking see it.

Then he started getting reports from inside Homeland. They had the stupid fuck on a camera, parking the car and walking away, and then it explodes. Then they had him again, getting into another car and driving off. Had the getaway car plates. Pretty soon they had Hardin's name, where he lived, and they were tracking his movements over the past thirty days from credit card bills. Had his phone records. Wouldn't be long before they were looking at Tiller.

From there things just continued to unravel. Even while they were tracking down Hardin, the feds had shifted all their resources away from finding the Jubilees and on to stopping future attacks. He had to assume that anyone he'd had in mind for tomorrow's strikes was under surveillance. Making things worse, he'd kept himself isolated from the Hardin types, letting his lieutenants handle the contacts. Then he lost all his lieutenants. So he only knew a few men to call and they were all being watched. Fucking Christ!

Final nail in the coffin was Big Nigger's speech. Tiller had wanted him contrite, broken, visibly burdened by the innocent Americans slaughtered because of his traitorous embrace of Jubilee. Standing there with blood all over him. Be like Jimmy the-wuss Carter—failed to keep his people safe. But what they got instead was fucking Churchill. Steely resolve. We will not be moved. Saying they'd already caught the Dallas bomber, now bound for lethal injection, same as Tim McVeigh. Same for anybody who even thinks of repeating today's attack.

Tiller didn't need any polls to know that the country was totally with Big Nigger and the Jubilees. Watched Crissom again, post-speech, and all the terror was gone. Now he was confident, righteous, patriotic and one hundred percent pro-Jubilee. Switched channels a few times and everywhere it was the same. God fucking Christ almighty.

Tiller had one more play—a contingency mini-nuke they'd hidden in DC—but he'd have to wait till tomorrow to get there. He wasn't even sure he could detonate it without killing himself, and he was no suicide bomber. But he didn't have anyone else to call. He'd figure it out in the morning.

If he made it that far. Because for sure they'd be coming for him tonight.

For the first time in his life, all his weapons and money were of no use at all. Harrow proved there was nowhere you could go to escape them. Carney, that there were no measures you could take to stop them. While he had shown that they could be beaten, he had no idea how he'd done it. No fucking idea at all.

All he knew was that they were coming for him.

Day Six

Friday, November 11, 2011

The powerful, with no check left on their greed and criminality, are gorging on money while they busily foreclose our homes, bust the last of our unions, drive up our health care costs and cement into place a permanent underclass of the broken and the poor. They are slashing our most essential and basic services—including budgets for schools, firefighters and assistance programs for children and the elderly—so we can pay for the fraud they committed when they wiped out $14 trillion of housing wealth, wages and retirement savings. All we have left is the capacity to say "no." And if enough of us say "no," if enough of us refuse to cooperate, the despots are in trouble.

—*Chris Hedges*

Chapter 51

Muriel couldn't remember the last time she'd had such trouble sleeping. She just couldn't slow her mind, spinning way faster than the still and quiet needed for lucid dreaming. Her thoughts kept returning to last night and the rush of fear, no, the soul-rattling horror she'd experienced when Tiller went after the woman. The woman who, Joss had informed her, had been real-world injured by it. Just like Andy, physically assaulted in a dream. A dream which she'd now been part of four times, but without any capacity for influence or control. Which meant that it could easily be herself who dies tonight with no way to stop it. She didn't even know why or how she joined the dream in the first place. She certainly didn't know how to fall asleep without going there. So her body-mind had dialed up insomnia as a survival tactic. If she was smart, she'd get out of bed, take a cold shower, and forget about sleep until this whole business was over.

But Andy was awake when he died, so no guarantees there. That thought triggered another round of restlessness, like her body just wanted out, fast, anywhere but here. She looked at the clock. 3:15. Another hour and—

She was in the room, standing behind a man in the chair, both facing the window, his back to her. She felt the other presence, the other man, just to her right and she was able to turn and look at him. He looked back at her and . . . he seemed ageless, a friendly face surrounded by a golden glow, he was smiling and nodding yes. He reached out for her hand and when they touched she felt a rush of pulsing energy, filling her, beaming from her.

Then the fire, outside the window, growing stronger, the room getting hotter, and the man in the chair turned, with the raging face, the piercing red eyes, and he started to howl and she felt herself shrinking, faltering.

Then she felt her new friend squeezing her hand and she squeezed back, then took the largest breath of her life and sent the exhale like a mighty wind—

Muriel awoke. Just laid there for several minutes, sweaty, the sheets drenched and fast turning clammy, but a glorious feeling because it meant she was alive. She looked at the clock: 4:15.

Though she would not know for certain for a few more hours, she was pretty sure she just helped murder Ted Tiller.

Chapter 52

After their conversation with Jubilee—Leo Sharpski, according to Alex—Carver had had to run to an official dinner for a visiting dignitary. "I hate to be spending time on something that's been rendered irrelevant by recent events, but the food will be good. And I can't remember eating today so I must be hungry. Then I'm turning in early because we need to hit the ground running tomorrow. It will be a day to remember, I promise you that. Something to tell the grandchildren about. Lots to do. Neutralize the anti-Jubilees. Move several revolutionary bills through Congress. Announce the Jubilee. And bring the American people along, every step of the way. So, Roosevelt Room at seven?"

They all said yes and then good-bye. Trenton decided to follow the president's lead and try for some sleep. "There's really nothing for us to do till the morning, nothing that the night crew can't handle. I'll be at Homeland by four to track the FBI raids and new Jubilee vics. Let's just hope to Christ that Tiller doesn't screw things up again. Six o'clock should do for you guys—time enough to get up to speed and then over to the White House by seven. Get some rest."

Joss had taxied to the White House, so Alex gave her a ride back to her car. Along the way, they debated stopping for a late bite, but decided instead on a five-fifteen breakfast at the all-night Starbucks. Sufficient sleep, then start the big day with a good breakfast—sensible rules for revolutionaries.

When they pulled up behind her car in the Homeland garage, Joss had a weird flash that they were returning from a date. Like Alex might lean over and try to kiss her good night. The moment passed and she got of the car, unkissed, into her car, and home to bed. Six hours of deep, dreamless sleep later, she sat bright-eyed and well-rested across from an equally rejuvenated Alex, munching a muffin and sipping her first latte of the day.

After settling in with their breakfasts, they had turned right to their Books for the early reports. The news was all good. FBI was calling the raids a total success. Nearly three hundred potential bad guys taken in and detained. Most of them weren't exactly hardened criminals and many were already talking, so further arrests were coming. Tons of weapons, including C4 and other explosives, would be locked down for as long as Homeland decreed. The goal was not to eradicate the anti-government movement—it was more important than ever that America behave like a genuine democracy, including showing tolerance for healthy opposition. But they hoped to eliminate once and for all the notion that violence was ever an acceptable expression of dissent.

As a sign that Homeland and Jubilee were following the same track, two of the perps the feds went after were found dead in their beds. Texas congressman Danny Whitehead was the loudest voice in the Texas Succession Movement, a proud gun-slinging militiaman who on a local broadcast yesterday afternoon said that the Dallas bomber "was just a poor, misguided but patriotic American trying to stop Jubilee Carver's big-government take over."

Ben Tucker lived in a heavily armed, off-grid compound in Utah, with his three wives, fourteen children and a dozen other polygamist families. He'd been a major force within the militia movement, in print, on the radio and online. His website, WateringTheTreeOfLiberty.com, had been calling for the blood of tyrants—just about anyone holding office in America—for years. His attempted arrest was the only serious firefight that the FBI got into, though it folded fast when the families realized Tucker had died during the night. Or, as even the feds were now putting it, "got jubileed."

Each branch of the military had also carried out selective detentions, focusing on officers who were known to favor armed insurrection. Here again there was a match with Jubilee: Major David Booth, General Carney's aide, who had taken the general's place in the coup plotting. When the MPs arrived they found he him dead of an apparent cerebral hemorrhage.

So three down, but no word on Tiller yet. Then Joss got the beep of an incoming skype, from Muriel Matson.

MURIEL: You up yet?

JOSS: You bet. How'd it go last night?

MURIEL: I was there, same dream, except the woman was gone. I communicated, I guess, with the man, a phenomenal experience, lucid dreaming to the nth, I can't begin to describe it. After we connected I helped him . . . can't believe I'm saying this . . . kill somebody. Felt like it was Tiller, but I really don't know. I don't really know if it even happened. Heard anything yet?

JOSS: Nothing, but will let you know as soon as.

Joss clicked off and then asked Alex, "You got anything on Tiller? Because Muriel says he is indeed dead and she helped."

"Wow . . . wait a second . . . I just have to get my brain around that."

"Pretty much validates their fears, doesn't it, if she could learn it in four days. Like Sharpski said in his first message: Imagine a world in which the ability to kill anybody, easily, without any chance of getting caught, was widespread."

Alex was doing that thing where he's nodding yes and shaking no at the same time. "It's like psi went straight from parlor games to the atom bomb. No wonder they were scared. And, if I read Sharpski right, they also suspect it gave his wife cancer." He looked at his watch. "Time to boogie."

Fifteen minutes later they'd taken their seats at the large conference table in the Roosevelt Room, just across from the Oval Office. Present were the Secretaries of State, Defense, Homeland Security, Commerce, and the Treasury, the National Security Advisor, the CIA and FBI directors, Vice President Riles, the Joint Chiefs chairman, and Attorney General Bellow, plus Trenton, Alex, and Joss. And, of course, the president, who seemed to Joss to grow more imposing every time she saw him.

President Carver had begun by explaining that he'd spoken personally with each Cabinet member who wasn't at the table, as well as a dozen key legislators. Everyone knew their role over this next critical twenty-four hours. But it was within this group that the heavy lifting would be done, and they had one hour to think it through and get to work.

They started with updates on the morning raids from Homeland Secretary Varnum and FBI Director Wilson. Though everyone at the table already knew how well things had gone, it was still a big lift to hear them go over it. When the president asked if they should be worried about more bombings today, or violence of any kind, Varnum answered without hesitation.

"No sir. Though of course we can never rule out the possibility of some isolated nut acting on his own, we have absolutely crippled any organized schemes. We've shut down every radical-right group in the country. And because of Dallas, not only are the American people behind us, so are some of the guys we arrested. Any positive veneer the militias ever had is gone. I have to say, all my time at Homeland, they've been the third rail; we couldn't go after them even though some of us saw them as bigger threats than al-Qaeda. Well, we're driving a stake through the whole movement now."

"And long overdue," said Wilson, "especially when they started showing up at political rallies with loaded guns. And you're right, Alan, they'd spun themselves into untouchable status. Had a lot of help from certain media honchos who are no longer with us. But they made a big mistake in Dallas, now it's up to us to make sure those deaths count for something good."

Varnum then ran through the morning's victims: they had four so far, the three Joss already knew about, plus—best news of an already great day—Ted Tiller. She suppressed her impulse to stand up and cheer since only she, Alex, Trenton, and Carver knew that Tiller was the missing sixth from yesterday, and most likely the man behind Dallas. She zipped off a quick text to Muriel: **TT confirmed**.

The president turned to Defense Secretary Locke. "Bob, I realize that the changes you're making won't be happening overnight and I have to think the Jubilees understand that too. You've got the old problem of turning a battleship around at sea, multiplied a million-fold. But I need to be able to say something later today that indicates we're moving in the direction of post-empire America. You've had two whole days to work on it," Carver said with a big smile. "What can you tell us?"

As a lifelong Republican, Locke was the most conservative man on Carver's team, and the president half-expected he would just quietly resign rather than go along with the Jubilee agenda. While he hadn't resigned, neither had he made any public statements or given any indication as to where he stood.

"Yes sir, Mr. President. To first answer the question I imagine many of you must have," he said, scanning the table, "consider me a convert to the goal of 'rational defense.' It's the right thing to do and the right time to do it. Because there is so much about our current system that is irrational in the extreme. In particular, our *offensive* posture and everything that goes with it." He held up one finger. "Weapons systems that the nation can't afford and that are no longer needed given the capabilities of potential enemies." Two fingers. "Foreign bases that no longer serve useful purpose for the host country—more money we can't afford and all we get is locals who resent America." Three fingers. "Supporting, encouraging, hell, economically depending on an arms industry that keeps the world constantly at war." Four fingers. "Worst of all, getting stuck in these long-term occupations. Nothing but death and sorrow and more people who hate us."

He paused for a sip of water while everyone at the table imagined an inoffensive America.

Locke continued. "General McAdams and I have been working together on this nonstop since the manifesto went out. The part that seems easiest—winding down bases in non-combat circumstances and bringing those troops home—will actually take the longest. However much they may want us gone, in places where we've been for a long time we are integral to the local economies. We believe our departures should be scheduled with enough lead time so that host countries can adjust. Could be as short as a few months, we just need to consult them on the timing.

"But as for Iraq and Afghanistan: Mr. President, we're recommending immediate withdrawal." A wave of fidgeting went around the table. Several looked to a stone-faced General McAdams, who answered with a barely perceptible nod. "We've looked at all the arguments for staying, hell, I've been out on point making the case—the insurgents will take over if we leave now; the Maliki and Karzai governments aren't strong enough to manage their own affairs yet; we're needed to hold Iran and Pakistan in check; we need a strong presence in the region to maintain access to oil; if we leave now and it all goes to hell, then the blood and treasure spent has been in vain. All good points, but the thing is, we could stay another ten years and spend a trillion dollars and five thousand more lives and there's no guarantee of any improvement. To the contrary.

"So, we take our lumps, swallow our pride, get out, and let this be a turning point for the world. Imperialism, super-powerism, one country dictating to everyone else—that's over. We're done and no one's taking our place. But we don't flip to isolationism. We call on the UN to start living up to its promise and we back up that call with a lot of money and genuine cooperation. So it's no longer us trying to nation-build and getting in the middle of civil conflicts; it's multi-national, well-funded UN peacekeepers, and they only go in when there's been a clear consensus among members to send them."

Kanofsky, who must have been a real wise-ass in high school, chimed in, "Good thing we arrested the black-helicopter crowd last night." Most everyone laughed, including Carver, who then raised a questioning eyebrow at McAdams.

The general nodded vigorously, and said, "Couple more points. The use of private contractors for military operations stops immediately. The government offers significant support to arms producers who retool for peaceful purposes, like mass transit, space exploration, renewables. And all four branches expand their training to include disaster relief and peacekeeping and whatever else is needed."

"If this is a dream," said Nathan Kane, "please, nobody wake me up."

It occurred to Joss that since Carver's "New America" speech two days ago, they'd been hearing similar tie-dyed language from the most unlikely people, first Kanofsky and Wilson, and now Locke and McAdams. The Jubilee mindset, the meme, was spreading, like a beneficial virus.

Now it was Carver who was nodding. "Naomi?" he said, turning to Secretary of State Galway. "So how does the world respond?"

"With universal approval, if heavy on the schadenfreude. We just need to finesse two big problems—North Korea and Israel."

Like the two women who preceded her as Secretaries of State, Galway too often come down on the side of the hawks, as if she had to show that girls can fight. At least so thought Joss, who was now thinking it'd be a good time for a less macho approach at State. Some of that old-time feminine.

"If we just up and leave South Korea," said Galway, "we can be certain that the tanks roll south an hour later. So we take it slow there, with ample warning, so that China and Japan can work with the UN to adequately take our place.

"As for Israel, it's my turn for heresy: we make it clear that Israel's security is still a top priority for America, but that we are no longer providing arms to Israel, Egypt, the Saudis, or anyone else. Israeli settlements stop, and enough are rolled back to create a viable Palestinian nation. Then we pump the cash equivalent of a few years of war into building something that the Palestinians can be proud to call home. We put the whole population to work, earning good wages. Along the way, they renounce suicide bombings and affirm Israel's right to exist. They cede custody of Jerusalem to the Israelis, while retaining friendly and cooperative access to the city and its many shrines and holy places. They learn to get along, while we and the rest of the world provide material support, whatever it takes."

"What about the extremists?" asked Kanofsky. "What happens when some refusenik from either side blows up a bunch of civilians? How do we keep it from triggering the next round of bloodshed?"

"Well, you know," she answered, "I've been thinking a lot about how Dallas, bad as it was, didn't derail us yesterday, how it just made us more resolute. All because of Jubilee and this dynamic they've set up. What they've managed to do, I think, is interrupt the cycle of violence—they've inflicted harm, engaged in violence, but without allowing reprisals. So presumably, when they stop killing, the cycle ends with them. I, um, I'm not sure where I'm going with this . . . but somehow, if we can approximate what they've done—"

"I don't see how," said Nathan. "It seems to me that their anonymity is the key to their effectiveness. The first day or two I'm sure there were plenty of people who would have struck back, eye for an eye, but they didn't know who to hit. Plus, the Jubilees mostly went after such unsympathetic characters. When ordinary folk are not getting hurt, when in fact they're getting helped, while the victims have all led these overfed, privileged lives, well, it's disarming, literally. It stops the cycle. But they really have to be anonymous or it all falls apart. Murder's murder. If the Jubilees and their bios were public knowledge, we'd see a ton of opposition to what they're doing. The right would be tearing them to pieces.

"So, if what you're suggesting is that the US government start jubileeing the Israeli and Palestinian extremists, or Ahmadinejad, or Kim Jong-il, it's really no different than the targeted assassinations we've tried for years. When everyone knows who pulled the trigger, it just feeds into the vengeance cycle."

"No, I agree, Nathan," said Galway, "and really wasn't suggesting that. I'm just saying: they found a way to break the cycle and it's working here. Now we need the same thing in the Middle East. Another batch of dead oligarchs or dominators or however you want to define it, and we could have the whole world speaking Jubilee."

The room got very quiet. Everyone was thinking the same thing, but no one was willing to say it. Finally, the vice president spoke up.

"Not sure how we go about this, but it seems like Jubilee's business is done here. What if we could get them to go global?"

Chapter 53

Good morning, America, and welcome to Jubilee Day Six and a special edition of the Morning Brew. I'm Annie McLaren, your guide through these crazy times. We've got another speech from the president to talk about, and an update on yesterday's bombing in Dallas, including the arrest of the low-life responsible. We've been getting a stream of reports all morning about FBI raids around the country—we'll give you the full story soon as we have it. We have yet another slate of dead dominators to talk about. And if all that weren't enough, the word is that the president will be launching the Jubilee sometime today. Plus, your calls, so pour yourself a cup and settle in for another three hours of the Morning Brew. First, these messages.

Annie pushed back from the mic and tried to slow her thumping heartbeat. Not bad, she told herself, you can do this. Relax. This was her third morning at "the golden WUSH microphone," sitting in for the illustrious but, as it turned out, *not* immortal Brew Tinsley. WUSH management couldn't say if it was temporary or long term because no one knew whether conservative talk radio would even exist in post-Jubilee America. Successful as Brew was, the demographics had been trending poorly for some time: his listeners were mostly old white men. They were an endangered species and were royally pissed about it, which gave Brew a committed and still influential audience. But their time was waning even before Jubilee made it dangerous to carry their flag.

The day after Brew's death, station management had to fill the hole fast and Annie was the simplest solution. She knew her way around the studio better than anyone because she'd been Brew's once-a-day foil for thirteen years. It had started out as a ratings booster—the conservative giant versus the milquetoast liberal in an ideological duel. For one or two segments they'd argue over an issue of the moment, she in measured, reasonable tones, he with bombast and humor and always an insult or two. *Don't be a femi-nitwit, Annie!* Always said with the practiced smile, his cover for anytime he went too far. *Just kidding. I'm an entertainer!*

The brewskis hated Annie from the start. Called in to say how they absolutely loathed her, using the most horrible terms allowed on AM radio—*the voice of a shrieking crone . . . the intelligence of a toad . . . wrong, pitifully wrong about everything.* Of course, they had to listen in to work up to such hostility, and listen in they did. Her little time on the air consistently had the best numbers for listeners and advertisers. She bided her time, enduring the doormat treatment because the pay was good and (here she was delusional) she thought the show was slowly transforming into something unique, the country's only ideologically balanced talk show.

That never happened. But she did eventually parlay her numbers into a fixed segment—the last half hour of every show. More important, she was permitted to argue in earnest and to make winning points, though Brew always got the last word. And the loudest. Add in the high six-figure salary and she found it easy to put up with Brew's harangues, as well as the complaints from her friends who thought she was selling out.

Though it was risky drawing conclusions from the past two days, what they knew so far was that the audience had remained steady, though calls were way down. The fear was that they were tuning in for reruns of Brew, or just out of habit, but that they still hated Annie and would switch off to the first conservative talker willing to step back in the ring.

Still, of those who did call in, many were encouraging. They'd identify themselves as longtime listeners and then indicate some way in which recent events had changed them. Some were even complimentary of Annie—that never happened before. If the Jubilees were gaining converts among the brewskis, then her notion of a fair and balanced show, with calm and deliberate discussions, was not so far-fetched after all.

Like the prez said, it's a New America.

Chapter 54

Joss stood outside the White House Press Briefing Room with her Book open, cramming in a few more details for the televised press briefing she'd be giving in a few minutes. Though the president would be doing his own appearance later in the day, that would be devoted entirely to rolling out the Jubilee and other items in the manifesto. Her job now was to provide updates and answer questions about Dallas, the FBI's morning raids, the threats of further anti-government attacks, and the new Jubilee victims.

Carver had taken her aside as the meeting was breaking up. "What I need you to do is put people totally at ease about these threats of violence. Make it clear that Dallas and the email and the 'blood on Jubilee's hands'—we're talking about a very small group of anti-American radicals. Stress the polling that shows that the people in the military overwhelmingly approve of the changes we're implementing and that approval among civilians is up to 96 percent."

"If they ask about our attempts to identify the Jubilees? Stopping the killings, bringing them to justice?"

He'd answered with a crooked smile that she interpreted as: don't tell them anything. Just say whatever you must to change the subject. And, by the way, the president didn't just tell you to lie.

Chances are they wouldn't bring it up. Reporters need something to write about and the Jubilee investigation had provided zilch in that regard. Whereas Dallas and the morning raids would keep them busy for days. Not to mention that in just a few hours Carver would give them Jubilee, tax reform, universal healthcare, and the end of the American empire.

Oughta sell a few papers.

Joss took a deep breath, let it out slowly, and stepped up to the podium. The room was packed. In the back was a phalanx of television cameras and she had the unsettling thought that she was now being watched by millions of people. She squelched the impulse to duck behind the podium, introduced herself, and then recounted the pursuit and arrest of Boyd Hardin, the Dallas bomber.

"Law enforcement was well aware of Hardin before yesterday, and for that matter, before Jubilee. Some of you may remember a Justice Department report on the danger of the anti-government movement—a report done by the Bragg administration—which Secretary Varnum drew attention to when he took over at Homeland Security. We were harshly criticized at the time for casting aspersions on so-called freedom-loving patriots. Well, Justice got it right. Homeland Security and the FBI took the report very seriously and we've been watching men like Boyd Hardin ever since. So we not only were able to arrest him within three hours of the bombing, we also had a good idea of who gave him his orders and who would be next in line to carry out further acts of violence.

"This morning the FBI carried out over a hundred raids, in thirty-five states, and took more than three hundred suspected terrorists into custody."

Carver had told her to avoid using the word 'militia'—it's hard to cast something as evil when it's in the Bill of Rights—and instead to go with 'anti-government' and 'terrorist'. He especially wanted the anti-government meme to be discredited, repudiated, and, once and for all, annihilated.

"Many of those arrested are cooperating, are naming leaders and co-conspirators, and a second round of raids is already underway. We are confident that not only have we prevented any organized effort to carry out the threats of more bombings, we have permanently crippled the movement to violently overthrow our government."

Joss paused for a moment and a few dozen hands went up. She nodded to the nearest, Charles Backly from the *Post*, one of the few she recognized.

"Are all of the people being arrested suspects in the threatened bombings? And if not, what are they being charged with?"

"They are all suspected of plotting terrorist attacks against the American people. For now, they are being held without charges, except for violations that occurred during the arrest." She nodded at another hand-waver.

"Is it true that they are all members of state militias?"

"No, though many are. We have also arrested employees of private security firms, as well as several US military servicemen."

She took a few more questions, more or less repeats of what others had asked, just fleshing out details. Then she got a toughie.

"Can you explain how some of yesterday and this morning's Jubilee deaths seem almost to have been coordinated with these raids? We're hearing that three of the men who Jubilee killed this morning were also raided by the FBI. And yesterday there were the CEOs of Taylor Dann and Kontrain, plus an Army general."

"Good question. We noticed the apparent correlation also. But it's really not that surprising. As I said earlier, we've had our eyes on these anti-government groups for years. As this past week has unfolded, we feared that Jubilee might be forcing their hand and pushing them into action, fears that were validated in Dallas. So, for our part, this morning's raids have been coming for a long time. As for the Jubilees, all I can say is that we have been impressed all along with their political savvy. They seem to have understood the nature of threat posed by the anti-government movement and have been attacking it from the start—"

"Are you saying that General Eisley was a terrorist?"

Shit. Didn't want to go there.

"No, just that all of Jubilee's choices, the men they've killed, taken together, have systematically removed resistance to their agenda. They're smart. So it's not at all surprising that they anticipated the possibility of violent reactions and that we both went after the same anti-government terrorists."

Time to change the subject.

Joss did a smooth segue into the day's Jubilee victims. First, she confirmed the reporter's statement, explaining that Major David Booth, Texas militiaman Danny Whitehead, and Ben Tucker, the Utah polygamist, were each targets of the FBI raids and all three died in their sleep. Then, with a minimum of detail, she named Ted Tiller. Finally, she announced that two more private security firms had lost their CEOs. With Taylor Dann and Kontrain reeling from the loss of their CEOs, Lawrence Flint of KKR and Duggal McCheney of Bally-Horten had been poised, however briefly, to move their companies to the top of the heap. Instead, they were jubileed. The top four private security firms in America were facing serious financial and legal difficulties.

With that, she called an end to the press conference. She noted that there'd been no more vigorously waving hands or voices calling out for one last question. They had a lot to write about.

Chapter 55

Source: The Sarah Meadow Show

SARAH MEADOW: Good morning and thank you for tuning in to this special edition of the show. Not only is it very early in the morning for me, the network has decided to make a day of it—we'll be here all day, sharing the hosting with Matt, Robert, and Suzanne. We've got a bunch of great guests lined up. We'll be talking some about the FBI raids that took place earlier today, but mostly about the monumental changes that are coming to America, all to be announced by President Wash Carver in a 3 p.m. speech before a joint session of the United States Congress.

First, we are really pleased to have a lead investigator for Homeland Security, Dr. Joss Morgan, who's just came from a press conference in which she talked about the FBI raids that have, we hope, neutralized the threat of any repeats of yesterday's horror in Dallas. Thank you for coming, Dr. Morgan.

JOSS MORGAN: Please, call me Joss. And it's my pleasure, I'm a big fan.

SARAH: Well, you're very kind. Let's start with these raids, for those who missed the presser.

JOSS: Sure. The main thing to know is that there has for a long time been an anti-government movement in this country that has managed to cover itself in a veil of respectability. So when Tim McVeigh killed 168 people in Oklahoma City, in April '95, even though he was an avowed member of the militia movement, the Clinton administration made little attempt to tie the two together, to rein in the militias, or to even point to their violent rhetoric as a contributing factor in McVeigh's evolution.

SARAH: I was just starting college when it happened. As I remember it, the militias were cast as true patriots, with First Amendment rights to say whatever they wanted and Second Amendment rights to arm themselves to the teeth. And Bill Clinton—well, he was trying to live down the draft-dodger rap and didn't have the support, really, to take on military culture.

JOSS: Sure, that was a lot of it. Plus, what had already happened at Ruby Ridge and Waco. So instead they tried to appease the militias and to treat McVeigh as an aberration. And I imagine they felt like it worked, because some of the militias did in fact disband, while the rest faded into the background. For a time. But it wasn't because of anything the government did, it was because of the ugliness of McVeigh's actions, the fact that he targeted civilians, including a daycare center.

SARAH: So they just took a few years to regroup and reload?

JOSS: Exactly. Fast forward twelve years, and the hard-right Bragg administration issues a report detailing the serious dangers of the militias, white supremacists, and other anti-government groups. These are people who profess extreme hatred not only for the federal government and all of its employees, but also for seventy percent of the American people.

SARAH: These are not friendly folks. Or good citizens.

JOSS: No, not at all. They are the very opposite and it's past time that we stop treating them with deference or respect. Oklahoma City and Dallas showed us who they really are: anti-American thugs.

Source: The Daily Liar

Today's the day, my friends. If all goes according to schedule, the President of the United States will announce a course correction like this country has never seen before. Bigger than the New Deal. Bigger than ending slavery. Bigger than the frikkin' American Revolution. Bigger than Jesus H. Himself. Like nothing the world has ever seen before.

We will, in one fell swoop, greatly reduce the gap between the overfed rich and the rest of us; convert to a simple progressive taxation system; fund the safety net of a 21st-century social democracy; erase everyone's debts (unclear for now just how far this one's going or how it will work); regulate lending to prevent the evils of usury in the future; reform campaign finance; end two wars; roll back the American empire; and channel a lot of the money saved into the environment and renewable energy.

Not bad for six days work.

As someone who has spent the past ten years in this space chronicling the daily lies of the politicians, corporate fat cats, banksters, generals, and pundits who run this country, I have to add that it's been a refreshing six days. While I suspect Wash Carver has not told us everything, I'm pretty sure he hasn't lied to us.

Nor have the Jubilees. In fact, quite the opposite: starting with their first Sunday morning message they've been delivering the all-caps TRUTH, straight up. *Here's what ails you, America, here's how we're going to fix it, and this is what will happen if you don't take your medicine.*

Carver's transition from liar-in-chief to Honest Wash has been a revelation to watch. His Day One remarks were classic high-official obfuscation. The next couple days he didn't say much, though you got the feeling his internal sands were shifting. Then came the Manifesto, followed by his Day Four speech. A once-in-a-lifetime presidential speech that was completely devoid of lies, hypocrisies, self-serving spin, and political compromises. And yesterday's speech was more of the same: an American president who looked his people in the eye and gave them the unvarnished truth and nothing but.

If this keeps up I may have to change the name of the blog.

Source: DC•PM

MATTHEW CRISSOM: Hold on George, you're saying she was covering something up? You're not sure exactly what, but you just know she's lying and whatever it is is enough to cast doubt on everything Jubilee and we should just shut it all down, forget the whole thing, it's time to reboot the status quo and power on?

GEORGE DEEDS: The reporter asked a simple question: How could the FBI and the Jubilees, two supposedly separate entities—how do they end up with at least three, and probably more, common targets? You might find refuge in coincidence, Matt, but I do not.

JUDY ROTHBERG: Sometimes a coincidence is just a coincidence, George. I mean, there's nothing mysterious here. As Dr. Morgan said, Bragg identified these guys as problems several years ago. We've been watching them ever since and if Dallas had happened in a non-Jubilee universe, we would have done exactly what we did this morning.

DEEDS: That explains *our* choices, Judy, but doesn't tell us how Jubilee came to choose the same.

JONATHON ROBART: Well, sorry, George, but it seems to me you're clutching at straws. I'm inclined to agree with Matt and Judy on this.

DEEDS: On this and a whole lot more, Jon. Lately, you're inclining like you've had few too many rounds of Jubilee Kool-Aid.

ROBART: Maybe I have, George, but better that than inventing ridiculous scenarios, like Franke come back to life. I just don't share your distrust of Carver or the Jubilees. And while some of the economic stuff goes against long-held conservative principles, the economy is in serious trouble and none of the usual fixes from the left or the right have worked. In fact, a tax break for the rich now, or cutting Social Security benefits, or further dismantling financial regulations—all these time-honored conservative fixes—they'd be the death of us, make no mistake, way worse than the '30s.

DEEDS: You can't have had too tight a hold on those principles to so easily flip toward an anti-wealth, income redistribution scheme that only a Communist could love.

ROTHBERG: Dear Lord, George, red-baiting is so twentieth century. And what Carver will propose today bears zero resemblance to the old Soviet Union. Or anything else that we've known. That's the whole point, the reason this can work—it's all new, George. A new America. Post-partisan. Post-oligarchy. Post-empire.

CRISSOM: And post-neocon, George. Good time for an ideology upgrade.

Chapter 56

Leo had always been early riser, up and going before six. He could not remember ever sleeping past seven, at least not since he was a teenager. But he and the others had all been sleeping as late as nine this past week. They'd just figured it was due to exhaustion: they were staying awake past midnight so that they'd do the sacs early in the dream cycle. After which, the assumption was, they were so energy-depleted they needed the extra downtime.

But when Leo popped awake in the pre-dawn dark, noted it was just past five and that he felt well-rested and ready to go, he realized that, at least for him, it wasn't exhaustion that had been keeping him asleep after the dreams; it was staying connected to Dorothea. Leo was awake now because Dorothea wasn't in the dream last night.

And then it went through him like a cold breeze—the Tiller fiasco, Dorothea's collapse, hearing the report from Dallas, her final moments—and he had to lie there for a long, long time, breathing in his new reality: waking up without her, facing life without her. *Dorothea's gone, Leo, she's really gone.*

Ah, sweetie.

What they say is true: you take it one moment at a time and eventually you stir, emerge, and move on, even from the hardest losses. After a while, his thoughts turned to last night's dream. Tiller had come at him again, stronger, even more ferocious, and if Leo had been alone he may very well have failed. But the observer was there again—Muriel Matson, he assumed—and they had linked up, combined forces, and were able to defeat Tiller.

Amazing, really. Pretty much confirmed Eva's concern that the dream could get out of the circle and into the wild. Still, Muriel must have been a strong dreamer to begin with since she'd apparently been present for her husband's death and every dream after that. Truly amazing.

Leo finally rolled out of bed, shaved and showered, made himself toast and coffee, settled in the den, and turned on the tube. Though he rarely watched TV, and never in the daytime, today was special, to put it mildly. So he also fired up the laptop—he wanted as many views into the American zeitgeist as possible. How were Americans reacting? What were they hoping for? What were they most afraid of? Was anyone resisting, protesting? Any serious threats to worry about? Would they need to do more sacs? Could they really have succeeded with just thirty-five?

They'd had years to ponder the shift and originally saw it taking much longer, months at least, while they'd be chipping away at the status quo, replacing old leaders with new, until they reached critical mass. He and Joe must have spent thousands of hours gaming the different scenarios in rambling, late-night conversations. Whenever they'd hit a serious hitch, they'd just dream on it, separately for several nights, then they'd co-dream it for several more until the issue resolved. In this way, they slowly fine-tuned the sacrifice dream, worked out the timing and targets, and came up with the language for the emails and the Manifesto.

Yet even with such refinements, the shift could still have taken months if not for the Internet. Though, as a bunch old fogies, they didn't really get it until Brett and Mia joined the group, the ability to communicate with the whole nation instantly, and then have a trillion simultaneous sub-conversations going on in blogs, tweets, texts, and forwarded emails—well, it all quickened the shift dramatically. So that, six days ago when they finally got started, the expectation was around ten days and sixty sacs.

Still, for all the years of dreaming and scheming and thinking it through, Leo'd never been able to picture this day, Jubilee

Day, when America changes its mind about all the big things. It wasn't that he didn't believe, but at this point so much depended on the actions of others. A flat and uninspired presidential speech today could queer the whole deal, as could a poorly-planned, haphazard Jubilee. Or the piggies who run the military-industrial complex could be just pretending to be on the team, while having no intention of letting their budgets be slashed or their wars reined in. Or the crazies who took over the House last year could pull together, realize the safety in numbers, and just refuse to pass the critical legislation.

Bottom-line, we were dealing with human beings under great stress and there was just too much you could not predict or control.

On the other hand, Leo was not at all worried about Carver. It wasn't just that his past two speeches had been so extraordinary; the president had perfectly modeled the shift to the American people and in particular to the wealthy and powerful. The nation had watched him change his thinking, shifting from his Day One outrage and pledge that "this will not stand!" to a bold and clear-eyed modern Moses, leading his people into a better world. Add a few other highly visible shifters—especially Ryan Weathers at Marsdale Lipman—and the Jubilee meme had spread like fire in a bone-dry forest.

No, if there was trouble today, Leo was sure it would not come from the Carver administration. Nor the military or the bankers or even the Christian right. It would be something they hadn't foreseen, some group they'd never thought about, mundane, low-level, some significant sector of the American population that just couldn't let go and shift.

Leo was clicking through channels and came to an interview with Joss Morgan. As she ran down the success of the morning raids, Leo felt himself relaxing, releasing pockets of stress he hadn't been aware of. Fucking Dallas. Though they had in fact foreseen such a possibility, they had dreamed it through, they'd fully resolved it. Never would have happened if not for Tiller, which never would have happened if not for—

The doorbell rang. He heard the front door opening seconds later and then Joe calling out, "Wake up, Leo, it's Jubilee Day!"

Chapter 57

Around noon the country fell into a pre-speech lull that Alex called "the eye of the Jubilee." The winds of mega-change were imminent, yet for these last few hours there was little to say and less to do. So America was holding its collective breath, awaiting the new reality. It was widely understood that the president would be announcing such monumental changes that by the time everyone returned to work on Monday—and that's where the thinking stopped. A whole lot of jobs, indeed, entire industries could be disappearing, while new industries were called into being. No one had any idea how it would all come down.

The president sent out a brief note to those at the morning meeting, saying: "You've all done exceptional work, all the more remarkable because you did it under such enormous pressure. My speech is written and I am absolutely, one hundred percent confident that this is going to work. We are taking a giant leap today, into a New America. The only unfinished business is legislative; the House, no surprise, is moving a little slowly. So I will be spending these next couple hours working with Speaker Tannen, dotting i's and crossing t's. We will get it done. After the speech, I want each of you making the rounds, doing interviews, answering questions, talking the American people through the changes. For now, however, it's better that there not be any further official statements before my speech. So I've set up a lunch for you in the family dining room. Please take a well-deserved break."

So it was that Joss found herself sharing a scrumptious meal with Alex, Nathan Kane, Zia Carillo, Secretary of State Galway, and CIA Director Kanofsky. Most of the others from the earlier meeting—Trenton, FBI Director Russell, General McAdams, and Defense Secretary Locke—were busy with the continuing take-down of anti-government factions within the military and militias. The vice president was on the Hill, twisting arms.

They'd settled around the table and then awaited their food with but a few perfunctory stabs at small talk. After the food arrived, they ate in silence for the first few minutes, each of them deep in contemplation of the rapidly shifting realities. Finally, Kanofsky took the words right out of Joss's head.

"Six days ago, the odds of us breaking bread together were too high to calculate." He looked at Nathan Kane as he spoke, then Naomi Galway. "Off-the-charts high. Never-in-a-million-years high." He flashed a big smile. "Last night, after they'd nailed the Dallas bomber and I knew that was it, there'd be no stopping this . . . this New America, I had a long video chat with my grandson, just turned ten. Never in my life have I laughed so much." Now his eyes slightly watered. "Until now, the odds of that happening were also. . . ." He shook his head in wonder.

It could have been an awkward moment but it just wasn't. Everyone knew what he was talking about.

Secretary Galway, who'd had a good shot at becoming President Galway if not for Wash Carver, nodded, smiled, and said, "I hear you, Tom. Whoever said 'There's nothing so powerful as an idea whose time has come' really captured this moment. This idea—that society's dominant share their wealth and power—has just, I don't know, infected us all. It's like mass hysteria, only this is what? Mass happiness? Trust? Faith in the human spirit?"

There was nodding around the table, except for Zia Carillo, who had the furrowed brows of nagging doubt.

"I don't know, maybe I've just been on the national security beat for too long . . . though, I know, some of you've been dealing with the same bleak and dangerous world as I have, and for much longer," she said, with a nod to Kanofsky. "So maybe it's just me, but this feels a little too storybook. Suddenly, all the aggressive and difficult and greedy people in the world decide to lay down their weapons and give their money to the poor? Universal kumbaya? I can't shake the feeling that some horrible push-back's coming, like Dallas but worse. And the thing is, intellectually I'm right there with it all, the full Jubilee. I want to believe, but. . . ."

As she listened, Joss took Zia's doubts to heart. How much has my thinking changed, really? How deep the "infection"? What would it take to throw me back into the pre-Jubilee dog-eat-dog, trust-nobody world? Have we really changed so much? She could sense the bare outline of an answer, something about the *shared* infection, when Alex spoke up.

"Naomi's not the first to describe what's happening to us as an infection. Past couple days I've heard it called a meme, a social virus, a virulent idea. The point is, it's something real. We're not just talking in metaphors or abstractions. I think we're looking at actual entities—virus-like packets of thought—that spread through society, person-to-person, just like ordinary viruses, or computer viruses. Only instead of disease or the latest malware, we get an improved outlook, a more benign political philosophy."

Zia looked unconvinced but Nathan was nodding vigorously. "I think you're right, Alex," he said, "and this could be what the Jubilees had in mind all along. Their whole message was directed at the 'dominators,' who, we might say, are infected with the 'domination virus'. People deciding things based on who has the most money or the biggest army or the greater willingness to use force. A very old social virus that's been plaguing humanity for millennia. You can see it in the cycle of violence, how hard, really, how impossible it is to stop once it gets going. A single act of violence infects the victims with viral domination, so the victims strike back, which strengthens the infection in everybody. Two thousand years later, the infection rages on, people keep killing each other because they're all too sick to see another way. Too war-sick. Too domination-sick."

"Greed-sick," added Alex, "Empire-sick."

"Look, I'm not quite there yet, but for argument's sake—" said Zia, "The Jubilees release their virus into the wild and in six days they've changed three hundred million people?"

"It's feasible," said Kanofsky. "We've got studies showing that a really nasty virus, or something like bubonic plague, could spread that fast these days. Computer viruses are even faster. And nothing's faster than the Internet, which the Jubilees have played perfectly. The first message achieved global saturation in a few hours. That, combined with their, uh, unique decapitation process, and they had ninety-two percent approval in four days. If we assume that approval is a sign of infection by the meme, then, yes, it can spread that fast."

"You know, I was in Israel on Day One," said Naomi, "trying, in vain, to get them to stop the settlements. The thing is, when you spend time with the Israelis, listening to their complaints, their fears, their justifications for what they do, there is a logic to it all that is hard to refute. You start thinking like them. Their most belligerent and bullying actions seem inevitable, unavoidable. Even righteous. Whatever hopes and plans I'd had for easing tensions, let alone bringing lasting peace to the region. . . ."

She paused, and closed her eyes for a moment. Then she turned to Nathan. "From the moment I stepped on Israeli soil I was infected—war-sick."

Nathan nodded. "Eye for an eye, tooth for a tooth. It may be the oldest meme in the world."

It was a sobering thought, because it was easy to imagine fallout from the Middle East overtaking all the good that was happening in America.

"Takes us back to this morning's big question," said Joss. "The Jubilees may have done all they need to do for us, but what about the rest of the world? If they don't make the same shift, won't they just reinfect us?"

Chapter 58

Speaker John Tannen. He just loved the sound of that. It'd been a full year and he never got tired of it. Loved the power of the office. Loved that he was second in line for the presidency. Loved that at the State of the Union he got to sit behind Carver with a serious mien and no applause, letting America know just how much he and his party loathed this one-term farce of a president.

When they took back the House last year, elevating him to Speaker, he'd been crystal clear about his job: make sure Carver did not get reelected. Period. Which meant, in turn, saying no to and actively blocking anything the man tried to accomplish. Didn't matter what it was. Didn't matter if it was originally a Republican idea. Didn't even matter—this part was tricky—if the country desperately needed it. All that mattered was getting Republicans back in control of the presidency and the Senate. Then they could get to work doing the nation's business.

Truth is, it wasn't personal. Tannen was not the racist that the left accused him of being, nor was Carver the flaming socialist that the right accused him of being. Tannen found Carver a reasonable enough man and a bipartisan centrist. Under other circumstances they'd be friends and colleagues. But politics was politics and it often got ugly. More to the point, politics was expensive and if you wanted to stay in office, then you quid pro quoed the people and corporations that paid your bills.

Just the way it was and, thanks to Citizens United, the way it would always be. Elections would just get ever more expensive and candidates ever more beholden to ever more corporate cash.

The best democracy money could buy.

His first year as Speaker had unfolded exactly as expected. Even in the rare instances when he wanted to throw Carver a bone, he had nearly eighty new representatives, most of them Tea Party certified, who insisted on throwing bombs instead. It'd been a year of gridlock and investigations. Though the public wasn't all that happy with it, they were less happy with Carver and the Democrats. Tannen's challenge was to push it as hard as he could, without going over the line that Gingrich crossed in the nineties.

All was going according to plan until Sunday, November 6th. Just five mind-boggling days ago. Like 9/11, today—11/11/11—would no doubt become part of the national vocabulary. Tannen had no doubt whatsoever which day would turn out to have *really* changed everything. It was certainly changing him.

At 8 a.m. on Sunday, he'd been enjoying his usual quiet breakfast with Marie, without a whiff or the faintest premonition of what was coming. Ronnie Barlow had called and given him a quick rundown, including the dominator message. He'd had Ronnie read the message four times, each time slower than before. Then he'd tried to explain it to Marie but couldn't get his brain around what he'd just heard. They turned on the tube.

Fox had already switched from their regular programming and were in Huge Fucking Story mode. They were talking about five confirmed deaths at that point: Dick Mallard, Howie Croft, Judge Griffin, General Eisley, and Chuck Davis. Tannen'd had two immediate thoughts: first, if there was a number six, it was probably a senator, and if he had to guess—Robert Tofer; second, why the hell did they kill Davis instead of himself, Mr. Speaker?

It was the oddest sensation. He was a quasi-religious man, but had never believed in the God who watches everything we do, sending rewards when we're good and punishments when we're bad. Just too much evidence against it. But at that moment, Tannen had felt that he was indeed being watched, judged, and would be punished or not depending on his actions. Again, he had the queerest feeling, an internal tingling, all over. A quick shiver ran through him.

Marie had been thinking along the same lines and had come right out and said it: "Why Chuck Davis instead of you?" The moment she spoke the words she'd started crying. He'd muted the TV and they'd clung together for a long time, Marie crying softly and he going over and over it in his head until finally he had the answer.

"They think I'm someone they can work with."

Chapter 59

Some people, the closer they are to the end of something, the harder it gets; so hard, in fact, that they may never get there at all. Their lives become an accumulation of unfinished business and unsatisfied expectations. Wash Carver was just the opposite. With the end in sight, he'd get stronger and more determined, like he was tapping into resources reserved just for finishing up. His life, from the poor and ragged streets of Roxbury to the posh private quarters of the White House, had been a tale of lofty goals met, each accomplishment setting the bar a little higher for the next.

Once he became president, however, that all changed. He came into office with so much that he wanted to do. Getting out of Iraq and Afghanistan. Fixing healthcare. Ending the war on drugs. Immigration reform. Rebuilding the nation's international standing. Dealing with global warming. Taking a strong lead on renewables. He'd wanted all of it, had set the goals, and after achieving the first big step—winning the election—he'd rolled up his sleeves, ready to work, fully expecting that he would follow it all through to a successful finish.

Talk about your rude awakenings. From election day forward, the economy and the goddamn banking crisis pushed everything else to the side. With real unemployment over twenty percent and millions of homes facing foreclosure and sixty million people without health insurance and the banks claiming they needed trillion-dollar bailouts or the whole global economy was going down—all of which Carver inherited from Bragg—it sucked up all of his time and political capital. That he nonetheless managed to push through the Health Reform Act was a huge achievement, though even there he'd had to give up on universality to get it passed, which diminished it considerably.

For the first time in his life, Carver had started to feel unlucky. Not in a self-pitying way—he'd never sink that far—but practically speaking, he'd had the misfortune to take over for the most incompetent president in history, who left behind a slew of mega-disasters, each feeding into the next, and no solutions for any of it. Carver had had a good laugh at the post-election political cartoon that showed him as the black janitor, mop and bucket in hand, entering the White House to clean up Bragg's mess. It stopped being funny in a hurry.

When they lost the House, things got even worse. Much worse. Becoming a one-term president started to look more like a reprieve than a failure. Even if it meant he left so much unfinished.

Then his luck returned—jubilantly so. Sunday morning, he'd seen the Jubilees as just one more impossible mess to deal with, but worse because this one could kill him. Over the next few days, he'd felt himself gradually listing in their direction; Howie aside, it was hard not to appreciate the effect that they were having on America. But Wednesday was the turning point. The first time he read the manifesto, it gave him goosebumps. As the day wore on, he slowly internalized it, thinking through each of the points, until he'd made it his new list of goals, better than the one's he'd started his presidency with, and dammit, he would see these through to completion. That evening, by the end of his conversation with Jubilee, he'd established a working partnership which left him feeling like, for the first time since he was elected, he was truly leading the nation.

In a show of good faith, and a concession to the fact that the speaker had more work to do at this point than the president, Carver had gone to the Hill to meet with John Tannen in his office. They were seated across from each other, sipping coffee, and feeling awkward. For three years, Tannen had shown nothing but animus for the president. Since becoming speaker, he'd become unapologetically belligerent. Like so many on the right, he'd been silent since Sunday, so no way to know where he stood, except that all of the Jubilee bills were stalling in the House.

"So John," said the president, holding both hands out, palms up, "where do we stand?"

Tannen took in a deep breath, then forcefully exhaled before replying.

"Mr. President, right now the House is divided into three groups. You've got 175 Democrats who are, with just three wavering, totally on board the Jubilee train. You've got 35 Republicans who, one week ago, were barely willing to call you their president, much less go along with this. But they're getting swamped with constituent calls and emails running at ninety percent approval, some even higher. Not to mention pressure from friends and family. Combine that with the danger of getting jubileed and, well, sure, they're ready to vote yea. Puts you at 207, 210.

"Then you've got 235 rock-solid conservatives who are angrier than hell at what's happening. Most of them think you're responsible, if not you then clearly liberals acting on your behalf. They don't approve of taxing the rich or ending the wars or cutting defense or regulating lenders or government healthcare or any of it. And I'm not talking casually held positions—these are bedrock principles, the whole point of being proud Republicans. You can't expect people to just abandon a lifetime of convictions, turn against everything they've ever stood for."

"Aren't they getting the same pressure from constituents?" asked Carver. "I mean, we're looking at 95% and up right now for the country, with no state below 85%. Sometimes you gotta ride the horse in the direction it's going."

Tannen just shook his head, not an expression of "no," but more "I just don't know."

"How about you, John?"

Tannen sighed. "Mr. President, every fiber of my being is screaming 'resist!' But, I have to say, I'm beginning to see that as a knee-jerk, automatic reaction, like I don't have any choice in how I react. And that doesn't feel right. I keep coming back to something you said after Dallas, to the bombers, about being on the wrong side of history."

They sat in silence for a long minute. Then Carver asked, "What's Marie want you to do?"

Tannen had to smile. Yes, he knew he was being manipulated. Carver, like so many of the great politicians, had a knack for remembering names and deftly applying the personal touch, but still. . . .

"Actually, last thing she said today was that if I didn't pass these bills, I wouldn't have to worry about getting jubileed, she'd kill me herself."

The president laughed. "Well, then, can't have *that*. Let's go find fourteen more yeas."

Chapter 60

Joss had never attended a State of the Union Address, or a Special Presidential Address, as they were calling this speech, but she'd watched enough of them on TV to know that over-long stretches of applause for the president were part of the tradition. She always found it tiresome and awkwardly self-congratulatory. But tonight, even as she registered that her hands were starting to feel bruised, she could not clap hard enough and didn't care if it ever stopped. Seemed to her that everyone in the packed House chamber felt the same.

She was standing next to Alex, up in the balcony with other invited guests. Down below were House and Senate members, along with most of the Cabinet, the Supreme Court, and the Joint Chiefs. President Carver was at the podium, smiling broadly, his hands held up, gesturing *enough already,* but clearly loving it. Behind him sat Vice President Riles and Speaker John Tannen. In a sign that something truly magical was afoot, Tannen was enthusiastically applauding, looking more like the president's number one cheerleader than the sour-pussed grinch of Carver's last State of the Union address.

When the chamber finally quieted, the president began by thanking the assembled legislators for "the most productive 48 hours in congressional history." While this triggered another long burst of self-congratulation, it was a stunning display of just how united the two parties had become. Carver continued, acknowledging a number of individuals and institutions that, in one way or another, "made this current moment possible." Turning somber-toned, he expressed his sorrow and appreciation for the thirty-five men who'd died, "decent Americans, one and all, whose lives were sacrificed for the greater good." Then, he came right out and said the once unthinkable: "Finally, we must thank

Jubilee, whoever you are. Though we may disapprove of your method, there is no question that you have acted out of a deep love of country. You have ushered in a national rebirth, cleared the path toward a New America, and for that we the American people will be eternally grateful."

There was an uneasy silence—Carver's words hanging in the air like a potentially toxic mist—but then a torrent of wild applause as everyone dared to breathe it in. The president then went to work making the case for the Jubilee and supporting legislation.

"In preparation for today, I had a long talk with our new treasury secretary, Nathan Kane. Now, despite his standing as a Nobel Prize economist, Nathan has long been disparaged as a radical leftist, a big-government socialist, and a Communist. Just about the worst things you can call an American, and I should know, I've heard 'em all."

That got everyone laughing. Alex leaned closer to Joss and said, "After this, our pundits are gonna need a whole new vocabulary."

Carver continued, "Secretary Kane suggested that I talk about America's second Civil War: the economic battle between our most wealthy citizens and everyone else. Now, this has long been a taboo topic in America, guaranteed to raise of howls of protest about class warfare. The idea being that just talking about the obvious class divisions in our society is un-American and an affront to the rich, or even worse, an act of war that empowers the lower classes at the expense of the wealthy. So we must never talk about it, should avoid even using the word 'class.'

"The net effect of our refusal to come to grips with wealth and income disparity is that we have failed to acknowledge, much less address, a host of problems caused by those very disparities. As Secretary Kane showed twenty years ago, when the income gap between the mega-rich and the average citizen grows too wide—when, say, a CEO is being paid a thousand times more than his workers—the whole society suffers. Physical and mental health declines. Incarceration rates go up, likewise rates of drug abuse, teen pregnancies, obesity, school dropouts. The wider the gap between rich and poor, the more the signs of a society under too much stress. And right now, of all the modern industrial societies, America has by far the widest, most socially destructive wealth gap."

Carver waited to let it all sink in. Joss had to appreciate the difficulty factor of making this case to so many millionaires.

"Now, here's the really bad news: the wider the wealth gap, the less democratic a society. Justice Louis Brandeis said it best, eighty years ago: 'We can have democracy in this country, or we can have great wealth concentrated in the hands of a few, but we can't have both.'" Again, he paused. "Clear as a bell: we can have democracy or we can have this ever-widening gap wealth gap. *We can't have both.* The hard truth is, over the past thirty years, as the merely rich grew into the mega-rich, America ceased to be a functioning democracy."

He waited while a jolt of unease rippled through the audience.

"That has to be the last thing you ever expected to hear from your duly elected President, I know. But believe me—America is no longer ruled of, by and for the people; it is ruled by the rich, for the rich, using the dominant powers of the rich. That makes us more a plutocracy than a democracy. We go through the motions of a majority rule democracy, but we are actually governed by our wealthiest one percent."

Another pensive pause. His audience remained quiet, hanging on his words, if not at ease with his message.

"Now, there's no big mystery to this. As we all know too well, it costs a lot of money to get elected in America; every election we spend more, and the person who spends the most money, most often wins. Once we decided that money was 'speech' and that we needed to protect the rights of the mega-rich to 'speak' without limits, well, so much for the power of one citizen, one vote. Turns out that a bucket full of thousand-dollar bills speaks a whole lot louder than a bunch of disgruntled voters. And we wonder why so many no longer bother to show up at the polls."

"Post-election, the power of money only gets stronger: every proposed act of legislation triggers a flood of contributions to key legislators. At this point, nothing gets passed around here without the financial blessings of the wealthy. Nothing. Just consider the two biggest acts of my administration to date: the financial bailouts and the Health Reform Act. In both cases, I made a series of choices and decisions that were, frankly, inexplicable to my longtime friends and supporters. Putting the very men who caused the crash in charge of the solutions. Giving approval as they engineered a massive transfer of money into their own pockets. Doing so little for the rest of the country as it became mired in a depression. Giving up on the public option and any hope for universal, nonprofit healthcare."

The president just shook his head, visibly pained.

"I am not offering excuses or asking forgiveness. Nor, really, am I casting blame, not on myself, the Congress, the courts, or the rich, for that matter. Our problems evolved over a long period of time and we cannot now point at any one individual, or event, or piece of legislation and say that that's the cause. Or that they're the villains. Rather, we gradually and incrementally shifted from the power of the people to the power of money. From democracy to plutocracy. Until a well-intended, starry-eyed president comes into office and discovers that the people no longer matter, that, in fact, the president himself only has the power to do what big money dictates."

Carver took a long slow breath, then a longer, slower exhale. Joss could sense him changing gears and moving on from what the pundits would call his 'anti-rich tirade.'

She whispered to Alex, "Enough with the diagnosis, time for some remedies."

"Our problem," continued Carver, "was 'how do we fix any of this, given that our legislative, administrative, regulatory, and electoral tools are all broken?' That was the question that was keeping me up nights and for which I had concluded there was no answer. There was no getting our democracy back and no stopping our decline. I'd become so discouraged that I was considering not running for a second term. Until this week, when everything changed."

The president stopped for a long look into the cameras and then a slow scan of the audience. His sorrowful mien gradually lifted, he seemed to grow bigger, then he spread his arms wide and flashed the patented Carver smile.

"So. Today we get our democracy back." Huge applause, with everyone on their feet. It went on and on until Carver reined it in.

"A short while ago, I signed a number of bills, all designed to reduce the wealth gap to socially-healthy levels. Jubilee Day is of course the centerpiece of the changes, and I'll get to that in a bit. But first, there were a number of moves that we had to make to set the stage. We know the Jubilee will hit some people harder than others, that there will be major economic dislocations, that some jobs, some entire industries, will disappear overnight. There is no way to avoid this. I truly regret the unfairness. But, frankly, far more—many, many, many times more—people are suffering, unfairly, in our current system, so, big picture, thinking as a nation, this is the fairest way to go. Moreover, we have taken a number of steps to cushion the blow for those who are hit hardest.

"Start with taxes. For years people have wanted a system simple enough that it could fit on a 3 x 5 card. Here it is: no more federal income tax for 99% of the American people." He waited for applause that was not quite enthusiastic—too many top-one-percenters in the room. Carver continued, "No taxes on the first $500,000 of earnings. The rate starts at 50% for everything above that, goes to 60% for everything above $1 million, 70% above $10 million, 80% above $100 million, and 90% above $1 billion. No loopholes, no deductions, except for charitable gifts, no special rates for the financial industry or capital gains or estates or corporations. Those who benefit so greatly from living and doing business in America will pay for the privilege and thereby help to keep this nation great."

He waited, nodding his head slowly, measuring the response among the legislators. The Jubilee might be the centerpiece of the proposed changes, but this move to progressive taxation went to the heart of the divide in American politics. That the Republicans didn't get up and march out of the room in protest was a very good sign.

"The hardest part of my job, by far, is the letters I write, sometimes phone calls, to those who have lost loved ones in war. We say they've made the 'ultimate sacrifice.' They surely have. And what they've given to their country, what they've sacrificed to keep America great, is so much more than we are now asking of our most prosperous citizens. If you make 50 million dollars, yes, you will be required to pay thirty-five million in taxes. But you will still have fifteen million for yourself and anyone who wants to argue that that is an unfair sacrifice, well, tell it to the mother who just lost her only son."

Okay, he wasn't quite finished beating up on the rich.

"The Preamble to the Constitution lists five purposes for government: establish justice, insure domestic tranquility, provide for the common defense, promote the general welfare, and secure the blessings of liberty to ourselves and our posterity. Taxation provides the funding to fulfill these purposes. Now, Americans have had a long debate about these terms, one that has coalesced in our current time as a debate between those who want a big well-funded government and those who say that the government that taxes and spends the least, governs the best. For forty years now the small government argument has been on the ascendent, winning the debates and driving policies. It was a Democratic president, after all, who declared 'The era of big government is over.' We were told that if we just removed government regulations and lowered taxes, then the magic of the free market would take over and America would soar to new heights.

"Well, as it turned out, America crashed badly and the only ones benefitting were the mega-rich. Small government favors the rich because, in an absence of regulatory limits and progressive taxation, those with money always win. In an unbridled, under-regulated marketplace, wealth trickles up. The rich get richer and everyone else gets poorer, as certain as night follows day.

"So, going forward from today, let us rejoin the Founders' vision of forming an ever more perfect union, where the role of government is seen as a force for good. Where we have free and open elections that bring big-hearted dreamers to Washington eager to serve the American people. Where the government that governs best, *does* its best, working hard, with determination and devotion to make America a better place. Let us proclaim that the era of big government is back, ready to take on the challenges before us."

A standing ovation erupted on the Democrats' side of the chamber and then rolled wave-like through most of the Republicans and the rest of the audience until everyone was up and cheering. Joss checked her watch; it went on for more than two minutes before Carver could speak again.

"Progressive income tax is the first step. It reduces the wealth gap and gives us the funds to do the important work of good government. We will also keep our current payroll tax, with some adjustments. Returning to the Preamble, think of this as the 'Promote the General Welfare' Tax. Everyone contributes because it funds society-wide benefits. This will continue to fund our retirement system and, over time, we may expand it to cover other social needs that are not well met by the marketplace. The first expansion, which as already been passed, is universal healthcare. Earlier today I signed a bill making Medicare available to all ages—effective immediately."

Another standing ovation rolled through the chamber, this one longer than the last. Carver then rather quickly went over four bills which he and the Congress were committed to working out in the very near future: universal secondary education, campaign finance reform, ending the drug war, and a massive jobs bill—putting Americans to work rebuilding infrastructure, restoring the environment, and "making America the world leader in the innovation, production, and use of renewable energies."

Then he announced the end of the American empire.

"Everything I've described so far will cost a lot, no question, more than we can hope to collect with taxes. So today we begin the process of greatly reducing our defense spending, with an initial goal of cutting it in half. This will not be easy. It will mean economic pain for millions of Americans, for countless businesses, for whole communities. But it has to be done.

"It would have been a lot easier to do this in 1959 when President Eisenhower warned us about the growing military-industrial complex. In essence, he tried to point out the first stages of our shift from democracy to plutocracy. Ike clearly saw what was happening—that 'national defense' was being driven more by big money and corporate profits and campaign contributions than by any rational assessment of threats to America. The dangers he so accurately described have had fifty years to metastasize and grow until, now—well, as all of you know, we spend more on defense than all the rest of the world combined. And what do we get for all that we spend? Fact of the matter is, the more aggressively we pursue our national security, the more international insecurity we create. And, because of the billions and billions wasted, we at the same time foster domestic stress and strife."

It seemed to Joss that Carver was struggling a bit with this part. Though she'd heard him rail against 'the beast' and the wars and the dangers of empire, he was still Commander in Chief and a military scholar and it had to be hard leading the greatest retreat in American history.

"Starting today," he said, "America is making a profound shift in its global identity. In the simplest terms, we are heeding the sage advice of the Founders when they cautioned against foreign entanglements. We are disentangling . . . everywhere. We currently have more than eight hundred military bases in foreign countries. Joint Chiefs chairman General McAdams is committed to closing all of our bases and bringing the troops home over the next eighteen months. This will give time for adjustments in both the foreign communities that we are leaving behind, and those in the US that we are coming home to."

The president stopped for a quick sip of water, his eyes sweeping the audience, gauging the response to what he'd said thus far. Then he took a big breath and uttered the blasphemous:

"Let me be clear—this is the end of the American military empire. The end of being arms dealer for the world. The end of intervening in civil wars. The end of using military force to control foreign resources. The end of preventive war and wars of choice and unwanted occupations.

"Going forward from today, the primary concern of the US military is rational defense of America's sovereign territories. The money and manpower that we've been spending abroad will all come home to secure our borders, to toughen our ports and transportation systems, to keep our cyber-security three steps ahead of the hackers—first and foremost, to keep the American people and their homes and communities safe from foreign invaders. We will redirect much of our military industry: from offensive weapons to defensive and non-lethal technologies; from nuclear bombs to safe and clean nuclear power; and from tanks and fighter jets to high-speed rail and windmills.

"At the same time, we will re-task the men and women of the military from the primary mission of making war to a new, higher mission of making the world a safer and better place for all. We will become experts at providing disaster relief. At environmental restoration and rebuilding infrastructure. People will join the services to be of peaceful service to others. They'll leave the services not with life-altering injuries and PTSD but with useful skills and newfound empathy and compassion."

Sounding a little too kumbaya, even for Joss. She couldn't imagine it was working for the macho boys and warrior class, and indeed, there was a lot of fidgeting in the audience. Hadn't been an ovation for any of this end-of-empire talk. Carver plowed on.

"Now, I know the world is still a dangerous place, filled with a lot of bad actors, hostile men of evil intent. They're not going away just because America's changing course. But let's be clear: what we've been doing was not working, has not really worked for decades. We were not making the world safer. We were not resolving the most threatening issues of our time. And we were bankrupting ourselves in the process. The simple fact of the matter is that no single country can be in charge of the world's security; not any more. America's days as the reigning superpower are over. It is time for the United Nations to start doing the work that can only be done through the collective, cooperative and coordinated efforts of all nations. And it is time for America to stop seeing the UN as a threat and to give it our full support."

Carver went on to explain that we would begin withdrawing from Iraq and Afghanistan immediately and that the continuing challenge of nation-building and peacekeeping in each country would be turned over to the United Nations. This did garner some applause, mostly from the Democrats. Americans had been living with the military-industrial complex for so long, its ways and means were so deeply woven into their finances, their communities, their ideologies, their personal philosophies—you could hardly expect everyone to immediately embrace such monumental change. But if they weren't wildly clapping, nor were they booing, or walking out, or reaching for their guns. They were listening intently to their President and, it seemed to Joss, were willing to follow him on this radical new path.

Still, Joss was not the only one to notice that he hadn't mentioned Israel. Carver would later explain that he'd decided to wait a few months before tackling the US-Israel relationship, allowing the world to change around it first. For now, he just wanted to keep everyone on board and moving in the same direction. It was time to declare Jubilee.

Chapter 61

In the early eighties, when the Wiggensterns and Sharpskis moved to the island, the plan was to find a house big enough to hold circles, which at that point were up to sixteen regulars. Since the others would be coming from the mainland, they'd need a good meeting space, plus decent sleep-over options. Joe and Eva immediately fell in love with their North Beach bungalow, a tiny three-bedroom which fit their needs perfectly, but with little room to spare. Fortunately, Leo and Dorothea preferred trees, meadows, and arable land. Just a twenty-minute walk inland from Joe and Eva's — five by bicycle — they'd found their fifty acres, thirty of it forested, with a rambling six-bedroom farmhouse and barn. A series of work-party weekends transformed the barn into a comfy, carpeted meeting space on the ground level, with four bedrooms above.

Mia was born in the house, on a wet and windblown December day in 1982. Dee always said, "it took a year of constant carpentry, but once the nest was ready, our baby came along." Like all good dreamers, Mia had vivid memories, going all the way back: floating across the fields on Leo's strong shoulders; running with Hershey, her chocolate Lab and full-time companion; going down to Uncle Joe and Aunt Eva's to scour the shoreline for beach glass and magic stones; walking everywhere with Dee and Hershey, through the woods, the garden, into town, down to the water, hand in hand, Mia and her mother.

It was just a few weeks ago that she and Dee had walked the land together for what would turn out to be the final time. It was post-diagnosis and the decision to go forward with the dream had just been made. Yet instead of discussing such weighty matters, Dee had gone on a stream-of-consciousness ramble, letting one long-ago moment after another bubble to awareness to be lived and appreciated once more. Though Mia had been hearing the stories all her life, she'd listened then as if for the very first time, while trying not to think *the very last time*.

Dee said, "Those first circles in the barn were really something. We were all still so young, so new to it all, the dreams were just taking form, like we were discovering mental muscles, flexing 'em for the first time, just starting to glimpse the possibilities, and Mia, even then, we sensed that we might be at the center of something big, like the world was revolving around us.

"Joe was the captain and Leo was the first mate, but Don was the shipbuilder." She'd had to stop and hold still, slightly hunched over and quiet until the sorrow passed—four years gone and Don's passing still hurt. Mia could only wonder how she'd ever get over—

Dee asked, "Do remember those camping summers, when Don and Jane, Rob and Susan, Tom and Jessie and—shoot, that other couple, what were their names?—they'd all pitch tents in the meadow and stay for July and August, and you'd have Dylan and Cassie to play with?"

Of course, Mia remembered. And it was so tempting to just stay there, to dwell in the house of the past, as Leo would say.

But not now. If there was ever a time to be fully present, this, their long-awaited moment, was it.

They were all in the living room, sitting around the widescreen TV Brett had bought just for the occasion. President Carver had been speaking for forty-five minutes, the last stretch detailing the closing down of America's military empire. In this roomful of lifelong peaceniks—well, Susan, Jessie, Ali, Leo and, of course, Brett, were all sniffles and wet faces, while Joe and Eva and Jane positively beamed, looking forty years younger. Rob had a look of utter disbelief, his head shaking the whole time, as if Carver had just announced that he was turning the government over to faeries. Even old taciturn Tom couldn't keep from smiling.

Then Carver said, "And finally, we've come to Jubilee."

While Carver's audience—in the living room and in DC—erupted into frenetic cheering, Mia found herself thinking about what Joss Morgan said last night, how it saddened her that Dee had just missed living to see this day. That she'd traveled so far and come so close. Mia thought Brett had it right—Dee was the necessary sacrifice that made it all work. Like a shipwrecked swimmer clinging to a piece of driftwood, Mia had held tight to that thought through last night's troubled sleep, this morning's weird and awkward world-without-Dee, and then the goodbye circle and burial ceremony.

The mainlanders had come over on the nine o'clock ferry, pulling up to the house at ten-thirty. They went right into circle, a short one as circles go, just once around with the talking stick. Then Eva led the group through a waking dream—part prayer, part meditation—bringing Dee into the circle and affirming her forever connection with each member of the group.

The circle is open but never broken.

Leo had used the backhoe to dig a deep grave that morning. They carried Dee's shrouded body out to the meadow, laid it in the ground, and held hands around the grave while folks said what needed saying. Then Jane started a soft chant and everyone joined in, eleven voices blending into one beautiful Song of Dee. After a time, Leo knelt at the head of the grave, scooped a handful of dirt and dropped it onto the body. Everyone followed in turn and then, still chanting, slowly made their way back to the house.

They'd had half an hour to shift gears before Carver's speech. While Leo went back to finish filling in the grave, the rest relied on a combination of humor, hugs, and food to move on from losing Dee to celebrating New America. Except for Mia, everyone, including Leo, seemed to have made a smooth transition.

For the umpteenth time, Mia dragged herself back into the here and now. Carver was going through each form of debt and explaining how it would be handled. As with the earlier parts of his speech, she thought he was trying to answer the most obvious questions people would have, while not going too deeply into details. He repeated several times that the country was making so many big changes, so much of it untested, there were just so many unknowns, that they must expect some rough edges and rocky times.

"As Benjamin Franklin warned: '*We must all hang together or, most assuredly, we will hang separately.*' Remember, the original thirteen colonies had a million reasons to go their separate ways. They disagreed on huge divisive issues. Yet in their wisdom they saw that 'The Separate States of America' was a recipe for certain failure. They understood: united they would stand, or divided they would fall. So they learned to compromise, to set aside individual agendas for the common good.

"Now, we didn't listen that well to old Ben and have since grown into two separate governments with two separate economies, one for the mega-rich and one for everyone else. We are more divided than united, some extravagantly wealthy and the rest struggling just to get by. The most important lesson of the day is that we can no longer sustain this separation. We can have the wealth gap or we can have a democracy, but we can't have both.

"And so I declare today, on behalf of the American people, that we shall have our precious democracy, that we *will* hang together, that we *are* the United People of America. I declare this our day of correcting injustice and finding balance and rediscovering the common good. I declare this Jubilee Day!"

Finally, even Mia had to cry. She looked at Leo, who was sitting with his head bowed and eyes closed. Hanging with Dee.

Epilogue

This was Joss's first time on a ferry and, she had to admit, it had its charms. Their trip had begun at 6 a.m. Eastern in a taxi racing to Reagan National. Then the direct flight to Sea-Tac and a two-hour drive up to the ferry terminal, followed by a ninety minute wait. Now, 3 p.m. Pacific, they were halfway through the sailing and as much as she wanted to get some work done, she found it hard to stop gawking at the view. The water was white-capped and choppy on this rainy March day, the sky a dreary gray. But the islands that slowly drifted past were green and gorgeous and seemed to be saying: slow down, take it easy, you're on island time now.

The long hours of sitting had made Alex antsy, so he bundled up and went for a walk on the outside deck that circled the cabin. Every couple minutes he would stroll by and give a little nod or make a funny face in her direction. Once he did a quick little soft-shoe. More of the strange Alex behavior that, she was happy to say, had its charms.

She turned back to her Book. The big news of the moment was the President's trip to China. In ways that nobody saw coming, the Jubilee had vastly improved relations with the Chinese. Turns out they were seriously worried that America's financial crisis would take down the whole global economy, with cataclysmic geopolitical ramifications. The fact that America was the sole superpower, that she was armed for Armageddon and in the grips of permanent war fever, that her democratic institutions were failing, that she was addicted to resources that belonged to other nations, and that her people showed no signs of grasping the depths of their dilemma, nor inclinations toward making necessary adjustments—well, the Chinese had come to view America as a huge craven beast, mortally wounded, fever-crazed, and liable to lash out in the most terrible ways.

So they had watched with great interest and building excitement as the whole Jubilee drama unfolded. While the world focused on America, few noticed China quietly undergoing its own transformation. The Chinese *loved* the Manifesto; indeed, within a day a Jubilee Manifesto movement sprung up on China's Internet—with government approval. They liked the progressive tax system and the emphasis on reducing the wealth gap, which was just starting to be an issue in China. The people who built the Great Wall had long believed in a small, defense-based military and well understood the wisdom of avoiding foreign entanglements. True to their Marxist roots, they favored the limits on usury and restraints on capitalism.

But the biggest surprise of all was China's position on foreign debts, in particular, the trillion owed by Uncle Sam. Carver originally called for the forgiveness of all third-world debt, but left the debts between developed nations vague, saying only that fair debts would be honored, while those deemed unfairly usurious would be recalculated, if not repudiated. He then asked the Chinese to maintain the status quo in their financial relationship for at least three months while America set about getting its new house in order. But just two weeks later, China declared its own Jubilee and announced that it was forgiving all foreign government debt, including America's. Finance Minister Lai explained that the huge sums owed by the US Treasury were but a capitalist illusion with no actual value: virtual money created out of nothing and worth nothing. The world would do best to forget it ever existed. Going forward, said Lai, the economies of the future must deal solely in real goods and services. Chinese workers were prepared to go on delivering those goods and services in abundance and it was to their advantage that America have a healthy economy.

Thus, in a two week period, the two largest economies on the planet, so very different, had gone Jubilee. The rest of the world held its collective breath, waiting, watching, and expecting—chaos? collapse? riots in the streets? That, as the bankers all warned during the crash, the wheels of commerce would grind to a depressing halt?

All those dire warnings—how the banks were sacrosanct, too big to fail, too powerful to regulate; the need to honor contracts; the dangers of moral hazard—turned out to be nothing but self-serving bromides from the financial industry. The only people hurt by the mass repudiation of debt were the mega-rich, and all they lost was a few zeroes off the end of their massive fortunes. Billionaires were reduced to millionaires, the poor dears. Life went on for everyone else, farmers farming and factories producing, merchants selling and consumers buying, only it was all so much easier without the burden of crushing debt.

Four days after China, the European Union went Jubilee, followed in turn by a rush of other nations. Thirty-six days from the first email, it was pretty much Jubilee Planet, a world without debt.

Of course, it had to be said that the process was not entirely voluntary. Three days after Carver's speech, at 04:10 a.m. Eastern, Leo and friends sent out a new message. The subject was the now-familiar "A Message to the Dominators." They then listed six men who had all died of cerebral hemorrhages just ten minutes earlier: an Israeli Knesset member, dubbed the "king of the settlements" in the papers, who was finishing a working lunch with several colleagues when he groaned and fell face-forward into his soup; the arch-conservative and Israel-hating Iranian president, who passed out during afternoon prayers; North Korea's Supreme Leader, while watching an American movie before bed; the Saudi Arabian king and the minister of justice, together on a plane in flight to Paris; and, though never confirmed, Osama bin Laden. After the names of the dead, a brief message: "**Share the wealth and end the violence. Jubilee**"

The message went out to all traditional and Internet media, was translated, and achieved global saturation in less than an hour. As the deaths were confirmed, that information spread even faster. It was proof that what had happened in America could happen to anyone, that the Jubilees could strike anywhere, and that it didn't matter what the victims were doing. Dominators everywhere started rethinking their positions.

Four days later, they jubileed another batch of six. North Korea's new Supreme Leader, who took over for his predecessor with blustery defiance. Similarly, a hot-headed, vengeance-swearing Iranian ayatollah. Two Russian billionaire arms dealers. Another Israeli Knesset hardliner and another Saudi prince. A new email went out, listing the names and reiterating the message. **Share the wealth and end the violence**. Four days after that, six more, same process. Then, a few days passed and China made the big leap, and the rest, as they say—

The Jubilees had been quiet since then. Which was the main reason for this trip and a source of some tension between Joss and Alex.

Right after his Jubilee Day speech, Carver had offered them both White House positions—Joss as Chief of Staff and Alex as Special Intelligence Advisor. While Alex was honored and excited, and accepted immediately, Joss had tried to turn Carver down, explaining that she was neither a politician nor an administrator and that her passion, and her skill set, was psychological forensics. But the president persisted, asking that she come on for at least one year—through the next election and, more importantly, through the coming wave of Jubilee change. Then he told her, point blank, that he needed her. How could she not say yes?

When the first six were jubileed, she had gone right to Carver and suggested that they contact Leo and explain that the Jubilees couldn't just start whacking foreign presidents and kings without clearing it with the president first. Carver had nodded, said something vague about letting things unfold, but "no need to take any action right away." She had understood in a flash that Carver was already talking with Leo, and was probably picking the victims. Also, that at least partly explained why she and Alex were being brought into the White House—as holders of Carver's big and potentially destructive secret, it was better that they be committed members of his team. Yet, if she was right and Carver was still calling the shots, he was also giving her and Alex plausible deniability by leaving them out of the loop.

That night over dinner when Joss told Alex her theory, it was his turn to go vague, while clearly avoiding her eyes and watching his words. She suddenly got that it was Alex, probably assisted by Trenton, who was actually picking the targets. Then either he or Carver was telling Leo. But much as she tried to get an answer out of him, he wouldn't budge. Clearly, he had his orders and, professionally, she understood. Personally . . . well, that this was happening just as they were tiptoeing into warm romantic waters was a tad chilling. It became a source of tension but hardly a deal-breaker. Just something to avoid talking about.

As the ferry approached the dock, they gathered their stuff and went down to the car. Soon they were rolling off the boat and then they followed a string of cars along the island's central road for several miles into the island's main town. A couple of turns and a short drive later they saw the Sharpski's Farm sign.

Though Joss had been left out of the Carver-Jubilee loop, she'd stayed in close contact with Muriel who—surprise surprise—ended up joining the Jubilees and was now living at this farm. Apparently with Leo.

The morning after the first international deaths, Muriel had skyped her with the news: since Jubilee Day "the dream" had continued. Each night Muriel would find herself back in the room, along with what she assumed was Leo's dream-self, and a third person sitting in the chair, his back to them. This happened for three nights. Then, on the fourth, the fire returned and she woke up knowing she'd just participated in another killing.

"Joss, I know this is all top secret and that you work for the president and all, and I don't want to get you in trouble, or get in trouble myself, but I really have to talk to this Leo guy. Can

I just have his skype name? If he doesn't want to talk to me, he'll just ignore my request."

Muriel had been involuntarily conscripted into the Jubilee execution squad by the man who killed her husband. Joss gave her the name. Well, Muriel and Leo apparently hit it off because a few days later Muriel called her from the island.

"After our first conversation, I knew, we both knew, that I belonged here. They, Leo and the others, think that Dorothea, his wife, basically recruited and trained me to take over if she couldn't go on. I know it sounds bizarre, but in their reality, which I'm starting to get, it all makes sense. A week after Jubilee Day they were having a big memorial service for her—she was a local saint and practically the whole island showed up—and when Leo told me about it, I started packing. Once I met him and the others, it's odd to say, but it was like discovering a family I never knew I had."

Though they had stayed in regular communication, Muriel was never any more forthcoming than Alex about a continuing Carver-Jubilee link. And once the international sacs stopped, it receded as an issue for Joss, who had more than enough on her plate. Until two days ago, when Carver made it an issue again and sent them on this mission.

Joss and Alex pulled up to a pretty, well-kept farmhouse and the front door immediately popped open. Muriel came down in the rain with an umbrella and after a couple of quick hugs they ran with their bags into the house. They were quickly introduced to the five Jubilees they'd already identified: Leo Sharpski, Joe and Eva Wiggenstern, Leo's daughter Mia and her husband Brett. It was, surprisingly, not at all awkward. Which was proof, Joss was thinking, that they'd become something of a team—the Jubilees, herself, Alex, Carver and Trenton. Like people who had survived an earthquake or hurricane by pulling together, or soldiers at war, they'd accomplished something that really mattered and would be forever bonded.

In her conversations with Leo to set up this trip, Joss hadn't explained the need for the meeting, though she'd had the sense he knew what was coming. The idea now was for eight of them to settle down with coffee and tea and have a chat about Carver's proposal. If necessary, then the rest of the Jubilees—who had all moved to the island after Jubilee Day—would come over and they'd have a full group powwow.

Alex got things started with a question for Joe. "So, that day when we thought we were interviewing you, while in fact you were misdirecting us, how did you keep from just laughing out loud?"

Everyone laughed. "Don't be too hard on yourself, Alex. We expected that I'd be contacted at some point, once you started looking at psi. So, I was ready for you, knew pretty much what I was going to say. But I have to admit, upon meeting your lovely partner during our video-chat"—this drew a soft elbow jab in the ribs from Eva—"ouch!—well, I just couldn't help flirting and said a few things that I later thought better of. We were lucky things worked out so quickly, since you did in fact track us down, didn't you?"

"He did," said Joss. "Can I ask something that's been on my mind all these months?" When Joe and Leo nodded, she continued, "I can imagine the discovery and development of lucid dreaming, and then of co-dreaming. I can also see, in Leo's writings, the evolution of your political philosophy, vis-à-vis dominators and the cycle of violence and predatory capitalism, and how that would all lead, especially after the financial crisis, to Jubilee. But what I can't see is how you made the leap to . . . uh—"

"Killing people?" said Leo.

Joss nodded and Leo inclined his head toward Joe.

"Well," said Joe, "that was me and Eva and one of those accidental discoveries that show up so often in science. It happened in two stages. You see, we'd been co-dreaming for a while, we were five married couples at that point, each couple sharing a bed, as couples do, and having a dream or two each night where we'd go lucid together, or, as we'd eventually say, co-dream. Then we moved to the island, only I was still working at the Seattle VA, so I kept an apartment and commuted, spending three days here then four days there. And that led to the first discovery: the co-dreaming gets stronger when the dreamers are not touching, and the further apart they are, the stronger it gets. This was a huge counter-intuitive breakthrough that we spent years exploring and understanding better.

"Accidental discovery number two came in 1990. A long-time patient of mine, Billy Dayes, a Vietnam vet who'd spent years working through his PTSD, was stricken with a brain aneurysm. Left him in a deep coma, the so-called vegetative state. Didn't have a living will, wasn't married, had no children, no one with power of attorney to take charge of what was happening. But I knew from years of conversations that this, this vegetative existence, was his worst nightmare, and believe me, Billy had some terrible nightmares. He must have said to me a hundred times: If it ever happens to me, just kill me.

"I was in Seattle then and went to the hospital after I got the news and spent two hours sitting by his bed wishing I could do . . . something. Wishing I could help him. That night, Eva and I came together in the dreaming in Billy's hospital room. We heard him pleading: 'just kill me.' And we thought, as one: *amplify the aneurysm*. And that's what happened. The room filled with fire and . . . he died."

Joe was clearly struggling with the memory, so Leo picked up the thread. "We—circle—spent the next six months processing it. Hours of talk, then we'd all dream on it, then come back the next day and talk some more. It was during those circles that the whole plan came together, the idea that we could remove key dominators from the world without, we hoped, *becoming* dominators, that we could engage in violence without feeding the cycle. Jane had an aunt, and Jessie a close friend, who were like Billy, in terminal but long-lingering conditions, but neither were from brain injuries. Both had expressed, in their own ways, 'just kill me.' And, after some trial and error, we did."

"We had to kill eight more people before we mastered the process," said Eva. "And then two more when Mia, Brett and Ali joined the circle. Thirteen altogether, and they were all similar cases, terminal, with do-not-resuscitate orders, or living wills, or clear and unambiguous communications to somebody close about what they wanted at the end of life. We also looked at the families and friends, and if there was someone—I remember a granddaughter in one case—who just wasn't ready to let go, then we passed. Most of them were like Billy—alone in the world and ready to die."

Joss was thinking of her paternal grandfather, who'd taken years dying, in and out of hospitals for one failed treatment after another, and how much that had colored her childhood. Who was she because of it all and who would she be if some group of mercy killers had shortened the process? She also did the math: these friendly folk had confessed to thirteen more killings to go with the fifty-three they'd jubileed. She looked at Eva—the quintessential sweet old lady—and, to her surprise, the two thoughts fit easily together. These were sweet, friendly people who had mastered the practice of killing for the common good.

She looked at Alex. He was frowning, his eyes cast down, clearly working something through. But then, another surprise, he looked up at her, shrugged, and smiled.

"What?" she asked.

"Well . . ." He slowly scanned the others, making eye contact with each. "For a moment there, I was reaching for my badge. The law is the law and bad guys are defined by their actions, not their intentions. It's hard for me to stop thinking that way. But . . . if we could actually discern one's intentions, if, say, we had perfectly infallible lie detectors so we could know exactly what was motivating a suspect, then we could start factoring intentions in. And that would make for much better law. Some apparent criminals would turn out, like you guys, to be decent people trying to do the right thing."

After a long silence, Joss said, "I assume there was no karmic blowback from these pre-Jubilee mercy killings. Why do you think Dorothea was so badly affected killing dominators?"

Leo answered immediately. "They didn't want to die. They didn't ask for help, never said 'please kill me.' It's like Alex just said—the power of intention. This only works if we are able to stay clear of the negative thoughts and emotions you'd usually associate with murder—hate, vengeance, punishment, retribution, greed, personal gain. Sociopathy, psychopathy.

"We see ourselves acting on behalf of the whole nation, indeed, all of humanity. We're not killing a bunch of awful people who we think deserve to die; we're sacrificing a few individuals for the good of all."

"And the thing is," said Brett, "and this is what convinced me: society is already sacrificing individuals, in much greater numbers. So, all we did was change the target group for social sacrifice, and vastly reduce the numbers."

Now it was Joss's turn to slowly scan the group, making eye contact with each, and confirming, for herself, that she was not looking into the eyes of murderers. She'd done that before and she knew the look. Nor was she seeing people torn by conflict or wracked with guilt. Though something was going on with Mia.

"My mother," said Mia, "got all of this better than anyone. But, and I'm just thinking out loud here—Leo, hang with me for a sec—I think it was bringing Brett and me into the group that undermined her. We were pretty resistant, like, we got the basic thinking, and were able to carry out the mercy killing, *but*— We couldn't really articulate it, but we just couldn't get past that 'but.' We argued for months and it was during that time she got sick, so sick that she would have died even if we didn't go forward with Jubilee."

"Ah, Mia," said Eva, and she pulled her into a hug, the two of them weeping softly. Everyone else sat in patient silence.

Joss started regretting the purpose of this trip. She'd made the case against it, but Carver, Trenton, and Alex had been adamant.

Leo must have been reading her mind. After Mia and Eva quieted, he said, "So Joss, Alex. Unless we're mistaken, you're here because the president wants to press us back into service. More sacrifices for the common good. True?"

"True," answered Alex. "Shall I tell you why, or do you already know that also?"

"We follow the news. We know that North Korea, Israel, Iran, and al Qaeda have been defiant, shrugging off last year's sacs like minor inconveniences, and fuel for their martyr numbers. We know that six months of silence from us is just strengthening them and emboldening others. We're guessing that there some other international issues that are worrying President Carver." He gave Alex, then Joss, a questioning look.

"Sounds like it's been worrying you also," said Alex.

"Some of us," said Joe. "But the truth is, Alex, we're divided right now, which for us is cause for inaction. I'd say about a third of our group is done with the sacrifice dream. The rest are persuadable, though only for international cases. We're all finished domestically."

"Because?" asked Joss.

"Because, like the Jubilee, saccing dominators is not the way to run a country. It was a one-time course correction. It achieved its purpose and now it is incumbent on America, and the other nations that went full Jubilee, to sustain this new reality, and improve upon it, going forward."

"Actually," said Joss, "Carver agrees. Though it didn't take long for his post-Jubilee domestic opposition to take form and start causing problems, including threats of violence, he says that if we can't work it through now, we'll never be able to. So, he's not asking for more domestic sacs."

"But internationally," said Alex, "what we did in November was more destabilizing than transformational. It's unfinished business. Well, what the president is asking is that we create the kind of comprehensive plan that you all had for America, and that we just keep saccing bad guys till we've won."

Mia let loose a loud sigh. Brett was frowning, as was Muriel, though Joss couldn't tell if they were disapproving or simply reflecting the gravity of the situation. Leo, Joe, and Eva, on the other hand, were clearly in agreement with Carver. As were Alex and Trenton and, she now decided, herself. There were still too many tyrants loose in the world, driving things, creating hell on earth for everyone else. They needed to either change their thinking, or be sacrificed for the good of all.

Leo was slowly nodding.

"OK," he said. "We understand the issues and the stakes. We have to take this to our full group for, I imagine, a series of long circles. We'll let you know as soon as we've made a decision."

That ended the discussion for Joss and Alex. Though they'd come prepared to spend the night, if they left now they could catch a ferry and sleep in Seattle. Felt best to leave the Jubilees to their process.

As they pulled away from the house, Joss gave a final wave to Muriel, Leo and the rest. "We really have to do this again," she said to Alex. "On vacation rather than official biz. Come back and stay for a few days and just hang out with these people."

Alex smiled. "Agreed. As nice a bunch of killers as you'd ever want to meet."

About the Author

Michael Sky is the author of *Thinking Peace, Breathing Lessons,* and *Dancing With the Fire,* all published by lulu.com.

He is also the creator and editor of thinkingpeace.com and commonhealth.us.

He lives with his wife and daughter on a small green island in the Pacific Northwest.

Michael can be reached at sky@jubilee-day.com.